September 28, 2010

To Angela Mulford

Dear Angela,

I believe we are fated to meet one day; I regret that we couldn't have lunch together when you were here in the summer. I know you will take good care of Liz. She is a precious friend.

See you in York one day.

Best wishes,
Patricia Björnstad

A Quiet Life in Bedlam

by
Patricia Bjørnstad

Eloquent Books
New York, New York

Copyright © 2009 Patricia Booth Bjørnstad.
All rights reserved.

No part of this book may be reproduced or transmitted in any form or by any means, graphic, electronic, or mechanical, including photocopying, recording, taping, or by any information storage retrieval system, without the permission, in writing, from the publisher.

Eloquent Books
An imprint of AEG Publishing Group
845 Third Avenue, 6th Floor—6016
New York, NY 10022
http://www.eloquentbooks.com

ISBN: 978-1-60860-212-4

Book Design: Bruce Salender

Printed in the United States of America.

To love, in all its guises

And with loving thanks to Carol and Jack Hidle, of Stavanger, Norway.

I would also like to thank:
Olav Guttorm Bjørnstad
Dorcas T. Helfant-Browning
Jeanne Hintz Culbert
Denise H. Powell
Dianne B. Cotnoir
Linda Bernice Booth
Pearl David Beatty
Melvin G. Berna, Jr.
Ingeborg Kristiansen
Laila Solberg
Kjell Amund Prytz
Geoffrey Colin Parkes
Eva Gjerde
Unni Karoline Bakke
Stephen Misner

Esther Smedvig
Magnhild Peggy Gilje
Aashild Naustdal Jacobsen
Else Merete Thyness
Siri Isachsen Ringe
Lars Falck-Jørgensen
Ann-Jorid Berg
William Sharp
Nancy Rohr
Pauline Burman
Sigrun Aukland
Anne Marie Garstad
Inger Fluge Maeland
The United States Navy
Google.com

> How much does a man live, after all?
> Does he live a thousand days, or one only?
> How long does a man spend dying?
> What does it mean to say 'forever.'
>
> —Pablo Neruda, *Life*

CONTENTS

CHAPTER ONE: *Escape* 9
CHAPTER TWO: *Cast Your Fate to the Wind* 32
CHAPTER THREE: *Carnal Knowledge* 57
CHAPTER FOUR: *True Grit* 76
CHAPTER FIVE: *Mystique* 96
CHAPTER SIX: *'Shout'* 120
CHAPTER SEVEN: *Love Can Make You Happy* 138
CHAPTER EIGHT: *The Kind of Boy You Can't Forget* 149
CHAPTER NINE: *Pretty Flamingo* 175
CHAPTER TEN: *Welcome Aboard* 197
CHAPTER ELEVEN: *Lovers of the World, Unite* 215
CHAPTER TWELVE: *Sing No Sad Songs for Me* 239
CHAPTER THIRTEEN: *On the Beach* 259
CHAPTER FOURTEEN: *He's Not There* 279
CHAPTER FIFTEEN: *Rose Garden* 302
CHAPTER SIXTEEN: *Key West* 327
CHAPTER SEVENTEEN: *Love Is a Dark Horse* 349
CHAPTER EIGHTEEN: *The Planets Collide* 369
CHAPTER NINETEEN: *Since I Fell for You* 386
CHAPTER TWENTY: *Total Eclipse of the Heart* 403
CHAPTER TWENTY-ONE: *The Edge of the Precipice* 425
CHAPTER TWENTY-TWO: *No More Crying Then* 444

The characters depicted in this book are entirely fictitious. Only the public figures are real.

CHAPTER ONE:
Escape

I measure the beginning of my life from the late summer of 1965 when I announced to my parents that I intended to leave home and move to Miami.

'Why Miami?' my mother asked me.

'Well, I just picked it off the map of the eastern United States,' I answered blandly, but I had my reasons. Mother didn't comment.

My parents were only mildly surprised at my pronouncement, and made no effort whatsoever to dissuade me from moving out. They had their own problems, God knew, and Mother felt that it was time for me to leave home.

Miami was far enough away, but not too far. I wasn't planning on coming back, but at least it wouldn't be impossible. Miami seemed as distant as Europe, but it wasn't really, if you studied a map.

'About a thousand miles to the southeast, it looks like,' I remarked to my sister, Annabelle, and measured the distance with my fingers as calipers, using the scale.

'Aren't you scared?' Annabelle asked me.

'What of?'

Annabelle drifted off. She preferred scary stories to ones with happy endings.

'Cast your fate to the wind,' I said out loud, and smiled. I took a red marker, and highlighted the best roads for driving. I had found another girl who wanted to move to Miami with me. She was a fellow worker at Southern Bell Telephone Company in downtown Memphis.

'Florida' sounded foreign and exotic, and the rumor was rife around the telephone office that operators were needed to handle the 'seasonal' telephone traffic in Miami. Winter was coming, and South Florida would be flooded with sun-seekers. Why couldn't I be one of them?

I had tried once before to move away from home—just across the Mississippi River Bridge to West Memphis, Arkansas. I knew I was risking my reputation when I moved there, but the new apartment was considerably closer to my job, and the rent was low. My mother did not approve of the address, but she didn't say anything.

West Memphis was seen as slightly 'naughty' because of the dog racing and gambling that took place over there, on the weekends. What I never could figure out about the dog racing and gambling in West Memphis, was why the radio announcers declared regularly, 'Miners not allowed.' That was mystifying. We were, however, familiar with the concept of discrimination in the South, so I thought, *Well, it's just one of those things. Miners not allowed.*

Gambling was against the law in Memphis, but that doesn't mean it didn't take place—games of poker and craps were played perpetually. Walking downtown, one could almost hear the ejaculated 'Hahhhh' sound, and the quick explosion of air that followed it as the dice were thrown. The concurrent bourbon drinking and Havana cigar smoking were conspicuous. The police looked the other way, of course, as long as there was no 'trouble.' Once, on a Friday night, Mother hit Daddy on the head with a frying pan because he had gambled away his whole paycheck.

My 'moving out' experiment did not work, alas—it was too easy to move back home when my salary would not stretch to the essentials, like food, clothing, and bus fare. I hadn't yet

Chapter One: *Escape*

learned to live on a budget. Actually, I never did learn it, God help me. I ate lunch in the Piccadilly Cafeteria too often, went shopping at Lowenstein's Department Store and at Gerber's, though they should have been off-limits to a poor girl like me.

At Lowenstein's, I threw caution to the winds and bought a 'Voyager' blouse and sweater. The 'look' was 'banana.' Groovy. The 'preppy' style in teenage clothes, was 'in.' I loved it then, still do.

One day at Gerber's Department Store, I bought six nylon half-slips in different colors and patterns because they were on sale. Needless to say, that broke the bank, but I wasn't sorry. I was sure I needed those petticoats. They were for shorter skirts, two inches above the knee.

But what was more telling, and cinched the return of the prodigal, was when the roommate got on my nerves by wearing my clothes and getting dark-colored make-up stains around the necks of my white shirtwaist blouses. So I threw in the sponge and moved back to Mother and Daddy's house, hoping to save enough money to buy a car. Riding the bus was getting me down. I was naïve; it was a mistake to try to move back home. Mother wore my clothes and then left them in a balled-up heap at the bottom of her closet. And that wasn't all she did. She asked me to pay room and board! What? Room and board, to live in my own house?

'Is that fair?' I fumed to Sherry, my youngest sister. She just gave me her gape-toothed grin and bopped on out the door.

'She has a nerve.' I stormed around, but unpacked my belongings anyway. At least Mother could not wear my shoes. I had a bigger foot than she did.

It was typical of my age, I guess, that Mother and I were at loggerheads on nearly every issue. I was the family trail-blazer, as much as if I had been born an Aries, the eldest child who has to get her parents used to all the new ideas that youth are prone to adopt.

My mother did not appreciate my independent spirit, although she plainly had one herself. 'Yakety yak, don't talk back!' I sang whenever Mother wasn't listening, and giggled.

A Quiet Life in Bedlam

If she sometimes heard me, she fell in with the joke and warbled off-key, *'Don't you give me no dirty looks ...'* [1] Tee, hee! She had a sense of humor.

But Mother didn't really understand me at all. She knew I was a scholar, and she wouldn't allow me to buy books! Women in the South were not supposed to be educated—at least, not more than a modicum. Mother tried to discourage me from reading of every kind, complaining that I spent too much time on 'frivolous pursuits.'

'You've always got your nose in a book,' she said. I don't know how she knew that. I had been reading with a flashlight, under the covers at night.

'What about doing the housework, your homework (when I was in school), the laundry, or looking after your baby brothers?' As she spoke, I could hear the squeal of the irreverent 'Yakety Yak' saxophone:

And when you're finished doing that,
Bring in the dog and put out the cat! [2]

Gad. Was I born to be a slave?

'Tote that barge. Lift that bale.'

True, I was a romantic and a dreamer and Mother was right that I needed to be grounded in some practical realities, but the situation at home was one from which we all would have liked to escape, and the farther away, the better. A trip into the twelfth century with Ivanhoe was just what the doctor ordered.

'People say that life is the thing, but I prefer reading,'[3] wrote Anglo-American, Logan Pearsall Smith, a man after my own heart.

Ever thrifty, my mother insisted that library books were good enough for my use, particularly for the voracious rate at which I consumed the written word. She refused to accept that

---

[1] 'Yakety Yak', by the Coasters, 1958. Written, produced and arranged by Jerry Leiber, and Mike Stroller.
[2] 'Yakety Yak.'
[3] Logan Pearsall Smith, 1865-1946.

Chapter One: *Escape*

I wanted to 'own,' not borrow—to have as mine the books I liked best.

Mother took to counting the books in my bookcase once a week to be sure I had not bought any more. I resorted to subterfuges to hide my new acquisitions from her—there was a secret place in the headboard of my bed; and the bomb shelter in our backyard was an excellent hiding place for the spanking new books, in colorful dust jackets, that I did not have the heart to make look ruffled and used—then place on the shelf with the old ones.

Mother censured my books, even the ones I checked out from the 'young adult' section of the library—presumably those were 'decent.'

'Would the Memphis Public Library try to corrupt me?' I asked her.

She gave me a look.

I will never forget when Mother caught me with my paperback copy of James A. Michener's recently released *Hawaii*. She rifled through the first pages of *Hawaii*—skipping right over the creation of the world—to where the Polynesians were getting into their love-rites, and burned the book (along with several others) in the incinerator—as trash and pornography—though I don't think she had ever heard the word 'pornography' and certainly, I hadn't. Imagine putting James Michener in the same category as Irving Wallace and Jacqueline Susann! It was pitiful.

While I was at home, my mother kept our incinerator as active as the heretic fires of Woodstock during the reign of Mary I of England. My books were her fuel. I never cried so much as when I saw them burn, along with my 'movie star' scrapbooks and *Seventeen* magazines.

She always read my correspondence, and anything that I, personally, wrote, but she did it in secret, and it took some time to find out about it. I can't seem to keep myself from writing things down. It is a weakness. I have been getting into trouble with my writing since I was about twelve years old.

A Quiet Life in Bedlam

Our grandparents used to give us diaries as Christmas presents. On New Year's Day, we ran off to our bedrooms to write in the diaries as a sort of celebration of the New Year. It was satisfying to snuggle up under the quilts there in the wan winter's light, chronicle our secret wishes, and make New Year's resolutions.

I wrote in my diary very conscientiously until about the twelfth of January, when I'd had enough, and started on the paint-by-numbers sets. My diary entries were only sporadic after that, about boyfriends and girlfriends and school:

Dear Diary,
    A boy named Charley Roberts walked me home from school today. I should not have let him, because he is a Catholic. Before we were in sight of the house, Charley pushed me into a ditch and made a concerted effort to kiss me. I resisted with all my might, in an attempt to be 'good.' I don't suppose I could have held out for long, and really would have liked to be forced, but Charley, who is epileptic, all at once went into a seizure. Poor Charley. I walked the rest of the way home alone.
                                  Your friend, Katharine

Mother thought it was her duty to police my behavior, actual or imagined, by reading my diaries. There was a lot of nonsense written in them (it embarrasses me today), and she read every silly word, then chastised me afterwards—once I had caught her out, that is. Why do people give children diaries? What good does it do to write one's thoughts if they can't be private?

Annabelle taught me how to make my diary entries in pig Latin. That was a hoot. It kept our secrets safe for a while, but Mother found the hiding place, no matter how well concealed, picked the locks on the diaries, and broke the 'code.' Our ingenuity could not match hers.

When I began learning real Latin in seventh grade, I used that as much as possible to make my entries, because the only Latin Mother knew was, '*Veni, vidi, vici.*' But as I grew older,

Chapter One: *Escape*

it began to be a serious infringement upon my privacy that she read my diaries, and I hated her for it.

I had to get away, and it should be for good. Memphis had become stifling, both figuratively and literally. As the humid summer of 1965 sweltered and passed, we were aware of turmoil in the population—what they called 'civil unrest.' We heard reports of the terrible Watts riots. There was a nationwide worry over civil disobedience, student unrest and the resumption of mass conscription. The newspapers said that American B52s had begun bombing North Vietnam.

The number of young men being drafted was speeded up for the first time since the Korean War. The far-away conflict in Southeast Asia was getting closer to home, to the concern of every mother's son. Young men had to make a decision to get married, go to college, or get drafted. It made me glad not to be a man—what a burden! Certainly, the draft laws were unfair. A poor boy could not afford to go to college, or even get married, and so, would be the first drafted, not having any exemptions or deferments available.

The conscription situation continued like that until a draft lottery was begun in about 1969. After the lottery started, everybody had an equal chance. If you pulled a high number, you were well assured of never having to go into the army. Still, every young man had to avoid getting labeled as a 'draft dodger.' It was as poisonous as being handed a white feather.

The complacent, prosperous atmosphere of the late 1950s had lingered on until about the time I finished high school in 1964. Then there seemed to be an explosion of 'psychic' energy that caused crisis and upheaval, and the situation got more disturbing as the so-called 'New Age' got underway. People talked about the planets lining up in Aquarius, far-fetched though that notion seemed. It was said that vast changes were coming in the universe, and the benefits to mankind would be great; but it was too fantastic to believe.

Some intellectuals spoke of the lost continent of Atlantis rising—there was even a song about it. Others spoke of 'counterculture.'

What is that? I wanted to ask somebody, anybody. *Does it have something to do with counterclockwise?* I mused, alone with my thoughts and confused.

'What's it all about, Alfie ...' [4] Cilla Black was singing on the radio. Good question.

'C*ounterculture* could be a synonym for abacus,' I surmised. Life on Earth held so many mysteries.

The term 'youth-quake' was coined in England; that was funny. Did teenagers really have that kind of power? I hadn't noticed that anyone took me seriously.

No one from the older generations could understand why young people (me, for example) had to have everything, *now. They* had to wait for their dreams. But in the post-World War II industrial boom-economy, anything seemed possible. The United States did not suffer through the post-war austerities that plagued Europe, and from approximately the year of my birth, 1946, the U.S.A. was the land of milk and honey. It was easy to get well-paid work just out of high school, with or without a diploma. Money gave freedom—that was a kind of power. Money bought cars. Cars provided privacy for courting—privacy never available before, and dangerous in its way.

Police cars patrolled the dark lanes of Chickasaw Gardens at night, and wickedly shined their flashlights on startled 'neckers,' caught like deer in truck headlights, and ordered them to move on. What state of undress the lovers were in, how far things had gone, would not become apparent until some months later. Nine, to be exact.[5] Not many girls thought of getting a higher education; they didn't have to. All it took was the right boy, at the right time, in the right car.

Everyone thought the Beach Boys sang about girls—it was a myth. Really, they sang about their love affair with cars—just listen to their lyrics with a critical ear, and you will hear, *'She's my little deuce coupe, you don't know what I got ...'* and *'she's*

---

[4] 'What's It All About, Alfie,' by Hal David and Burt Bacharach, not actually released until 1966, but what's another year?
[5] 'Get me to the church on time! If I am dancing, roll up the floor ...' Lyric from My Fair Lady, Lerner and Lowe, 1956.

Chapter One: *Escape*

real fine, my 409.' Although 'America's band' used the feminine pronoun (as was the custom of the times) it's not a girl they are bragging about, no indeed, it's a vehicle. Though I guess it is not unusual for American boys to love cars and girls. Certainly, Motor City, Detroit, had been pumping out 'finny' cars as if people had the money to buy them.

'New vibrations?' 'Age of Aquarius?' What nonsense, and yet they were exciting concepts to the young of America, who, if the popular music was any indication, were really only looking to find true love.

I adored listening to the various and myriad-named 'Girl Groups' of the 1960s, like Ruby and the Romantics, the Ronettes, the Shirelles, the Chiffons, the Toys—*'How gentle is the rain, That falls softly on the meadow ...'* [6]—to name but a few. Some of the girl groups were from 'Motown,' Motor City, as Detroit was dubbed by the autoworkers. The weight of the music business seemed to be shifting from Memphis to Detroit. Strangely. Didn't anybody remember Elvis?

The girl groups sang endless wistful ballads about finding 'that perfect boy' and marrying him, after a courtship that was as pure as the driven snow, conducted by all the special rules laid down on women in a patriarchal society in days gone by.

The girl group genre suited my sensibilities exactly. Those songs could take me some place that I wanted to go—oddly, into a world where mathematics ruled (*not* my favorite subject). Happily, I had a natural sense of rhythm in my body that circumvented the need to master arithmetic, or even to read music. I learned every song by heart, and picked out the melodies on the piano, by ear. Mother offered me piano lessons, but stuff like *Für Elise* did not appeal to me. I chose singing lessons instead.

What would have really appealed to me (but nobody would listen) was learning to play the percussion instruments (specifi-

---

[6] Lyrics from 'A Lover's Concerto,' sung by the Toys, 1965; written for them by Sandy Linzer and Denny Randell. The melody was adapted from the composition, Minuet in G, by Christian Petzold.

A Quiet Life in Bedlam

cally, the timpani) in the school band, or mastering the viola; but Mother and Daddy would have thought I had run mad to ask for that—those instruments were not for girls. I was sorry; there was something about the mellow, deep voice of the viola, something fundamental about the steady pulse of a drum that appealed to a tribal nature deep inside of me, calmed and soothed me in hard times.

When people are uncertain about the future, they often turn to religion or clairvoyants. Both avenues seemed reasonable to me. The predictions of Edgar Cayce, a world-renowned psychic and clairvoyant, were much consulted during the 1960s. But that kind of mystical mumbo-jumbo was heresy in the Bible Belt South, and we weren't allowed to know much more about Cayce's predictions, than that there would be dramatic changes in the Earth's surface; and the turmoil would last until the turn of the century.

'Turn of the century,' I exclaimed. 'I'll be fifty-three!' Good heavens. 'Will I live to tell the tale?' There had already been dramatic changes in the Earth's surface: the Iron Curtain covered one-half of the landmass, and spy stories were all the rage.

Would the Earth rock (and roll) on its rotational axis? Were sun spots causing good vibrations? Would 'smile on your brother' become the global motto after 2000 years of strife and a proliferation of the seven deadly sins? I had gleaned some of these exciting, if spurious, 'information' tidbits from the information operators where I worked. They were inveterate gossips, but dependable in their way.

'Peace and harmony?' I said. 'Well, show me.' Only a short time ago, November of 1963, President Kennedy had been shot. The nation was still getting over the shock and trauma. It was tragic, though I was a Republican, and would have been glad to see Goldwater elected.

It had long been clear that my set of encyclopedias were not up to snuff when it came to the subject of 1. Astrology 2. Soothsayers 3. The Space Age. 'What space age?' the encyclopedia editors would have asked; i.e. 'The Russians have put a

Chapter One: *Escape*

dog in orbit, and a man in orbit. Is that so special?' The Cold War was on—no need to give the Russkies any credit. *Ignore them, and they might go away.*

By 1965, in the United States, it was another kind of revolution that people were thinking of—not like the one in 1776, or even in 1789. It was a social revolution, a revolution in ideas, a kind of latter-day 'enlightenment'—a new morality. Before the end of the decade, there were at least four popular songs naming 'revolution';[7] but it was difficult to pinpoint the exact dates of the coming uproar *('got a revolution, got to revolution,'* [8] sang the Jefferson Airplane). Astrologers were some of the first Cassandras out with predictions of change—causing a new wave of public interest in astrology, and anything to do with 'star signs.'

I threw myself headlong into the study of star signs. Though at first I was skeptical, I was interested in anything that would help to explain the enigma of 'myself.' The 'research' gave me many interesting insights into the peculiarities of everyone I knew. It never occurred to me that I was being 'nosey'—*I practically have a license to steal,* I thought. If anyone gave me their birth date, then they were fair game: I had 'permission' to check them out.

Anyway, people only laughed at me, not taking my guesses about their inclinations seriously at all: it was disappointing. I would have liked to surprise my friends and family with some amazing predictions. I found out that Mother was a Scorpio, and therefore my opposite. That explained a lot. Opposites attract, and then they fight.

In the turbulent social and political atmosphere, everything at sixes and sevens, I got a feeling of 'Hey, what's happening?'

    a. What is causing the rumbling that seems to come from the center of the Earth?

    b. Is this what adult life is like?

---

[7] The Beatles, 'Revolution'; Buffalo Springfield, 'For What It's Worth'; Thunderclap Newman, 'Something in the Air'; Jefferson Airplane, 'Volunteers.'

[8] 'Volunteers,' Jefferson Airplane, 1969.

c. Is that the school air raid siren being tested again? Or have the Russians arrived?

d. Is it hormones?

e. Does chocolate cause pimples?

f. Is 'sonic boom' the same as 'lower the boom?'

There was no one to talk to. In such cases, one must resort to one's library.

'Jules Verne might know,' I remarked to Annabelle. He had made some astounding prognostications. 'It's time for a re-reading of *A Journey to the Center of the Earth.*'

'BORING!' she said.

Hmmm. Not on the bookshelf.

'Have you seen my book?' I asked her.

'Not me,' she answered with a laugh. 'I only read horror stories.'

'Edgar Allan Poe?'

'Yeah, for choice.'

'He was insane!'

'So what?'

'Can't you find something better?'

She ended up reading 'true crime' when it started to be marketed. Mother did not approve, but at least 'true crime' did not have 'sex' in it. Neither did the new romantic fiction, Annabelle's second choice for brain food: one extreme to the other. That was my family, down to the ground.

I was restless, unhappy, tortured by my parents' incessant quarreling at night. Often we couldn't sleep because Daddy was drunk and rambled about the house, kicking the walls, cursing everything that was in his way, shooting his rifle through the ceiling sometimes, and knocking Mother around, though he never touched any of us.

When things got really bad, my sisters in hysterics, and my little brothers cowering under the bedclothes, I tried to call the police. Daddy yanked the telephone cord out of the wall to prevent me, and abused me verbally until I retreated. Invariably, the next morning, Mother would wearily ask me not to do it again, because it cost money to get the telephone recon-

Chapter One: *Escape*

nected. And it was embarrassing, to keep calling out the repairman.

It had been a year since the breakup with my boyfriend, Roger Douglass, the love of my life. The rosy cocoon I had lived in during high school had disintegrated, and I was alone. I wanted Roger, but he didn't want me. I knew from the very beginning—the eleventh grade— that of all the boys at Messick High School who might make me happy, Roger was the most likely to succeed.

Roger Douglass was one in a million. He made me feel my worth and value as a person, and as a woman. He applauded my accomplishments in scholarship and my performance in the high school activities—while Mother did not seem to be particularly impressed. I could not have been happier had I been captain of the cheerleaders.

I had always known Roger Douglass, but we did not notice each other until we were about sixteen. Roger and I went steady during high school, a time when my life revolved around study, music, and my relationship with him. He did not kiss me until we had been going out together for more than six months; but after he did, the kiss seemed to become the token of a pledge. Roger put his heavy, gold class ring on my finger and anchored it there with my own class ring. The red stone settings in the rings represented the Messick colors of red and black; but in my imagination the red stones were also two crimson hearts entwined together on my ring finger—two hearts that would love forever.

Other girls had three or four boyfriends during high school; I had only one. But he was the best there could have been, one of life's blessings. Because Roger was there, I was able to remain more tolerant of being 'betwixt and between' as the saintly Pat Boone[9] called it: the time in late adolescence when I was forced to live inside the walls of that madhouse in Memphis with Mother and Daddy.

---

[9] See, *Twixt Twelve and Twenty,* a moralizing book by teen idol, Pat Boone, that we all read avidly.

A Quiet Life in Bedlam

Roger and I were actually engaged, and I still had the engagement ring, the prettiest jewel I had ever seen. The white gold of the band swirled delicately in a waltz of metal right up to the illusion setting. The diamond couldn't have been more than a quarter karat, but it meant the world to me.

There was no hope, however. Roger had joined the U.S. Air Force, rather than be drafted and have to face out his 'year' in Southeast Asia as a common infantryman. He was gone to basic military training at Lackland Air Force Base in San Antonio, Texas ... or, so I had heard from Roger's father, a man who didn't like me. Or rather, he did like me—he just didn't like my plans for Roger.

Mr. Douglass thought his son and I were too young to marry, and so, quite cold-heartedly, set up the conditions for us to part. He was aided and abetted by the conflict that was beginning to be known as the Vietnam War.

Roger's mother, a model of propriety, stayed strictly out of the conspiracy, bless her. Mrs. Douglass's given name was Blanche; I believe she would have asked me to call her that, but Mr. Douglass wanted to keep it more formal. Blanche Douglass had a serenity about her, a quiet, cool look that could uncover all liars. She had a certain elegance, even though she dressed in nothing more formal than day-dresses; and she had a thick crown of prematurely gray hair that seemed to echo her name, 'Blanche,' white, pure.

Blanche Douglass was one of those rare women who did not begrudge the girl her eldest son was dating. She always had a kind word for me when I came around, and she was very free with handing out Coca-Colas, too. My sisters and I appreciated her generosity; we didn't get Cokes very often.

My youngest sister, Sherry, met Mrs. Douglass as frequently as I did, because she was a good friend of Jimmy Douglass, Roger's younger brother. When Jimmy asked Sherry what she wanted for Christmas, she replied facetiously, 'I want an oil well, and a Corvette.' Ask for the best and you might get it, was Sherry's philosophy.

Chapter One: *Escape*

On Christmas Eve, Jimmy Douglass presented Sherry with a model car—a tiny, fiberglass Corvette Stingray coupé. In addition, he brought a twelve-foot-tall wooden 'oil well' he had built with his own hands (the darling), and a can of motor oil. I would have been jealous, but that was the Christmas when I got a diamond ring in my stocking.

I knew vaguely at the time we parted company that Roger's father was pushing him to break the engagement, saying, 'Son, just wait a few more years; you're so young. If it's right, it will wait. Go to college, or join the Air Force—give it more time. Please.'

But I thought I would win out; I didn't. Encouraged by his father and in a spirit of testing the waters, a Friday night came when Roger took another girl to the drive-in movie. They 'made-out' in the most wanton fashion, so the reports of friends said—behavior Roger Douglass had never indulged in with me!

The police looked the other way.

'Who cares,' I said, as I punched my bed pillow at night. Roger broke my heart. He had also broken faith. I would never get over him. I couldn't see where I had been at fault, although I did throw a jealous fit—*not* my noblest hour. 'Hell hath no fury ...' I ranted and raved; it was shameful. I was so insecure. I needed Roger's love so desperately; and so I drove his love away.

I will never do it again. I just thought that sort of scene was expected from me. Roger Douglass and I turned our backs on each other, leaving serious misunderstandings on both sides.

During that year, 1964, there was a great agitation for civil rights in Memphis. I rode the bus to and from work each day, boarding at the corner of Park and Highland, in East Memphis. The trip took about an hour and a half because of all the stopping and starting that buses did en route. It was fifteen miles to work, and then the same distance back again, to where I lived at the curve of Radford Road and Walthal Circle.

One night after work, when I was about twenty minutes from home, the bus stopped to pick up passengers in Melrose, a 'colored' neighborhood a few miles from my stop at Park and Highland. Until that pause to pick up at Melrose High School, the bus was virtually empty. My sleepy head had nodded against the window as I napped during the long and boring journey; a person practically had to pack a lunch to get through such a trip.

Suddenly, everything changed. A football game played at Melrose Stadium had let out; a jubilant crowd of fans got on the bus, packing us in like sardines. They were mostly teenagers, and very excited; I guess they must have won the game. Anyway, I found myself surrounded by a sea of shining black faces, some faintly hostile. There had been a lot of rumors flying around the town about what blacks were doing to whites when they caught them in isolated situations.

Fear walked abroad among the white inmates of Dixie in the mid-1960s. Segregation had been a way of life. People who do not remember segregation or never had to deal with it, will find it hard to imagine. It seems as odd, now, as being forced to wear whalebone corsets, or having to ride a mule to the farmer's market. Everything had seemed so peaceful only moments before, in time. *First there were tremors, then there was an eruption ...*

Growing up, as I did in the fifties and sixties, I was like everyone else—ignorant, you could say—living with blinders on—not understanding the injustices, ignoring the undercurrents, innocent of the coming changes: shocked when the changes did come.

In the mid-1960s, we white Southerners painfully awoke to the realization that a rebellion was brewing, a civil rights movement was seething, just below the surface of the steaming streets, and was ready to crack open, pop out and scare us, like a jack-o-lantern on Halloween.

I might have taken it seriously, if I hadn't been so young.

The racial tension in Memphis that autumn was palpable. Dr. Martin Luther King Jr. and the NAACP had been stirring things up. There were demonstrations—not as nasty as in other

Chapter One: *Escape*

cities, but worrying enough. I was not an anarchist, and tried to stay out of all that 'protest' stuff.

'Let them fight,' I said, 'let them demonstrate, let them riot, let them eat cake; just leave me alone—I have other things to do.' Politics was not my bag.

After the Melrose students boarded the bus, there was a tension in the close atmosphere; it was electrical, almost. I could feel it prickle my skin. I became a little bit nervous, and ever-so-slightly afraid. I was the only white person on board that evening.

Then, I exacerbated the tension unknowingly. Holding my head high, and glowing with something like 'white superiority,' I turned my back on the jubilant teenagers, and stared pointedly out of the window into the dark night. Because of my growing fear, I suppose I had some idea of showing those kids that I was not to be trifled with.

I did not really think that I was in danger; the bus driver was white. It seemed to me that he would be on my side in any conflict; and I had been thoroughly indoctrinated in the White Supremacy Notion so prevalent in Memphis. Then I did the wrong thing. When two black teenage boys sat down on either side of me, I haughtily got up, and went to stand beside the driver at the front of the bus. I had seen other people do that, but never my mother, who was an egalitarian and treated people as she expected to be treated herself.

Well, the current of feeling in the bus moved every one of those youngsters toward me. It's the world's wonder that the bus didn't tip over forwards. The weight of a whole load of angry teenagers, plus the bus driver, plus me, was unaccountably at the front end. Suddenly. *Was I dreaming?*

The crowd of children, all at once, had turned into a mob. They surrounded me, moved me bodily to the middle of the bus and pressed themselves against me, mashing me as much as they could, and pinching me, causing a great deal of discomfort and humiliation until my 'stop' came, and I was allowed to get off the bus.

A Quiet Life in Bedlam

I say 'allowed,' because that is exactly how it happened. They could have held me on the bus. The bus driver could not have done anything to help me, even if he had wished to. I felt chilled that he showed a clear lack of interest in my dilemma. Plainly, I had put myself into that pickle-barrel, and had to find the courage and dignity to get myself out. I have always been bull-headed. And like a bull, I charge into the china cabinet, not knowing how much china will break, or what the cost will be.

Later on, when I was thinking about it, I referred to it as the time I got 'stomped'; but I didn't really get stomped. Those kids did not hurt me, and I got off the bus intact, a valuable lesson learned. I hadn't really noticed when the Civil Rights Act of 1964 passed through Congress; the incident on the bus got my attention. Painfully.

When I told Mother about it, she did not have the least sympathy. She was very good at pointing out how I came to get my just desserts, and said that I had better be more careful about whom I chose to snub the next time. Wise words.

At least I had a job. I began working for the telephone company right after graduation. Within a very short time, I was bored to tears by the sheer tedium of the automated work, but was more or less trapped in it. What else was there? Girls were supposed to get married. I hadn't made the grade. What now?

During lunch hours and split-shifts, I reread my abridged edition of *The Red and the Black,* by Stendahl; by chance, I found the quotation, *'Past loves ... they are like old campaigns. The outcome can never be changed.'* It was an omen. I was certainly not better than Napoleon.

Afternoons at the telephone company, I cried into the switchboard, and scribbled bad poetry when the Chief Operator was not looking. After losing Roger, I had few marital prospects and very little social life. I had not stayed in touch with the boys my own age.

'They are *drips* anyway,' I told Mother. She laughed. We were fondly remembering the time when my mother had swallowed a dozen raw oysters on a dare from Roger Douglass.

Chapter One: *Escape*

Those were the days. I shed a tear.

'*Southerners*,' I said, 'with their Southern attitudes to women, not my cup of tea.'

Mother was amused. She knew what I meant, the 'pedestal' thing: having to behave like a delicate piece of china, an object to be looked at, admired and used. It wouldn't hurt if the piece of porcelain could give birth to baby boys, either. My mother did not subscribe to that traditional Southern-female role. She grew up on a farm where she had to carry her own weight, wear overalls, and work just as hard as a man. But to be contrary, she said, 'Your daddy is a Southerner.' She knew I loved him, in spite of his weaknesses. But I would never marry such a man.

'I will not marry until I am thirty,' I mumbled, but I was lying through my teeth, and she knew it. It has been a lasso around my neck, keeping me from being truly free, that I have always, in the deepest recesses of my heart, even when I wouldn't admit it, wanted to be married. That was the ideal of the 1950s when my character was formed; the decade of Ike and Mamie in the White House. The Eisenhowers were a picture of placid domesticity that many American girls were encouraged to emulate. It is not easy to escape 'character,' God knows. I was told over and over by my mother and others, that strength of character is plainly visible in your face when you are fifty, and it had better be a pretty one.

On days when Mother and Daddy were at work, but I wasn't, we kids imbibed iced tea all day long and huddled by the one lonely window unit of an air conditioner to escape the omnipresent heat and humidity. I cooked spaghetti or chili con carne for my brothers and sisters from a recipe learned in Home Economics, and baked one-layer cakes from a box, using the rest of the cake batter as icing. We were permanently out of powdered sugar; Mother was always on a diet.

When Mother came home from work and saw the homemade one-layer cake with 'batter' icing, she actually said, 'I can't understand you at all.'

A Quiet Life in Bedlam

The only exercise I got was running for the bus, and playing tennis with my friend, Martha Boston. I was so proud to have a real tennis racket with a good press on it: that put me above the ordinary run of nineteen-year-olds, which was where I wanted to be.

Martha (pronounced 'Moth-ah') and I would get up before five o'clock in the morning to beat the heat and humidity, and bicycle or walk the few miles to Audubon Park to play tennis before the sun got too bright. It was thrilling to watch the pink glow of dawn as it diffused the sky, became apricot and then golden—then flaming orange as the sun burst upon the world, bringing a new day all the way from China. I became so emotional over the stunning summer sunrises that I cried sometimes, and spoiled my game.

That wasn't all I had to cry about.

*You don't have to be a ba-a-aby to cry
All you need is for love to go wrong* [10]

The tinkling tones of the Caravelles' duet rang through my head whenever I was feeling sorry for myself. So I did. Because it had. I sobbed like a baby and wrote 'mourning' poetry with the blue ink running, by the switchboard, there in that cold, efficient telephone building for hours at a time:

*When love is lost
A sadness there is ...
That fills the soul
And mind of you
And digs a well of emptiness
That nothing of this Earth can fill ...*

Snuffle, snuffle.

---

[10] 'You Don't Have to Be a Baby to Cry,' words and music by Bob Merrill and Terry Shand, 1963.

Chapter One: *Escape*

By some sort of electro-magnetic wave magic, I could hear a faint signal from the local radio station coming in over my headphones. Listening to the music made the time pass more quickly. When Gary Lewis and the Playboys sang, *'This diamond ring doesn't shine for me anymore,'* I cried even more, and put myself in danger, I am sure, of electrocution from the wet telephone circuits. But I didn't care. I wanted to die.

And this diamond ring doesn't mean what it did before...[11]

'Crikey,' I burbled, 'how long does it take to get over a broken love affair?'

In a daze, I had accidentally answered a call, and the customer said, 'Information? Information? Will you give me the number for a pawn shop?'

Pawn shop! Did I have the courage to pawn the ring and get some money out of it? *Serve him right,* I thought. 'Certainly!' I said to the customer.

Florida and a new life beckoned over the fronds of a palm tree. What an opportunity: I had nothing to lose. I would do it. At least it would be a different switchboard in Miami, a different chief operator. Any change might help. The surge of new creative energy hitting the universe was striking me, making me adventurous. What the heck?

'I wasn't born to be a broken-hearted, love-sick fool,' I announced to the room at large, and everyone looked at me like I'd gone crackers.

So I said to the service assistant, 'Miami or bust,' and applied for the transfer. It was granted almost immediately.

As abruptly as I decided to go, I left. My last morning at home gave a taste of autumn, my favorite time of the year. The early air was cool and damp, with a sky that was clear and high. A cold white moon hung in the west, full and bright, beaming at me. The flashing stars winked, and then snuffed out, one by one, as the dawn came. My ride was already waiting in the car outside. I could hear the motor idling.

---

[11] Lyrics from 'This Diamond Ring,' sung by Gary Lewis and the Playboys, 1965.

I opened the kitchen door and stepped out onto the porch into the moist air. The wind pushed by me, ruffling my dress. I clutched at my bag, steadying myself. The resident birds roosting up in the sycamore trees were just starting to twitter with their waking-up noises, but all else was dark, still, quiet and calm. A new start, a turning point.

'The turn of the screw,' I chivied myself.

Could I do it, could I turn? What else was there—a miserable life at home with Mother and Daddy until I married? I couldn't bear to think of it.

My parents stood behind me, waiting. My brothers and sisters crowded around, pulling at me. I would miss them. I had been their 'little mother' for as long as I could remember.

Stalling for time, I watched brown leaves scudding along the gravel driveway; then I raised my eyes to the treetops in search of a gray squirrel. Unbidden, the words of the Episcopal liturgy came to me, 'Lift up your hearts.'

'We lift them up unto the Lord,' I murmured in response. It seemed as if my heart-center opened, and my spirits soared. I felt an intense excitement. I thought, *If I had wings, I could fly away, like those darn pesky mockingbirds up in the sycamore tree.* Those feathered devils had pecked me so many times, when I was hanging out the wet diapers and clean sheets ... I would not miss them!

Are there mockingbirds in Florida? I wondered.

'Birds, high up in the trees, serenade the clouds with their melodies, oh, oh, oh.' [12]

'No, now I remember,' I said aloud. 'It's egrets they have down there. If they're not extinct.'

'What?' said my mother.

I glanced at her fondly. *If only I could be as strong as she is!*

As suddenly as the exhilaration grabbed me, it ebbed away, and I was left standing there, bereft and forlorn, just a home-

---

[12] 'A Lover's Concerto.'

Chapter One: *Escape*

sick hulk, wondering what in the world I was doing, moving so far away from home.

'Are you out of your gourd?' That's what my grandmother would say if she knew about it. But there was no turning back. My plans were made, the transfer was given, my portmanteau was packed, and my ride was out there waiting in the shadows.

I believe my father shed a few tears—he was sentimental—but my mother handled it all philosophically.

'Take care of yourself,' she said, and kissed me.

Annabelle, whispered, 'Wish I could go with you!'

I grinned at her.

'We would only fight,' I said. It was the truth, but I would miss our sparring matches. Annabelle and I were as different as night and day. I used to tease her that she was adopted.

Sherry said, 'Bon voyage,' and hugged me.

My sleepy brothers had gone back to bed. Cinnamon, our dachshund, was still there, waiting. I reached down to pat his head. He was an old dog now. Would I see him again?

I got into the car.

***

Through the years that followed, I returned home from time to time for brief visits, but from that moment, I was truly gone from them, never to return. The responsibility for my life passed to my own shoulders, and however well or badly it turned out, I have to blame or credit my own choices and decisions.

I walk that way sometimes in my dreams, coming up out of the darkness and mists. And stepping onto the porch that is still shaded by the sycamores, I find only desolation and despair. It is just a house, but the scene of so much unhappiness that I approach it feeling fraught with emotion, taunt with fear, even in my sleeping state.

How can the period of our youth, which is so short, have such an impact, such a hold, over the rest of our lives? It is a puzzle for the Sphinx.

CHAPTER TWO:
Cast Your Fate to the Wind

I left my home in East Memphis that early August morning in 1965. My unlikely companion into the unknown was another information operator, Linda Black. Linda had also elected to transfer to Miami, where she and I would be employed by the Southern Bell Telephone Company to answer a thousand and one calls a day, 'eight days a week.'

Linda had never been out of Tennessee, either. We had arranged to travel together hoping it would make us braver. We did not know each other at all; it was just the luck of the draw. Linda too, was nineteen. She was a Roman Catholic, the first I had ever known.

The low hills of West Tennessee undulated gently as a woman upward from the mighty Mississippi, and eastward to the lazy, winding Tennessee River far in the distance— the peaceful land languishing in the humid, hazy sunshine, undisturbed by progress, unmoved by events that were bothering me, and a whole parcel-full of other people.

The Tennesseans that I knew moved with an indolent grace through unhurried lives—gentle, hard-working, God-fearing people, benighted and insular, their whole existence being their burgeoning families, their farms, their livestock, their jobs. Lit-

Chapter Two: *Cast Your Fate to the Wind*

tle else existed for them; they barely acknowledged the world outside.

'Will I return?' I asked myself. *Will I ever return?* [13] God only knew.

Tennesseans had always seemed like Innocents Abroad to me, their transitory lives untouched by the sordidness and wicked ways that came with Adam's apple to the rest of the world, including me, as soon as I fled the protecting Tennessee borders.

Escape. Try your luck elsewhere. It seemed the only way forward. 'See what is in the world out there!' I knew there was one. I had seen it in *Life* Magazine. 'It has to be better than Tennessee.' But leaving childhood is like leaving the garden called Eden; knowledge comes.

As soon as we were outside the Memphis city limits, Linda Black informed me about her reverence for her church, her gratitude for a strict Catholic upbringing—and she was just bursting with homilies about her numerous brothers and sisters, the sanctity of her honored parents, and the hallowedness of her Catholic home. It made me wonder why she was leaving it.

Why leave a place where you have been happy? I thought. I didn't get it. But, no matter—I had a ride to Miami.

As we drove south along Route 55 in Mississippi, we fell quite naturally into discussions, and then verbal debates, from which no victor emerged. It took little time to find out that her values were not my values, her interests not my interests, and from there we fell into some dreadful quarrels—all before reaching Alabama!

Ye gods! I thought I had left the fighting at home in Memphis. But here we were, no farther along than Columbus, Mississippi, and we were going at it hammer and tongs! By the time we reached the Mississippi-Alabama border, we were nearly into hellfire and brimstone; the atmosphere was *hot*.

---

[13] A famous refrain from the song, 'M.T.A.,' by the Kingston Trio, 1959.

A Quiet Life in Bedlam

You wouldn't think that anyone but sisters could find so much to argue about.

Our first fight (nearly a fist fight) began when Linda informed me, in her most self-righteous tone of voice, that since I was not a Roman Catholic, I could expect to go to Hell when I died! And she was serious. *Well, that was conducive to friendship!* I thought angrily. Was she trying to convert me?

Though I wasn't planning on dying anytime soon, I believed in Hellfire then, and Linda's pronouncement upset me a lot. I could not persuade her, by any amount of reasoning, that I was as 'saved' as she was—administered sacraments of the R.C. Church, or not.

I was baptized, wasn't I? I had joined the church, hadn't I? We were both Christians, weren't we? But, no, that was not good enough!

'You're bugging me, Linda!' I said, and then tried to shut up. I thought *I* was stubborn, but she had it over me in spades.

Why we should have reacted to each other in the way we did, I do not know.

I believe the only bond we had in those first days was the new and profound experience we were undertaking together. Our first encounter with the open road was exhilarating—Birmingham, Alabama ... *oops, there went Montgomery* ... stopping for french fries in Columbus, Georgia ... then, *goodbye to Macon ... Macon rhymes with bacon, Linda, I'm hungry* ... 'Bye, honey!' said the lady at the drive-in just outside of Macon, Georgia ... and so, on and on, *on and on*.

'Two wheels a-turning, one girl a-yearning, big motor burning the road,' [14] sang Roy Orbison on the radio. It was still summer, and we were each burning with a temper, so we had to have the car windows open for fresh air.

There were flies and mosquitoes, sweat bees and wasps; there was brown dust, red dust, then yellow dust. We were soon windblown and grimy and travel-stained and bitten from the residue of the highway, but we didn't really care. The trip

---

[14] 'Ride Away,' Roy Orbison, 1965.

Chapter Two: *Cast Your Fate to the Wind*

was undoubtedly a once-in-a-lifetime thing, we knew, and soon we would be too interested in the changing scenery to quarrel much—we hoped.

I wanted desperately to drive, but Linda would not trust me behind the wheel of her new car. She needed a navigator, and I was it, discovering I had a talent for reading maps. The highways and byways of the Deep South rolled by our wondering eyes, and we were enchanted. *'Look at that! Linda, look at that!'*

Linda's car had an unheard-of luxury, a stereophonic radio, although many of the songs came across in mono. We listened all day long to the popular music of 1965, and some of it was sung by the Beatles, a mop-haired group I had little experience of.

'I wanna hold your hand ...'

How I had laughed when the boys in my senior class grew their hair long and left it shaggy, with bangs. Then gradually, as money and mothers allowed, the senior boys changed their clothing styles from our traditional 'Ivy League' look, of V-neck cardigan sweaters and cuffed pants, to casual but neat two-piece suits with no collars, peg-leg pants, and skinny ties. They wore narrow pointed boots called, apparently, 'winkle-pickers.' *Queer*.

'To each his own,' I said in disdain, and tossed my head.

They just grinned at me like idiots. I wasn't known as a fashion plate.

'The senior boys look silly, like rubber stamps of John, Paul, George and Ringo,' I had commented to Roger Douglass. He gave me an indulgent smile, and held my hand. Roger was impervious to fashion changes.

'Beatlemania' had swept through our school like a virus late in 1963; but I didn't like the sound of 'British Invasion,' and just ignored it.

As a result of the senior boys' perfidy, I admired all the more Roger Douglass's carefully-styled, upswept blond wave, his buttoned-down collar, Oxford-cloth shirt and canvas belt.

A Quiet Life in Bedlam

Roger was so much more mature than his classmates! He didn't have anything to prove.

'Just look at the shine on his mahogany penny-loafers,' I murmured to my best friend, Sally Hedges. We had known each other since early childhood.

'Yes, ummm,' she replied distractedly. The captain of the football team hove into view. Sally was the best-dressed girl in school. She had 'personality'—*'walks personality, talks personality, smiles personality, charms personality, loves ...'* [15]

Sally could do better than Roger Douglass: little sympathy there. And off they went together. At least she had chosen the Captain. He had some aptitude.

'Was that a cut?' My eyebrows shot up, though I knew that Sally would never try to hurt me.

'British Invasion, my eye,' I had said to my sister, Annabelle, when I got home from school. But it was no use—she was enamored of the Beatles like everyone else, and worshipped them for years, even sporting purple bottle-top glasses at one time and talking about gurus and India. It was sick-making.

'It's been a hard day's night, and I've been working like a dog ...' sang the Fab Four joyfully in stereophonic on Linda's car radio. Perhaps I had to reconsider. Adults maintained that Beatles music was decadent. I couldn't see any harm in it. The newspapers reported, 'The Beatles, and their haircuts, were banned by the government in Indonesia as a form of mental disease, and proclaimed that the people should wage war against it.' Too right!

In Cuba also, the surging wave of Beatles' madness was seen as subversive—as dangerous as Capitalism. In Japan and Israel, it was condemned as breaking down traditions and values—more dangerous than Communism. Even a ninny like me could see that the Fab Four was a force to be reckoned with.

'Can't buy me love, everybody tells me so ...'

---

[15] 'Personality,' a song by Lloyd Price, 1959.

Chapter Two: *Cast Your Fate to the Wind*

Curious beat, I thought as I listened, but I was tired of being a 'longhair' (classical music buff), and ready for a change, a big change. I wanted to change like a snake sloughing off an old skin.

It was actually Roger Douglass who liked classical music, not me. I just went along with it because I loved him. I would have said I liked Dave Brubeck and the Quintet, if Roger had espoused them. That number, *'Take Five,'* wasn't bad though. 'Roger gave me my own hi-fi, so then I have to play his records, don't I?' I had said to Mother when she laughed at my eccentric musical tastes.

'Get hep,' she teased me, and I choked. What did she know about it? Mother had a tin ear. And she was too old to know about the Beat Generation anyway. Then Roger left me, and I could form my own opinions.

'Do you like the Beatles?' I asked Linda. She was driving like an automaton with her knuckles gripped tightly to the wheel. Was she nervous or something?

'Oh, yes, the Beatles are wonderful,' she enthused, 'and the Catholic Church allows it.'

'Oh.' I was puzzled. 'What do you mean by that, the Catholic Church allows it?'

'Well,' she explained, 'for Catholics, not all forms of entertainment are permitted. There is a censor who decides what books we can read, what movies we can see, what music is appropriate to listen to.'

Jumpin' Jehosephat, I thought, but I didn't say more (though I could have).

Then Linda remarked, *'The Sound of Music* was very popular with the censor. I saw it five times!'

'I liked it too,' I said with a smile. At least we could agree on that.

'Did you see *Lawrence of Arabia?*' she asked me.

'Yes.' Oh, the pain! *Lawrence of Arabia* was my first date with Roger! Why did she have to mention that? A flood of memories came welling up, and my eyes spilled over with tears. But I did not let her see it. She wouldn't have understood

A Quiet Life in Bedlam

... Maurice Jarre's dignified music, the movie theatre like a night full of bright stars ... Omar Sharif ...

Gosh, here I am on the way to Florida. I pinched myself.

Finally we stopped at Waycross, Georgia, to spend the night at an inn which looked exactly like Tara in the movie, *Gone With The Wind*. There, sitting in the tiny, spotless restaurant, we marveled that we were surrounded by 'Georgians' as if they were so many Martians—and bravely extended our hands out the open window to touch the silvery Spanish moss.

'Is it slimy?' Linda asked me.

'Surprisingly, no.'

The moss was drifting from a live oak tree which was growing right out of the terrace. It was a huge tree, obviously ancient—might have been a hundred years. It made me think of being in a dream, or lost in a book, *'Last night, I dreamt I went to Manderley again ...'*

The waitress came to take our order. The inn's specialty was 'breakfast,' so we ate 'hamandeggs,' grits, red-eye gravy, and hot biscuits.

'Umm, good,' I said, and smacked my lips.

That night, we went to bed in a state of happy exhaustion, and no more angry words were spoken until dawn.

'Goodnight,' said Linda peacefully.

'Nighty night,' I said.

We were up early the next morning, and off for the Florida State Line where we would meet perpetual summer, and (perchance) some handsome millionaires. Linda wondered if her parents would be worrying about her, but I knew mine wouldn't. Neither of us would have dreamed of stopping at a phone booth, to telephone home. We were on our own now, mature adults, expected to fend for ourselves. And so we would.

Jacksonville, Florida, St. Augustine—splendid! *Daytona Beach, Melbourne*. 'Perfect weather!' *Palm Beach*. 'Oh! Look at those palm trees!' Fort Pierce whizzed by our shiny faces. Lordy, Lordy, a new world.

Chapter Two: *Cast Your Fate to the Wind*

Linda's car was performing beautifully. It was a plain four-door blue Ford, 1964 model. No frills, except for the radio. The contents of my 'hope chest,' china, stainless steel flatware, pots and pans, linens, rattled in the backseat and on the floorboards. It was my Earthly treasure.

I had two suitcases full of clothes in the trunk of the car, and Linda had one. I asked her if she had brought any of her old school uniforms, and she didn't like that.

We stopped only for gas and to give close scrutiny to the first few coconut palms growing alongside the road. As we cruised through Fort Lauderdale, rapidly approaching our final destination, Linda and I were only slightly annoyed with each other, and still willing to try to get along. Everything was costing so much money it looked as if we would need to pool our resources for some time to come. That required peace.

An angry goose named Toulouse
And a furious moose named Bruce
After fighting so much, said "what's the use"
So they got together to call a truce ... [16]

Dream on ...

As we swooped into Miami, it was our dual intention to drive straight to the ocean front at Miami Beach, park the car, and wade in the water. This, we did. *Wade in the water, children!* 'Wade in the water ...'

The green waters of the Atlantic Ocean made a lasting and powerful impression on me that day—I have rarely been able to leave the proximity of the sea since. *La Mer, the sea.* It was love of the mighty deep at first sight. The waves rolled in, rocking me. The warm, white foam ebbed out, rolling me. The cradle of seawater buoyed me up and held me as fresh water never could. Drowning would not be as easy in the sea.

The next wave laid me down in the manger of the sea, the sand. The salt spray splashed me, hit my mouth, and with a

---

[16] Verse found on a greeting card. Author unknown.

shock I realized that there really was salt in the sea! *Saline solution, imagine that.* Whatever next. Nothing works like 'experience' with yours truly. The ocean was deep and wide, mysterious. What was under the surface?

Next, I thought good-humoredly, *I'll have to go to the moon and see if it's made of green cheese.*

After only seconds in the surf, we were wet through, but not cold—no, not cold! Exhilarated! We were sandy and salty—we didn't care. What a lark!

Linda, in a burst of good humor, chanted, 'And we'll have fun, fun, fun …'

I shrieked with delight. Then, I spied something: 'Oooh, Linda, look at those boys! Those baggy pants they're wearing, have you ever seen such a thing?'

Linda was goggled-eyed. 'What are those funny boards they're carrying?'

'Could they be surfboards?' We had never seen the real thing. 'And are they wearing beads?'

Linda screeched, incredulous.

'Quiet, Linda,' I giggled.

Sing out!

Let's go surfing now,
Everybody's learning how,
Come on and safari with me!
(Come on and safari with me …) [17]

This was more fun than monkeys.

Nobody carried surfboards under their arms in the confines of the big 'Bluff City,' Memphis. It was more like 'banjos' in landlocked Tennessee. Clearly there was a different breed living here in South Florida.

Exciting! It was almost unreal.

---

[17] 'Surfin' Safari,' music & lyrics by Brian Wilson and Mike Love, 1962.

Chapter Two: *Cast Your Fate to the Wind*

On with the journey, and cruising into Homestead, Florida: we were to be put up for a few weeks at Linda's sister's house near South Miami. We were lucky at the start of a new life in a strange town, to know somebody. That was a real advantage. Otherwise, where would we go on *no money?* We couldn't expect to get a paycheck for at least three weeks—that was an eternity.

Linda's sister, Peggy, was an altogether nicer person than Linda was, though Peggy took little interest in me personally. I didn't mind, however, because she seemed to be an 'older' sort of person, and in addition, she was married—therefore out of my orbit entirely. Linda was Peggy's baby-sister, and had grown up after her big sister moved away to get married.

Peggy's husband, Charlie, Linda's brother-in-law, was an Air Force sergeant assigned to the Homestead Air Force Base located in south Miami-Dade County. Charlie had been sent to Homestead late in 1962 from George Air Force Base, California, during the Cuban Missile Crisis of October that same year. He had lived through some tense times.

It was such a short time ago, too! 1962! Three years ago the United States had been on the brink of war with Cuba—only 90 miles off the Florida coastline, only a little over ninety miles away from the ground where we stood, Charlie said. So, Homestead A.F.B. had been at a strategically important position in the military scheme of things.

The way Charlie put it, was that Cuba had all but been invaded by the U.S. Army, using Homestead Air Force Base as their launching pad. Clearly, Charlie had relished the idea of a fight, and had been sorry when the Soviets backed down.

A shiver went through me. 'He must have been the only one though, from what I heard!' I whispered to Linda. It was probably just military talk, man-talk. I wasn't interested in war, so I didn't listen.

'But what about the red telephone on the President's desk?' Linda asked him. 'Was that a true story?' Charlie wouldn't commit himself.

A Quiet Life in Bedlam

As is well known, the Cuban Missile Crisis was precipitated by the infamous Bay of Pigs *(Bahia de Cochinos)* episode of April 17, 1961. For years afterwards, U.S. Navy submarines and aircraft prowled the territorial waters of South Florida, guerilla fighters trained for future landings in Cuba, and other armed services stood their time of readiness.

The little naval base at Key West had experienced an epiphany. Florida had not witnessed such ferment in a long, long time. Sleepy, colonial Key West started jumping. There had even been NATO ships docking at the base in Key West, lending their support to operations. The missile crisis had the whole world sitting up, glued to the TV, waiting for news and developments. All was confusion. Televisions became indispensable.

'And Kennedy was President. Just think. Another era entirely.' Linda wanted to have her share in the conversation. 'He was a Catholic.'

So what else is new?

I remembered (could never forget) where I had been when I got the news of the Kennedy assassination: sitting with Roger Douglass in the study hall at school. We clutched at one another. It was like hearing that war had been declared. The world changed, that day in Dallas.

During one long afternoon of mint juleps and piña coladas, Charlie regaled us with tales of reconnaissance in Key West and environs during those frenzied times. (I think he was a bit of a ham.) He said:

'We were welcomed by the Navy to the Key West Base with open arms and great hospitality.' Charlie took a sip of his Budweiser. 'The military operations being carried out were astounding, even to us, but I won't go into that.

'What might interest you girls, is my personal observations from forays out on the streets and in the bars ... that was fascinating.'

We perked up.

Chapter Two: *Cast Your Fate to the Wind*

'The Cuban population was very visible in Key West. They seemed to be constantly animated and loud, passionate about everything—seemed to be angry when they weren't.'

Linda and I were cautious about the alcoholic drinks we had in our hands. Neither of us had ever drunk one before. Most likely, the Catholic sensor would have been against it. My piña colada was delicious, and I slurped it up. The next thing I knew, my head was spinning, then nodding. I heard Charlie say before I drifted off,

'I speak a little Spanish from my time in San Diego, but the Cuban dialect is different.' Charlie lit his pipe. Ooh, it was Cherry Blend! *Roger, oh Roger ...*

'Still,' continued the sergeant, 'I was able to talk to people, and they wanted to talk! It seemed as if fifty per cent of the population in Key West was Cuban, the most of Spanish descent, so they said, professional people and middle class. Some of the refugees had just arrived, some had been there for a while. The occasional *muchacho* was willing to buy me a drink for the chance of learning a little English; and I observed three kinds of money changing hands in the bars—American, Cuban, and Spanish!'

Money. Gosh. Where am I? I awoke with a start. Rum was a dangerous thing—delicious and deadly. Better watch out. I had heard people say that our family, with its Cherokee Indian blood, could not tolerate liquor. Could that be true?

Linda was yawning. It was time for bed, but Charlie wasn't finished with his dissertation. He had had a few beers. I didn't know it then, but the 'military' is a drinking culture: if you can't hold your liquor, don't join up. And if you can't spin a yarn, remain a civilian.

'What was the most intriguing, though,' Charlie laughed, and looked as if he expected us to join in, 'was that each bar seemed to have its Cuban "Rosita," who was ready to fall in love for the price of a drink. It made me think of the Old West, the frontier. Miss Kitty. *Gunsmoke.*

'As you may imagine, I wondered what sort of impact all of this had on the ordinary Conchs (natives of Key West). Well, they seemed to take it in their stride. The life down the Keys is mostly fishing, beer, swimming and eating. I was surprised that the Cuban presence was not resented more, but it seemed that the local populace was so used to the influx from Cuba that they didn't care, other than enjoying the increased business opportunities!'

Yawning so that we nearly swallowed ourselves, we said goodnight, and made our way to the guest bedroom.

'What a curious thing that we are in Florida!' I remarked to Linda. I wouldn't be there at all if I had gotten married. *The best laid plans of mice and men ...*

'Amen,' said Linda. She had called home, and talked to her parents. I heard her crying on the phone. I suspected that Linda wasn't enjoying the adventure as much as I was.

Linda and I didn't get to talk to Sgt. Charlie anymore in the three weeks we stayed there near Homestead A.F.B. with Peggy's family, but I heard later—much later—that Charlie went with his fighter squadron to *Tuy Hoa* Air Base in South Vietnam. Perhaps he was glad to see active duty, I don't know.

Within a week, we began working in downtown Miami at the enormous old telephone company building, commuting together in Linda's car. Luckily, we were assigned daytime hours, 8:00 a.m. to 5:00 p.m. I had disliked the split-shifts we worked in Memphis: 8:00 a.m. to twelve noon, four hours off with nothing to do, except go to the USO, or a movie; then back to work, 4:00 p.m. to 8:00 p.m.; afterwards, dinner in the canteen, if I was lucky. Finally, home to a short night of sleep, with Mother and Daddy moaning in the background.

In Miami, we were offered the possibility to work all night, and sunbathe during the day on the roof of the building if we wanted to, but that kind of life did not appeal to me at all. 'Might as well become a sardine at once and be finished with it,' I said to Linda. She agreed with me. Linda's skin was very fair.

The extra money for the night shift would have been nice, but money wasn't everything. I disliked the automated telephone work—even in the daytime. 'Working at night would be

Chapter Two: *Cast Your Fate to the Wind*

like being buried alive,' was my immediate reaction to such an idea. Still, I was very lucky to get the transfer to Miami, *'The land of dreams, ahhh,'* I sighed. The Bell System allowed, and even encouraged, transfers to other cities. It was a safe means of 'running away.' That's what I did! *Run, run, run, run, runaway ...* [18] Del Shannon's pulsing moog synthesizer-type rhythms danced through my blood. I wiggled my hips.

'*MIAMI!*' I threw up my arms to the sun. The whole city of Miami seemed splashed in vivid tropical colors and perpetual sunshine—except during the occasional rain storms that rolled over the pedestrians like a rumba rhythm, taking everyone by surprise and drenching each one to the bone.

'Doesn't anyone stay dry in Miami?' I muttered one day to no one in particular. *At that rate, my hair will mildew,* I thought. My hair was a constant problem, because though it was thick, it was baby-fine and straight as a stick. Humidity made it flop. A girl had to work hard with her hair. A girl wanted to attract a boy.

An even more fascinating weather phenomenon in Miami, was when a brief storm burst—always with the sun shining brightly—on *one* side of the street, while *your* side of the street, *hah, hah,* was dry as a bone, and baking hot. But your turn was coming—'Linda! Better run!! Here comes a black cloud!'—and pedestrians scattered like geese in all directions.

Lunch hours out in the town were fascinating—walking those streets was like being in another world—everything was hot pink, and cobalt blue, canary yellow, luscious peach. Jasmine perfumed the air, and bougainvillea tumbled over painted stucco walls, flaunting itself, mocking the winter that was coming to North America.

People were singing, '*Guantanamera, guajira, guantanamera ...*' everywhere, and popular music was blaring away in the stores. People were nearly dancing in the streets, but I didn't know what they were so happy about ... it must have been the atmosphere of Miami in the mid-1960s.

---

[18] Lyrics from 'Runaway,' by Del Shannon, 1961.

The exuberant Cubans were already there in numbers, but I did not realize it at first. It seemed as if Miami was already 'Spanish' before the Cubans got there: the architecture made me think of Spain. Ponce de León brought his expedition to Florida in the early sixteenth century, and a 'Spanish' atmosphere had permeated the east coast from early days. Not least, the climate in Florida was reminiscent of Spain. At the tourist bureau, Linda and I received information that the Fountain of Youth was at St. Augustine, but we didn't need it.

Lunch itself was exciting—sampled Cuban dishes, chicken and yellow rice being something we could always afford. Someone told me that there was saffron in the rice, but I didn't know what saffron was (still don't). The smells on the streets, the noise of the streets—the Spanish language everywhere—was a complete departure from all we had known before in hick town Memphis.

After our first paycheck, we went apartment hunting, and found one right away. It was clean and modern, furnished, carpeted, with one bedroom and a double bed. We signed the lease, feeling very grown-up. We paid our September rent, and a deposit of one month's rent in advance. We received two keys.

On our first night there, Linda, the only one with a camera, snapped a picture of me sitting in the middle of the double bed. I was wearing turquoise blue nylon baby-doll pajamas, looking winsome and very young. Even so, my tortoise-shell glasses lent an owl-like air to the sweet baby face.

'Smile,' said Linda once more, pointing her Brownie. I gave her a grin, and yanked my glasses off.

Later, before we slept, Linda nailed a crucifix over the bed, so she had the last word on that particular day; but I didn't mind so much, it made me feel safe to see the cross there.

'G'night, Linda,' I said.

''Night,' she answered. And so we dreamed.

The apartment was not far from downtown Miami—it was on N.W. 71st Court or something—it is difficult to remember the address. Miami was easy to negotiate because of the 'num-

Chapter Two: *Cast Your Fate to the Wind*

bering system' on the streets and avenues, but a number is just a number, and for me, not easy to remember. A Spanish street name would have been easier to hold in the memory, or a typical Florida-name, like 'Seminole,' for example, or 'Everglades.'

The apartment building did not have a swimming pool— that was a disappointment— but there were other pools all around us. We would have to get to know somebody! Our new pad was just a twenty-minute bus-ride away from work. Ostensibly, we had a car, but I suspected that someday I might find myself dependent on the bus services—some day in the not-too-distant future, if I didn't watch out. So the location was practical in terms of distance to the job—however, it was not a prime consideration. Cost *was* a consideration, because we each made only sixty-five dollars a week. That had to cover all expenses.

We should have had a boat, though. Our court flooded regularly. Southern Florida is just a big coral rock; the rainwater runs off it, and pools in hollow spaces. It got to be no surprise, in the mornings, to have to wade out to the car barefooted, past palm fronds, driftwood, beach balls, coconuts and rubber duckies. But that just made Miami more special.

Linda and I liked our new apartment and felt very glamorous, actually supporting ourselves financially for the first time. We tried hard to keep our bickering to a minimum. Often, we were successful: many new things claimed our attention. I reckon Miami was a bit of old Europe, stuck like an oversize-stamp on the mangrove swamps of southeastern Florida.

It was with some trepidation, a week or so later, that we realized we were entirely surrounded by Cuban immigrants. We were 'in the ghetto.' And so we had our initial contact with the first wave of those poor exiles, that beleaguered people, the educated and well to do of Havana, the ones who fled from Cuba in the early 1960s, the ones who were the original targets of Fidel Castro's persecution shortly after the Communist consolidation of power in 1959. They were new to Miami, as we were, and had not integrated into the society as yet. And they were poor; but they were rich in spirit, as we later discovered.

There wasn't a soul who spoke English for miles, but we didn't know enough to be afraid. And moving again was quite out of the question, so we settled in as roommates, and attempted to get along as friends. Wary friends. But it was true to say that we were living on the wrong side of town.

Linda had led a rather narrow, restricted life, which included a convent education cloistered with girls at St. Anne's Catholic School in East Memphis. She was one of the youngest of eight children.

Linda never had a boyfriend. Linda wasn't worried. She said to me, 'Nice Catholic girls marry nice Catholic boys after being introduced by a nice Catholic priest.' I did wonder if she was teasing. Could it be that easy?

'And what about love?' I queried.

'Love will come,' she replied, looking almost wise.

In my opinion, her great advantage in life was that she had lived near the public library. I had had to drag my brothers' little red wagon two miles every week, rain or shine, to fetch my usual ten books from the young adult section of the Highland branch. Sometimes it was a misery to be an intellectual.

Linda wasn't a reader. I wondered what that felt like. And I wondered what it could be like, never to have known any boys except for your brothers.

I myself had been somewhat protected as far as living in a nice, quiet, middle-class neighborhood—not likely to come to any harm—my parents hardly ever locked the front door. Linda and I did not suppose that we were in any danger, and probably, we weren't. We exhibited friendliness and trust before strangers, and generally conducted ourselves like country bumpkins well on the way to becoming sitting ducks.

But the weeks passed, and the only problems we had were with each other.

'My field of dreams is not your field of dreams,' Linda said one day, apropos of nothing.

Chapter Two: *Cast Your Fate to the Wind*

Oh? What the heck does she mean by that? I was thinking. *Is she some kind of a philosopher?*

I liked philosophy, 'that something intermediate between theology and science,' but I didn't want to hear any from her. Bertrand Russell was more to my taste.

For a while, I thought I was entirely dependent upon Linda for transportation, and she held this as a mallet over my head. Why be dependent? You ask. It may have been that I did not want to tackle the Miami metro-transit system—another new thing—when there were so many adjustments to make.

I hated riding the bus, and hadn't bothered to find out about the bus schedules—memories of taking public transportation to work during the racial tensions in Memphis were still fresh and painful. And I wanted a companion. I had never been alone in my life, God knew. I had four brothers and sisters, a plethora of aunts, uncles, cousins, and grandparents; but they were all in Tennessee, leading boring lives. And I was alone with Linda in Miami. I would have to cope.

Linda and I needed to make some acquaintances, find some friends—build up a kind of 'network' for safety's sake as well as for social intercourse. But how to go about it? We were so young, we didn't understand the new place where we had landed—we might have been from another planet.

In all that vast city of Miami and its suburbs, we did not know a single soul except for Linda's sister. We had been 'catapulted out of our context,' as the percipient author Kennedy Fraser said about the time when she moved to New York City at a similar age.[19]

We wanted to meet some boys—marriage was the object—they had to be our age or slightly older. Anyone else was a fuddy-duddy. It did not take long to meet some Cuban boys, but they did not speak English, and we didn't want to learn Spanish.

'¡Hola!' they said cheerily.

---

[19] 'Ornament and Silence,' by Kennedy Fraser, copyright 1989. Originally in *The New Yorker*.

A Quiet Life in Bedlam

'Holy Cow!' There were those nitpicker boots again—oops, winklepickers. Couldn't I escape? And they were wearing cravats, in Miami's heat! Weird.

'Hi!' we said, moving towards them.

'Uh oh,' Linda and I breathed in unison. They had pimples; too much chocolate.

Even with pimples, the Cuban boys were attractive. Olive skin and raven hair, *ooh*. And they would certainly be Roman Catholic. Maybe they were the sons of doctors, who knew? We could flirt a little.

'Cómo está inglés?' I said in my best *El Camino Real* Spanish.

'No.' The boys looked abashed. That was as far as it went, really. Without communication, love is hopeless.

Well, we did spend some time with them, drinking cherry cokes at the drug store. They taught us how to count in Spanish, *uno, dos, tres, cuatro, cinco, seis, siete, ocho, nueve, diez, once* ... A lot of good that did.

The Cuban boys, who were about nineteen or twenty, made me smile at the machismo of the Spanish male, their overt sexuality, displayed in each move of their bodies, every twitch of their faces. It was mildly threatening—American boys would never behave like that.

'Every move you make, every breath you take ...'

We resisted their overtures—there was no future in it. Still, we were invited home to meet their mothers, who cooked enormous meals for us and helped to hold the starvation-wolf at bay. They really were so kind, those Cuban families. They shared what they had.

When this episode was over, Linda asked brightly one day, 'Where could we meet someone?' She didn't have to say which gender.

Jeez, I dunno. Doesn't the Catholic Church have a social center?

I shrugged. '*I know notheeng,*' parroting the Cuban boys' accent.

Chapter Two: *Cast Your Fate to the Wind*

We needed something to do in our spare time—any distraction to keep from squabbling.

'Beats me,' I said again, but I was concerned. Time was slipping by. In half a year, I would be twenty. Spinsterhood loomed. I already knew there was a USO in downtown Miami—I had checked it out, had counted on it—but that was my ace in the hole. I wasn't mentioning the USO until desperation set in.

Soon, Linda and I made a few friends in the apartment complex—hallelujah—most of them quite spectacularly exotic and vastly different from the people we had known in Tennessee. In Miami, I truly could not find any 'good old down-home Southern boys,' whose attitudes to women I could not abide: that was refreshing. But there was no 'boyfriend' material, either.

I remember there was a family of trapeze artists from the Barnum & Bailey Circus living across the court from us; and in our building, a professional heavyweight boxer, a flamenco troupe, a pair of luxury-cruise-liner stewards, and a French chef who worked at one of the art deco style hotels down on Miami Beach.

'Would any of them make a boyfriend?' I asked her.

Linda rolled her eyes and tossed her head like a restive mare. 'At least it has to be someone respectable. My mother would never approve of a trapeze artist.'

She had a point there. Mine probably wouldn't either.

Our neighbor, the French chef, who lived two apartments down, made wonderful 'flan' (crème caramel, or caramel pudding), which he brought as a 'welcome' present. We let that flan slide down our throats un-chewed, as if it were raw oysters! We did have some fun before the final falling-out.

The French chef's other specialty was fried plantains, a tropical fruit resembling a banana, which nevertheless, was like eating hot caramel candy when one put it into one's hungry mouth. I don't know if 'fried plantains' was considered to be a dessert or a vegetable—it could have been either one.

A Quiet Life in Bedlam

That 'French chef' had another talent, and it was for deception. Though I was an innocent, I had some savvy, and I suspected that the French chef was not French at all, but just pretending to be, to keep his job at the fancy hotel. 'Raoul' certainly knew a lot about Spanish cuisine:

'Linda,' I said, 'taste that paella! Good, huh?'

'More, more!' she cried.

Raoul's paella had a little bit of everything in it, including shellfish, chicken, rabbit, vegetables, tomatoes, rice, seasonings, and the inevitable saffron. Raoul told us that paella was called 'poor man's food,' and therefore made up of anything that happened to be laying around in the kitchen at the moment of cooking—but Linda and I felt rich as Croesus just having such delicious and nutritious food served to us, steaming hot from Raoul's black skillet. And though he fed us well many times, he never asked for any sort of payment; we were privileged indeed. But we had to observe the Valencian ritual before eating, and say 'bon mot,' after sprinkling the paella with lemon juice.

Another clue to Raoul's true identity came in the form of his very interesting, and handsome, roommate, a gentleman named Mario Fiqueroa, who was of Spanish descent, a native of Key West. Mario just laughed when I asked him if 'the chef' was really 'French.'

If it was so, I said—that Raoul was French, I wanted to ask him exactly what a 'French kiss' was. (Yes, I said that, little Miss Naïveté.) I can't remember that I was teasing. I wasn't asking for a demonstration—just explain it, please.

I really wanted to know. I had never encountered anyone who knew exactly what a French kiss was, or would tell me, anyway—and it was not in the dictionary. I don't think even Mother knew, and she would have slapped me had I inquired.

Mario replied ironically that Raoul was about as 'French' as he was, that they were cousins, and that he, Mario, could French-kiss me if I would be patient and wait until we knew each other a little better. Mario's beautiful brown eyes were

Chapter Two: *Cast Your Fate to the Wind*

smiling, but his demeanor was as serious as a judge, as he handed me my first *piropo* .[20]

Well, I got that back in spades, I thought, as I gulped.

Mario, looking relaxed and tanned, and possibly looking for love, was sitting like a young god on the sofa in our apartment. He wore Bermuda shorts, and I could see the black hair on his legs.

Coincidentally (or was it), a 45 rpm record was spinning on my phonograph at the exact moment of the French kiss interchange, and it was Jewel Akins, 'The Birds and the Bees'*:*

*Let me tell ya 'bout the birds and the bees
And the flowers and the trees
And the moon up above, and a thing called 'Love' ...*[21]

All at once, I realized how shameless I was being, and blushed scarlet. I would have blushed again, right to my liver, had I gotten the connection between 'The Birds and the Bees,' and what Mario was proposing. Mother used to say that I didn't have 'the gumption of a billy goat,' and I guess I didn't.

Linda was beside herself with pique as I stole Mario right from under her nose. I had been thinking in terms of 'boys,' but here was a man. With Mario in the picture, Raoul's food was of less importance. I didn't feel so hungry anymore. I felt like being on a diet. I stood up straighter, and washed my hair more often. I began putting a dab of toilet water between my breasts.

Well, this little exchange about the French kissing endeared me to Mario, and he decided to see what could be done about introducing me to the ways of the world. He would be gentle, he would be kind, he would be thorough. I would find out what a French kiss was, and more. Soon, my education would be

---

[20] Roughly translated, 'courteous pass'; also 'compliment' or 'flattering phrase.'
[21] Lyrics to 'The Birds and the Bees,' words and music by Herb Newman, 1965.

taken in hand. And if I didn't like French kissing, it wouldn't be his fault!

Mario Fiqueroa made life easier for Linda and me by squiring us around to the various tourist attractions in Miami, which we would have had little chance, or money, to visit in the ordinary run of things—without a little help from a friend, that is.

The three of us visited Miami Seaquarium, and Parrot Jungle. We trudged around the everlasting sandy beaches with picnic baskets full of *criollo* cooking prepared by the excellent Raoul. It seemed a shame that the sand around Miami wasn't white like I had been expecting, but a yellowish-brownish color instead.

Where did a body have to go to get white sand? I wondered.

Still, the sand was warm, and in any case, I wasn't interested in lying around on the beach. I was beginning to think about lying in bed with Mario, but squelched such thoughts as unworthy.

What would Mother say if she heard I was in bed with a Catholic? I thought with alarm.

Then we went to Vizcaya on S. Miami Avenue, the previous winter home of James Deering, an industrialist. It was almost as good as being at the Pink Palace in Memphis, that house/museum I loved so well. The proportions of Vizcaya House were elegant, the grounds spacious, the furnishings impressive (not to mention, imported). The style was a tasteful combination of Baroque—that I adore—Rococo and Neoclassical, with some Renaissance thrown in for good measure. I felt an immediate affinity to the place.

If only I could move in at once, I thought to myself. *Fat chance.*

I began to feel warmer towards Mario Fiqueroa. I appreciated the kind of 'old world' charm that was represented by Vizcaya and Mario. Everything Mario did was self-assured and graceful. He moved with a languid ease, and smiled like an angel. He dressed well, and danced like Gene Kelly, but slower. I

Chapter Two: *Cast Your Fate to the Wind*

remember he used to say, 'How beautiful it is to do nothing, and then to rest afterwards.' [22]

It gradually became apparent to everyone, even the French chef, that Mario preferred me to Linda, though he was generous and gracious to us both. Linda was tall, angular, prim and proper, and wore her naturally curly hair in a bouffant 'flip'—it looked like a tulip turned upside-down, just the mode of the moment.

Linda had dresses in the same shape as her hairstyle, with a kind of ballooning fullness to the skirt, and a constricted hemline at the knee. *Trez chíc,* but I would have looked awful in such a concoction. Linda's blue eyes sparkled and she was vivacious and attractive.

As for me, I used to think of myself as a Marian-the-librarian type, but I wasn't really. It created a scandal in my neighborhood when I had my ears pierced—it marked me out as 'avant garde,' something a respectable girl oughtn't to be. I had long dark hair in a pageboy style, and wore it in a ponytail whenever the weather was hot. Many girls at my age had a 'beehive' hairdo, but that wasn't for me.

I was of medium height, slightly plump in the way that healthy youth can be, with a fully developed woman's figure—something Mario Fiqueroa appreciated, apparently. Traditionally, the Spanish male believes that plumpness indicates good health (and fertility), thinness, bad health. I had fallen into some luck.

Though I was becoming more aware of fashion, I wasn't so very fashionable. I favored A-line skirts that hid my hips, madras blouses, and brown leather penny loafers with shiny copper pennies in them: that was what I could afford.

My eyes were green, I wore glasses, but I wasn't shy. I was ready to fall in love, but how old was he?

Mario and I began to go out as a couple, while Linda *fumed* back at the apartment, not at all consoled by the attentions of the pugilist or the 'French chef.' The boxer was *not* a Roman

---

[22] Old Spanish proverb?

Catholic, Linda pointed out to me. He was Eastern Orthodox. She would have to get a dispensation to marry him. And Mario *was* a Roman Catholic, if lapsed. Therefore, the case was clear: to Linda's mind, that surely meant that Mario was destined for *her*, not her greatest rival in the world.

As we both were well aware, 'mixed' marriages were frowned on in 1965 if not forbidden altogether. 'He's mine,' Linda declared. Her eyes shot blue blazes at me.

'Mine,' I stated categorically. But did I want him? *Let me think ...*

That song was running through my mind, over and over, that one called 'Cast Your Fate to the Wind'*:*

A month of nights, a year of days,
Octobers drifting into Mays;
I set my sail as the tide comes in
And I just cast my fate to the wind. [23]

'Cast your fate to the wind, girl. See where you fetch up.'

---

[23] Words and music by Vince Guaraldi, recorded, 1962; also recorded by Sounds Orchestral, 1965.

CHAPTER THREE:
Carnal Knowledge

I remember my initial surprise and dismay when I discovered that Mario was much older than anyone I had ever dated before—twenty-six years to my nineteen—and that he had recently been divorced. I had never known anyone who was divorced, except for a woman at home who lived across the street from Mother and Daddy, and that we never spoke of, even in whispers.

Divorced! Well, that ruined it! I wasn't going to marry a divorcé. Thereafter, I regarded Mario, for a time, with the curiosity that would normally have been reserved for a freak. Still, his European veneer, his worldliness and sophistication, his sheer gentlemanliness, appealed to me, and my pleasure in his company increased as the weeks went by.

I didn't have to marry him, did I? I could enjoy his company. I had never understood the dating game, and here, right in front of me, was a good chance to experiment. What could be easier? *'Practice makes perfect.'*

Mario's divorce definitely put him off of Linda's list of candidates, and she was a little easier to live with for a week or two. For a Roman Catholic like Linda, Mario was still *married*, and all but taboo for a pure virgin like herself. It showed what a sinner I was that I liked him, but she knew I was fallible. And in a way, all Linda and I had was each other for companionship and help. A female is a female, and different from a male: solidarity and cooperation must take the place of competition in time of need, we thought.

Then something happened to upset the balance, but I believe that Linda did not know about it. One night at the apartment, Mario was paying me too much attention, and Linda stomped off to bed in disgust. Rudely, she turned out the living room lights. In a flash, Mario had me on the floor and my clothes nearly off me. He was a smooth operator, certainly no green boy as Roger Douglass had been.

I never thought of resisting, I didn't have time! He began to make love to me, and I was in the throes of delight. But I became afraid, and made him stop. It was happening too fast, my conscience was bothering me. What if Linda came back and caught us? I couldn't think of what she might do to me in the dark of the night in that apartment, after the doors were locked.

I really had to try harder to make the roommate-thing work out—that was the only way to protect myself from having an affair with Mario: such an idea could not be entertained. I did not love Mario. He was older, he was Roman Catholic, and he was divorced. Three strikes. And anyway, I was only nineteen and a virgin, even if Linda thought she was the last one in the world (apart from the Queen of Heaven). I must try to save myself for my husband, as I had been taught.

So, making an effort at togetherness, on a beautiful Sunday in late October, Linda and I took a trip to Bayfront Park in downtown Miami to visit a U.S. Navy destroyer, the U.S.S. Bigelow. It was open for inspection. We could try to meet some sailors.

I wore my most beautiful and expensive outfit, a coordinated, Jackie Kennedy-type two-piece suit with a turquoise-blue silk skirt, and a sleeveless sweater heavily embroidered with multi-colored crewelwork. It was the perfect choice for autumn in Miami. I had a golden necklace with a tiny chain, and *Katharine* was spelled out in a script made of gold plate. It was just a shimmering dot on my throat. There was lots of gold

Chapter Three: *Carnal Knowledge*

jewelry like that necklace in Miami, you could find any name you wanted. The Cubans loved the glitter of gold. So did I.

Linda had on one of her tulip dresses in blue to match her eyes, plus spiked heels with pointed toes, and a string of pearls. We must have made quite a pair.

At the very moment we got on board ship and everyone was looking at us, Linda pointed out to me a silk string that was hanging from the hem of my skirt. She reached down to pull the string away for me, and voilà, the two-inch hem of my skirt fell out, leaving me wearing an unnaturally long dress with frayed edges.

A kind of 'chirrup' burst from Linda as she clapped her hand over her mouth, and I all but fainted. In those days, no one dared to have the hem of their dress *one centimeter* longer or shorter than anyone else—individuality was strictly for kooks. (And if your slip was showing, it could get you thrown out of church.)

I was so embarrassed, I could have cried; but I tried to keep my chin up and inspect the ship. It was a half-hearted attempt, though. I wanted to get off that boat as soon as possible, and go back home: so much for meeting a sailor on that sunny day. *Rats.*

Linda was smiling from ear to ear, enjoying my discomfiture. 'Shall we go?' she asked sweetly.

We didn't drive straight home after visiting the ship. Linda wasn't satisfied yet. As long as no one was looking at me, I could tolerate the frayed skirt for a while. It was nice to be out of the apartment, lovely not to be at work. We cruised around Miami, up Biscayne Boulevard, down Biscayne Boulevard … East Flagler Street, W. Flagler Street, N. Miami Avenue, S. Miami Avenue.

The royal palms lining the Avenue of the Americas were superb; we craned our necks. Linda and I were wide-eyed and wondering at the beauty that never seemed to stop. The traveler's palms in the park beckoned us on towards the beach. We walked barefoot into the sand, stockings and all. Linda and I were like two Alices. We dipped our fingers into the green water and baptized ourselves, not a care in the world.

We went to a drive-in for hamburgers and Cokes; the 'skating' girl carhops looked so pretty with their lithe bodies and tanned legs. Then, when darkness came, we drove over to look at the huge, solid concrete, dismally gray structure—sitting there like a giant bug—that was the electrical power building. In daylight, what a monstrosity! But in an utter change after dark, it became a fantasy all night, lit up with colored electric lights and decorated by swaying palm trees.

In the evenings, the lighted 'transformer' building was lovely and quite unexpected. Other people like us drove there at night to see that display. Weren't the sub-tropics wonderful? Warm weather and sunshine all the year round, balmy breezes and a sort of magic in the soft air after darkness fell. A person could live outside and rarely feel the cold—wear shorts, eat plantains, and feast on roast pig. I loved Florida as much as any native Floridian could do—I could have stayed there forever.

Perverse as it seems, I did get homesick about once a month, and cried, long distance, to my mother across the pulsing AT&T long lines from a phone booth down the block, so as not to run up mine and Linda's joint long distance telephone bill. It did not help my homesick feelings when Mother informed me that my dear friend, Sally Hedges, was to be married in a big church wedding in Memphis, and I knew I was too 'broke' to go home for it. What would a plane ticket cost anyway? I couldn't imagine.

My astonishing relationship with Mario was flourishing however, and though I would not think of marrying an elderly divorcé, I was having a wonderful time, and in some ways, felt as pampered as a princess. There was a dull pain each time I thought of my old flame, Roger Douglass, but it was easing, it was easing! I was young—surely I had time enough to find the man of my dreams, a wonderful man who would marry me and make me an honest woman.

Sally was marrying at nineteen—*eat your heart out, Kate*—but maybe I could tie the knot by twenty or twenty-one.

Chapter Three: *Carnal Knowledge*

Stranger things had happened, God knew! And I had no intention of being an old maid.

Even though she didn't really want him, Mario's attentions to me instead were a bone of contention between Linda and myself, and the rows became more frequent and violent. Strangely, we could not stop ourselves from fighting. We both did try.

Late one November evening, Linda and I had been out cruising in her car, driving around in our new-found confidence and knowledge of the city, when we started the worst quarrel we had yet begun. I believe it was the worst quarrel of my life, and the consequences could have been dire.

She started it. She said, 'You couldn't possibly have gotten a decent education at a public school. Only Catholic schools are any good.'

'What do you mean?' I protested. 'I made straight A's. I was in the Honor Society!'

I was proud of my education. *Don't you dare attack my school*, I fumed inwardly. Was smoke coming out of my ears?

'That just shows the standard,' Linda answered spitefully.

'How dare you!' I said under my breath, my indignation aroused.

Roman Catholics in Memphis had not mixed with Protestants. Why was Linda mixing with me? Roman Catholics went to parochial schools in the 1950s and '60s. We Protestants were protected from them, and they were protected from us.

Well, there was this one Italian boy in my class; his name was Michael LoPicolo. Mike was dark and handsome. We fellow classmates tended to look at him as if he were some kind of rare bird, and figured there must be a sinister story attached to why he was there with us in a public school. Mixed marriage?

Before plain, unvarnished Linda Black came along, I hadn't known any people who weren't just like me—folks were what you could call 'homogeneous' in Memphis, Tennessee.

A Quiet Life in Bedlam

Our family had been close to one black woman, our maid Honey Bunch, who cared for us, and the household, for many years when we were little. Honey Bunch taught my sisters and me how to shimmy. We shimmied for hours to the 'boogie-woogie' on the radio. Honey Bunch managed to shimmy and get the housework done all at the same time. She was amazing.

'The shimmy' was our little secret. We made a pact that our uncle, who was Church of Christ, should never get to hear about it. Uncle Lawrence had given us hell when we danced the bop at his house. Why did he have the radio on then? I said to him, 'I think you should examine your soul and stop casting stones.'

I got a spanking for it, of course. It was disrespectful to talk to an elder and better that way. 'Presbyterian' and 'Church of Christ' couldn't get along. It was like mixing oil and water. I didn't know why Lawrence Hitchins had married into our family. He and Aunt Dale had eloped, causing a scandal and no end of trouble.

Linda, jerking me back into our argument, said caustically, 'I've been meaning to tell you—it's only pigs who don't wash out the bathtub after shaving their legs!'

I was aghast. Applying tremendous self-discipline, I had *never* told Linda that she squeezed the toothpaste tube in the middle. I should have. *And* she left the cap off, letting it dry out, Miss Priss.

'You are very holier than thou!' I retorted. I did not want to fight, but my gorge was rising. *Ratfink!*

'What about the way you spend an hour in the bubble bath, and get the mirror all foggy, and everything damp? And then it mildews afterwards. And as to schools, how can you learn anything useful from nuns and priests?'

'Ho!' Linda got huffed up. 'My sister is a nun,' she said haughtily.

'Well, lah di dah!' I spat at her, 'Papist.' That was the worst thing I could think of. I had heard my grandmother speak darkly of papists. (That was the Presbyterian in her). How can

Chapter Three: *Carnal Knowledge*

you call names when you don't know what hurts somebody? Even after three months, we were still strangers to each other.

Odd, that I should have said that word, 'papist.' I never had before. It hadn't been long since I'd known the difference between papist and Baptist. In the Memphis of my childhood, I was not aware of different religions. There was only 'Met-dist' and 'Bab-list,' with a sprinkling of 'Prezbeetering' (Presbyterians) and those zealots, the Church of Christ. Oh, and Pentecostal Holiness, that one of Daddy's sisters belonged to. Aunt Clarice could speak in tongues, and we were mightily frightened by it. I remember, my mother did not know whether to laugh or take it seriously. I thought Aunt Clarice was weird because she wouldn't let her daughters shave their legs.

As far as I know, there were not many Roman Catholics (Catlicks) or Jews in Memphis—well, I guess there were a few third-generation EYE-talians who spoke with a drawl as broad as your hand, and maintained their own little conclave on one side of town. They attended the Sacred Heart Catholic Church or Saint Anne's, and sent their children to the private parochial schools. And those families had been Southerners for so long, that they hardly knew they were Catlick.

The only 'Jews' I knew about were the ones fleeing from perils and pestilences within the horrible inky-colored picture pages of our huge King James Bible. The engravings in that Bible made one afraid to think of what it must be like to be born a Jew, though I had never seen any Jewish people, and was hardly aware that there were any in Tennessee. I thought they most likely lived in Judea or Arabia or New York, if they existed at all.

Roman Catholics married among themselves. If, by chance, one of them picked *you* as being worthy of marriage, you had to convert. You had to swear to bring up your children Catholic—something we Protestants thought was blasphemous. And you had to read a Catholic Bible, which was apparently different, and, worst of all, you had kow-tow to the Pope.

If you married a Catholic, you had to fight with your family over the marriage; you had to fight with your mate's family about the conversion and the future children. It was said that your own family wouldn't be allowed to go into the Catholic Church for the wedding, because non-Catholics were not allowed inside a Roman Catholic Church. And Catholic girls could not be bridesmaids in a Protestant wedding (i.e., better not make friends with one). I'm not saying those were the actual facts of the matter, but it is what Protestants believed. Plainly speaking, it wasn't a bed of roses to fall in love with a Catholic, or to have anything to do with one, apparently. Holy Mother Church did not allow for lesser beings.

'Growing up in Memphis' does not prepare you for broader horizons. Linda Black was a broader horizon. I did not know how to answer anyone as bigoted as she was. I could not match her for self-righteousness. We were the Odd Couple, two mismatched roommates, one uptight and the other slovenly, much the same as in that famous Neil Simon play on Broadway.

Actually, I probably would have made a good Roman Catholic, had I been born to it. Guilt came easily to me. I felt constantly repentant, even when I hadn't done anything. I would have relished the difference between venial sins and mortal sins. In religious matters, I wanted to follow the rules. I wanted to know where I stood with God: was '*He who must be obeyed*' up there keeping score somewhere? I liked clear guidelines, as long as they were not too harsh. (And what a boon to have some reason to feel superior.)

I could countenance the idea of a priest for counseling, but did not know how I would have felt about 'confession.' Would I have told lies? I love beautiful vestments, mystery, ceremony and Gothic churches. For me, it would have been pure pleasure to go to mass every Sunday and holy day, and see the priest and choir come marching down the center aisle, carrying the cross and waving incense.

Linda, one of the more canting of Catholics, had more vitriol to pour on me (*gasp, gag*), as the time of reckoning unfolded its multi-headed self: *Just keep it up and see what happens,* I steamed ... Was I strong enough to throttle her?

Chapter Three: *Carnal Knowledge*

'Holy Moses,' I cried aloud as I listened to Linda Blackheart, astounded that anyone could hate me that much.

'*Poison ivy, poison ivy, late at night while you're sleeping, poison ivy comes a-creepin' around ...*' [24] sang the Coasters inside my roaring head. Help! I need somebody ...

She comes on like a rose, but everybody knows,
She'll get you in Dutch
You can look, but you better not touch ...

How can I defend myself? I wondered wildly. I felt as if I were gargling wasps; I was stuttering with rage. Oddly, I can't remember exactly what she said, I blocked it out: something about 'burning in Hell,' and 'only Catholics go to heaven,' and 'the Protestant Church is not a real church.'

I could not defend myself. I simply did not possess her corrosive nature.

Then, adding insult to injury, she said in a steely voice, 'You'll never get married, no one will want you.' That was below the belt! The prospect of never getting married was my worst nightmare. How could I bear a life alone? Did what she said, have the power of a curse? I was surprised at the murderous wrath that filled me. Somewhere out there in the ethers, my grandmother commanded, 'Shield yourself from the evil eye.'

'Holy Mother Church ... ' Linda said, beginning anew.

All at once, I felt the suffering of the Incas and the Aztecs when the Spanish Conquistadors forced a cross up their rumps. I was practically foaming at the mouth. I could not control myself. I was so furious about the abominable things Linda was saying (and I haven't listed them all), that I jumped out of the car in an unknown section of town, about five miles roughly from our apartment. It was just one of those knee-jerk actions that is done before you have time to think. I had never been so angry before. The injustice of Linda's remarks could not be

---

[24] 'Poison Ivy', by Jerry Leiber and Mike Stoller, sung by The Coasters, 1959.

borne. She hurt my pride, and that is the worst thing anyone can do.

I had to put distance between her and me, immediately. The car door fell open, as if by magic. Then, there I was on the sidewalk, boiling mad, stunned, disoriented. Linda was so unreasonable that she just squealed her car away like a hell-bent dragster, and left me there stranded, alone in the dark with no protection, the hostile eyes of strangers staring at me from every window I was sure—and my heart in my throat. What had I done? What could I do?

I had very little money on me, which was good in a way, as I knew there must be plenty of unscrupulous, desperate Cuban refugees around, just waiting to get at my life savings, if I had any. But then again, without any money—maybe I had some coins—how was I going to take a taxi back to the apartment, and what would I find when I got there? It just didn't do, to think about it. I must act, and quickly.

I started walking. It would take some time to get back to the apartment, all night perhaps, but I could manage it as long as I wasn't interfered with. The numbered grid of Miami's streets and avenues would take me home as surely as a streetcar if I could count, and I could. As my mind cleared, I knew I should tackle it. I knew I could do it. The weather was warm and calm, a quiet night of quiet stars. *Home, walk home,* I told myself.

Some minutes had gone by when a car pulled up beside me, and I heard filthy language. I ignored it, and just kept walking. I had been alone at night on the streets of Memphis before, and though I had been afraid, I was never threatened in any way.

Minutes passed, and there was more harassment from these guys, and a few half-hearted attempts to get me into the car. I suppose the men decided that I wasn't a streetwalker, and they left. But then they came back. This time, I fully sensed the danger. Mercifully, there was a dime in my pocket. I dashed into a telephone booth, and called Mario. Thank God he was at home. Mario agreed to come and rescue me, and said he was leaving

Chapter Three: *Carnal Knowledge*

leaving immediately. But I had at least five minutes to wait until he could arrive.

Is this what people mean when they say take a walk on the wild side? I wondered.

I stayed in the phone booth, and remained relatively calm. The men in the car were laughing and jeering, waiting for me to come out. *They can wait,* I thought. I wasn't budging. The men began to climb out of the car one by one and surround the phone booth. It was very frightening, but I was resolved, they weren't taking me, and I knew that help was on the way.

'Thank the Lord for Mario!' I said fervently to the glass doors. I closed my eyes and held on tight. '*Hey baby, take a walk on the wild side. Hey sugar ...*' [25]

What would I have done if Mario had not been at home? I hadn't a clue what the telephone number was for the police. I could have called the Operator even without a dime, but I didn't know if she would believe me. People pulled all sorts of tricks on operators.

Time passed. I was sure it was more than five minutes. A taxi went by, I wished I were in it. A policeman pulled up. Mario arrived simultaneously. Whew! For the moment at least I was saved from 'a fate worse than death,' as they used to call rape. That particular fate finally cornered me years later—but for the moment, I was not aware of any future. I only knew it to be the present hour, 11:00 p.m. on a dark night in downtown Miami, early in November of 1965, and that Mario had possibly saved my life.

I was aware with my pounding heart, and through a mild feeling of shock, that Mario had come when I needed him, that I could trust him and call him my friend—clearly, the only one I had in that lonely city. As he got out of his car, he looked grim, an uncharacteristic furrow on his otherwise placid brow. He called me 'Kit,' the first time he had done that. It sounded strangely like 'sweetheart.'

---

[25] 'Take a Walk on the Wild Side,' a song made famous by Lou Reed in the 1970s, but the history of it goes much farther back, to 1962, at least.

'Tu amor.'

The would-be rapists had absconded. Cowards.

We drove to the apartment building to find that Linda had locked and bolted the door. My key got me nowhere. Linda Black had no intention of letting me in; the chain-lock was on. I could see her glaring at me through the window. I banged on the door. Nothing. It did no good to threaten or cajole.

I screamed at her, 'Linda, let me in!' No answer. 'I live here!'

Apparently, I didn't anymore.

Linda was immovable, implacable, her rage as blind as mine had been. She might have been 'Half-Dome' at Yosemite. What a mess!

Mario, bemused, left us then, and went back to his own apartment to await the outcome.

'He's a brick,' I murmured, and threw him a backward glance. *'Silver-footed ironies, veiled jokes, tiptoe malices ...'* [26] Somehow that passage from Edith Wharton jumped into my head. Obviously, I was still in shock.

Linda would not let me in; I did not know what to do. Her jewel-blue eyes blazed like sapphires, and just as hard and cold. I ran down to the corner phone booth and called my mother at home in Memphis. Feeling very sorry for myself, I sobbed over the long-distance telephone lines for fully half an hour, collect:

'Mother, she won't let me in ... what can I do?' I rambled, nearly hysterical.

Mother talked to me reasonably, quietly, until I calmed down and gathered my wits again.

It never occurred to me to catch a plane for home, and Mother did not offer me a plane ticket, or even a bus ticket. She had her own problems. She had set me free. She hadn't thrown me out, but I could not go back. I was on my own.

Anyway, I wanted to stay in Miami; there was nothing for me in Memphis, 'that sad place of sorrow,' as it seemed to be.

---

[26] Edith Wharton's *'A Backward Glance,'* Chapter 8.

Chapter Three: *Carnal Knowledge*

Linda and I would go our separate ways, and though the rent would be hard to pay alone, I was ready to begin looking for another apartment right then and there, at midnight.

'Could there be any "for rent" signs in the windows?' I asked myself. I had noticed some a few days earlier. That neighborhood had places for rent I knew—studio apartments, mostly. I realized there was no point in asking obstinate, headstrong Linda to move, so I would have to be the one to take the initiative.

Taking the initiative has never been a problem for me, but I do tend to miscalculate the odds at times and bite off more than I can chew. At twelve a.m. on a Saturday, it was a cinch that all of my prospective landlords were in bed.

Slowly, I climbed the concrete stairs to the apartment, and sat down on the top step of the landing to the second floor where I had lived. That was as close as I could get to my own things, my own bed, my precious 'hope chest'—even though I didn't like the Melmac dishes my mother had given me—and my privacy.

Maybe I could cry. Maybe I could stare dry-eyed into the night. It was chilly. I had on a sleeveless blouse. What could I do? Where could I go? I was very tired, and emotionally spent. Nothing makes me more exhausted than a bout of crying, and what good would *'Crying'* do now? (*Shades of Roy Orbison, again.*) I would have to behave like the grownup girl that I was and get on with life, even if it had to wait until tomorrow morning.

People used to say, 'Tomorrow is the first day of the rest of your life.' It almost makes me laugh to think of it now. Was it? Was Saturday morning the beginning of a life that would be worth something? A married life with children? I didn't know. Things looked pretty bleak.

I'm probably not the first one to spend the night on a top step, I thought sadly. I did not know it then, but my mother spent many nights sleeping in the shrubbery, outside the house, when Daddy just would not leave her alone.

'Adam, please ... ' I heard her say.

Poor me. The dawn would come; but, I really hate to sleep on concrete—I'm not the ascetic type—didn't even have a pillow. They hadn't started inventing those mouth-inflatable plastic ones yet. I liked to sing. To give myself comfort, I began softly to sing.

I should have sung a dirge, if I knew one, but instead I sang a bossa nova melody that was running through my head. I was always singing, inside myself. I could not stop it somehow, there was this perpetual music swirling around in my brain like the perpetual motion of a (syncopated) clock. As a teenager, and for years afterward, I thought everyone experienced the same thing, and that it was totally ordinary to have a jukebox inside your head.

I listened to the inner music, and started to hum, then to sing *'Wave,'* by Tom Jobim:

So close your eyes, for that's a lovely way to be
Aware of things your heart alone was meant to see
The fundamental loneliness goes whenever two can
dream a dream together.
You can't deny, don't try to fight the rising sea
Don't fight the moon, the stars above, and don't fight me
The fundamental loneliness goes whenever two can
dream a dream together.
When I saw you first, the time was half past three
When your eyes met mine, it was eternity.
By now we know the wave it on its way to be
Just catch the wave, don't be afraid of loving me ... [27]

Then there he was, Mario looking for me, with his head sticking out of his apartment door a little further down the corridor. 'Kit?' he said, looking both ways, like Janus.

---

[27] 'Wave,' by Antonio Carlos Jobim, Corcovado Music Corp., composition date unknown.

Chapter Three: *Carnal Knowledge*

And so, the events of the evening led me to Mario's apartment, and into his protective embrace. It was as simple as that, the turning of fate.

Mario was waiting for me; he knew I would come. 'Are you hungry?' he asked, and welcomed me with paella and sangria. Raoul was out, but he left food.

I was hungry, but not for victuals. I needed loving, protecting, petting, comforting. Mario Fiqueroa was more than willing to do it, if I would let him.

What an ordeal! I fumed. When I remembered Linda's behavior, Jane Austen's words came to mind, *'I would have that woman whipped through the streets!'* All I wanted was a quiet life, and what did I get? Bedlam!

'What happened?' Mario asked.

'I don't want to talk about it.' I could not hold my grief back any longer. Then I looked at him.

'Come and get your love, little baby,' he seemed to say with his slow, gentle smile. He put his arms around me.

And so, my lover made the loving as pleasant as it could be under the circumstances. He was tender, and patient, and kind. It was not terribly romantic, because I did not love him and had no illusions that I might marry him. The sensations were entirely pleasurable; I can't remember that it hurt at all. I kept my eyes open the entire time, so as to see how it was done.

Carnal knowledge. It seemed as if the whole world had been conspiring to keep me innocent until wedlock of something so simple—the act of coupling—and in the human instance, such a natural expression of love and care. *But so forbidden.* The closeness and warmth, the intimate contact with a man, the smell of his aftershave lotion—it was intoxicating. I remember it even now.

There were other girls of my generation who did not know the consequences of the sex act; but I did. I had watched through the seasons the animals on my grandfather's farm, and made the connection. I wanted to ask my mother if I was right, but she didn't care to talk about it. When I persisted, Mother told me, in the coldest possible way, the bare biological facts, with no embroidery and little humanity. I cried. I was fifteen.

I believe that Mother was rather nervous about it. No one had told her the facts of life. Well, she had to tell me, the eldest of three girls. There was no place else for a teenager to learn. Usually a bride found out on her wedding night. It *was* a relief to hear that babies didn't pop out of your navel, as my friends had said. Certainly the details concerning the birth of a child were as shrouded in mystery as the location of the Holy Grail.

To spare herself more embarrassment, my mother expected me to inform my younger sisters in their turn before they got much older, about what happened after marriage, and I did. I hope I was kind. They didn't know whether to believe me or not, I was always telling stories.

I never could understand why Mother did it in that abrupt way. She did most things in a harmonious, gracious and pleasing way. She seemed to be unaware of my deeper feelings and emotional needs. It was as bad as hearing that there was no Santa Claus—it took the romance out of my imaginings. It gave me something to think about, and ultimately, something to worry about.

And so I lived in fear of pregnancy from that day on, and in an agony of guilt that I was no longer a 'good girl.' But I did not regret the experience—I knew I had to find it out sooner or later—was sort of looking forward to it. The event changed my consciousness in a kind of 'awakening.' My body had been sleeping through childhood, and now it was awake, to passion.

I thanked God profusely each month as my menstruation arrived, and made many foolish promises to the Almighty about how really well I would behave in *every other aspect* of life if *He* would grant that I should not become pregnant; but I knew that I would never be able to give up the lovemaking once it had begun; I liked it too much.

I had been a reluctant virgin ever since Roger and I undressed and got into bed together before graduation—then didn't do anything more than just look at each other. But I would not have admitted to it even under torture. Nice girls did

Chapter Three: *Carnal Knowledge*

not have those thoughts. I really wanted to obey the rules, be conventional, conform to the demands of society, but things kept happening to derail me—quite unaccountably.

Mario Fiqueroa did not seem to suffer any qualms about taking advantage of a poor virgin, and I guess one could say that we became lovers out of mutual need. Mario had only recently finalized his divorce—if in fact, it *was* finalized—especially traumatic for a Roman Catholic, to whom marriage was a sacrament and divorce not recognized or allowed.

Mario was probably not ready to remarry; anyway, he never mentioned it, and months went by before I even thought to discuss the possibility with him. Mario Fiqueroa was just not the sort of man I had in mind to marry. I wanted someone nearer my own age, someone who was Protestant, because people mixed religions at their peril.

Different sorts of people intermarry so easily nowadays—different religions, different races, different nationalities—that it seems quite commonplace to produce children who don't know what they are: and since there are few barriers now to race, creed or color, I suppose it hardly matters. But I remember when it could tear a family, a neighborhood—even a town apart, for a Protestant to marry a Catholic, a Christian to marry a Jew, a black person to marry a white one. Some of the aforementioned couplings were not recognized by the church, some were not recognized by law. It was a different world in the first two-thirds of the 20th century.

I wanted to marry someone whose heritage was completely American and therefore, familiar, not strange or foreign. Oh yes, that formula sounds very dull, but it was what I wanted at the time: poor stupid creature.

'*Poor little fool, oh yeah, I was a fool, uh huh,*' [28] sang Ricky Nelson on Mario's hi-fi as I stood in his living room wondering what to do next.

---

[28] 'Poor Little Fool,' written by Sharon Sheeley and recorded by Ricky Nelson, in 1958.

A Quiet Life in Bedlam

'Uh huh,' I nodded absentmindedly, and wondered what Raoul was cooking for dinner. It was the next day after the debacle, and I was as hungry as ever.

I stayed three nights with Mario, and walked the streets of the neighborhood during the daytime, looking for an apartment. What I found could not compare to the one I had rented with Linda—one paycheck would not go so far as to buy such luxury as a separate kitchen and bedroom. I got what the English call a large bed-sitter, or 'studio apartment' in American English, for sixty-five dollars a month, one week's salary.

I lived there at the bed-sitter for several months, and listened to pop music every morning on my clock radio as I got dressed for work; that was when I heard 'California Dreamin' [29] for the first time. I was thrilled.

'All the leaves are brown, and the sky is gray ...' Well, it would have been, if I weren't in Florida. Actually, the weather was quite nice—good thing, too. There was no heat in the studio apartment, and the floors were terrazzo.

The advantage of the bed-sitter was that it was only two blocks away from Mario. So close, and yet so far away. I had to get out of Mario's apartment quickly, for Raoul's sake (who was staying with friends), and for my own. I had not been living with Mario for more than forty-eight hours before he wanted to photograph me—in the nude! It's a slippery slope, so they say.

The landlord for the new apartment was a deeply dodgy-looking critter, and I felt forewarned to stay away from him. I left my rent money in his mailbox, upstairs.

The separation from Linda had been wild and bitter. We were both immature, and there was no love lost between us. She watched me move out, scowling like a wraith, then gave up the apartment within the week and moved in with her sister in South Dade County.

---

[29] 'California Dreamin',' sung by the Mamas and Papas, written by John and Michelle Phillips, 1965.

Chapter Three: *Carnal Knowledge*

Linda had not wanted the apartment, but she did not want *me* to have it. The abandoned pad was a peach, and so near to Mario, just two doors down the corridor from the landing. Months later, I heard that Linda Bernadette Black had gone home to Memphis. *Great,* I said to no one in particular, *good riddance to her. Her parents deserve her.* I had never met such a stubborn person in my life!

She eventually married. One hopes it was a good Catholic. Enough about her.

CHAPTER FOUR:
True Grit

It was hard to live independently on what I made at the telephone company, even though they paid me 'a good wage for a woman.' Money was always a problem. I remember walking into Woolworth's in Miami for some sewing needles, and gazing longingly at all the various notions pocketed around the long aisles of the store. They were inexpensive, but cost more than I had. Even a 'tomato pincushion' was out of my reach.

I rarely got a decent meal unless Mario took pity on me, and carried me out to dinner at the Kentucky Fried Chicken. The only day that I personally could splurge on food was payday when I allowed myself a hamburger, French fries and a milkshake at the Burger King. That was heaven. Otherwise, I lived on mayonnaise sandwiches, scrambled eggs, and pot pies. Oh, and Campbell's Soups—they were a blessing.

Smoking was popular among my contemporaries, but I knew I could not afford to sustain a habit like that, and didn't start. My friends said smoking would help to keep the weight off, but I didn't get enough food as it was. What luxury, to gain weight.

I scrounged around other peoples' trash containers looking for cola bottles that I could cash in for the deposit: that way, I had my bus fare at least, for I had to get to work, and my only

Chapter Four: *True Grit*

transportation was the municipal transit system. Mario had a car, but he worked in the opposite direction. I didn't, at first, tell him about my desperation. I was proud. I did not want to become what was described as a 'mistress.' There was a fine line.

At the telephone company, on the bulletin board, I advertised for a roommate, and got one. You could trust just about anyone who worked there, they screened their employees carefully. My new roommate, Joyce, was a perky little thing, and she was ideal as a roommate, because she worked all night. That way, we rarely saw one another.

But I had to make more money. I did not want to be dependent on a roommate to live. The position of information operator at Southern Bell Telephone was considered to be an entry position for girls and women. Southern Bell had to find out if you were dependable before they would let you in to the inner sanctums of the telecommunications monopoly.

Men starting work at 'Ma Bell,' as the firm was affectionately called by the employees, could become linemen, climbing poles, stringing wires, digging trenches, etc. A prerequisite was that you liked to work outside. When Glen Campbell sang that song, 'Wichita Lineman,'[30] I really thought he was talking about a telephone man, but a manager at the telephone company squelched that. 'No,' he said, 'it's an electrical power lineman.'

'Are you sure?' I asked him.

'Sure.' End of discussion.

But I still think, after all these years, that it's a telephone man:

I am a lineman for the county, and I drive the main road
Searchin' in the sun for another overload.
I hear you singin' in the wire,

---

[30] 'Wichita Lineman,' is often referred to as 'the first existential country song'; written in 1968 by Jimmy Webb, and recorded by Glen Campbell.

77

A Quiet Life in Bedlam

I can hear you through the whine
And the Wichita Lineman is still on the line ...

A lineman who wanted to get out of the weather might start work as a 'frameman' at the telephone company. Framemen worked in a noisy hot room with huge batteries and lots of colored telephone wires. And these wires, called 'pairs'—one positive, one negative—were being pulled and reconnected all the time as orders came in to connect phones—or disconnect them, especially if someone hadn't paid their bill. [31]

Plus, in 'the frame,' there was lots of carrying to and fro of very heavy equipment. The din of the machines spinning and heaving and clacking caused hearing problems for some of the framemen later in life, but what they didn't know wouldn't hurt them, and framers were considered by us operators to be lucky dogs. They got paid eighty-five dollars a week on the Miami pay scale—a fortune.

At that time in history (yes, only a few years ago), women were thought not to be physically strong enough for the heavy work of framemen, and were effectively barred from the job until women's liberation came along.

In 1965, women were still 'the fairer sex,' and had to be protected. *'Male chauvinism'* is what people called it at the time. Such was life in the big city, and all across the land. Again, the 1950s lasted well into the 1960s, as far as attitudes toward women were concerned.

The most well known woman in the world, apart from Eleanor Roosevelt, Jackie Kennedy, and Marilyn Monroe, was Bridget Bardot, acknowledged by most to be the universal 'sex kitten.' Not only was Bridget well known (and well-endowed), she was widely admired and emulated. What does 'sex kitten' mean? It means 'sex object,' plain and simple.

Didn't you want to be a sex kitten? I did, but kept it as a dark and hidden secret. In my humble opinion, it *is* within the

---

[31] There is nothing worse, in my opinion, than to pick up a telephone receiver and find the line dead. I paid my telephone bill, always.

realm of possibility for a brunette to be a sex kitten; only blonds are bombshells—that's the way of the world.

After 'women's liberation,' women took the job of frameman, but they were not, in many cases, strong enough to lift the heavy equipment. Some of the male framemen had to help them, with the result of hidden resentment and strained employee relations. But no doubt, afterwards, women went on to greater things within the upper echelons of the telecommunications industry. Southern Bell Telephone was one of the first of the monoliths to promote women. Beginning a career anywhere within the confines of Ma Bell was considered to be a fortunate turn in any person's life.

Men at Ma Bell progressed from lineman and frameman perhaps, to switchman, repairman, and other skilled jobs by making a 'bid' on an open position. That position could be located anywhere around in the greater suburban area—Hialeah, Coral Gables, South Miami, etc.

Operators who wanted to advance had some choices too, for a kind of 'promotion' (as regards salary) or 'parallel move/lateral move,' as they called it, through the inner channels of Southern Bell.

I had a strict upbringing, and learned discipline early in life; so, in many ways, was well-suited to working at what was considered by the general population to be a benign institution—up there in importance, say, with some of the public utilities like Memphis Light, Gas and Water; or the Federal Government—a paternalistic employer, a lifetime job, a pension and a gold watch at the end. *BORING!!* as that character on *Rowan and Martin's Laugh-in* would have said, but it was what a lot of people wanted.

In Memphis, I had been chased about, virtually persecuted, by a union representative who desperately wanted me to join the telephone workers' union. In the lives of so-called 'blue-collar workers,' labor unions mattered very much—solidarity and all that. (Though we at the telephone company never considered ourselves to be blue-collar workers.)

A Quiet Life in Bedlam

I was bound and determined not to join the telephone workers' union, because I could not afford to pay the union dues. I became opposed to unions after that. It was like having a hostile figure chase me through my dreams. It took many years before I understood that a union was there to protect you and not to hound you to death.

I was resentful of the regimentation at the telephone company—the 'machine' mentality, as I saw it—a kind of 'Taylorism.' We worked with the precision of those on an assembly line, becoming smoothly functioning units, like at the Ford plant in Detroit. But being so young and inexperienced, considered myself lucky to get work at eighteen, just out of high school. Everyone congratulated me on landing such a good job.

For once, my mother was proud of me. People respected me more when I said I worked for Southern Bell Telephone Company. I could get my paychecks cashed at any bank with no problem; I only had to say the check was from Southern Bell. It was like gold.

I was punctual, plus had perfect attendance, and so I was qualified to be offered a better position within the concern. 'Perfect attendance' was very important at the telephone company. The operators joked about pregnant women having to give birth during their split-shifts, so as to be back at work by 4:00 p.m. The trouble was, I thought they were serious.

The American comedienne, Lily Tomlin, when playing the role of power-mad operator, 'Ernestine,' caught the spirit of the institution when she mimicked, 'We are the telephone company. We are omnipotent.' That line made a lot of people laugh, including me—I laughed while I cried.

When I applied for the position of 'service representative' in the telephone business office at Coral Gables, I got it. I was overjoyed. The job paid eighty dollars a week, but it meant forty-five minutes of riding the bus from where I lived near downtown Miami. It was a 'lateral move' to the clerical department where the billing, service orders and complaints were handled.

Chapter Four: *True Grit*

I was jolly tired of being an operator anyway. The job was monotonous and repetitive—so boring. And people called up with stupid questions, like:

1) 'Do you know how long it takes to drive to California from here?'

'Haven't got a clue,' I answered.

2) 'Can you give me a fool-proof recipe for homemade biscuits?'

'I can't cook,' I replied.

3) 'Do you know if I'm pregnant?'

'How should I know that?' I asked, rather shocked.

I was hoping I wasn't pregnant myself, and didn't have any idea what signs to look for. I only knew that your stomach grew. *Look, you weird people,* I was thinking, *I'm supposed to give you telephone numbers!*

The telephone service assistant, a kind of 'floor supervisor,' reprimanded me later for not modulating my voice tones on that call. We operators were closely observed, and given demerits for service errors. The chief operator was often listening secretly to our calls. She was a terror.

Anyone who has ever seen movies or film-clips of old-style telephone operators throwing those long black insulated cords around, and singing into the mouthpiece, 'Operator!,' as they stab the plug into the tiny hole, will have an idea that the job was more fun than it actually was. It was stymieing, stultifying, fossilizing. I felt as if I were turning into a vegetable. Or a stone.

There were a few times when I arrived at the switchboard soaking wet from inclement weather, and never really believed the service assistant when she assured me that I could not get electrocuted as I sat down, headset in place and plugged in, to answer a call.

Everything was always worse in the 'traffic' department, where the operators worked, during the full moon or foul weather, don't ask me why. At least, on those busy days, it was more exhilarating to deal with the challenges that came in, fast and furious. One lived through a few zippy, happy moments during the creepy-crawly eight-hour stretch of the workday: in some ways, it was like being a doctor in the emergency room at the hospital.

The day of the full moon seemed to be when 'the crazies' came out from under their rocks—though this has never been scientifically explained. The 'information' calls came in from the public by the thousands.

'Can you tell me where to get a skeleton for Halloween?' inquired a customer one October 30th, a night of full moonlight.

'No,' I answered shortly.

'A broomstick for a witch?' asked the man brightly.

Silence, my end. Then I disconnected him. *Was he kidding me?* The chief operator came flying down on my position like a bat out of hell. That was disconcerting! I looked up at her, all innocence.

'Yes, ma'am?'

'It is not allowed to be rude to customers,' the old harpy hissed into my unharnessed ear.

'Yeh yeh,' I answered, but she didn't hear me. *'Yakety yak, don't talk back.'*

The next customer asked me, 'Can you tell me how to break up with my boyfriend?'

Determined to be polite, I answered, 'It's a good question. I wish I knew. If you find out, would you call me back? Operator number 13.'

'Okay. Bye.'

'Bye.'

In Memphis, in the winter, I dreaded working on the 'snow days.' Memphians were not used to snow, and the city authorities did not plow the snow away quickly enough, if they did it at all. People got panicked and confused when they couldn't get to the store even to buy beer. You guessed it—on snow days, there were many more calls to the information operator, presumably a kind of 'personal assistant' to the public, as it were:

'Information.'

Chapter Four: *True Grit*

'Dew yew know whurr I can gooo to buyyy a new snow shovel?'

'No, sir. But I can give you the number for a hardware store.'

'That'll be peaches.'

'The number is, umpty-en, umpty-to, umpty-tree.'

'Thank yew. Bye honey!'

'Bye.'

When it snowed, in Memphis, we operators were strongly discouraged from going home for the night after work. Instead, we were offered beds inside the big brick buildings near Central Park. We were then roused early enough to go on duty at 8:00 a.m., manning the switchboards to answer a minimum of a zillion calls an hour. We had, beside us at our positions, a little 'pegging' device for counting calls. Any wise operator would peg a few extras each hour to keep up the averages.

I disliked sleeping at the telephone company overnight, because I only sleep well in my own bed. There is something about lumpy mattresses and foreign pillows that I cannot abide. Some people think it is exciting to sleep in a strange bed, but not me. One night at the telephone dormitory, I slept on a pillow that was so fat, and put my neck at such an odd angle, that I dreamed of being strangled by the neck until dead. It was a kind of 'gallows' scene from a past life: that scared me. It was so real.

Miami, that darling city, did not have any 'snow days,' hah. Floridians had an easy life.

The Omniscient Telephone Company later changed our job descriptions from information operators to 'directory assistance operators,' presumably to more clearly identify our function, and weed out some of the dumbbell customers. The 'old' telephone monopoly was never lacking for customers.

We even got a slight raise in pay, and automatic switchboards where we didn't have to throw the cords and risk electrocution. That was progress. But I hated working in the traffic department—temperamentally, I was unsuited—and was much happier when they sent me along to the clerical department where my problem-solving abilities were appreciated.

The position of 'service representative' proved to be more challenging than even I wanted. During my working hours, I was as busy as a one-armed paperhanger, selling 'color telephones,' extensions, 'Touchtone,' 'Princess' phones, and bell chimes. In addition to that, I solved every 'billing' problem known to man, and weathered the storm of complaints from people who perceived themselves to be mistreated by a monopoly.

Memphis, my own little town, is famous for the lines of a song sung by Johnny Rivers: *'Long distance information, give me Memphis, Tennessee.'* I miss Memphis whenever I hear that song. I was young in Memphis, unformed. And I was as lonely as the long distance runner. God knows, at the age of eighteen or nineteen, I had a long distance to run.

As for my remarks about the telephone company, they gave me well-paid work for many years when I needed a job, and I do owe them some gratitude. I was never sexually harassed once when I worked there, and I *was* at other places where I was employed.

After I had moved away from Linda Black, and Linda went to live with her sister in South Miami, my love affair with Mario Fiqueroa reached full flower. Mario began to take me out at night to elegant, expensive places where the Maitre de's bowed us to our table and the over-blown Cuban women, dressed in full fig, rolled their eyes at him and switched their tails like hussies.

I felt like a fish out of water in a nightclub. I couldn't even drink. No one asked me my age though, and once, I drank a Planter's Punch and was deathly sick afterwards.

Mario drank very little. Because of a popular song, *'Tequila,'* I asked him, 'Do you drink tequila?' I figured it was something the Spanish drink, like the Japanese drink *sake* and the Russians drink vodka.

And he answered, 'No. That's low class.' I raised my eyebrows.

Chapter Four: *True Grit*

I tried to learn from Mario's sophisticated behavior; was impressed with his knowledge and control; flattered that he had eyes for no one else but me in that bright company. Mario Fiqueroa was just the sort of man to inspire confidence and bring out the best in a moulting female. I wanted to be more beautiful. My parents were both handsome—I didn't see why I couldn't be.

After having worn glasses from the age of eight, I managed to order contact lenses by giving up some of the pot pies and Campbell's Soups. The contacts were the hard plastic kind, and sat right on the cornea of my eye, waiting to cause trouble. I never in my life had such excruciating pain as when a bit of grit got under one of them and I fell out of my chair by the switchboard in agony. That gave the service assistant a turn. She kindly sent me to the nurse.

A person who was as near-sighted as I was had to carry an extra piece of luggage, nearly, to tote all the paraphernalia that went with contact lenses. It wasn't just 'the contact lenses and me,' by any means. No indeed.

In my purse was a tiny, ocular-looking storage case for the contacts, plus a bottle of saline solution, some cleaning solution, my regular glasses, my sunglasses, and my prescription sunglasses. It was worth the trouble though, because contact lenses were revolutionizing the way girls looked—*men seldom make passes at girls who wear glasses*—and all that, as Dorothy Parker wisely noted.

Contact lenses had been around for some time, but it took the general public a few years to accept them. Some people thought contacts were prohibitively expensive, and they did gouge quite a hole in my budget. It was more than a week's salary, more than the rent for a month.

I loved the way I looked without the four-eyes, but I could not keep the darn contacts *in* my eyes and *under* my lids. One night, a contact lens flipped right across the table into Mario's lobster. Another night, my 'left eye' flew across the floor and landed under a neighboring table. Mario rose, sauntered over to

A Quiet Life in Bedlam

the surprised diners, and asked their permission to search under the table for my contact lens.

Everyone knew in those days how much contact lenses cost, and how important it was to locate a lost one. A myopic person owned only *one* precious pair of lenses at a time, and guarded them like garnets. The amused diners at the guilty table scooted back their chairs—and there Mario was, down on his hands and knees, looking for my lost lens. He found it, and I was forever grateful.

He is a brave man, I thought. Imagine having the nerve to do that!

There *was* one thing Mario did that was disconcerting: he enjoyed taking me to the movies—not just ordinary movies with John Wayne, Rock Hudson or Doris Day. No. Naughty movies, 'art movies,' or 'French art house films,' as they were euphemistically called—and by today's standards, they would probably be labeled 'soft porn.' In 1965, they were known as 'blue movies,' or XX-rated. Upon brief reflection, I thought ... *Mario is trying to corrupt me!*

I had not known that 'art house' films existed, could not watch them, couldn't look—I was mortified. I thought that Satan must be breathing down my neck as I sat there beside Mario's warm body. What if someone found out that I had seen a blue movie! There would definitely be a smudge on my reputation. But I did not want Mario to leave me behind at my bedsitter—I spent too much time alone—so I went with him, hiding behind my big tortoise-shell sunglasses, at night (and that was long before the fashion for it), until we got inside the theatre, and I could breathe freely again, dropping the 'movie star' pretense.

I was so ashamed to be observed there, as if my name and social security number were printed on my forehead along with the names of my parents. I did not dare to meet the eyes of the other patrons, who were probably libertines and perverts. Actually, I had never heard those words—*libertine* and *pervert*—but I knew which category my mother would put the ticket-holders into—*the damned.*

Chapter Four: *True Grit*

When the X-rated film started, I firmly clamped both hands over my eyes so that, as I sat perfectly straight facing the screen, I could not see a thing, and suffered through the film's entirety for Mario's sake alone, hoping that he was not embarrassed by my lack of composure. I wanted to be sophisticated, but just wasn't.

Once or twice as the film reel spun around and the non-existent plot revealed itself, I would spread the fingers of my hands a fraction or two, to see what was happening on the screen. It seemed as if, each time, there was a woman's bare breast in a man's sweaty palm, and kissing, in odd places; or a well-manicured, white-cuffed male hand going up a frilly stockinged-and-gartered female leg (the 'maid')—and she had no panties on! I would squirm violently, nearly fainting from the palpable sexual tension in the theatre, and not a little, in myself. *Gad, even now, I feel nervous, just thinking about it!* Really, I should have just let the experience wash over me and make me wiser, but I was too young to know ...

Whenever the moans of the actors and actresses got to me, I groaned myself sometimes, and with a quivering hand, reached for Mario. He good-humoredly obliged me by placing his own hands over my ears, to block out the disturbing moans. But he thought it was awfully funny that I should behave like that, little ass.

Mario never begrudged me the money he wasted, getting me into the theatre. I was his girlfriend, and he took me places. Those films were quite an initiation into the adult 'mysteries'—I had never even seen a 'girly' magazine, except once, at my aunt's house when I was babysitting for my cousins. I found a *'Playboy'* tucked between the cushions of the couch. I tried to tell Mother, but she didn't want to hear it.

A couple of years later, I saw the Swedish film *'I Am Curious (Yellow)'* [32] and it didn't bother me much. In fact, it was rather boring. I remember seeing a lot of pale-skinned, naked people clambering around on rocks. The viewing public for

---

[32] Directed by Vilgot Sjöman, 1967.

this so-called semi-documentary, was said to be upset by the pubic hair, but I didn't see any. Would blond pubic hair have been visible?

Curiously, *I Am Curious (Yellow)*'s star and poster girl, Lena Nyman, looked very much like I did at the time, but prettier. The resemblance may have been because of the shoulder-length straight brown hair, the bangs—or 'fringe,' as the British call it—the freckles, and perhaps the sweet young face.

Whatever his faults, Mario Fiqueroa had beautiful manners, and a courtly way of behaving towards a woman. He made me feel beautiful and desired. Oh, I needed that kind of treatment at that time! I felt so unworthy of a man's love. The breakup with Roger Douglass had crushed me. He had walked away so coldly, with no seeming reason! I had an affectionate nature. I was dying to be held tenderly, made passionate love to, courted and feted. Mario was Johnny-on-the-spot and wooed me into womanhood.

Sometimes, without being able to help myself, I found I was being swept off my feet by my Latin lover. Mario was fluent in Spanish; it was his mother tongue. By turns, he called me *mi niña* (girl, apple of my eye), or *mujer* (woman, wife)—it was charming. Once, he even said to me *'enamorado compasión,'* but sadly, I did not know what it meant, and so the moment passed.

Mario Fiqueroa knew the Latin dance steps, and was willing to teach me, though I felt very nervous about dancing in the arms of a man—so close, in public! Where were his hands?

'Ven a bailar conmigo,' he said. 'Come dance with me.'

The dances I had done before, the Twist, the Jerk, the Frug, the Watusi, the Swim, were danced facing your partner, but mostly not touching. Of course there had been the odd 'House of the Rising Sun' [33] 'slow dance' at the USO in Memphis, and 'Goodnight, My Love' [34] was de riguer as the last dance at

---

[33] American folksong, sung in 1964 by the English group, The Animals.
[34] As performed by Jesse Belvin in 1956, and used for years as the closing theme for American Bandstand.

midnight before closing the USO, but I had had so very little training in following a lead. It was difficult—*I* wanted to lead. I always had, when waltzing recklessly with my sisters at home. I was a brave leader, but not such a good follower.

I wanted to dance with Mario, but I felt like an elephant in clogs. It threw me off balance to keep stepping on his feet. Mario's shoes were the best Italian leather, the kind of shoes you kiss, and not trample all over.

On a night in December, Mario and I danced the rumba to *Bésame Mucho* ('Kiss Me A Lot'), one of the most beautifully romantic of Latin songs and one that I love. I felt the nearness of his body and his fondness for me, but I could not let myself fall … what would it lead to if I fell in love with him? I must have had a very cold heart.

Then we watched while other dancers began the tango to *El Choclo*, and I felt myself nearly strangle as the passion rose up within me. How had I changed so quickly from a girl into a woman? I wanted a man, I wanted Mario, at least for the moment—he was a very good stop-gap—but how did I live with the shame of being the 'mistress' of a gentleman to whom I was not married? Had other women faced this dilemma? What would Bridget Bardot have done? And what would I be afterwards? 'Damaged goods?' That was the label for girls who had sex before marriage. It was a hard world for women in 1965.

The tango dancers continued to negotiate the steps, and it was erotic. *Oh God*, I thought, *what will happen if I let myself be swept away on a wave of passion and say 'Let the devil take tomorrow,'* as Sammi Smith did in that song, 'Help Me Make It Through the Night,' [35] though the song came out later, in 1971, and I had not heard it, but the morality themes in it were omnipresent in the lives of girls and women in the 1960s.

Will it kill me, I asked myself, *will I become a wanton—if I give way to sensuality?'*

---

[35] Country music ballad 'Help Me Make It Through the Night,' written by Kris Kristofferson, 1970.

You may think I am making a big deal out of it, but I was under-age, and had visions of my parents (my mother, at least)—first, killing me, and then sending me to a home for unwed mothers; then turning her back as my bastard was snatched from my breast and handed over to adoptive parents. That was what happened in many cases—it's true—before birth control became widespread, accepted, legal, and allowed—i.e. the 1970s, the Sexual Revolution. I did not know that I was in the vanguard. I never meant to be rebellious—I wanted my mother's love.

And if Mario and I married—could a person join his or her life with someone so different, and make it work? It was not likely, I knew, because the very society we lived in would not sanction it, would make us miserable. I was a romantic, but not so much so that I would fly in the face of reason. I did not want to live outside of religion, and that was what I would have to do if I married a divorced Catholic. I did not know the answers to any of these questions, and didn't want to find out. Parents used to tell us about 'ruining our lives,' if we did this or that. They seemed to know what they were talking about.

As these jumbled thoughts swept through my fevered brain, we witnessed the end of the dance. By that juncture, there was only one couple dancing, swaying to the music, and the partners seemed to be meshed into one another. I could feel the heat.

There happened to be a fresh gardenia in my hair. Suddenly, its heavy scent overpowered me. I was frightened. 'Mario, take me home,' I said weakly. He did. Of course we made love. What's a girl supposed to do if she needs closeness and intimacy, if she needs union with something greater than herself? Read the *Kamasutram*? Cloister herself before marriage, like The Lady of Shalott in her turreted castle? Wait for the knight in shining armor to arrive on his white horse? *Would* he arrive at some point in time? Would he *recognize* me? I kept looking over my shoulder, so to speak, for that one, and I knew he would have blond hair.

Chapter Four: *True Grit*

Meanwhile, back at my studio apartment, Mario liked for me to sing to him in bed after we made love. Surprisingly, he wanted hillbilly songs. His favorite was *'Your Cheating Heart,'* by Hank Williams, and the irony was not lost on me.

I liked to sing the blues—I sang in my sleep before I could talk. When my sisters and I were in junior high school, we were in lots of musical productions; our favorite was the minstrel show when we got to black our faces, wear snow-white gloves, and glow in the iridescence of beribboned costumes styled to shine in black lights *up on stage*, up where we *belonged*. There, we would tap-dance away to *St. Louis Blues,* the pulsating rhythms punctuated by our tap, tap, trip, trap, I'm-gonna-take-a-little-nap, in 4:4 time.

Those songs and routines, trotted out in that amateur way, became a part of my consciousness, produced in a time of life that was pure and sweet and uncomplicated. The worst thing I had to worry about was a case of stage fright.

I liked it enough, that I thought of becoming a professional dancer, but I knew later, at work at the telephone company, that we in the business office routinely asked 'dancers' and airline stewardesses for large sums of money (deposits) before we connected a telephone for them. That was because there were some types of work that were not respectable; those customers could not be trusted to pay their bills on time. It was Southern Bell policy, don't blame me.

Feeling that phosphorescence dance over me though, hearing the breathing of the troopers, sensing the approbation of the crowd, I could have been persuaded to have a career on the stage, if I thought there was any money in it. But alas, many blues singers died in poverty. To die in poverty is not what I want from life.

I could belt out *'Beale Street Blues,'* and *'Cry Me A River'*—but not in bed. I had to stand up for that, to sing properly, to get enough air. My diaphragm had to have enough room to go up and down.

Beale Street papa, why don't you come back home?
It isn't proper to leave your mama all alone.

A Quiet Life in Bedlam

Sometimes I've been cruel that's true,
But papa, your sweet mama never two-timed you!
Boo-hoo I'm blue, so how come ya do me like ya do
I'm cryin ... [36]

Once long ago, I dreamed that I had been a blues singer in Chicago, in another lifetime; and was surprised, this go-around, to be born into a white body, a woman's body. But white body or no, I had a good voice for singing in a minor key.

I could sing country music too, of course, which was my father's preference, to say the least. No other music existed for Daddy except country music and Strauss's *Blue Danube*. My father had a life-long dream of becoming a country music star in Nashville at the Grand Ole Opry. I don't think he would have minded having daughters, if we could sing like Brenda Lee, but we couldn't.

I often sang for Mario a country song my father taught me, 'I'm So Lonesome I Could Cry.' [37] Mario liked to hear me wail and drawl. It put him in a good humor. But Mario liked bluesy songs well enough. He often talked about having seen blues singers perform in 'Chick-a-go.' (That was the way he pronounced it.)

He sometimes asked me to sing 'When I Fall In Love,' by Edward Heyman & Victor Young, or *'Skylark,'* by Hoagy Carmichael and Johnny Mercer.

I laughed every time Mario asked me to sing in bed, and that was plenty of times. I suppose we found it comforting to rock in the cradle of the blues when we were feeling guilty—at least I was—for spending those intimate moments together. Mario and I could still be light-hearted, even in our state of moral collapse. I wonder if God loves people who laugh?

We spent very little time lying on the beach, though we were living so close to the famed resort area. My skin was so

---

[36] *Beale Street Mama*, as sung by Bessie Smith, 1923.
[37] 'I'm So Lonesome I Could Cry,' written and recorded by Hank Williams in 1949; and notably sung by B. J. Thomas, in 1966.

Chapter Four: *True Grit*

white; sunning myself caused freckling instead of tanning, or I burned and peeled—that was no fun. I really did not have the desire to acquire a tan. It was boring, just to lie there soaking up the rays. I had had enough sunbathing after an hour, so it hardly seemed worth the trouble to go all that way. But Mario was perfectly willing to take me to the beach, since that seemed to be the fashionable thing to do, and we mounted an expedition sometimes, packing a picnic lunch, and renting a cabana.

I was afraid of sun poisoning—it had happened to my sister with dramatic results—so we took along copious quantities of suntan lotion, even though people thought it was unnecessary and that only baby oil was needed—with some iodine in it. And because Mario was wise, at times we took cover-up clothing and great striped umbrellas. After a while, it became a joke that we only wanted to lie close together, and did not really enjoy the gritty feel of the sand, mixed, as it was, with small stones and suntan lotion. Nor did we care for the merciless heat of the sun's rays in that southerly latitude. We stopped our treks before full summertime, and stayed at the apartment in bed. Mario had an almost permanent suntan anyhow, since he was naturally dark.

But yes, we went to the beach sometimes to swim, as anyone would expect us to do, and I got a bit of a golden glow. The salt water made a mess of my hair, and I didn't like that. Afterwards, lying in the sand, listening to my trusty transistor radio, I wrote letters on blue vellum stationery with a fountain pen to my friend Martha Boston back in Memphis, describing the beach, the day, and what we were doing. I tried to keep the letters very up-beat.

Martha was studying nursing and working very hard, living a Spartan life, and was so jealous when she read my letters. She needn't have been jealous—she turned out better than I did; and I would have liked nothing better than to get a proper education.

A Quiet Life in Bedlam

At the seaside, Mario Fiqueroa made splendid photographs with his tripod and Canon camera, of sweeping vistas, and sometimes, of a nineteen-year-old girl whose eyes were gazing beyond him to someone she could not yet see. The palm trees swayed, and I struck a pose, but I did not like being photographed, was very insecure about my looks, and did not have a photogenic face. During the time I knew him, Mario Fiqueroa went from being an amateur photographer to a professional one.

He eventually turned the camera away from me, and towards my beautiful younger sister, Sherry, when she came to visit us in Miami in the next year after school was out—but not before he had dressed me in a full-length, flowing candy-striped kaftan, with ruffled neck and elbow-length fluted sleeves, set a long braided fall, plus chignon, at the back of my upturned hair, tucked tropical flowers behind my ears, fitted me with false eyelashes, and snapped a lovely picture of an exotically-dressed dark-haired woman who didn't look a lot like me.

Mario sold my portrait to a firm that provided unending pictures of pretty girls for the uncountable record album covers of the 1960s. Thus I finished up, quite anonymous, on the cover of the hit record album, 'Guantanamera,' by the Sandpipers (LP, A&M Records Ltd. 1966). I liked the Sandpipers' music, so it wasn't such a bad end, after all.

The Sandpipers were one of the many groups/vocalists who recorded the classic 'Somewhere Beyond the Sea (La Mer).' The song was on that album, 'Guantanamera,' and it is a favorite of mine:

Somewhere beyond the sea, she's there watching for me
My lover stands on golden sands, and watches the ships that go sailing.
Somewhere beyond the sea, she's there waiting for me

Chapter Four: *True Grit*

If I could fly like birds on high, then straight to her arms, I'd go sailing. [38]

It was prophetic.

---

[38] 'Somewhere Beyond the Sea (La Mer),' English words by Jack Lawrence. Music and French words by Charles Trenet, copyright 1945.

CHAPTER FIVE:
Mystique

'Kate,' my mother said to me, 'stop frowning.' My mother refused to call me 'Katharine.' She said it was some highfalutin' name my father had given me, and she wasn't going to be a party to it.

That was all right. When I was six years old, Kate was much easier to spell than 'Katharine.' I would have liked to be named Ramona, but no one thought of that.

'You must stop all this frowning, Kate. It's not good for your looks. You will get permanent wrinkles on your face.'

'Yes, ma'am,' I said as respectfully as possible. I did not want any wrinkles. More wrinkles, less beauty; less beauty, no marriage. No marriage, and spinsterhood beckoned a boney hand. It was a domino effect.

When I was young, I supposed that Mother wanted the best for me. I made a real effort to carry around a bland, expressionless face in order to thwart the early onset of wrinkles. This was difficult, because I had a tendency to throw temper tantrums. Naturally, I got thrashed for them, but actually, I would have liked to please Mother if I could.

This homily about frowns producing wrinkles was one of my mother's favorite pieces of advice. She used to say it to me

Chapter Five: *Mystique*

all the time. Another one was, 'You can't hide a piece of broccoli in a glass of milk.'

It took a few years to find out that I was born nearsighted—could not really see well from infancy. So I went about scowling, squinting, screwing up my eyes and wrinkling my forehead in an effort to *see*, unconsciously believing the world was just a fuzzy place, sort of soft-focus, like an Expressionist painting; and that it was natural to have to get right up to a thing in order to see it. What everyone else took for granted, was beyond me from birth.

The day I got my first pair of glasses was one of the most exciting of my life. The world literally came into focus, and pressed around me with startling clarity. I could see individual blades of grass, different shapes of leaves on trees! I could see sunbeams dancing. I could see wrinkles on faces! I saw freckles on my face when I looked into the mirror.

'Why didn't anybody tell me?' I said to Annabelle.

Annabelle did not answer, but she gave me a snaggle-toothed smile, as if to say, 'Does it matter?'

For the first time, I saw a mosquito as well as felt it bite. I saw fireflies sprinkling fairy dust. I could see the blackboard at school. The teacher had thought I was a slow learner, but I just couldn't see. I noticed that I did not have much in the way of eyebrows, two dots and a dash, as Daddy called it. That was before I spotted the cowlick.

Mother once told me that I had inherited my inferiority complex from Daddy. It could have been true to some extent: certainly, my father had not wanted daughters, he wanted sons—but the top layers of the inferiority complex, or 'extremely low self esteem,' as my psychology book calls it, was laid on by my mother, herself.

My beautiful mother, who could not find beauty in me: I wondered what she would say when I told her my picture was on the cover of a record album. She probably would not believe me, but I could show her the album jacket when I could get hold of one.

True, a record album wasn't the cover of the *Rolling Stone*—a pinnacle not likely to be reached by my warbling alto in this lifetime—but gee, it proved that I had inherited something from Mother, a certain 'chutzpah,' perhaps, even if she could not recognize it.

I was working all the time on self-improvement, and if I could form, somehow, a better opinion of myself, then it helped in the fight for survival—one didn't abuse oneself so roundly, peering into the bathroom mirror in the early morning light. One could drink one's *Metrecal* bravely, and go out to face the ravening world.

Daddy rarely showed his inferiority complex; he compensated for it with a slight swagger, a dash of arrogance, a ready charm, and he could smile you right into a flutter. I tried mightily not to show my lack of confidence, smiled broadly whenever it seemed appropriate, and sashayed about as much as I dared. I was schooling myself on how to be feminine and beguiling, so that eventually, I could find 'fulfillment as a wife and mother,' as the women's magazines said I should. It was my destiny. And yet, I was longing for something more. An education perhaps?

'You don't need one,' my mother had said.

A malicious fate gave me intelligence instead of beauty. In 1965, nobody trusted a girl with brains, least of all her mother. 'Knowledge,' in a girl, smacked of emancipation. People are slow to change, and believe or not, women's liberation was still dreaded by a majority of both men and women: independence meant responsibility.

What a female needed was 'sex appeal': large breasts and even, white teeth. Well, I had both of those, but it was no guarantee. Was I married? *No.* Was I nearly twenty? Yes. Did I have to get a move on, or what?

Out on a date with ordinary boys (not Mario), a girl had to be gah-gah and stupid, practically a geisha if one was truly well bred in the Southern manner. I had not learned so much, at that early stage, about play-acting and dissembling, but I was

Chapter Five: *Mystique*

born a woman and a woman I would be. I would glory in my own femininity, might as well. What else did I have?

It was easy to play helpless—Southern girls were coquettes in the grand manner—but I could not play 'dumb.' I would use my intelligence to get ahead in the world—anybody who was smart could learn to do things the way other people did. I would develop 'mystique,' though I did not know what it meant, or where the idea came from, unless it was in the vibrations of society at that moment in time.[39]

I could imagine what mystique was—I liked the sound of it—and I was sure it could be developed. Why ever not? I would work with it, along with my calisthenics. *'You must, you must, you must increase your bust!'*

Certainly, my mother did not trade on 'mystique.' She definitely didn't tutor us in the beauty arts and seduction wiles thought necessary to catch a man— *'tickle him here, honey.'* A con artist would get short shrift from her: poodlefakers, even less. But she was not against beauty or femininity or fashion; and she absolutely, unconditionally, believed in marriage as the way forward for women.

I was late, catching on to the idea of 'mystique.' By 1965, the female consciousness was moving away from that. Despite my intelligence, I was conservative, recalcitrant, late catching on to fashion changes, stubbornly hanging on to what I liked of the status quo. I have been a reactionary about the subtle force called 'fashion,' usually the last one to convert.

The new buzz-words were 'visionary,' and 'space age.' Fashion was beginning to dictate a very bare-of-frivolities, boyish, flat, unpadded look, compared to the early 1960s when I was in high school. Short dresses were cut all of a piece, with no seam at the waist. There were alarming peek-a-boo windows and cut-out holes in clothes around the midriff, or at the bodice. And the designers were turning out shorts (!), and slim 'hipster' trousers—geometric shapes, clean lines and no extra, superfluous materials or decoration.

---

[39] See *The Feminine Mystique,* by Betty Freidan, 1963.

Gone were the wide, gathered, belted (feminine) skirts of the 1950s, the Peter Pan blouses, the busty brassieres with their forward thrust that enhanced, and sometimes made ridiculous, the female figure.

The new, simplified, square, triangular, trapezoidal, rectangular, octagonal clothes were for young bodies—a symbol of women's liberation that was staring at us all with an unforgiving eye. I looked the other way.

How much mystery could there be when so much skin was showing—boat necks, sleeveless dresses, hemlines four inches above the knee? Mystique? when panty girdles, long-line corsets, stockings and garters, had no wealth of luxurious fabric to conceal themselves under? When the derrière was barely covered?

Whenever I could afford it, I began to go shopping. Lo and behold, stockings and garters (which I hated), could be replaced by a latex 'panty' with concealed hooks inside, around the boy-leg. The one I bought was blue, in a kind of woven, stretchy fabric. And specially made hose (stockings) *caught* the hooks in reinforced patterns around the tops. That left an opportunity for a whole lot of leg to be exposed. Risqué? Yes! *Exciting*.

Stockings and garters had actually left red imprints on the legs, and they were so obvious, you had to be careful how you sat: 'knees together, please.' Men say garters are sexy, but they never had to wear them, I'll warrant. It was with a struggle worthy of Sampson, that a lady got herself into stockings, garters, and a well-fitted girdle each morning. Girdles had been de rigueur for respectable women since long before I was born.

After the winter of 1965–1966, I stopped wearing panty girdles and stockings with garters. The Cuban women did not wear them. Why should I? At first, I felt a bit, well, naked; but of course, I wasn't. Even in my poorest days, I was well, if conservatively, dressed.

I had been shocked when I first moved to Miami that none of the Cuban women wore girdles. It was little short of appalling to see the way Spanish women's derrières were left free to

Chapter Five: *Mystique*

wiggle at will, underneath their fitted clothes. The ladies were not self-conscious about it, however.

Now I found myself in the same shameful position. It was just not possible to wear a girdle, or garter belt and stockings, underneath a short skirt—there almost wasn't any 'underneath' to it. So pantyhose, or 'tights,' a new fangled garment soon on the market, seemed to be the answer to the problem of what to wear for an undergarment with short skirts; but no one seemed to know whether a girl was supposed to wear panties underneath the panty hose. I did. Others did not.

The existing American fashion business seemed unwilling or unable to deal with the sudden demand for 'young' fashion. For as long as possible, they kept churning out modifications of Dior's New Look; and after that, copies of Oleg Cassini's clothes for Jacqueline Kennedy. Until about 1964 or '65, teenagers wore exactly what their mothers and fathers did.

Though I hate to admit it, the young fashion designers in London seemed to be way ahead of designing 'what was happening' to youthful style in Britain and the United States. I saw it all in *Vogue* magazine: Mary Quant in her workroom, the 'Mods' running around on their Vespa scooters.

In 1965 there were new fabrics and materials, dacron, rayon, terylene, and others, that were favored for their lighter, more durable qualities; and best of all, those materials needed little upkeep and care, almost no ironing! Clothes could be sewn in a different way, worn in a different way, maintained easily. It was all very convenient, really.

I have noticed that people still make jokes about that old type of lingerie elastic—the kind that wore thin and broke, allowing one's most intimate garments to fall down, and off, at the most inconvenient of times. My sister told me that the correct thing to do when your panties fell off was to flip them into the gutter with a neat flick of your pointed toe shoe. Thank God it never happened to me.

But Annabelle knew what she was talking about. Once, at the sock-hop in the school gym, her red net bouffant petticoat fell off, right in the middle of Percy Faith's 'Theme From a

Summer Place.' [40] Annabelle was caught in mid-whirl, and fled the scene of humiliation with a face as scarlet as her petticoat. People remembered the incident for years.

Vogue magazine said that the miniskirt was born in Britain, but I don't know. The French claimed credit, too—Courréges, I think his name was. Who knows? It seemed to be one of those brilliant ideas that flower several places in the universe simultaneously, like Darwin's theory of evolution.

Right up until the mid-sixties, men did not wear colorful clothes—just navy blue, brown and gray—but wool suits, which every man wore religiously up until the sixties, were beginning to go by the boards. Well-dressed men did not wear 'loafers,' which is probably just a slang word for casual shoes. Daddy was a snazzy dresser. Mother had a terrible time getting him to wear loafers; but once he tried them, he never looked back.

'Moccasins,' for everyday use, were unheard of among non-Indians. And it was only cool dudes who wore sport coats with shawl collars and pink carnations.

As everyone knows, it was Jack Kennedy, that sexy thing, with his full head of exuberant hair who did not wear a hat, that stopped men everywhere (even in cold countries) from wearing wool fedoras, stiff bowlers, velvet derbies, straw panamas, walking hats, etc. The only hat-wearers who didn't give up, after Kennedy blazed across the fashion sky, were the cowboys in their Stetsons. I miss seeing men in smart hats. I hope the fashion changes again.

When I found out that Mario was thinking of hiring me as a model for his 'life study' drawing and painting classes at Miami-Dade Junior College—*Mario, you want* me *to do* that?—I considered it briefly. It scared me stiff, of course, to think of taking off my clothes and standing quietly in front of strangers

---

[40] 'Theme From a Summer Place,' Percy Faith Orchestra. Written for the movie, *A Summer Place,* lyrics by Mack Discant, music by Max Steiner, 1959.

Chapter Five: *Mystique*

while they dabbed at their canvasses or sketched my silhouette, but the money would buy me some new clothes. The times, they were a-changing. Skirts kept getting shorter, and high-heeled shoes were on their way out.

I dearly wanted a boxy purse to wear with my new low-heeled, square-toed shoes. The one I coveted looked like the lunch box I used to carry to school. *Far out!*

'Money to buy clothes, just think.' I smiled when I remembered the first night I lay with Mario, and had nothing to wear to bed. My nylon 'shortie' pajamas had been locked up with bloody Linda at the exact moment when I needed them.

In the event, I wore Mario's striped pajama shirt, like Doris Day in the movie musical, *The Pajama Game,*

The pajama game is the game I'm in
And I'm proud to be in the pajama game
I love it ... [41]

while Mario wore his draw-string trousers, as John Raitt had done in the musical play and the movie.

'You're cute,' I had said, smiling into his brown eyes; and he kissed me.

(It seemed so long ago.)

Ummm, I speculated, *what if I had enough money to buy a silk négligée!* Sh-Boom! *Would I dare to wear it? I don't know*—(feelings of horror at my audacity)—it would take some guts. To my certain knowledge, my mother had never worn a négligée.

'Jezebel,' I called myself, but I was tempted.

'Now look, Katharine, you have to stop this!' I commanded. 'Pull yourself together.' I tried to feel penitent.

Oops, talking to yourself. Watch out. Next, you'll be drinking alone, hoarding hot-toddies behind closed doors. I could

---

[41] *The Pajama Game*, musical score by Richard Adler and Jerry Ross, 1954.

not keep that schmaltzy ballad, *'Hey There,'* from wending its way 'round in my head; it was insidious:

> *Hey there, you with the stars in your eyes*
> *Love's never made a fool of you*
> *You used to be too wise ...* [42]

Wise? Not me. The false eyelashes I bought for the photo-shoot weren't helping my femininity crusade, alas. The eyelashes caused my contact lenses to eject like a World War II co-pilot out of a cockpit. I was determined to use false eyelashes; it was stylish. But I couldn't. In a way, that was okay, because the better ones—furry, like a pair of tarantulas, or wispy and spider-like, a la Cher Bono—were dreadfully expensive.

And, with *some* false eyelash sets, you had to glue each eyelash on separately—just take a look at a photograph of Twiggy, or Penelope Tree, to see the big-eyed effect. Eye makeup took a lot of patience. I had patience, but not enough for such delicate procedures as individual eyelashes, one twig at a time. It was bad enough to have to put on liquid liner—I could not see well enough to do it properly. After the application, I looked like I hadn't slept. That was not glamorous. Forget the eyeliner!

'Smudge a little kohl around your eyes,' wrote the beauty editor for *Vogue:* 'Mata Hari! Swell,' I commented.

Every sort of beauty treatment I scouted out seemed to cost an arm-and-a-leg. The expense was crippling. Take, for instance, the 'fall' and the 'wiglet.' I spent thirty-five dollars on a fall of natural, long dark hair that exactly matched my own 'sinuous and serpentine' locks. But would it stay on my head? Not without suffering the agonies of the damned, it wouldn't.

The fall was attached with a little knot of hair that made me look like I had a pointed head. But, no matter. On a good day, I resembled the young trend-setting models in *Vogue* magazine

---

[42] 'Hey There,' from *The Pajama Game.*

Chapter Five: *Mystique*

(definitely artificial, wide-eyed and innocent). Super. And I was a Breck Girl, washing my hair twice a week. I believed their advertisements, hoping to turn from an ordinary person into a goddess.

The wiglet that I bought from Burdine's wasn't much better than the fall, because it required so many hairpins to stay in place. A-shaped hairpins popped out like baby birds from the nest with each nod of my head. It was disconcerting to suddenly see tiny bobby pins flying past my face on their way to my eyes.

My co-workers at the telephone office in Coral Gables had a mania about going to the beauty shop once a week and getting their long hair pinned up on the tops of their heads. The caught-up hair was then formed into large loose curls. They looked elegant, like ladies. I wanted to be a lady. How those girls could afford 'hairdressing' so often, I do not know. (Were they getting money from men?)

The name of this stylish coiffure was *'Up ... in Curls.'* (That was the only name I ever heard it called.) I did not like it for myself, because I could not sleep on that hairdo without getting a neck brace from the health aids store—which meant … I couldn't sleep, and I had to have my sleep! *But a wiglet,* I thought, *might solve the 'style' problem. (Wiglet rhymes with piglet.)* One just popped the little wiglet onto one's cranium each morning like a little *chapeau*, and *voilà*, one had loopy curls on the top of one's otherwise flat head.

Sadly, the reality of the wiglet, was somewhat different, sigh! It seemed likely that I would develop a bald spot where the little comb went in and out and the hairpins speared me. The bare nape of my neck got a chill from the cold air-conditioning. I would not suffer for beauty—or anyway, not much.

In the end, I was stuck with my own plain, baby-fine, albeit thick hair, so I got it 'frosted,' with blond streaks throughout—especially in the front. I wouldn't go all the way, with bleached-blond hair and a scalp-full of hydrogen peroxide (it stank to high heaven). 'Bleached blond' was too reminiscent of

Marilyn Monroe, and I wasn't sure about her. I heard that she had been photographed in the nude for a calendar. That was shocking. What ever could have led her to do such a thing? Did her mother know?

The frosted hair added a gleam to my chutzpah that I had not seen before. I was almost pretty. The 'blond' around my face went well with my complexion. When Mario saw me, he rolled his eyes and said, *'Ooh, la la!'*

I laughed. *'You're a bombshell,'* I said to myself, not believing it for a minute. Pharmacists around the world sold millions of bottles of hydrogen peroxide after Marilyn Monroe's debut as a blond. I was a sucker, just like the rest. I liked it, but the bleached parts of my hair put an end to swimming. Who had the nerve to dive into a chlorinated pool, when the end result would be green hair?

'Big hit now, lips all softly sheeny!' ran a Cutex advertisement in *Vogue*.[43] It seemed that everything was frosted in the mid-1960s—even your baby's bottom, I shouldn't wonder. Did people realize they were probably painting ground-up fish scales on their eyelids and lips? I doubt it.

Did girls understand that they were putting strong chemicals on their scalps and faces? Probably, no one cared. Certainly, I didn't. Women in the 1960s did not realize that anything could be dangerous. Cosmetics were seen as a sure-fire way of luring a man into marriage. The 'look' was everything. At nineteen, I halfway believed I would live forever, with many more chances on the roulette wheel of life. I was willing to try what ever would improve my outlook for being beautiful and desirable.

The 1960s were a great time to be young. Everything was experimental. An unconventional person (like me) wasn't as likely to be labeled 'kooky.' There was this explosion of new creative energy. It affected us all. Some people went off to San

---

[43] Author's note: I must acknowledge a debt of gratitude to Yvonne Connikie, author of Batford's *Fashions of a Decade, The 1960s*, whose book, one of a series, has been invaluable to me in the research carried out for this novel. B.T. Batsford, London, 1990.

Chapter Five: *Mystique*

Francisco, and became 'far out' drug addicts and hippies. I only wanted to become dynamite.

Though customs were slow to change in the South, taboos were beginning to break down: *'No white shoes before Easter, or after Labor Day.' 'Do not wear black to a wedding.' 'Don't wear white to a wedding, unless you are the bride.' 'Women should not wear flaired pants to church.' 'It is blasphemy to say* the Civil War; *it was the War Between the States, and don't you forget it, child.'* Yes, Grandmother.

You could say that the clothes people wore in the mid-sixties began to split along generational lines. When I was in high school, Mother and I wore the same clothes (though I did not like it), but after I started to work and bought some short skirts, mother's shape didn't fit into them at all.

Mother loved rich food, and her weight yo-yoed up and down: a compulsive eater, a compulsive dieter. She became nervous and fidgety if things were not moving fast enough. She got bored quickly. She would enjoy parties to the hilt, eating everything in sight, talking a mile a minute, then go through a period of asceticism, self-denial and introspection. She starved herself then. It was difficult to fathom. She would not let me into her world.

Mother, whose given name was Brenda, was so rounded and curvaceous, that the fifties fashions, the Dior look of full-on female, with its bows and furbelows and lots of jewelry, hadn't suited her, though she tried to wear them. The women in my family had 'hour-glass figures,'—all the rage in the Edwardian Age, but not much use to a Mod.

My mother was not slim like Jackie Kennedy, but she wore similar, elegant, paired-down Oleg Cassini (inspired) fashions. And she got them all on sale, or sewed them herself from Vogue Patterns. Mother *did* wear girdles, garters and brassieres with pointed cups, and pointed-toed, high-heeled shoes—as all well-dressed women did.

Though she did not have a perfect shape, I thought that Mother was more attractive than Jacqueline Kennedy. The two of them had that same sort of intense, dark-eyed, dark-haired, black-eye-browed, stunning-glance beauty and grace. One noticed her 'presence' before one noticed her figure.

She needed lots of clothes, two wardrobes in fact. Two sizes at least. She worked at her bookkeeping job to keep the household running, but also to buy clothes. She was feminine and mysterious, but hugely practical and matter-of-fact. (I don't understand her any better now than I did then.) My mother could be so light-hearted and airy, that I believe she put on weight as sheer ballast. She was a people person, but not a people eater (*'one-eyed, one-horned, flying purple-people eater'*). They don't always make the best mothers. Neither do one-eyed, one-horned, flying purple-people eaters. ('Purple-People Eater' [44]—why on Earth did I think of that? It was one of those nonsense songs popular in the late 1950s.)

My mother seemed to enjoy visits with our childhood friends, and was gracious to our boyfriends, winning them over completely with her adult-to-adult manner. But with us, her children, she seemed to have such a low opinion of everything we did, and everything we said, that we became reduced to imbecility on any confrontation. Or maybe it was only me.

Blunt and energetic, Mother was compelled to tell the absolute truth, even when it hurt. But she was delightful to know—could get away with murder. Few could resist her. Whatever she did, you would forgive her. If you were mad at her, she would talk you out of it.[45]

I had worn some makeup since the age of sixteen: a pat of powder, a smudge of lipstick—because Mother worked for the Fuller Brush Company in Memphis, where she received, regularly, boxes full of make-up-and toiletry samples. Mother got cosmetics, cologne, hand cream, even boars' bristle hairbrushes for nothing, and handed the booty on to us, her daughters.

---

[44] 'Purple People Eater,' a novelty song performed by Sheb Wolley in 1958; written by Barry Cryer.
[45] With thanks to Lyn Birkbeck for his ideas about 'Gemini Rising,' as researched in his book, *Do It Yourself Astrology,* Element Books, 1996.

Chapter Five: *Mystique*

'I have to get you married,' she had said, winking at Sherry, the youngest. Mother's porcelain complexion and expressive eyes were so arresting that she did not need makeup, though she wore a little moisturizer. Sherry resembled Mother, only more beautiful, if that was possible.

We girls practiced brushing our hair *one hundred strokes* a night with the boar bristle hair brushes, and rubbed as much hand cream into our arms and hands as the skin would hold. It was amazing! In our late teens, we had beautiful hands with strong nails! And we all had long lustrous hair, which we then pinned up in curls, or set in big rollers. We sat under the hair dryer for hours and *hours*.

I must have gone through two dozen sample tubes of 'soft blue-pink' lipstick in the years before I left home. But by December of 1965, I had run out of Mother's samples, though I still had my hairbrush; so I took myself off to the Merle Norman Cosmetic Studio in Coral Gables—an unusual thing for a girl of my age to do—where they made me over into a new and more glamorous nineteen-year-old.

Merle Norman's frosted blue eye shadow is the bees knees, I thought. I didn't care a fig whether it went with green eyes—though by that time, I had started calling my eyes 'hazel' instead of green. That sounded more romantic. I could not understand why the Merle Norman make-up artists suggested I should wear brown mascara instead of black.

'What do you mean, black is "too old" for me?' I asked. I felt very old.

When I was in high school, a girl who wore a lot of make-up was considered to be 'fast.' What the heck? I didn't know any of those people anymore, tra la!—no one to pass judgment on me. *Lah!*

In my frivolous moments, I considered buying a car. I knew from the experience with Linda Black that four wheels would set me free, and I envied the mobility that other telephone workers had. *They* went out to *lunch*: no lonely sandwiches in the canteen.

A Quiet Life in Bedlam

It was difficult, and expensive, to get around Miami by bus—the city was vast—and the frequent tropical downpours were ruining the few nice clothes I owned. Peasant blouses looked pathetic when wet. Madras dresses bled their colors. I should have been considering buying a sewing machine to make my own clothes, but could not bear to think of it; I was not domestic.

One day after work, I was standing out at the corner by the bus stop about two blocks from the office building where I worked. Into a clear blue sky, there floated a gray cloud with a greenish underbelly. *Eek!* Soon the sharp rain needles came hurtling down, and I was instantly drenched to the bone.

'Not again!' I groaned. Why couldn't the weather gods leave me alone? Who could afford a raincoat? Not me. A London Fog would have been my choice, but such a coat was too hot for Miami. All I had for protection was one of those fold-up clear plastic bonnets that women used to wear, hideous thing.

It wouldn't have been so terrible to get wet if I had not been carrying my portable stereo phonograph. It was my most precious possession. Would the portable phonograph be ruined by the deluge? Certainly it would be if I stood there much longer. The darn thing weighed a ton; my hand was raw and numb from the downward pull of the handle. I had carried it to work only as an accessory to a presentation made at my office. How on Earth would I get home with my stereo intact?

'A life without music ...' I moaned. What to do, *what to do*? I was stuck, stuck and wet, phonograph ruined, catching cold, mascara running. My contact lenses were foggy. I was utterly miserable and shivering, ready to drop into a deflated heap. I did not yet have enough 'service' at the telephone company to get paid sick leave, *woe is me*. And anyway, I had better not 'report out,' unless I was in the hospital, near death, or otherwise incapacitated.

I had never been in a taxi in my life, and certainly didn't have the money for one. I watched dejectedly, resignedly, as the people in cars rolled by. Then, a miracle happened. A man

Chapter Five: *Mystique*

drove up in a black sedan, stopped, rolled down the window and asked me, 'Do you want a ride home?' He looked like a nice, respectable businessman, one who would not harm me for the world.

Could appearances deceive? I had to make a quick decision. Though I had not hitchhiked before, it seemed wise to accept his offer. It could have been dangerous, going with him, but somehow I trusted the man. It was just an instinct.

'Hop in,' he said again, and opened his passenger door. 'I can take you where you want to go.'

Hmmm.

I got into his car. He drove me home. We exchanged, perhaps, two words. I never saw him again. Whew.

I started looking at automobiles. To purchase. I knew I should get a Volkswagen Beetle, because that was the cheapest car on the market. It was really ugly though. What I actually wanted was a 1965 Ford Mustang—I had never seen anything so cool—those lean lines, low-slung and sexy-looking. I stood with my mouth open every time a Mustang drove past me—but it was out of my orbit financially. Only a dream.

So I took the bus across town to the Volkswagen dealer to discover if I actually had the means to buy a car. The way the salesman figured out the monthly payments, I could have just stretched to it; but I could not get a radio in the car for the right price. Well, access to a radio was essential to living a decent life. I decided not to do it. No Volkswagen. No car that year. It was the bus, or nothing, until I married. Such was the life of a single girl in 1965.

I was still thinking about Mario's proposal of an extra job. Money from a second job would come in handy when I went looking for a new apartment, as I soon had to do because I was living too far away from work. I was already a Fallen Woman, what difference did it make if I posed nude for a college class to paint me? It would be honest work, wouldn't it?

'*Sophism,*' my puritanical self cried out.

What it boiled down to was that I did not have the courage. It was going too far. What would I tell my grandchildren about my young days?

Another problem was 'shame.' I could not say who it was that made me ashamed of my body. It probably wasn't Mother. She often walked around half-naked, even in front of our friends sometimes. My mother had such presence as she strolled around unclothed and barefoot through the rooms of our house, that the situation did not become too mortifying for anyone concerned, for as long as we stayed innocent. Mother was simply the barefoot contessa. To my relief, she stopped doing it when I brought Roger Douglass home.

And it couldn't have been Grandmother who made me ashamed. We had been bathed by her, in a tin tub, in front of the fire, in the kitchen, with uncles and aunts running around, cooking and cleaning. Certainly, we were expected to keep ourselves decently clothed at all times, and we had never seen Daddy naked—but no—I think it was at church and Sunday school that I learned to be ashamed. The naked body was connected with ... ooh, wicked to think of such things!

Shame. Mario and I did not live together, but the neighbors seemed to know what was going on. Possibly my guilt feelings were giving me a dose of paranoia: I felt that the Cuban boys were laughing behind their hands, and the honest matrons were affronted by my presence in their neighborhood. I could see the living room curtains twitch in the window across the street.

We fear, more than hunger, more than pain, the psychological pain that comes with the censure of our own kind. I could not articulate the reason why I had to move away, but I had to flee. It would have been a fine thing if I had known what I knew later, that the 'Latins,' the Roman Catholics, were generally more tolerant of love affairs than we 'White-Anglo-Saxon-Protestants' seemed to be.

I know my self-flagellation is hard to understand with today's 'free love' attitudes being what they are; but I could not have felt worse about my situation if I had been a criminal on the run. My conscience was killing me.

Chapter Five: *Mystique*

'Sex is sin,' the preacher called down from the pulpit of my childhood, and I jumped.

I have hardly mentioned 'sin,' because it is not a part of my consciousness today, but I must have feared the fires of Hell and they were real for me. Hell-fire and damnation had been a recurring theme at church, and we girls were given to understand that if we were not 'good,' and did not refrain from 'sin,' that we would each be thrown into a fiery furnace where we would burn forever and ever, amen, with no marriage available unless it was to Beelzebub. And what was worse, we would not be allowed to wear white dresses.

I had to find a way to get myself out of the 'affair.' But how? There was no one to turn to for help, no one to ask for advice.

Though I was continually anxious, the only actual problem with the neighbors was the landlord who lived in the same building. He was fond of walking about with his trouser fly unzipped. I heard from other girls living nearby that the landlord was a 'flasher'—was working his way up to a demonstration of his special talent for *my* benefit.

'Will he open his trench coat?' I asked myself, and ran whenever I saw him.

In Memphis, 'child molesters' had lived on either side of us. There was Mr. Smythe, next door on Walthal Circle, and Mr. Jones across the street, on Radford Road. Mr. Smythe, who looked like a bespeckled toad, actually cornered Annabelle in his garage, and she had to stick her fingernails into his eyes to get him off her.

Mr. Smythe was not so rough with me, but I had to stay out of his way. You wouldn't think he would put his hands on me outside in broad daylight, in the sight of God and everybody, but he did. I had to be very quick.

When I mentioned Mr. Smythe to Sherry, she cursed. She said it had served Mr. Smythe right, when, years later, his grandchild had died in a tragic way. 'The sins of the fathers,' she said ominously. I thought she was harsh. The death of that child broke more than one heart.

Mr. Smythe was interesting to talk to, and I loved to talk. So I learned to dodge, to bip and bop. I told Mr. Smythe about the collection of Nancy Drew books I was making, and that I needed a bookcase. Well, he built me one! It was my first. I suppose he thought that the beautiful little bookcase would buy him some favors, but it didn't.

Mr. Jones was the more dangerous. He offered to give me a ride to school each day since he was going that way anyhow. Mother thought it was a good idea—I would have time to wash up the breakfast dishes before I headed out.

The first day I got into the car with Mr. Jones, he waited until we were out of sight of the house, then he stopped the car and grabbed me. I was out of that car like a shot, screaming like a banshee. I went home and told Mother, but she pretended not to believe me. When I mentioned it to Annabelle a few years later, she said that adults, in those days, rarely credited such stories: it was not to be believed.

I could handle my landlord, Mr. Bills, but the situation was unpleasant. Before Mr. Bills had an opportunity to flash *me*, or worse, I felt it would be wise to move to one of those quiet tree-lined streets in Coral Gables, near the Miracle Mile, close to the telephone business office on Alhambra Circle, where I worked. But I could not think of moving until after the New Year. I had a six-month lease.

Sadly, I lost the battle with my conscience time and again, and life with Mario as lover became an accepted condition. *'Hell in a hand basket, damn.'*

Mario Fiqueroa was a delightful companion, anybody would tell you that. I settled down to my work, which took half of my time, and waiting for 'him' at my apartment, which took the other half.

When I was young, I was a terrific 'waiter' where the man of my choice was concerned. If he did not come to me when I wanted or expected him, I just settled down to wait, even if it was for hours, or days or months, until he came, knowing that he inevitably would.

Chapter Five: *Mystique*

When my lover came to me, all my longings would be fulfilled, my loneliness assuaged. I would have that support of love and care that was missing from the time I spent with my parents. I did not look for strengths in myself, which might have sustained me through a life alone. I had no calling to be a nun, and it would take some education to become a teacher, or nurse, the two professions designated for spinsters of my caliber.

Lonely. That was a new experience for me. Life with my family in Memphis had been constant sound and activity—the one who talked the loudest was the one who got heard. But I found that living alone was a different kind of life, with as many disadvantages as advantages. I found out that loneliness was my enemy. What did one do to pass the time? *Sleep. Wait.* Just wait, wait for Mario.

Usually, I did not have to wait too long. He came to me almost every week-night, and there I would be, decked out in my best négligée, smelling of perfume. I did not allow the word 'amoral' to enter my head.

The only times Mario left me for more than a day were the holiday weekends, when he drove to Key West to visit his parents, Mario Sr., and Carmen Fiqueroa. It was disappointing that he never asked me to drive down with him. I could not understand why he didn't, but was too proud to ask.

I suffered such agonies on those long weekends while Mario was away in Key West. I cannot describe how sick it made me to be left there on Friday afternoon in that horrible apartment without him, no money to go anywhere or do anything. But back he would come on Sunday afternoon to take me out to dinner. At such times, he was my godsend. I can't believe that I did not fall in love with him, but I didn't.

Christmas 1965 was rapidly approaching, and Mario deserted me to spend the holidays with his family in Key West. It was to be Christmas without a Christmas tree, Christmas without presents. Christmas without friends or family, though Mother thoughtfully sent me some new ornaments, in case I should decide to set up a tree.

Surprise! In the package there was a pink sugar gumdrop man, an elf, and a red and gold Austrian blown-glass sphere. That was exciting. My first Christmas ornaments! But it didn't help much. I could not afford a Christmas tree. The weekend stretched before me like desolation.

There was one more gift in the parcel. It was an 8x10 color portrait of my sisters and me in taffeta dresses, sitting like stair-steps on a piano bench, and smiling. I did not like the picture because my hair was in a ponytail, my ears stuck out, and my lipstick was too red; clearly, I had been too young for lipstick. Annabelle looked like an angel (which she wasn't), and Sherry looked like an elf (which she was).

I folded the picture in half, and laid it carefully in the trash. 'So much for that.'

'Melancholy Christmas,' I said to the walls. Joyce, my red-haired, freckled-faced roommate, wouldn't be coming home that night.

I had no Christmas magic to sustain me, so I spent time thinking of the Yuletide as it had been when I was a child, and of the Pink Palace. The Pink Palace, located in Chickasaw Gardens in Memphis, was designed in the early 1920s for Clarence Saunders, a businessman who went bankrupt before its completion. In the late 1920s, the City of Memphis acquired the Pink Palace for use as a museum, and it was open to the public when I was a child.

The Pink Palace was a mansion built of pink Georgian marble, a material that had been admired by the gentleman's wife, and which he secured for the construction at great trouble and expense. In the summers, my sisters and I begged to visit the Pink Palace every Sunday. There was no admission fee for children.

We wandered awe-struck through rooms full of mahogany cabinets, their drawers open and filled with hundreds of mounted butterflies. We admired showcases stocked with silver spoons, archeological artifacts, precious china, and exotic dolls. Thick oriental carpets adorned the wood floors.

Chapter Five: *Mystique*

There were bird rooms with displays of stuffed parrots, and safari rooms with preserved monuments to African wildlife. There was a huge dancing Shiva, and other memorabilia from India. There were doll houses such as you have never seen in your life—I fancy that even Queen Mary, George V's consort, would have been impressed.

Everywhere in the Pink Palace, there was antique furniture, mahogany, teak, ebony and rosewood. There was carved ivory, jade, grand pianos, Chippendale chairs, and Edwardian clothing displays of such opulence. There were jewels and diadems. There was a little girl, her small pig-tailed head spinning every second, accumulating memories to carry with her always.

The Chickasaw Gardens around the Pink Palace mansion fairly dripped with magnolias, camellias, azaleas and rhododendrons, all in the peak of health and obvious horticultural happiness. For those who believe in the 'planes of existence,' it was like being on the Astral Plane—heaven.

All of these wonderful things, I thought of, and felt warm inside. People who have been in concentration camps say that what sustained them through the dreadful times were memories of happy childhood days when they were safe. I was safe in the Pink Palace—and safe, in believing that there were miracles and magic—so long as I did not mention it to anybody else.

I listened to my taped recording of *The Nutcracker Suite*, as arranged by André Kostelanetz, and marveled anew at the combination of Tchaikovsky's music, and Ogden Nash's verses[46] written specially for *The Nutcracker Suite*. The poems were spoken with spirit and chortled with glee by Peter Ustinov, so,

A little girl marched round her Christmas tree,
And many a marvelous toy had she.
There were cornucopias of sugarplums,
And a mouse with a crown that sucked its thumbs,

---

[46] Ogden Nash's poems published by Curtis Brown, Ltd. As heard on Columbia Records, recording date unknown.

And a fascinating Russian folderol,
Which was a doll inside a doll inside a doll inside a doll.
And a posy as gay as the Christmas lights,
And a picture book of the Arabian Nights,
And a painted silken Chinese fan,
But the one she loved was the nutcracker man.

It was lovely.

Right before I went to sleep on Christmas Eve, I told myself a story of Christmas:

'Long ago, and far away,' I said, 'I believed in Santa Claus. Santa Claus was magic.

'Nobody ever talked about magic in my family. It was considered to be kid stuff, phony. The adults, and therefore the children, seldom put the name *magic* to anything.'

'Magic' had to do with rabbits jumping out of hats, eating fire, levitation, birds popping out of the magician's mouth, beautiful women being sawed apart, and little else. Nobody believed that magic was real. But I did. It had to be magic that Santa Claus, the Mighty Elf, delivered presents to all the children of the world in one long Christmas night.

'Magic was not mentioned at school, either,' I continued for my own benefit as I drifted off with the fairies, floating around in Never-Never Land. 'Perhaps it was anti-Christian. *Miracles* were a different matter. They were *religious*—nothing to do with the secular. It was completely respectable to believe in miracles. Miracles were well documented in the Good Book. How could the miracle of Christ rising from the dead be anything but true?

'Though she did not believe in magic, my mother must have believed in Santa Claus—though she said she didn't—because, every Christmas Eve, she made a gorgeous coconut cake from scratch, even grating her own coconut. The finished cake, made with the fresh coconut milk, was luscious. We could not wait to get at it, but weren't allowed to, before morning came. The fresh cake was for Santa Claus.

Chapter Five: *Mystique*

'Mother set a slice of coconut cake on a china plate, and placed it on the dining room table, along with a glass of milk— as an inducement for Ole Saint Nick to stop in at our house and leave presents. Mother did this every year; and each year on Christmas morning, the slice of cake was gone, and the milk drunk up. And there were presents under the tree!'

And so there would be, next year, when I was married ...

'Goodnight. Merry Christmas.'

CHAPTER SIX:
'Shout'

Two days before Christmas Eve, I was riding the bus home, feeling more forlorn than ever I had in my life, when God sent me another small miracle. Sitting across, on the aisle seat, was a sweet-looking Cuban girl who happened to get off at my stop.

'¡Hola!' she said with a smile.

I grinned. We took to each other immediately, and in the good will of the season, she brought me home to meet her family.

Lalulalia Navarro spoke only broken English; I spoke little Spanish—*uno, dos, tres, cuatro, cinco, seis,* like reciting a poem.

Lalulalia's family spoke no English at all. They had only lately arrived from Cuba but somehow, someway, we communicated, and I was invited to spend Christmas Day with them. I was so touched by their kindness that I began to cry. The next thing I knew, they all had their arms around me in a crèche, rocking me back and forth as if I were a foundling just brought in from the doorstep.

'Gracias, gracias,' I sobbed.

'De nada, de nada,' they responded.

Chapter Six: *Shout*

Señor and *Señora* Navarro did not mind that I wasn't a Catholic. I told Lalulalia right up front, in sign language and broken Spanish, to be sure that I would not be damned and thrown out of the house before dinner. Then I cried again. It was the Navarro family's first Christmas away from Cuba, and they seemed to understand my desolation.

My Cuban family did not celebrate Christmas in the manner to which I was accustomed, but it was a good time, it was good food, it was fellowship. It was even a Mass celebrated in Spanish at the Roman Catholic Church, all memories of the hated 'Catholic Linda' long forgotten.

I soaked it up, and basked in the warmth of their true Christian love, while they fed me black beans and rice, and picadillo, a traditional Latin American dish made with ground meat, tomatoes, and other regional ingredients.

'Eat!' said *Señor* Navarro, and handed me a bunch of grapes.

Lordy, is it the Saturnalia? It was just a passing thought. *No, of course not. It's Christmas. God rest ye merry gentlemen.* It was the custom to eat twelve grapes for good luck in the New Year, one for each month. That was fun. But then I choked when *Señora* Navarro told me to swallow the seeds for fruitfulness.

We danced some sort of 'round dance'; and, oh yes, we ate roasted pig! But it wasn't just the head, the glistening eyes, and the burnt ears of New Year's at home with Mother—no! My mother's spirit must have been laughing at me though, thinking of years gone by when I had refused to eat hogshead, black-eyed peas, and squirrel stew at New Year's, and took a whipping instead.

So Christmas that year brought me new friends and unexpected blessings, gifts of the Magi. It also brought me to my lowest ebb, alone on the New Year's holiday. There would be no one to celebrate with, or toast with champagne—not that I had ever tasted a drop of the bubbly—there were no dear ones to stay up with 'til midnight while we brought in the New Year together. I was so lonesome I could die.

Where was Mario when I needed him? Here I was, facing a year in which I would be twenty, and because of my upbringing, could not see a future except as a married woman. It was tragic. I blame my parents for it. What a cripple I was, to think of only being happy if I married. But I guess they were not the only ones who thought like that.

In my own mind, at the end of 1965, I was marking time until Mr. Right appeared.

'Marriage is forever,' I told myself. Only one chance to get it right! I was deeply unhappy. Was I so brave as to move to a thousand miles from home, only to find the winter of my discontent?

I could not understand the conflict within me, did not know how to resolve it— thought I was the only one in the world to suffer so. *What would Julie Christie do?* I asked myself. She was the new sensation, because of *Dr. Zhivago*. I noticed her, an English actress, when Mario said, 'You move like she does.' Oh, that was interesting. *But what does it mean?* Was he saying that I was beautiful?

Julie Christie was beautiful, certainly, but she seemed so cold with those blue eyes. I watched her with new eyes as she moved on screen, trying to discover something in myself, something about mystique which I knew she embodied. After watching a number of Julie Christie movies, I decided that what she embodied was controlled passion. Hmm, I could relate to that. Wild, unrestrained, 'cast your fate to the wind' passion, I knew little about.

With holiday-time and year-end celebrations, Mario had deserted me again for his family in Key West. I was desperate. I sat, turning over a pile of old records, and put one on the spindle. Maurice and the Zodiacs sang:

Oh, won't you stay
Just a little bit longer ... [47]

---

[47] 'Stay,' by Maurice Williams and the Zodiacs, 1960.

Chapter Six: *Shout*

Drat. In a fit of frustration, I emitted a piercing peacock shriek that reverberated in the chandelier, provoking the notice of my landlord, who banged on his floor directly above me with his cane.

Had I known it, I was experiencing the typical 'mistress' syndrome of being left alone on all the important days—the only thing I did not have was his financial support.

'Is our relationship so shameful that he cannot introduce me to his family?' I asked myself. 'Is it my own attitude of not taking his love seriously that prevents an introduction to his nearest and dearest?'

Who could say? Certainly I was nursing a grudge on December 31st, that day of endings and beginnings with *Janus* looking both ways; there was plenty of room for doubt about Mario's love and devotion.

Where can I meet some nice lonely young men? I wondered idly, but I already knew. I removed a TV-dinner from the freezer, and resolved on a course of action. Lulu's *'Shout'* was rocking its frenetic way through my living room, via the radio. I could not resist it. I began dancing like a Zulu, my feet hitting the floor in what I imagined would be the same stamping rhythm a beaver uses for packing river mud around his house. *'You make me wanna shout, shout, shout, shout!'* [48]

On New Year's Eve, what better time?

'I'll do it.'

Can you surrey, can you picnic, oh oh,
Can you surrey, can you picnic, c'mon c'mon ... [49]

I surreyed on down to the USO in Miami, that friendly, protected spot of the rarefied atmosphere, where girls and soldier-boys, or sailors, could dance away the lonely afternoons. I

---

[48] 'Shout,' performed by Scottish singer, Lulu, in 1965. Written by The Isley Brothers.
[49] 'Stone Soul Picnic,' written by Laura Nyro, 1966, and famously sung by *The Fifth Dimension* in 1968. Author's note: There is some disagreement over the way 'surrey' should be spelled.

had done that in Memphis when I was eighteen, during my split-shifts away from the telephone office, or in the evenings, after work. It was exciting for a while. A person could go down to the USO to meet people, as I wished to do now—and not be considered as 'cheap,' or as having compromised oneself in some way.

Petula Clark's 'Downtown' began tripping its happy way through my head. *'When you're alone and life is making you lonely, you can always go ...'* [50]

It brightened my spirits. I felt inspired. 'Forge ahead! Don't be scared.' I marched out my front door. I had to think positive thoughts or I would go back in and hibernate. *Why do I have to fight my way through life?* I thought. *Could it be true, about karma?*

When I first started visiting the USO in Memphis, a year previously, I had just broken up with my boyfriend, Roger Douglass, and was full of self-pity. I felt as worthless as a Buffalo-head nickel. *I will console myself,* I thought, *by dancing the night away.* That was in the September.

Try to love again, I told myself. That was in the October. *Don't wallow in your misery.* Easier said than done. I couldn't help it; I was pining for Roger Douglass.

Dancing at the USO, I quickly discovered that I could not follow a lead. Though I liked to 'fast dance,' I had never done a lot of 'slow-dancing' because of a lack of partners. Not having an older brother constituted a handicap when it came to learning basic dance steps that were popular in high school. At home, dancing with my sisters, I naturally played the 'man'-part, being the elder and taller.

Mario was a wonderful dancer and I could have asked him to teach me, but *that* was all ballroom stuff, mambo, samba, bolero, and I was not interested in it at the time. Pity. I would

---

[50] 'Downtown,' performed by Petula Clark, 1965. Author unknown.

Chapter Six: *Shout*

pay a lot to learn, now. *'It's too late, baby, now it's too late ...'* Sigh.[51]

The only dances I could do after high school were the bop, the polka, the Charleston, the *cha cha,* and the waltz––not acceptable on any dance floor in the U.S. in 1964. Roger Douglass did not like to dance, and hadn't even taken me to the Prom. Fie! Consequently, I had not learned any of the new dances that succeeded the bop. Well, I could do the Twist—but I didn't like it, my breasts swung in too wide an arc.

When I was in junior high school, I had a boyfriend named Carl, and he could do the bop. Carl had a feeling for rhythm. At the hop, he thrust his pelvis forward to the beat of the music in a way that was almost obscene. But, of course, you don't know how to be obscene when you are only twelve years old. Still, his parents believed that rock 'n roll encouraged unworthy thoughts of physical contact, and would have stopped us dancing if they could. But they couldn't. My mother was at work, so she didn't know.

In those good old days, I wore full skirts, sometimes made of felt with an appliquéd poodle on it; and bobby socks, with lace-up black and white saddle oxford shoes. That style sounds so dated now, but at the time, I was the cat's meow. I knew girls who envied me.

Little Richard screamed, *'Good golly Miss Molly, sure like to ball ...'*[52]

Carl threw me up into the air, petticoats flying, and then sliced me between his legs, the way they used to dance the jitterbug in the 1940s. I was too worried about showing my panties to actually enjoy all that tossin' and turnin'. (Darn it.) But actually, it was great fun. Sadly, I lost Carl to another school after he finished the ninth grade.

I thought 'the bop' was a funny name. Was 'bop' short for 'bebop,' that Beatnik rhythm, like they used to talk about in the

---

[51] Lyrics from 'It's Too Late,' performed by Carole King, 1971, on the album, *Tapestry*; co-written by Toni Stern.
[52] 'Good Golly Miss Molly' performed by Little Richard. Written by John Marascato and Robert 'Bumps' Blackwell.

A Quiet Life in Bedlam

1950s bars and coffee houses? *Bebop,* a kind of jazz? I missed out on it—the coffee house, calypso, folk music, arty-party scene, because I was too young for the era of café society, Beatniks and beanies: but in many ways, I was still a child of the fifties.

Everyone was expecting Rock 'n Roll to die, but it didn't. It metamorphosed into something worse, the sixties dances. I was acutely self-conscious, that first time in 1964 when I went into the USO. I felt my inadequacies, but would not be defeated. With an effort, I controlled my trembling, breathed in, breathed out, and pretended to be Loretta Young making an entrance. I swished through the door.

'Hello,' I said to the senior hostesses. A senior hostess welcomed me, offered me coffee and an egg. I declined politely. Then on to the main problem: How do I break the ice and get someone to ask me to dance? The place was chock-full of naval airmen from Memphis Naval Air Station at Millington.

It was pretty spooky standing there looking at all those naval airmen, and them looking at me. I was wearing a short skirt, almost to the mid-thigh—that was daring. The 'mini-skirt' accented my long legs. I say 'mini-skirt,' but it was actually a dress with no waist in it—a pity! I had a small waist. My hips were cleverly hidden beneath the A-line of the skirt, and while I stayed slender, fooled everyone about my true shape—far too womanly for the 1960s; girls were supposed to have a 'boy' shape.

The fabric of my dress, that first time at the USO, was a racy hot-pink-and-chartreuse paisley cotton-blend number, what they used to call 'loud.' I am surprised I had the nerve to wear it, but I wanted to be noticed. Working at the telephone company had gotten me a few nice, basic things. Paisley has a swirl in it, and so do I.

I'm in circulation! I thought excitedly. *Whatever that means.*

I adored 'paisley,' and wore it for years, as often as I could find clothes like that. Paisley became very popular in the late 1960s. Originating in Scotland by way of India, it probably

Chapter Six: *Shout*

came onto the American fashion scene from Carnaby Street in 'swinging' London. In the States, the paisley pattern became almost a symbol for 'free-love' and Woodstock, and the anti-war movement that was gathering speed right on the doorstep, waiting to break out— lying in wait to go down in history as a social upheaval.

'Well, no use standing around, dear Lord, what do I do?' The pause was pregnant. The servicemen, those that cared, were still looking at me. Available girls were not in the majority at the USO. It was rather like being on a stage. 'That's what I have to do—pretend I am on a stage.' *Fluff up your hair a bit.* I went to the ladies' room.

Finally, I took the plunge, and concentrated on making the men feel manly by walking up, and meekly saying with eyes downcast—*play helpless*—'I don't know how to dance—will you teach me?'

They fell for it every time—unless they were really 're-tarded'—more shy than I was. Or too snobbish: there were precious few of *those* at the USO during the Vietnam era. It was a veritable silver groove of promising young men. The popular song, 'I'm In With the In Crowd,' by Dobie Gray, had a ripple effect among native Memphians later on (Memphis was a snobbish town), but a young guy away from home is an insecure guy. An insecure guy needs a girl. *What about me?*

Once I got over my self-conscious feelings and let the rhythms of the music take over my body, I managed very well as a junior hostess at the USO in 1964; but it was the sailors from Millington Naval Air Station who taught me to dance—those sweet boys. They even taught me a few of the other social graces, I'm not afraid to admit it.

The best dancers were the guys from New York City—*'oo ah, oo ah, oo oo, Kitty, tell us about the boy from New York City'* [53] — though their 'accent' was hideous; and the boys from California, who were easy-going and eager to please.

---

[53] 'The Boy From New York City,' performed by the Ad Libs, 1965. Written by George Davis and John T. Taylor.

A Quiet Life in Bedlam

They were little beauties, those Californians. They danced their hearts out, one and all. And I did, too. It was great fun, and I began to feel like a full-fledged member of the 'Age of Aquarius.'

That was before rock music got so loud and obnoxious. I was safely married before the 'psychedelic' movement had gone very far, thank God. But until 'psychedelia' came along—electronic music, rock, pop, singing, dancing, body painting—and before 'marriage' when I became more conservative, it was just the original sixties dances at the USO, the Crawl, the Pony, the Stroll, the Funky Chicken, the Zulu, and so, on and on—one fad after another. The steps to new dances were mapped out in magazines for people who wanted to learn. I bought a magazine when I could afford one, and practiced the steps with my sisters.

But with the advent of psychedelia, in about 1966, I was out of my element—I just wasn't that wild, even in my most unrestrained moments. I believe that one *would* have to take drugs to enjoy that kind of stuff. The blaring, acid, minor key musical 'reverbs' gave me a headache. The flashing colored lights and 'strobes' crossed my eyes, and put me in bed with a migraine. The exotic instrumentation of 'psychedelic' was strange, to say the least. What on Earth was a sitar? The surreal lyrics did not set well with me. 'Lucy in the Sky with Diamonds,' I ask you. Donovan's 'Hurdy Gurdy Man' made me nauseous, though in general, I liked his songs.

I was not progressive enough for psychedelic, I suppose. Not liberal enough. As I got older, too much jerking and wriggling and bumping on the dance floor caused me to have muscle spasms, though everyone said it was great for physical fitness. 'Physical fitness' had never been much of a priority with *me. Psychedelic,* psychotic. Still, I loved to dance; it was a way to expel my passion. Otherwise, I did little to keep myself fit—nice girls didn't do that—there was a danger of breaking the 'hymen.' It was sacred. *Where was it?*

I did try to learn the new dances for as long as I remained single, no matter how difficult they proved to be. I wanted to

Chapter Six: *Shout*

be active and meet new people—needed a challenge to ward off the boredom. But it is surprising how dancing can become boring if you have nothing else to do.

On New Year's Eve, 1965, I tried to stay at the USO in Miami until the stroke of midnight and closing time; and that night, *everyone* danced to the last number, 'Goodnight My Love,' including yours truly. I was slow-dancing with a marine who seemed a nice enough boy. I tried not to lead.

'A whistling girl and a crowing hen will always come to a bitter end,' I heard my grandmother say in my ear. Go away, Grandmother. *Groan.* In other words surrender, be feminine. 'Well, okay, if that's the only way.'

'What?' asked the marine.

I smiled mysteriously.

When the USO closed, the marine and I took the bus to the airport for lack of anything else to do, and there we walked around, drank a cup of coffee, talked. I didn't usually date marines, because somehow, they did not seem to be intellectual enough. I preferred sailors, don't ask me why, but there weren't many 'swabees' at the Miami USO on that last night of the year. They were probably all at home with their families in Wyoming or somewhere ... sniff.

'Everyone's gone to the moon, everyone's gone to the moon...' [54] I felt, rather than heard, the singing over the airport PA system.

No challenge with a marine ...

I quickly knew that I was not interested in this boy; he didn't have 'charisma.' His mind seemed to be elsewhere. Perhaps he was thinking of home, of South Carolina, the state he had recently left: the Marine Corps was no respecter of holidays.

Streets full of people, all alone
Rows full of houses, never home

---

[54] 'Everyone's Gone to the Moon,' performed by Jonathan King, 1965. Words and music by Kenneth King.

A Quiet Life in Bedlam

*Church full of singing, out of tune
Everyone's gone to the moon.* [55]

The marine and I talked about Lyndon Johnson's perfidy to the South—and Johnson was a Southerner, by jingo! pushing through more Civil Rights laws!—against all common sense. I was suspicious of the consequences to the South and its traditions. I did not suspect that I had been corrupted by a mid-South upbringing—never guessed, did not recognize it for years. Some things come by osmosis, and leave only with acceptance of the Golden Rule. (And that ain't easy for a Southerner.)

Spouting a popular theory, I asked the marine, 'Was it something left over from the Kennedy Administration, the new law?'

'I don't know,' he replied. I don't think he cared much.

'The Voting Rights Act,' from Johnson's 'Great Society,' we decided the new legislation was called. Where ever it came from, and whatever its intention, the marine and I both believed anarchy would be the result; more rioting in the streets.

'Didn't they learn anything from Watts?' I asked.

It was a quiet night in Miami, however, and at two o'clock in the morning of January 1, 1966, the Marine escorted me home. Shortly after, he shipped out to Vietnam. We had no agreement to correspond with each other. I wasn't sorry.

The date was a dead loss. There was one thing he said that provoked further thought—about having been drafted, then joining the U.S. Marines instead; and then still not having the right to vote. That made me remember how sore I felt when Lyndon Johnson had been elected by a landslide, in 1964, and I had not been allowed to vote for Goldwater (the lesser of two evils), because I was only eighteen.

I was, however, considered to be an adult for other intents and purposes—Mother asked me to pay room and board in 1964. 'Why can't I vote?' I remember fuming as I rode the bus

---

[55] 'Everyone's Gone to the Moon.'

Chapter Six: *Shout*

to work early one November morning after the 1964 election. The colored women sitting around me seemed well satisfied with the result, I noted.

As is well known, it became a point for protest, that eighteen-year-olds who could fight (the most common age of being drafted) were disenfranchised by unfair laws. By the time another presidential election came along in 1968, I was old enough to vote, and gave my ballot to Nixon.

Before I slept on New Year's Eve, I thought about how disappointed I had been in my first 'New Year' away from home. How could I make my life better? I did not want every New Year to end up like this one, walking around an airport, for God's sake.

Should I make a resolution? With the passing of New Year's Day, my sisters and I made resolutions that had to be repeated to family members, who acted as enforcers in seeing that we stuck to our resolves.

I was a child no longer. There was no one to watch over me. I would skip it. And I wasn't starting back to church, either. How could I face it? Anyway, I was not sure where I belonged. I wanted to be an Episcopalian. Mother said I was Cumberland Presbyterian.

But still, I could smile, reflecting on New Year's celebrations in the Memphis of my childhood when, on the stroke of midnight, each citizen to the last man sprinted to his vehicle, and blasted away on his (or her) car horn with hilarious abandon in recognition of the mystical and significant hour: twelve o'clock. In Memphis, there was a city ordnance that forbade the blowing of automobile horns in any situation barring a life-and-death traffic incident. But at midnight on December 31st, the police in Memphis became, considerately, stone-deaf.

One of my best memories of the USO (in Memphis) involved a marine who asked me to marry him. Yes! Early in 1965, at the USO! I was just out of high school, and very unsure of myself. But I was ready to take a chance. My ex-boyfriend, Roger, did not love me, so what did anything matter? might as well throw myself away on a marine.

This little U.S. Marine, David, asked me to slow-dance. Uh oh. I ignored him, turned away, and talked to the senior hostesses. But he was persistent. 'Dance?' he asked me again.

I didn't answer; tried to wander off.

At the USO, not being able to slow-dance with a partner was an impediment: slow-dancing was conducive to getting to know someone more quickly if you had to put your arms around his neck. Still, there were the fast dances, plenty of them, and I was so enthusiastic, throwing my arms about and slinging my hair in front of my face. I beat my feet so hard on the floor, laughing sometimes like a maniac for sheer joy, that those 'mashed potatoes' were well and truly 'mashed' when I got done with them!

It is easy to make a fool of yourself on the dance floor, easy to forget who you are; and for once, I didn't care. For once, I was uninhibited:

Do you love me (do you love me)
Do you love me (do you love me)
Do you love me (do you love me)
Now that I can dance ...
Watch me now! [56]

It was okay to ask a boy to dance if you handled it delicately. The naval airmen seemed to like me—I was lively enough—and I teased them with saying that I was looking for 'my boyfriend, Throckmorton Daffy-down-dilly Snitzelfritzel.' They couldn't resist that come-on. They had to get to the bottom of it.

I never said: 'Throckmorton Daffy-down-dilly Snitzelfritzel is the name my ex-boyfriend, Roger, called himself, when writing semi-erotic letters to me, before graduation.' No. That would not have helped my case. That was a secret.

'Have you seen him?' I would ask.

---

[56] 'Do You Love Me (Do You Love Me),' sung by the Contours for Gordy/Motown, October, 1962.

Chapter Six: *Shout*

'Who?' was the usual reply.

'My boyfriend, Throckmorton Daffy-down-dilly Snitzelfritzel.'

'Oh. No, I don't think so. Is he at Millington?'

I was no dumb cluck. With that sort of banter, the ice was soon broken, and I got asked to dance, but *usually* accepted only the 'fast' ones. If a boy asked me why I would not dance with him, I told the truth, I could not stop myself trying to lead. They accepted it, to a man.

So this little marine who twice asked me to dance at the USO in Memphis—he was lonely and scared. He didn't *really* want to dance. He was nineteen, and on his way to the Vietnam war. He told me about it, all in a rush, after I had refused his second request to slow dance. We spent much of the evening together while I considered his proposal. David explained that he needed, wanted, to get married, so that he would have somebody, something, to hold on to, while he was away in Vietnam.

I was flabbergasted. *Could things be that bad?*

Delicately, I asked him to dance. He was shorter than me, but I didn't mind. The 45 rpm record playing on the phonograph was the Animals' 'House of the Rising Sun,' a sad song. The chords of the organ solo throbbed and moaned, the backbeat pricked at me as we danced:

It's been the ruin of many a poor boy, and God, I know I'm one. [57]

I knew nothing of the reality of war, did not have much of an opinion, one way or the other, about Vietnam. It was the government's business, not mine. It did concern me that many of the men my age were off fighting, preventing them from being in a place where I could meet them; but though my entire high school class may have been, at one time or another, given over to the draft and the military, I did not know of anyone, at any time, who died in Vietnam. I guess I was lucky.

---

[57] 'House of the Rising Sun.'

David had a lovely smile, and beautiful teeth. I found out later that the teeth were false, his own having been knocked out in boot camp. I met more than one marine with no teeth, and I think 'boot camp' should have been called 'teeth camp.' Anyway, I came close to falling in love with David, because, *first*, I was on the rebound, *second*, he seemed to need me, and *third*, he could play the piano beautifully. To his credit, he wasn't stupid, either.

David Thornton played for hours on the baby grand piano, in the afternoons, before dinner and before the serious dancing started. There in the roomy premises of the USO in Memphis, I sat as if under an enchantment by his side, wearing a drop-waisted navy-blue pleated skirt and a sailor (middy) blouse. I looked pretty, if I do say so—but only recognize it now because someone snapped a picture of me. I still have that photograph in an old album. It could very well have been David who took that picture.

What a thing, I thought, as I looked at my album. *I am attractive. Gosh.*

Where is David now, I wonder? Do I have his picture somewhere? I don't think so.

Finding the picture sent me off into a paroxysm of reminiscence, of longing. It occurred to me, that, in 1965, I had been in danger of turning from a girl into a turnip, because I would not give my love. The piece of music I remember specifically that David played, was part of the score from the musical, *The Fantasticks*,[58] which was then a hit off-Broadway. The music was unforgettable, the words poignant. I shivered with delight each time he played and sang,

> *Try to remember the kind of September*
> *when life was slow, and oh, so mellow ...* [59]

---

[58] *The Fantasticks*, music by Harvey Schmidt, lyrics and book by Tom Jones, 1960.
[59] 'Try to Remember,' from the musical, *The Fantasticks*.

Chapter Six: *Shout*

That kind of life, slow and mellow, *'when grass was green and grain was yellow,'* I had known only as a child, before my father's insurance business failed, before he lost hope and became an alcoholic; before our family life became a nightmare from which I wanted to escape forever.

It was a golden time, my early childhood, an era I associate with autumn, my favorite season of the year. But in 1965, I was not a child anymore, and could not marry a boy just because he sang of a charmed life in an unreachable place—evoked a memory, more illusory than real; or because he was beautiful in his soul, and obviously talented and thoughtful.

'Try to remember when life was so tender that no one wept except the willow ...' [60] the ghost of David sang to me as I went to sleep on the night he asked me to marry him. I did not love him, so I told the truth. David found a girl in Memphis who *was* willing to marry him, and I never saw him again.

It's funny how a melody can bring a recollection of days gone by: I rarely think of David now, except when I hear that song. And yet, I think of him with affection, wondering what ever became of that little marine with the memorable fingers.

David was from some strange place in Texas—Galveston. He was a Southerner. I felt sure there must be a lonely boy from somewhere else, a northern place, a western place, who valued the wits of women more than Southern men could do.

'Anyway, who knows if I would like his mother?' I said to my reflection in the bathroom mirror. 'Better to be safe than sorry.'

Going to the USO in Miami got old, fast, the same as it did when I was in Memphis. There's only so many times you can say, 'Have you seen my boyfriend ...' And yet, there I was again, late in December of 1965, dancing with marines. Well, it could occupy some of my time until I decided what to do next. Also, there was the remote, the faint possibility that I might meet someone who would be worth marrying.

---

[60] 'Try To Remember.'

A Quiet Life in Bedlam

My sister, Annabelle, had lucked out, had met her fiancé, Ralph, from Laconia, New Hampshire, through my contact with the USO in Memphis. I brought Ralph home, with a gang of other sailors, in October of 1964. It was my intention that he should be introduced to Sherry, my youngest sister. But it was Annabelle, the middle one, who snagged him. Ralph and Annabelle were to be married in August of 1966.

But in general, it was expecting too much from those poor lonely boys, so far away from home, cut off from everything they knew, so desperate for a little affection—a bit of attention—just as I was. Annabelle too. Would the marriage of Annabelle and Ralph work out?—It remained to be seen. Ralph's mother, a Roman Catholic, was dead-set against the match. And she was a Yankee. God forbid.

I did get a few nice dates out of the USO. There was this one sailor from California—he was twenty—who won my trust completely. I believe I would have married him if he had asked me. Instead, he told me that I made him realize how much he loved the girl back home.

Was that a compliment?

His name was Joel. Joel got leave, caught a flight home to Santa Barbara, and married his girl. *Rats.* I liked him. I liked his sense of humor. I thought it was very novel when Joel told me, 'On my wife's fortieth birthday' ... ah ... *(oh, ancient age!)* ... 'I'm going to slap her on the rump and tell her she's a good kid!'

Would, that I could have been that wife. Californians are a bit of all right, in my opinion. But I lost him. It was just a summer romance.

The USO was for enlisted men. The idea that such a breed as 'officers' existed, had never occurred to me. I really was so naïve, so innocent of what sort of man might suit me— ignorant of what fish were out there waiting to be caught, and the consequences that a marriage could have on my life. I only knew that *my* man should not drink, should not be violent, should respect my intelligence, be generous, and make me belly-laugh now and then; it's good for the soul.

Chapter Six: *Shout*

Altogether now, one, two, three:

Fish gotta swim and birds gotta fly
I gotta love one man 'til I die ... [61]

---

[61] 'Can't Help Lovin' Dat Man,' a controversial song from the musical play, *Showboat,* 1927. Music by Jerome Kern; book and lyrics, by Oscar Hammerstein II. Based on the 1926 novel by Edna Ferber.

CHAPTER SEVEN:
Love Can Make You Happy

The year 1966 arrived, and I was still not making enough money. It was slowly born in on my consciousness that if I wanted to have a better income, I would have to get a college education: that was a jaw-breaker.

It was true that people could move up through the ranks at the telephone company, but it took years. What would give a sure-fire promotion was an associate's degree, or a bachelor's degree, in almost any subject. Ma Bell would pay part of the tuition.

College education! What luxury. I didn't have time or money for it. Higher education wasn't an option women had that I knew of—except for some few cases where affluent parents with only daughters sent them off to college hoping they would find a husband. My friend, Sally Hedges, was such a one. That lucky girl; she had everything.

And I knew of a woman twenty years older than me, Micki Merrifield, who had worked her way up from long distance operator, to district manager, in AT&T Long-Lines Engineering in Miami (that had to do with drawing charts for laying telephone cables under the sea and technical stuff like that). But such phenomenal advances were very rare.

Chapter Seven: *Love Can Make You Happy*

My best hope was to become a 'supervisor,' but for that kind of promotion, you had to be more conventional, more biddable, more of a conformist than I was. Behind my back, people called me 'fey'; but I didn't learn of it until years later, and therefore could not correct myself.

I had developed negative feelings about higher education when I was enrolled briefly at Memphis State University in the summer of 1964. I wanted to attend Memphis State because Roger did. Maybe then, he would love me. The outcome of the summer term was dismal. I contrived to flunk 'English.' God. It was disgraceful—my favorite subject. I could never respect myself again, I was sure. To fail a subject was the worst thing that could happen to anybody at school; it had never happened to me before.

What I heard about it—it was a rumor—as the reason for the deplorable situation—I wasn't the only freshman who failed—was that there were so many new students, so many kids in the crop of 1946, that Memphis State had to get rid of some of them by any means available. Any weakness was exploited.

Well, it was easy to intimidate me. My mother did not want me to go to college. She discouraged me as much as she could. 'A sensible girl would work, make money, find a husband, and not think of silly things like higher education,' she told me time and again; 'What do you need it for?' though she knew my penchant well enough.

When my English professor at Memphis State told me I was stupid for asking a question during the lecture, I believed him. My mother had said the same thing to me, many times. She did not really think I was stupid, of course, she just thought I did not have common sense, or 'the gumption of a billy goat,' as she called it. Mother's higher education was the school of hard knocks. She valued common sense above rubies.

After a month and a half of fighting a losing battle with Memphis State and Mother, I *did* do something stupid. I stopped going to class. Since I was a 'part-time' student, I did not have an advisor. Because I did not have an advisor, no one told me to 'drop' the English class. I didn't drop the class, did not attend, did not take the exam, and flunked. It was as simple as that. I almost never got over it.

My English teacher at Messick High School, Miss Rogers, had positively doted on me, if Miss Rogers could be said to dote on anyone. I would have given my life for her. After two years with Miss Rogers, that most exacting of teachers, who made me, and the whole senior class, memorize *Ode on a Grecian Urn,* by Keats, I thought I could pass English anywhere, anytime, asleep and with one hand tied behind my back.

I don't know if the story was true, about Memphis State trying to weed out students—press them out any way they could—but failing English upset me so badly that I actually had nightmares about it for years afterwards. In those dreams, I was sitting in English 101 at Memphis State, trying my best, then flunking out, over and over again. It was as distressing as dreams where something is chasing you, and you can't escape, but you can't turn and face it.

In another dream, there I was, Miss Katharine Co-Ed, walking through the study hall in tight skirt, pageboy, twin set and pearls. The Fortunes sang out over the building's intercom, *'Here it comes again, that feeling, here it comes again ...'* [62] Uh oh.

And what to my wondering eyes should appear but Roger Douglass, my ex-, kissing an attractive blond girl behind a bookshelf. He did it only to upset me. I felt as if someone had punched me in the stomach. I awoke with a start, realizing I couldn't breathe.

The lyric, *'You know, you know, you broke my heart ...'* [63] was spinning around in my woolly head. Roger had passed English with an A. I had failed.

Gee whiz, I thought, *isn't life strange?*

'Oh, man,' I moaned, and held my head. I did not have a hangover, but it sure felt like it. In that book, *All the Rivers*

---

[62] 'Here It Comes Again,' sung by The Fortunes, 1965.
[63] Ibid.

Chapter Seven: *Love Can Make You Happy*

Run,[64] by Nancy Cato, the author proposed that an onion sandwich would cure a hangover. Was she joking? Would an onion sandwich cure depression? Would anyone kiss me afterwards? If I had been interested in alcohol, I surely would have started drinking. That anyone would dare to fail *me* is too incredible to express, even in English.

The nightmares about failing English (and various other subjects) continued right up until the time I actually passed English at Miami-Dade Junior College in the spring of 1966. What a mercy! I proved that I really could pass, and I had the ability to go further. It probably saved me a round of psychoanalysis: that time.

It was not easy for me to carry my nervous body down to enroll at Miami-Dade College, but I did it. Mario was proud of me. He had his Master's Degree in Fine Arts already, and was a great believer in higher education. I think he felt it would not hurt me to get some exposure to situations that would broaden my horizons, help in the maturing process. He discounted his own influence.

Mario had a fine baritone voice, and he sang to me sometimes. I could hear him, like an echo, as Michael Nesmith chortled on the radio in my living room,

> *Beyond the blue horizon, waits a beautiful day.*
> *Goodbye to things that bore me, love is waiting for me.* [65]

I opened up my semester transcript and saw an 'A' in both English, and algebra, my bane (Who cares if $a + b = c$?). 'Jeepers creepers, I'm a scholar.' I was jubilant. Hi-de-ho!

By and by it became more apparent, even to a blind baby like me, that 'my close friend,' as I described him to Mother, Mario Fiqueroa, was a gifted artist. My awakening knowledge

---

[64] *All the Rivers Run,* by Nancy Cato, 1958.
[65] 'Beyond the Blue Horizon,' by Frank Harling, Leo Robin, and Richard Whiting, composition date unknown.

of his talent and vision quieted my bad conscience a little bit. I needed that.

'Everyone knows that artists do not live by bread alone!' I reasoned one day in April of 1966. 'Of *course* they have mistresses.' Or muses, whatever you wanna call 'em.

And on the next day in April, my twentieth birthday, I did an about-face, and thought, *How can Mario fly in the face of public opinion, the social laws, and probably God's laws as far as I know, and still sleep at night?* It was a conundrum. I knew he had been photographing semi-clothed women at his studio. He developed the pictures himself in his darkroom. (You couldn't get it done at the drugstore.) What else went on in there? I have been in a darkroom; it's the perfect place for groping.

'Try not to be intractable!' I instructed myself. 'Don't be jealous!' I commanded. 'Remember, you don't love him.'

Well, okay, but I was uneasy.

The trouble with being obstinate is that you don't know you are, and it only gets worse if someone tells you not to be that way. It is one of life's vicious little circles.

There was still the constant worry of unwanted pregnancy. I made one feeble attempt to seek out information about birth control. That took courage. No one ever talked about contraception. It wasn't a subject that was broached in polite society.

I was well aware that no reputable doctor would prescribe contraceptives to an unmarried minor. At work, I spoke to a young married woman about the indelicate matter I had on my immoral mind. She suggested that I lie to a doctor.

Lie to the doctor! I could not believe it. How could I consider such a course as lying to the doctor?

Could I get away with it? Would it be a venial sin, a carnal sin, a moral sin, or a fatal sin?

I did not have a wedding ring, I didn't have a marriage certificate. Those European movies where you see the cheeky unmarried woman waltzing confidently into the doctor's office wearing a borrowed wedding ring, getting examined, and walking out gleefully with a prescription for a diaphragm, are con-

Chapter Seven: *Love Can Make You Happy*

trived nonsense. It just wasn't done. I would not be surprised if birth control was actually against the law in 1965. I *know* abortion was.

I hadn't a clue what means for birth control were available to me. Nice people did not practice contraception, though it may have been that the Catholics were already talking about the 'rhythm' method. I believe Mario spoke to me about it once. He said, 'There are times of the month that are "safer" than other times. When are you having your period?' I was horrified at the mention of my menstruation, and did not answer him. I threw up my hands. *Let's not talk about it.*

Even educated women knew little about birth control. Most married women pushed aside the thought as being slightly immoral. There was talk of childless couples as going against God's law. Married women had babies; that was the way it always had been. Unmarried women were pitied as 'old maids' and even denigrated in a card game.

I did not know that condoms existed, and I don't think Mario did, either. Condoms used to be called 'prophylactics.' I had heard the word in a childhood joke, but never thought to look up, in the dictionary, what I believed was a made-up word and nothing to do with me. With hindsight, that would have been the solution, I think. Prophylactics. A pity, that I didn't know, but I wasn't meant to know.

Our lovemaking could not have been very satisfactory to Mario; his idea of birth control was *coitus interruptus*. Yuk.

I had overheard whispered conversations among the older women at the office about some 'other' ways of prevention. So, after lovemaking, I jumped up immediately and walked briskly around the apartment, trying to dislodge any miscreant sperm. Then afterwards, I took a bath in water and vinegar.

Mario, laughing, exclaimed, 'Would it be so awful to have my baby?'

'Blasphemy!' I cried out from my secret heart, but silently, sadly. So he wouldn't hear me sob, I put on the record player. Astrud Gilberto sang sweetly,

A Quiet Life in Bedlam

'How insensitive I must have seemed when he told me that he loved me ...' [66]

Scream! Get me out of here.

The episode with vinegar and water did not make me feel confident, so I summoned up my courage, steeled myself for awkward questions, dressed in my most sober-looking clothing, and approached a druggist about an item that I didn't even know how to pronounce.

When I asked for a 'duce,' the pharmacist looked at me as if considering whether I wanted a pack of cards; then to my surprise, chuckled kindly, and gently informed me, 'Young lady, you won't be needing such an item as a douche until after you are married.'

Cringe! I could feel my face turn beet-red. Trying not to show how mortified I was, I accepted his wisdom, and tripped over my feet as I retreated. Did I really look that young? I felt old. Ancient as an Inca. Desperate as a dying dodo. Decrepit as a dried-up Druid.

'You gauche fool,' I chastised myself. *'Why couldn't you pull that off?'* It was the end of my trips to the drugstore. After that, I wouldn't even buy Bayer Aspirin.

I did not become pregnant during my affair with Mario, but I suffered every day the anticipation of it. My fear was intense. Round and round in my head—I could not make it stop—ran that song by the popular Californian college group, 'We Five,'

'I can never go home again, never really find my town ...' [67]

An outcast. I held my head and shouted 'Stop it, stop it!' My life was beginning to take on the quality of 'snowball rolling wildly down hill.' I did not know where to turn.

Was I going mad? Clearly, I needed to re-route some mental energy. I put on some music—the magic formula. The talented quintet, 'We Five,' looked so beautiful on their debut album cover—strolling down the beach, not a care in the

---

[66] 'How Insensitive' ('Insensatez') by Antonio Carlos Jobim, composition date unknown. English lyrics by Norman Gimbel.

[67] 'I Can Never Go Home Again,' performed by We Five, *1965*. Composer unknown. From the A&M album, *You Were On My Mind*.

Chapter Seven: *Love Can Make You Happy*

world. Lucky them. They were young in a way that I could never be.

In extremis, I always go back to religion. I recited regularly, along with the 23rd Psalm, a prayer of confession that I had learned at Sunday School:

> *Almighty and most merciful Father,*
> *We have erred and strayed from thy ways like lost sheep ...*
> *We have followed too much the devices and desires of our own hearts ...* [68]

It helped. I believed in forgiveness. Had I been a Catholic, I probably would have been hissing 'Hail Marys' through my teeth, day and night.

Essentially, I was a survivor. Having an affair with a lovely man like Mario Fiqueroa was probably not the worst thing that would ever happen to me: I made up my mind to keep on working, keep on truckin,' pray for a miracle, plan an escape route in the event that the worst happened—for I knew, without a doubt, that if I asked my mother for help, she would call me a slut and worse, and turn me out on the street to fend for myself.

Because of my fear, I sometimes turned cold to Mario's lovemaking. I don't believe I ever truly appreciated his skill as lover—I was too inexperienced and too awed. Mario did things to me that I hardly dare dream about now.

I rue the number of times I said, 'No!' to him. He was my best lover, there has never been his equal since, and I as good as threw him away. Whoever heard of a girl that was not willing to marry her first lover? It was practically the law of the land.

To think—I could have entered 1966 as a married woman if I had wanted to, if I had not been so idealistic and naïve. I knew where City Hall was located. I could have been counting my babies within a couple of years—Mario was a twin.

---

[68] 'Prayers of Confession and Pardon,' *The Book of Common Prayer*, 1946.

But no, I wanted a church wedding. The city hall was not good enough. I just knew that one did not jump up and marry the first person one went to bed with. There were other reasons for marriage than 'sex,' weren't there? I had seen that amply demonstrated by couples on television, like Ozzie and Harriet Nelson, for example. Although, 'sex' *is* a very good reason. It is a primal urge, like singing. Both can be done in bed.

Mario was easy-going. He was willing to string along with my multiple eccentricities. After his divorce, he had no fixed plans for his life, other than to live and work. Time was on his side. He had many interesting pastimes. I was one of them.

A certain element of love involves surrender, and I wouldn't. I would not surrender.

Thinking back on it, I cannot believe Mario Fiqueroa could really have been in love with me—my affectionate nature would not permit me to ignore a man who was plainly in love. I probably just pretended he was sometimes, to ease my conscience. Certainly, he never *said* he loved me.

At times, my shame and guilt were overwhelming, but not enough to make me stop. My essential loneliness and need for love drove me back into his arms each time I resolved to end it. *'Every time I try to say goodbye, his lips get in the way,'* [69] sang the Shirelles cheekily, on the stereo, as I stewed over the problem.

'Right on, sister,' I giggled. 'That was a beaut!'

Glutton for punishment, miss, my conscience said. 'Shut up,' I said.

'Why couldn't I have been born a boy?' I mourned. That was what Daddy had wanted. Nobody cared what boys got up to. 'They can go cattin' around.' Men were not branded as 'scarlet' if they happened to knock somebody up. People just patted them on the back, and said, 'Well, well,' as if they had proven their virility, or something. *'She's got a bun in her*

---

[69] 'His Lips Get in the Way,' Helen Miller/Howard Greenfeld, Sceptor single 1267 (B).

Chapter Seven: *Love Can Make You Happy*

oven, you say? Haw haw.' Men were practically encouraged to sow their wild oats. It wasn't fair.

Paradoxically, if anyone had asked me, 'Why do you do it? Why do you let him make love to you?' I would have said, 'That's what women are made for.' And I still think it's true, even though I have found, in latter years, that there are some few other things worth doing with one's afternoons.

I trusted Mario to do his best for me. He was ardent and tender; and now that so many years have passed since I have seen him, I wish for all that could have been while wrapped in his warm embrace, and wonder what it would have been like if I could have let go of my inhibitions.

Mario gave me something no other lover has ever done, not even my husbands: he loved me freely, without reservations, giving all of himself, and was not ashamed to do so. Mario Fiqueroa did not view sexual relations between consenting adults as disgusting or sinful—it was just a natural part of life.

None of the men I have been involved with has treated me badly. Certainly Mario did not. I have been singularly lucky in that way. When I think of what my mother suffered at the hands of my father, I wonder why I have been allowed to escape her fate. Even the men that I wanted, but who did not want me, rejected me in a kind way that did not hurt too much—and they were invariably right that we were wrong together.

Maybe Mario and I were right together. I don't know. If I had been older, perhaps I could have seen things differently. But I was fixed in my intentions, unmovable as a boulder; I would not yield.

So I made up my mind. I would take the long way home. I did not give my relationship with Mario a chance. I have made that mistake more than once—I did not know what I had, until he was gone.

And so, I have my sadnesses. Whenever I listen to those clever and perceptive lyrics of 'Foolish Little Girl,' by the Shirelles, I recognize myself:

A Quiet Life in Bedlam

> *Foolish little girl, fickle little girl*
> *You didn't want him when he wanted you*
> *He's found another love, it's her he's dreaming of*
> *And there's not a single thing that you can do.*
> *But I love him ...* [70]

I love him, the idea of him, of Mario—he gave me a good start in life, almost like a father.

---

[70] *'Foolish Little Girl,'* performed by the Shirelles, 1963

CHAPTER EIGHT:
The Kind of Boy You Can't Forget

Life with Mario became regular, serene, uncomplicated—even happy in a guilty, clandestine way. I moved, early in 1966, to a one-bedroom bungalow on a tree-lined street in Coral Gables near the Miracle Mile, close to the office where I worked. I ate Spanish mackerel for lunch, shrimps, or fried grouper. I walked up and down those streets in Coral Gables like I owned them.

Miracle Mile was fascinating. There was every wonderful thing you could think of in the shops—I almost did not mind that I couldn't buy them, it was lovely just to look at the wares. Best of all, there was a second-hand bookshop, where I bought a hardbound copy of *Hawaii,* the Michener novel that Mother had destroyed. And there was a whole shelf of Enid Blyton's adventures in their original colored dust jackets. I bought them all, at one per payday. Treasures.

Life. It went on. For me, it wasn't even wartime. The Vietnam War escalated, but I didn't pay attention. There was rioting everywhere, so I heard: 'everywhere' was apparently north of Miami. Lyndon Johnson's policies became a focus for protest, violent and otherwise. Civil unrest, racial tensions, civil disobedience, demonstrations, marches on Washington, marches through Mississippi, Black Panthers forming, 'swing and sway' with Cassius Clay, Molotov cocktails, 'The Eve of Destruction,'

A Quiet Life in Bedlam

sit-in's, love-ins, 'Exordium and Terminus'—all of these things rolled over me during the months of 1966, and I had no more qualms about the national situation than a few tremors over the fates of the victims of Richard Speck. It was a pretty pink bubble I was living in.

The weather was hot—hot as the blazes. At home, I had a huge electric fan that stayed on all the time. Women had not started wearing shorts like they did later on, in the 1970s; so after work, I stripped and donned a muumuu in a wild Hawaiian pattern. That was cool and comfortable, especially with no clothes on underneath; then I wrapped my long hair in a turban to keep it off my neck. I liked the way I looked in a turban—other worldly, like a Turkish Delight (odalisque).

Mother had taught us that under no circumstances were we to look at ourselves unclothed—there were few mirrors in our home—and, taking a gamble that lightening would not strike me dead, one day when I undressed, I stayed that way. There was no one around, no one to catch me.

The bungalow had a cheval glass in the bedroom. I could look at my full length, naked as a jaybird—all five feet, five and one-half inches of it. Sweeping a critical eye over my unfashionably white body, I suffered a few pangs of regret for choosing a life as a 'paleface.' It was difficult, when out and about, to avoid looking up at the ubiquitous billboards showing a beautiful blond teenaged girl in a bikini (not polka-dot): and this bronzed goddess was lofted on high by the adorable, unattainable Coppertone boys, their outsized figures dancing down a mythical beach. Urrgh! I should have been green with envy over her skin tone, as the Coppertone Corporation would wish me to be; but one must make decisions in life, and then stick by them.

The cheval glass revealed that I had good legs, amazingly good legs. That was a consolation. Should I have them insured? I would continue with short skirts and the shorter, the better. Where was my modesty? my grandmother would have asked. 'Oh, it's only tucked away ...'

Chapter Eight: *The Kind of Boy You Can't Forget*

Without my family's near presence my self-esteem was developing apace. Nothing makes me bloom faster than the attentions of a good man. But all it would have taken was one reproving look from my absent *mater* to wilt me back to nothing. Why, why, why?

The bungalow was charming—open and airy, with flagstone floors and early American furniture. There was a vaulted ceiling with beams, a fireplace we never used, and paneled or stuccoed walls. There was a gate-leg dining table that did not get used much, but stayed against the wall with its gate-legs folded tightly together, as any modest young lady should do.

The cottage was fresh and clean, and surrounded by palm trees, pine trees and dense vegetation. There were insects, of course, as there always are in the tropics. I spotted *large* insects like I had never seen before—they were pretty frightening: palmetto bugs (two-inch-long flying cockroaches), and huge black beetles with horns. Occasionally, a tiny house lizard similar to the ones we used to call 'chameleons,' defied gravity and blazed a trail across a corner of the ceiling.

My roommate, Joyce, began working the dayshift in Miami; but she was not difficult to live with when we were at home together. It was Joyce who borrowed the car that helped us move away from the sleazy landlord, Mr. Bills.

Joyce's boyfriend, a lovable, freckled-faced chap called Tommy, visited us regularly and took us riding on his Honda. As we rode through the lanes of Coral Gables, we sang a Beach Boys tune at the tops of our lungs, *'Help me, Honda, help me get her out of my heart!'*

And then Mario left for the Easter weekend. He should not have done it. I met someone. It was on the Saturday night. Joyce was working. I felt desperate, so it was the USO or kill myself. I walked into the USO dressed in a black silk-crêpe drop-waisted dress that had a swirly pleated skirt—perfect for dancing. That dress would have done Lucy Baines Johnson credit, or even Lynda Bird.

One look around the room told me it was going to be a dull night. Most of the boys were simply that, 'boys,' pimply-faced, no rank, little sophistication. It was enough to make me race back to Mario. But I had made the effort to get there; it would be stupid to turn tail and run.

'Can I dance with you?' they said over and over. 'Alright.'

'Too, too depressing to go back home,' I murmured disconsolately as I circled the dance floor. I had taken such care with my appearance—my make-up was heavy in all the right places, my hair was flipped just so. I had on my contact lenses and my mascara, and wore no rings, so as to avoid misunderstandings as to my status. My purse and shoes matched my dress to perfection. I looked like a Sixties chick—yes, that was some consolation.

Suddenly, something happened to jar me out of the doldrums:

'You look like a Mod,' remarked a young man with an English accent.

'Hmmm, do I?' *Mission accomplished?*

I said, 'Do you mean those "hip" English girls in tights, who hang onto the backs of Vespa scooters by their fingernails, as their "clean-cut" turtleneck-clad boyfriends speed them around town, buying clothes at designer boutiques?'

It sounded flippant, but I didn't mean it that way.

No offense taken. 'Righty-ho, you got it. The Mods, or alternatively, the Rockers, their rivals who hate them, are about all you see around Soho these days. I don't know why, but girls are pouring into London right now.'

Early in 1966, London was gripped by 'Mod fever.' I knew about it, from reading the glossy magazines. Understanding better than he did, I suggested an answer as to why girls were pouring into London: 'To be part of the scene; to find a boyfriend; to "escape"?'

'I suppose so. In England, you know, children and teenagers are totally supervised by their parents and teachers. There is no room for rebellion or independence.'

'I didn't know.'

Chapter Eight: *The Kind of Boy You Can't Forget*

'It's been that way since the world war and the rationing. We want to escape, it's true. I escaped by joining the Royal Navy.

'The Mods,' continued the young Englishman, 'they take flats together, and live by their wits. London has gone mad.' He grinned, 'Or Mod.'

'Oh,' I said, smiling at him winningly, I hoped. 'Have you been there lately, to London?' *London, a world away.*

'Yeah. A while back, on leave. I saw the Rolling Stones perform at an underground music bar, The Roaring Twenties. That was amazing.'

'Rolling Stones? The only ones I know about are the ones that gather no moss.'

'Exactly so.' He beamed.

'And, did you find a girlfriend in London?' I batted my eyes at him.

(*Sadly*) 'No. London girls won't even look at a Navy man.'

'Then they don't deserve you. What are Rockers?'

(*Shrugged shoulders*) 'I only know that they wear leather jackets, ride motor bikes instead of Vespas, and pour scorn on the Mods, whom they despise ... *(By way of explanation)* I've been in the navy since I was sixteen.'

(Wryly) 'Lucky you!' *(Thinking)* 'I can look up "Rockers" in my *Funk and Wagnall's*, if I need to know.'

'You won't find that in a dictionary.'

'Oh, I don't know. You can find anything in the dictionary, if you know how to look for it,' I assured him.

'You really don't know about Mick Jagger and the Rolling Stones?'

Well, so I was ignorant. I wasn't going to admit it. 'Where are you from, sir?' I asked politely, changing the subject.

The sailor raised his eyebrows at the word 'sir.' His accent seemed to require it.

'Originally from Yorkshire, but right now, I'm out of Portsmouth.'

Oh, that was interesting. Certainly not boring. Why not idle away some time by talking to him? It was going to be a long evening.

Several British sailors happened to be at the USO that evening. It was most unusual. *Not* 'boyfriend' material exactly, but, I have always been fascinated by folk from other lands. I want to know how they live, what their ideas are. For example, how can they bear it, not to be Americans? (Contrariwise, I was a sneaking Anglophile.)

Some of the English sailors were in military dress—the uniform was so different from the American one. It had a medium blue flap/collar around the neck instead of the white or navy blue that our guys wore. And their caps were different—not the white 'Dixie-Cup' that I was familiar with. The English sailors had quite a jaunty cap with a ribbon on it, a round shape with a flat top; but it looked strange, like they were little boys. Or Scotsmen.

Discreetly glancing at their 'fly' I saw it was the button-up one that American sailors had. And the uniform pants leg was flared—quite the reverse of current male fashion, poor them—more along the lines of what girls were wearing. American sailors had the same bell-bottomed pants-leg flare. Apparently it was a design that made it easy to get off one's clothes quickly, if thrown overboard into the sea.

A few of the English sailors were in dressed civilian clothes—they had on 'drain-pipe' trousers—very tight and narrow all the way down to the ankles; neat, casual jackets and turtleneck sweaters. And, the inevitable winklepicker boots, alas.

I teased them, 'Where did you get those awful shoes?'

'Oh, in London, on Carnaby Street near Oxford Street—the center of the universe! They're a bit of alright—Italian leather,' answered Sailor #2, who had a Cockney accent. He beamed with pride and flexed the toes for me. The shoes probably cost him a month's pay.

'Are they comfortable?' I asked, knowing what the answer would be.

Chapter Eight: *The Kind of Boy You Can't Forget*

'No, but who cares? It's better than being in uniform.' *(Joking, pointing)* 'Look at those nerds.'

'Why?'

'Because girls run from us when we are in uniform.'

'Oh. I wouldn't run from you. Where do you all come from?'

'Our ship is out of Portsmouth.'

'Portsmouth, Virginia?' I asked, all big-eyed innocence. (I was still teasing.) Next, I would be asking them if they had seen my boyfriend, Throckmorton Daffy-down-dilly Snitzel-fritzel.

The Brits were good-humored about the teasing, 'No, you Yank lass—Portsmouth, England. The United Kingdom.'

'Oh,' I winked, not at all offended. I had watched enough black and white war films to understand that I wasn't being called a 'Yankee.' So it was okay.

'You're furreners,' I said.

'I wouldn't say that,' Sailor #3 answered loftily. 'We speak the Queen's English! You are the foreigner.' Sailor #3's accent was educated.

'Do you? Am I?' I could not suppress a giggle. I had them going.

Everyone laughed. Six pairs of eyes were on me. I had them in the palm of my hand. Could I really be that charming?

'Do you wanna dance?' I asked the educated one. In spite of his pride, he seemed to me the most promising.

'I don't know how to do the American dances,' he murmured, alarmed.

'Could they be that different? It's all the same music, isn't it? The Beatles, et al.'

'Well, at home we don't get to hear that much popular music, because it's not legal to play it in England. Not legal to broadcast it, either. Pop music is thought to be morally corrupting.'

'Morally corrupting! Gad, I've heard that before. But no one over here worries about rock music causing moral corruption anymore. I think the grownups stopped being concerned

A Quiet Life in Bedlam

about pop music in about ... oh, 1964. What they are more upset about over here, is "long hair," the Beatles haircut.'

'They're upset about it over there, too, believe me. You can almost get thrown into jail for sporting long hair.'

'In America,' I added, 'you can hear pop music anytime you want. There are a hundred stations. Across the nation.'

'Lucky dogs,' said Sailor #1, the one from Yorkshire. He had never stopped tapping his foot to the music.

'Pop music, not legal—how can that be true?' I asked them. 'Can't the radio stations play whatever they want? They do over here—within reason.'

'Nay, woman! The only legal radio station in the U.K. is British Broadcasting; anything else is unauthorized,' answered Sailor #3. 'The BBC is owned by the government. The government has decided: NO POP MUSIC. The teachers at boarding school didn't want us to listen to it either, I don't know why. I can't see anything wrong with it.'

I remembered that a couple of songs denigrating teachers and school had been banned in Tennessee. And the Beach Boys were stopped from singing the words, 'spend the night together,' in their song, 'Wouldn't It Be Nice.' That was understandable, I supposed. One mustn't hint at such things to the young and impressionable.

I listened to the conversation with interest. Life in faraway lands ... blue British sailors ... flat caps with ribbons ... strange customs ... love rites in Hawaii ... jungle drums in Africa ... pineapple in the South Pacific ... my imagination was running away with me. *Lovely.* I wondered at the diversity of people and places, the variety of sounds and smells. What a beautiful world. *'Sometimes I imagine myself as a drifter, a seeker of fortune, connoisseur of great wine; dashin' through meadows of yellow and green, tryin' to reach the impossible dream, leaving the straight life behind . . .'* [71]

---

[70] Lyrics from 'The Straight Life,' Bobby Goldsboro, 1968.

Chapter Eight: *The Kind of Boy You Can't Forget*

'I knew a boy at school that loved pop music,' said Sailor #3—we were dancing by that time; he could do a fair waltz—'and the boy had a radio that needed an aerial. He didn't have an aerial, but he figured out how to attach a wire to the radio. The wire acted as an aerial, or antenna, when he touched it to the radiator. The radiator conducted the radio signal, and the boy played his music whenever a teacher wasn't around!'

'Ingenious! I've been sneaky like that when my mother wouldn't let me read. What's your name?'

'Geoffrey. Yours?'

'Katharine.'

'To finish the story,' said Geoffrey, 'as soon as a teacher was sighted, the boy just pulled the wire away from the radiator, and there was no sound. He was clever!'

'I'll say. Improvisation. But how did he tune in to a pop radio station, if all there is, is the BBC, and they won't play pop music?' The dance was finished. *Oh, look.* I'm surrounded by Lymies again. *Groovy.*

'Oh, don't you know about Radio Luxembourg?' exclaimed Sailor #4. He had a Scottish burr. 'They broadcast rock 'n roll music twenty-four hours a day! It's fantastic. Radio Luxembourg is the lifesaver for all the youth in Britain! It's the biggest commercial radio station in Europe.'

'Yeah, we can't live without it when we're at home. Everyone's mad about Radio Luxembourg!' Sailor #1 chimed in.

Or Mod.

'Luxembourg. Hmm. Does that have something to do with the Grand Duchy of Luxembourg?' My European 'geography' was foggy.

'Yeah, it's broadcast from there—all over Europe. All over the world, if you have a short-wave radio. They send English-language programming at night.'

'I think all this is very odd,' I said. 'What about free enterprise?'

'Free enterprise! Are you kidding, in Harold Wilson's Labor government? Hardly.'

A Quiet Life in Bedlam

Sailor #3, Geoffrey, the educated one, said, 'There isn't any free enterprise when it comes to radio stations (or railroads, and many other things). Young people in Britain are very frustrated over the situation …'

'We want our own music,' exclaimed Sailor #2.

'I have heard,' Geoffrey continued unperturbed, 'that some enterprising people have anchored a ship off the coast of England, and are making money supplying a demand—namely, pop music. It's called "pirate radio".'

'The authorities are furious!' added Sailor #1. And he laughed an 'English' sort of laugh.

Pirate radio? Whatever next. This was all crazy.

'Censorship.' I said. 'That is hard. People should be allowed to make their own decisions. A life without music …' I broke off, hardly able to assess what it would have been like to spend my childhood without rock 'n roll, the bop, and *'shimmy shimmy cocoa pop.'*

'The BBC plays plenty of music; it's just not pop. I actually like some of it,' remarked Geoffrey, his nose in the air.

Oh, a highbrow. 'Well, why doesn't the electorate (the voters) do something about it?'

'Because pop music is not approved of by the elders! I don't know why. My father thinks it's terrible music, and won't allow it at home—not even Radio Luxembourg—won't let us listen to it; so usually, I don't do it. But my brother does. He listens to pop music as much as he can.

'Sometimes I stand at the edge of the room and listen in, as my brother is enjoying the music program (there are two different ones). But when I hear my father's car arrive home, I leave immediately, and go into my room to study.

'My brother doesn't move an inch though, he just keeps on listening, even though he knows there will be a scene with my father—and there always is. When Father comes in and sees my brother sitting, listening to Radio Luxembourg, he shouts and carries on. He is convinced it is bad.'

Clearly, Geoffrey wasn't the rebel I was. Or that his brother was.

Chapter Eight: *The Kind of Boy You Can't Forget*

'When I was at home,' Geoffrey concluded, 'I couldn't understand why my brother allowed these scenes to happen. It wasn't worth it, in my opinion. All he had to do was turn off the music before my father came in, but he never did.'

'Well,' I said, 'I have been through scenes like that with my mother. It was like she didn't trust me, did not have confidence in my judgment. (That's why I moved to Miami.)

'Last year, before I left home, one day I came in from playing tag with my boyfriend in the woods of Audubon Park, near where I lived. I was covered in leaves—they were sticking in my clothes, in my hair. Probably, I had mud on my face. My boyfriend and I had been rolling around in the leaves, running, getting rid of some energy—we had just finished exams. It was perfectly innocent.

'You can't believe it, but my mother slapped me, and made out like I was some kind of a ...' I stopped suddenly, in midflow. I did not dare articulate the word, 'slut.' That was what my mother had called me. I almost never forgave her for it.

Embarrassed by my outburst, I drifted away. 'Cheerio,' I waved. The conversation had turned too personal; my fault, of course.

You're beginning to go off your rocker, I told myself. *Nobody cares about what your mother did. Just try getting married from an insane asylum, you imbecile.* It was fun at first, talking to boys from another place, another culture, another way of thinking, believing. Well, it was a cinch I couldn't marry an English boy. I wasn't that desperate—didn't even want a pen pal. I was wasting my time getting involved with guys who would just sail away to that other world, in Europe.

I drank a cup of coffee, looked at the clock. I hadn't danced more than a couple of dances. It was tedious now, going to the USO. I would not do it again, even if I died an old maid. There must be some other way.

Midnight was rapidly approaching. I felt something like the despair of the damned as I reflected, 'I spent the evening without meeting anyone of particular interest. Damn.'

At about 11:30 p.m., at practically the last moment, two very eligible-looking sailors walked in, and they stood out from the crowd immediately. They were petty officers! *Wow.* I felt shock and delight. They had chevrons on their sleeves! (Magic insignia.) What were they doing here? Good golly, Miss Molly.

Petty officers rarely condescended to dancing at the USO, because, in general, they were older, had their own clubs to go to, did not want to waste any time on 'teeny boppers.' But with Vietnam in full-tilt, the petty officers, and even the chiefs, were getting younger and younger. I walked up to them, a seasoned and hardened 'junior hostess,' twenty years old.

I flashed them my undeniably gorgeous smile, extended my hand and said, 'Kate Bamber,' by way of introduction.

Just one look, that's all it took ...

Terry Muszyka was twenty-three. He was blond and blue-eyed. He was thoroughly American (though his grandfather had been Polish). He was Protestant. He was single. Mind you, I did not find out all of this immediately, but it didn't take me long. Terry was slim, spiffy, looked grand in his white cotton uniform. He stood in a more-than-upright manner, as though he were on parade, with one hand behind his back. And he danced the last dance with me.

'What a nice name,' I said to Terry as we danced. 'Muszyka,' I articulated, trying it out, testing it.

'You like it? You must be the only one. Even my mother doesn't like it.'

I rolled it around in my mouth, 'tasting it'—'MYOO-SEE-KAH.'

Terry laughed, 'Well, that's almost right.'

I pulled a face. 'It's better than my name, Bamber—I get teased about it all the time.'

'Oh? Why?'

'Can't you guess? Bambi. The fawn.'

Terry smiled. His teeth were like freshwater pearls shining in a stream. His eyes were periwinkle blue. He had a mischie-

Chapter Eight: *The Kind of Boy You Can't Forget*

vous look on his face. He was from Bangor, Michigan. *Aha.* A northern place, a western place ...

Terry and his 'buddy' had ridden a motorbike up from Key West where they were stationed at the naval base. It occurred to me to wonder if they had passed Mario on the way!

Terry and his friend (can't remember his name for the life of me) rode up to Miami only on the weekends, as it was such a long, dangerous ride up the Florida Keys; anyway, they had to stand 'duty' during the week.

Of course I fell in love with Terry, virtually at first sight. He was 'suitable'—and *hallelujah,* he liked the look of me, too. For that first hour we were together, we did not intend to, but we completely ignored Terry's friend—which was not a good policy. It was his motorbike.

Terry walked me to the bus stop at 12:30 a.m. and waited with me the short while it took for the 1:00 a.m. bus to run. In the interim, there was a brief downpour of warm rain, unusual for Miami in April, and we both (all three, I should say), got soaked. That would not have been so bad—almost romantic— except that my silk crêpe dress immediately shrank upwards to approximately my waist, leaving a little bit of the skirt around my hips, and my long legs entirely exposed. I imagined I looked as if I were wearing an old-fashioned 1950s bathing suit, with a skirt on it for modesty.

Blimey! It was embarrassing—I was feeling extra sensitive. If I had not been so thrilled at meeting Terry, I suppose I might have died from sheer mortification. *Thank God I am wearing black panties.* I sent a prayer upward.

Question: After this incident of the shrinking dress, could I still say I was a lady? Cripes. Legs up to my bottom! Whatever next. But that instant of chagrin was when I found out that Terry had a sense of humor, an item of character I appreciate. He made some hilarious remarks about the dress and the situation—I can't remember what now; and in no time at all, I had forgotten my embarrassment and gracefully climbed the steps into the bus, feeling happy and expectant.

A Quiet Life in Bedlam

As I sat on the bus riding home, the Toys intruded on my reverie right out of the blue, and sang merrily in my ear, *'Keep this day in your heart eternally!'* [72]

'Do you think I am likely to forget it?' I asked them. There was no one on the bus to hear me, no one to think I had gone crazy (and have me locked up). That was nice. I wanted to savor this moment. I had found my man.

Terry and I agreed to see each other on the following weekend if he could get away from Key West and meet me. As I lay me down to sleep that night and was just drifting off, a voice deep within said, 'Dream boy, do you love me?' And the answer from her dream boy was 'yes.'

He's the kind of boy you can't forget ...

I remember when I first saw him
(Diddle-diddle-diddle-it)
Something told me I couldn't ignore him
(Diddle-diddle-diddle-it)
And I've been dreamin' of him every night,
Ever since we met
'Cause he's the kind of boy you can't forget ... [73]

All week at work, I lived in a state of suspended animation. To see Terry again on the weekend was what I wished and hoped for more than any other thing. No more lonely weekends! No more holidays alone. No more bleak future! If only Terry could contrive to, somehow, get up the 150 miles of the Keys without any transportation of his own ...

Gotta tell him that I adore him
(Diddle-diddle-diddle-it)
There is nothin' that I wouldn't do for him
(Diddle-diddle-diddle-it)

---

[71] 'A Lover's Concerto.'
[73] Lyrics from 'The Kind of Boy You Can't Forget,' performed by the Raindrops; songwriters, Ellie Greenwich and Jeff Barry, 1963.

Chapter Eight: *The Kind of Boy You Can't Forget*

*I won't be happy till I make him mine,
And a wedding day is set
'Cause he's the kind of boy you can't forget ...* [74]

Terry and I corresponded by letter during that first week, and then, there he was, standing on my doorstep on Friday evening. Did he fly?! I cannot begin to tell how thrilled, how excited I was. Terry was 'the one.'

It was ironic and perverse the way I kissed Mario goodbye on the Friday afternoon, and kissed Terry hello on Friday evening. I figured the two of them *must* have passed each other on the way—two destinies pointed in different directions: one towards me, one away from me. Yes, they must have passed each other; there was only the one two-lane highway up and down the Keys: U.S.1, the Overseas Highway.

So Mario went south and Terry came north, one leaving me, the other flying into my arms—but of course, Terry was in love with me, too! He seemed to adore me, and I did not question it at all—certainly, the 'chemistry' was there. I was attracted to Terry physically, emotionally, and intellectually—I was hooked. He was like a drug—better than champagne, I was sure, though I had yet to try any. (Among innocents, champagne is seen as the original aphrodisiac.)

Terry had a winning personality, golden good looks, and an agile mind. I could envision fair-haired, blue-eyed babies by the score. Terry told me later, much later, that he loved me simply because I would have him. That was ominous, but how was I to know?

My new love and I saw each other regularly on the weekends for the rest of April and most of May, and we went *groovin'* on Sunday afternoons. We saw all the parks, beaches, open-air markets, and whatever did not cost very much. Terry was as generous as he could be on his limited pay. He took me to Coconut Grove, which I remember as being bohemian, full of coffee houses and jazz, and girls in black tights.

---

[74] 'The Kind of Boy You Can't Forget.'

I lived those two months in a dream-like state, a trance, hardly knowing which end was up from weekend to weekend. It was truly baffling, amazing to me that Mario, whom I still saw most weekdays, did not realize that something was wrong. I suppose he did not really know me.

Terry and I spent each weekend in a rapture of love and kisses. Kisses, however, was as far as it went; for at Terry's prompting, we agreed not to make love until after we were married. That we would be married was a foregone conclusion. The question was, 'when and where.' Terry was awaiting orders to a new duty station. He had to find out about the destination on his orders before he could make any other plans.

Then too, a second-class petty officer (he had just received a promotion) did not make a lot of money. And I would have to arrange for a transfer with the telephone company to whatever place, where ever, that we would live. Where would it be?! Presumably, a sailor would keep me by the sea.

For one month, until I was sure of Terry, I managed to see Mario most nights of the week, after which, he invariably left for Key West. For one month, I ushered Terry 'in' on the Friday night, and we spent the weekend billing and cooing.

'Hold me tight, never let me go,' I breathed into his neck. Terry seemed too enraptured to say anything much, but he held me as tightly as he could. Our bodies fitted together perfectly. Neither of us was what you could call 'statuesque.'

My 'two lives' must seem contradictory, in the face of the continuing affair with Mario, but I felt that the relationship with him was a thing apart from 'real life.' 'Real life' was a man I could marry. Real life was Terry Muszyka. Mario was 'on the side,' though it seems callous to say so.

Thinking back on it, I realize now that it was odd that Terry and I were not tempted to 'make love.' We spent each Friday night and Saturday night in bed together, fully dressed (mostly), close together, waiting for dawn. But we both knew the rules of our society. We wanted to start out as we intended to go on: with a proper, chaste courtship, and a legal, binding

Chapter Eight: *The Kind of Boy You Can't Forget*

marriage blessed by the church. Then, we would have all the time in the world to make love.

Or so I thought. I was not aware of it then, but this beginning to our courtship, with the long weeks of waiting, the delirium of reunion at the weekends, the celibacy, was a pattern that our married lives would assume. It was a Navy life. It was the Vietnam era. It was bigger than both of us.

In May, Terry was transferred to Charleston, South Carolina. I then confessed to Mario that I was 'in love,' and had promised to marry; and told him, very firmly, that we must end our affair.

Poor Mario. He was completely taken aback. He said, 'How did you keep such a great secret from me for such a long time?' but Mario was kind and understanding—just a dollbaby, a perfect pet, as he always had been, and we agreed to remain friends.

I did not know where or when I would see Terry again.

I liked it there in Coral Gables, and began to think of South Florida as the most fascinating place on Earth. What a pity I would have to leave it! The natural colorings of my surroundings were more vivid and lush, than even in Miami. It was 'Flaming June' all the year around.

Living in the tropics was like inhabiting the Garden of Eden, without the snake. Each day was dazzling and brilliant, and achingly beautiful. Each night was indigo velvet spangled with bright stars, and humming with crickets. There was a complete palette of colors at every turn. It stimulated my artistic instincts—I didn't even know I had any.

Within a short time, Mario and I became more like friends and companions than former lovers. He did not hold it against me that I wanted to leave him. Mario constantly carried his camera, sketchpad or watercolors with him on our jaunts. He had enough sense to hold a regular job and not try to live off his art. I greatly respected his ability, and was happy that here was a man who appreciated the beauties of the Earth as much as I did.

A Quiet Life in Bedlam

The people in Coral Gables were more laid back than those in Miami had been, and our neighbors left Joyce and me to our daily routines with no interference. The Cuban Navarro family, and Lalulalia, I never saw again. They were too far away in space, and there was a considerable language barrier as well. I would not take the trouble to learn Spanish, and it seemed unlikely that *Señor* and *Señora* Navarro would learn English in their lifetimes.

I was close enough to walk to work, which was great, and I rose from my sleepy bed at 8:00 a.m., to get to work by 8:30. For breakfast, I drank chocolate-flavored Carnation Instant Breakfast instead of Metrecal, and after my repast, sprang out the back door like a wind-up toy, running fast along the sunny lanes to my job.

The only unpleasant surprise I had sometimes, was when the heavens decided to burst their buckets during the five minutes it took me to walk, or run, to work. I arrived at the office many a morning so wet you could wring me out.

Another surprise I had later on was that the neighborhood was full of peeping-toms—strange men, who liked to stare directly into the kitchen window at night, as I was washing dishes. I did not like that a bit. Unfortunately I could not afford curtains—'Miss Bamber' was saving for a wedding, so I learned to stay out of the kitchen.

Needing something to keep me busy, I bought some oil colors, paint brushes, a stretched canvas; mixed the pigments with turpentine and linseed oil, and dabbed out a landscape of my paradisical neighborhood: it was so beautiful, I had to capture it somehow. I had always known my days in that place were numbered. I just *had* to distill the essence of Coral Gables in oils on canvas. My need to create something was intense.

I did not understand what I was doing with the oil paints—totally untrained, a mad scientist with the turpentine and linseed oil. Thank God, I did not blow myself up; and in the end, I sought help from a local artist to finish the painting. The problem was with the 'perspective.' 'How do I make it look three-dimensional?' I asked him.

Chapter Eight: *The Kind of Boy You Can't Forget*

My perception of St. Augustine Lane, where I lived, interpolated/transposed itself onto the canvas as if a wee creature had thrown itself down on its stomach, propped its head up on its hands and elbows, and was gazing contentedly out over the yellowed grass and up toward the crotons, hibiscus and day-lilies.

The kindly local artist, who lived nearby, added clouds to my otherwise blue sky, painted in a bungalow with chimney to the background, and with a deft hand, made the crotons and hibiscus three-dimensional. *Voilá,* I had an oil painting with my name on it! That was neat. I still have the picture and my friends brag over it. Silly them.

I still did not have enough to do, however, so I decided that a television was the answer. Taking a loan from the telephone credit union, I bought an 18-inch TV with rabbit-ears antenna. There wasn't much on TV that appealed to me, but the variety shows were entertaining: *Andy Williams,* the *Glen Campbell Good Time Hour*, the *Smothers Brothers' Comedy Hour,* and *Hootenanny*.

Then there was *Rowan and Martin's Laugh-In.*[75] *That* was a hoot. What shocked me, was the body-painted bikini-clad go-go girls in cages. Goldie Hawn was one of them. How could they do that wild gyrating with so many people watching? It was beyond belief. Didn't dancers have scruples? I almost had to shield my eyes; and there was quite a lot of risqué humor being bandied about. Where were the censors? Call in the BBC! The let-it-all-hang-out mid-Sixties was having its wicked way with me, and my attitudes were evolving.

There came a day in mid-summer when it seemed natural to become a model for Mario. Though I was very nervous, he photographed me semi-nude.

I was enchanted with the black-and-white pictures of myself, but simultaneously ashamed. I would not have admitted

---

[75] *Rowan and Martin's Laugh-in* did not air until January of 1968, but its fractious, helter-skelter tone was a feature of Sixties living from late November, 1963, when Kennedy was shot.

for the world that I liked the pictures. I did not want anyone else to see them. Still, for a girl who never had any confidence in her beauty, it was little short of astounding to look at those delightfully formed pictures of a woman's torso, the long dark hair cascading over fair shoulders, covering her face, rendering recognition of person unlikely. 'So I am something more than a hank of hair and a piece of bone,' I mused distractedly.

'Have courage, don't give up, don't tell Terry,' went 'round, and around in the ole noggin.

The pictures were graceful and harmonious. The pose was, I fancy, similar to that of Matisse's 'Blue Nude,' an anonymous figure folded in on itself. I wouldn't have called the pictures sexy at all.

I was sort of proud. At the same time, I was sort of horrified. Had I sunk so far into immorality as to pose nude for a photographer who was not my husband? Whatever next?

Mario smiled at me, a slow sweet smile, knowing what I was feeling but said, 'I am taking them to a photography exhibition.'

Holy mackerel, Andy! 'Can you do that without my permission?'

'I know you will give your permission.' He winked.

Prizes were handed out. Mario won second place. Others wanted to know, 'who was the model?' but Mario only smiled politely, and kept his secrets.

Mario Fiqueroa's art classes at Miami-Dade Junior College needed a variety of subjects for drawing and painting. He seemed to think that I could fill the job of 'subject.' Eventually, my resistance broke down. With a little friendly persuasion, I agreed to sit for his drawing classes.

I must admit at first, I was put off by the idea. It was one thing to pose for his eyes only; quite another to let a class-full of strangers look at me 'uncensored,' as it were. The job paid forty-five dollars a week, was at night after work, and I was still in need of money. It was the thin edge of the wedge ... forty-five dollars seemed a huge sum for part-time work and just sitting there thinking about the grocery list, which was all

Chapter Eight: *The Kind of Boy You Can't Forget*

it amounted to. I made only ninety-six dollars per week at the telephone company. That was for forty hours.

Feeling queasy, I gave it a lot of thought—*best to consider exactly what I am doing here. Will I feel sorry later? What will be the consequences?* God knows.

And then, a few days later, I thought, *Shall I seize the day? What the hell.*

Mario did not understand why I was making such a fuss. To him it was just Art, and everyday opportunities! There had always been nude models. Women were a representation of Eve.

To convince me, though it was not entirely logical, he showed me some black-and-white glossies that he had taken of other women. 'Look at these. Aren't they nice?'

'Lord have mercy, when did you do that?' my wide eyes asked, glancing up at him.

No answer. I did not like it that some of them were full-frontal. It didn't help to see that there had been other women. *'Was it before me, or after me?'*

Mario was still waiting for an answer. 'We need you.' He smiled again his old, sweet smile. I melted.

'Are Fallen Women allowed to have scruples?' I asked him.

'No,' he said. 'And you are beautiful.'

Disbelieving, I heard the magic words. *Believe in yourself. You are beautiful.*

I tried to concentrate on being 'in it for the money.'

Think of the nice wedding you can have, I rationalized.

Even so, I used another week getting up the nerve. I must confess that I had this primal urge to show my body and reveal my youth and beauty, but I wanted to do it in a socially acceptable way. Was 'nude modeling' for life study classes at a junior college socially acceptable? I doubted it. Well, I could 'condition' myself by buying a bikini, couldn't I?

Women in the United States were slow to wear the bikini—we did not know if it was actually 'lewd.' What other ways were there to be nearly naked? (No more 'sanctions,' please.) I decided to buy a two-piece bathing suit—try that out, discover if I could live with my midriff. The only bathing suit I had was a one-piece black number with a modesty panel at the crutch, very old-fashioned.

The two-piece white bathing suit I bought looked quite nice, but I could not make my stomach flat, no matter how hard I sucked in. I definitely had a midriff, alas. Ursula Andress, I could never be. *Sigh.* In my heart of hearts, I adored the James Bond films: *Dr. No, From Russia With Love, Goldfinger*, but was electrified by the sexual innuendo (which, I am sorry to say, I did not fully understand) and the near-nudity. Those actors and actresses were certainly testing the limits of decency. The Bond movies were not X-rated!

I wondered, *How could people be so sexy and not be ashamed of it?* And, I wondered, *Is it okay to 'like' James Bond films in public, to talk about them at lunchtime?* I had noticed people carrying Ian Fleming thrillers on the buses, with brown paper wrappers covering up the titles. Sooo, there was a hint of mint in the air …

My new two-piece bathing suit was, in my opinion, provocative—it had one-inch lace-up slits at the hips, and a long lace-up V between the breasts. I kept it tightly laced until I got used to it. The more I looked at my body, the more I was able to accept it. But the Sex Symbol of the 1960s, I would never be.

Mario finally convinced me that it was a small matter to become a 'figure study' for the Enlightenment of the World Through Art. The world's need was far greater than my false pride. Who did I think I was, the Madonna?

I guess I wanted to yield, so I did, but the prospect of 'opening night' terrified me. I believe, somewhere down deep inside, I must have loved Mario, wanted to please him, or I would never have agreed to his request. Normally, I am a very modest sort of person.

Though it was Mario's intention that I should eventually sit for all of his classes, on the first night I was to sit for the draw-

Chapter Eight: *The Kind of Boy You Can't Forget*

ing class, so that the new art students could get their 'feel' of the female form.

I walked to the pedestal wrapped in a white terry cloth robe, very self-conscious. Shivering internally, eyes averted from the audience, I felt as though I were a Christian being thrown to the lions. Suffused with blushes, I disrobed and sat. Slowly, I turned to survey my tormenters. They looked innocent enough.

I sat for a few more minutes, trying to think of something, anything, that did not have to do with what I was doing. I looked up again. There were numbers of beady eyes just staring, looking at me intently, taking my gauge it seemed, and I broke out in hives all over. I knew I could not continue; so, with as much dignity as I could muster, I rose, donned my terry cloth robe, and walked back to the dressing room.

Minutes went by. Mario came to fetch me. He was gentle. 'Have you changed your mind?' he asked.

'So much for *mystique*,' I said.

'Mystique? What are you talking about?'

'Didn't you know that I have been schooling myself in how to be mysterious, how to be ... feminine, and ...'

'*Ay, caray!*' He laughed out right. 'You have never been mysterious a day in your life ... except once ...'

'Well, don't go into that. I don't want to cry.'

He looked as if he might cry.

Poor Mario. I knew he was being considered for Head of Department, and that the retiring Head had plans to visit the drawing class that very evening as part of the evaluation of Mario's competence. With an effort, I willed myself to be calm. It took about half an hour. The hives went away. I attempted to discover the inner stillness of a yogi in contemplation, practiced letting my mind wander.

Meanwhile, the class was drawing 'still life'— I had to laugh when I heard. There was some humor in the situation—I definitely was *not* still life. I was pulsing, throbbing, gloriously alive life, as vibrant as one could get and not burst apart from the sheer joy of it.

So, for Mario's sake, as well as my own—I did not want to live with regrets—I detached myself from the situation in a mental kind of way I have, and walked back out to the studio to face the ravening beasts. As I sat, I considered what I might do with the extra money I was earning. Buy some clothes? The idea of a savings account did not occur to me. I was so distracted—I did not remember the coming wedding—it didn't seem real somehow.

The lights were strong. It was hot. I curled up and went to sleep.

'Think of the Bluebells Dance Troupe of Paris,' I told myself, as I drifted between waking and sleeping. 'They were toasted by the richest men in Europe, weren't they?'

'Yes, but were they respectable?' My conscience was working overtime. No, they were not, not then and not now.

The Blue Bells were hardly an apt comparison to the just cause of The Enlightenment of the World Through Art. Hardly. My grandmother had said the French were not respectable, even when sleeping.

'Well, dance is art.'

'Hold your horses,' said my grandmother, tartly. 'Wait a minute. Don't think you can "semantic" your way through this, you hussy.'

Ignoring her, I just went on sleeping. It is a good way to forget.

Gradually I became accustomed to being looked at. My embarrassment subsided and a few days later, I sat for the painting class, feeling only a few qualms from looking into strange eyes. When it was over, I left them like Venus rising from the sea, feeling regal, and fully in command of the situation.

God almighty, I thought, *this must be a dream. I dreamed I was a nude model in my Maidenform Bra ...*

The next week I sat for the watercolor class, and then the sculpting class. By this time, my nudity did not bother me too much, and I became comfortable with it. Fairly quickly, after that point, it became positively tedious just to sit and sit with

Chapter Eight: *The Kind of Boy You Can't Forget*

nothing to do—not a lot different from sitting at the switchboard in the traffic department at work. *I sit all day just taking plugs out and sticking plugs in ...*[76]

'Operator, could you give me the formula for Love Potion Number 9?'

'Wake up, Kit.'

Wake up! My eyes popped open.

'Uh, I have to change my pose. I'm stiff.'

Thankfully, I got permission to hold a book, and read or study while I posed. The art students liked that. 'Props.' It gave them new angles to catch, new dimensions. One day, I had a cold, and Mario trained a fan heater on me to keep me warm. I had to search for poses so as not to strain my muscles. I had to dab at my nose occasionally, take Vick's, and drink warm liquids, sassafras tea.

'Enough!' I gave it up, vowing not to do it again. Some kinds of work could never pay enough. By that time, Terry and I had agreed to marry in December, the next time he could get leave of absence. I had to think of him.

Mario was good enough to show me the results of the classes' attempts at catching my essence. It was riveting to thumb through the stacks and stacks of drawings and paintings, viewing the various interpretations of my face and form. I had not expected to be beautiful.

I hope it will not sound immodest when I say that some of the pictures were very fine. I became fascinated with one or two, and wanted to scoop them up, take them home, and hang them on the wall! To think that I had ever been ashamed!

Well, I was still ashamed—it was something that welled up from the gut, like jealousy.

Mario just graded the various interpolations of my body, and handed them back. I never saw any of them again.

After I was married, I corresponded with Mario, asking for copies of his original black-and-white photographs of me, but

---

[76] Paraphrase of Carl Sandburg's *Manual System*, 'Mary has a thingamajig clamped on her ears ...'

they were not forthcoming. Mario kindly wrote back, but ignored my request for the pictures. He was married too, and I suppose he wanted to circumvent trouble with his wife.

Perhaps this is surprising, but Mario and I were together again, as friends, a few years later, in Key West, where we both lived with our spouses. That Christmas, of 1970 (?), Mario made me a present which I will treasure all my life. It was a torso of my twenty-year-old self, molded and sculpted by him out of clay, painted a shiny black, then fired in a kiln.

The statue is a beautiful thing, an original signed by him who later became famous and much admired for his work. The gift is a treasure, more valued by me than rubies. When I look at it, I readily recognize myself as I was then, but never will be again. I have not told anyone but my husband who the model was. I wouldn't dare.

I don't know why Mario's wife was not jealous of his gift to me. It seemed as if the figure fairly shouted that we had been lovers; but I never saw a ruffle in her composure. She was heavily pregnant, and went into labor as we played canasta by my dining room table.

Mario Fiqueroa was an adept at making a silk purse out of a sow's ear—that's certainly what he did with me. His wife, Leigh, took on a special beauty after he married her too, though she started *out* looking like a model, and I had to be *made* into one!

I believe Leigh was pregnant before the marriage, tut tut. What a wonder that I avoided that particular fate—Mario was just so virile.

You have no idea how much I wanted to tell her—idiot that I am. But, by that time, I was good at keeping secrets.

CHAPTER NINE:
Pretty Flamingo

When she walks by
She brightens up the neighborhood
Oh, every guy would make her his
If he just could, if she just would ... [77]

My baby sister, Sherry, barely seventeen years old, was coming to Coral Gables for the summer. I was looking forward to it for more than one reason. It had not been easy to get Mario out of my bed. Even when I was tempted to lie back down with him—which, of course, I wasn't—the horrific thought of my little sister Sherry, an undoubted innocent, finding out that her adored older sister had had an affair before marriage, quickly squelched any libidinous impulses.

When my roommate, Joyce, and I first moved into the bungalow, I was sure the 'twin bed' single-bedroom arrangement would be enough to discourage a love affair, dampen the fire; but nothing cooled Mario's ardor until my engagement to Terry was declared. That did the trick. But one never knew about 'backsliders'—when it might happen in the cold of a warm

---

[77] Lyrics to 'Pretty Flamingo,' a hit song by Manfred Mann, 1966. Written by Mark Barham.

night, that someone needed a little kiss and a cuddle. Better safe than sorry. Even when Joyce was at work, Sherry would be there. Sherry was going to sleep on our two-seater 'loveseat' sofa in the living room, thus making it impossible for erstwhile lovers to creep in.

Sherry was due to arrive at the Greyhound Bus Station early in July. Mario and I went to meet her. That old gray dog of a bus slung itself into the terminal whimpering from the heat, the dust, and the stress of making a long hot trip from Tennessee. But there was a bright face and dancing eyes at the window, and a little fluttery wave. Then suddenly Sherry was off the bus, hurling herself into my arms.

'Precious angel, give us a kiss!' she cried, and hugged my neck. Then she kissed my face and Mario's. Sherry gave large kisses, the same way as my mother did.

Mario was delighted. 'This is your sister?' he said, his eyebrows in dark arches as big as McDonald's. 'Enchanté,' he bowed, kissed her hand.

'Oh, my goodness gracious me,' breathed Sherry, gobsmacked. Sherry had not encountered Old World courtesy before.

She wanted to see the sights at once. Though she had been traveling all night, it hadn't suppressed her spirits. The one time I rode a Greyhound bus that same distance, I had been worn to a frazzle and tired to death—but not Sherry. She loved travel in a way I never could; and she had such constant energy, such dynamism, that I used to say she had been born in a thunderstorm.

Sherry was hungry as a wolf, and Mario and I were peckish, so we took her to a café for broiled scallops, fried clams, baked potato and coleslaw. The huge variety of Florida seafood put to shame the landlocked-Tennessee freshwater fish of my childhood: bream, bass, catfish and crayfish. Those were good, all right, when battered in cornmeal and fried in a skillet; but Florida seafood was often served broiled or grilled—nonfattening, I was sure. A person felt virtuous and svelte after such a repast; I ate as much of it as I could afford.

Chapter Nine: *Pretty Flamingo*

From the first day of Sherry's visit, we three rollicked our way around the town playing like children. Sherry was a flirt, and she flirted outrageously with Mario, but he seemed impervious to it. He was dignified. He was avuncular. He was not, however, impervious to Sherry's photogenic qualities, nor her beauty—she was as luscious as a ripe peach—and I ended up acting the role of photographer's assistant, carrying Mario's gear around while he made stunning pictures of pastel landscapes with my little sister Sherry gracing the center portions.

A few years ago, I read a gardening piece in British *Country Living,* which was an inspired description of Sherry Bamber at seventeen years old. The article was about growing peaches. Yes, peaches. It ran, 'The perfect peach is sensuous and feminine, delicately perfumed, tender, juicy, voluptuous and plump, sometimes with a pronounced cleavage.' [78] I could not have invented a better description of Sherry; it suited her to a T.

She was not averse to posing, seemed to love the camera, and if truth be told, would not have been ashamed to take her clothes off for a man like Mario Fiqueroa. Sherry had not learned the concept of 'modesty' in the same way Annabelle and I had. Younger children are invariably spoiled; I know that, because Sherry proved it time and again—oh yes, I saw the way Mother treated the younger ones differently.

How Mario endured all this provocation without breaking down and making as pass, I couldn't say, but he didn't. He certainly was an honorable man, one Sherry and I both could trust to do the right thing.

Sherry wanted to see a flamingo. *A flamingo?* Sherry Bamber—a hundred and one pounds of fun, with a wiggle in her walk and a giggle in her talk—who could resist her? In some ways, I was the only one; I have a severe side to my disposition that only shows itself when I am provoked.

'A flamingo!' I was puzzled, but not provoked. The provocation came later on, when Sherry took a job with some encyclopedia salesmen, and stayed gone all night because their ter-

---

[78] *Country Living,* August, 2000; (female) author unknown.

ritory was too big to actually make it back home by quitting time. It was suspicious. I had called the police, the hospitals, and the ambulances.

'Florida is famous for flamingos, isn't it?' Sherry looked at Mario as if he should know.

'You could say that,' he answered, winking at her. 'I don't know why, exactly.'

'There are a lot of plastic ones around,' I said, 'stuck in front yards, mostly. They look tasteless and tacky.'

Mario was thoughtful. 'I know where we can see some real flamingos.'

'Where?' Sherry and I chorused.

'At a Miccosukee Indian village near here.'

'Can we go?'

'Sure. Why not? It's still early in the day.' Anything for pretty girls.

The three of us, Mario, Sherry and I—*all* with April birthdays, *lah!* April 6th, April 9th, and April 26th, lucky us! (Did that mean we were just alike?)—drove away to the Miccosukee village together, to see a flock of flamingos, of all things.

Isn't a big bird just a big bird? I was thinking.

No. I didn't realize what I was missing. Flamingos are magnificent, whimsical creatures that graphically illustrate God's sense of humor. Well, didn't Alice in Wonderland use one as a golf club? Or was it a croquet mallet?

At the Miccosukee Indian village we watched entranced as the gorgeous hot pink birds pranced, danced, stretched their wings, and honked at us like geese. The flamingos were quite tame. We could touch them—gently. I jumped back when one of them looked me hard in the eyes. Was it looking for a mate?

Mario had to take pictures, of course, and Sherry was quick to pose. Then, we sat for a group photo, snapped by the kind native American villagers. After some refreshment, an Indian guide came up to give us a little speech about flamingos. His name was Tecumseh. He was older, but he looked something like my brother, Alun. Alun, the youngest Bamber, with his black eyes and angular face, was the most 'Indian'-looking of

Chapter Nine: *Pretty Flamingo*

us all. In his senior year, Alun was voted 'most handsome' at Messick High School—no mean feat: he was practically set to be a movie star. Too bad he ended up an alcoholic. Alun 'lives' at the Union Mission in Nashville. What a waste.

Alun's resemblance to a native American sharply increased in the early 1970s when hairstyles for men were long—to the shoulders sometimes. Mother had never allowed me to wear my hair long until I was past eighteen, and I was deeply resentful that she let Alun and Duane wear theirs shoulder-length. *It wasn't fair!* Her only stipulation was that they should wash it every day; and they did. Alun and Duane both were Breck girls.

Tecumseh, accepting a small donation for his guide services, recited his flamingo speech, 'Nobody knows for sure when flamingos came to symbolize the Florida tropics. We do know that John James Audubon, the famous painter and naturalist, saw a flock in the Florida Keys in 1832.'

Tecumseh swatted at a wasp, looked around him, and began again:

'Later, Audubon traveled to London where he had subscribers to his work. He was constantly in need of money, and so kept very busy producing watercolors, drawings, a few oil paintings, and many engravings. But his primary project was charting the birds of America.

'Audubon was putting together a book about birds, with his own illustrations and observations. He deeply regretted not having had the opportunity to illustrate the flamingo in its habitat, which he assumed was the Florida Keys.

'From London, Audubon wrote repeatedly to his friend John Bachman in Charleston, South Carolina, imploring Bachman to shoot a flamingo for him, and send it to England.

'Six years passed before Audubon received a flamingo specimen from Cuba. It was dead, of course, but Audubon gave it a kind of mortality. His painting is the most famous rendition of the bird ever captured on canvas. And that must be how the "flamingo" legend came to Florida. No one has ever discovered if they were a native bird like the egret, for example, though certainly flamingos have been sighted nearby in Cuba, and all around the islands of the Caribbean, for a very long time.' [79]

Mario asked Tecumseh, 'Do you know how they get their pink color? I have seen some that weren't quite pink.'

'The pink color comes from the blue-green algae they eat.'

Tecumseh stopped his speech. He waited, looking at Sherry, who was springing up and down like a jack-in-the box, hyper-active.

The tour seemed to be over.

Oh well, it was grand; I was satisfied. Golden days, in the sunshine of our happy youth. [80]

I began thinking about black walnut ice cream.

Before we walked away, Tecumseh said, almost as an afterthought, 'Flamingos eat little things, shellfish, insects, tiny shrimp, little girls—searching in the watery muck of the bay with their heads upside down, using their bills as a scoop.

'Parents feeding their young often lose their rich pink color. All their energy is going into the development of the baby.' [81]

Finale.

I did not register what he said about flamingos eating little girls until later. Maybe I imagined it.

Towards the end of July, just before Sherry should leave for home (but no date was fixed) I received a letter from my sister Annabelle, asking Sherry and me to come home by August the third. Her wedding was to be on August 6th, the same day as Lucy Baines Johnson's wedding to her Catholic fiancé, Patrick Nugent (for whom she had converted). That proposed

---

[79] With thanks to google.com, for providing various unattributed sites, with oodles of information, about the fact and fiction of flamingos.

[80] 'Golden Days in the Sunshine of Our Happy Youth', Sigmund Romberg, *The Student Prince,* 1924.

[81] With thanks to Jeff Klinkenberg, *St Petersburg Times* Staff Writer, for his interesting ideas about flamingos, in his piece of October 29, 2002. Found on google.com.

Chapter Nine: *Pretty Flamingo*

union had caused some consternation among Protestants. The Johnsons were Episcopalians.

Ralph had not asked Annabelle to convert, which was just as well. There would have been a whole hullabaloo about it. Ralph's parents had a mixed marriage, religiously speaking, and therefore Annabelle was allowed to slip through that net. Subsequently, she raised her children with no religion whatsoever: Sherry and I were aghast. *No religious instruction?* Of course they turned out to be heathens.

Annabelle's letter read:

Dear Katharine,

We need you and Sherry home in time to finish your bridesmaids' dresses. Mother and I have decided to set the hems at one inch above the knee.

(One inch above the knee! That was practically antediluvian.)

They can't be shorter, because then your garters and girdles will show, and that wouldn't do. Because it is so hot, you will want to wear half-slips. I hope you have a white one.

(I had them in every color.)

I know it is a problem to wear a girdle and keep the half-slip where it should be—the slip keeps turning around and around because of static electricity—but it just has to be done. You can't go without a slip. It wouldn't be decent. Mama can line the tops of the dresses so the outlines your bras won't show through.

(That was a relief.)

Mother has your measurements, but she thinks you might have grown. Certainly Sherry will have grown. I hope she hasn't gained weight. We don't have any more silk crepe.

Your dresses are so pretty. Mama sewed them from Vogue *patterns. The dresses are yellow, my favorite color. And you will be wearing pillbox hats, as I will. Mother has made those, too—she sews like a dream. Then you will complete your ensemble with white shoes and white gloves.*

Oh Lord, were they still wearing girdles in Tennessee? How dreary. It would take a boot-horn to get me into one. How tiresome.

And forever taking up hems, letting down hems. Lordy, lordy. Such a bore. Every dress I bought in Miami had only a tiny skirt. I didn't have to bother much with the hems going up and down. I was sick of sticking my fingers with needles. (Mending bra straps was the worst.) Maybe I could get Mother to re-hem the skirt of my bridesmaid dress before I came back to Florida, although she certainly wouldn't approve of the length I wanted. I could not cope with hemming A-line skirts—there was always some extra material that I didn't know what to do with.

And pillbox hats! Gruesome. I hated them. Pillbox hats looked fine on Jackie Kennedy—she could carry them off. I looked like a cream puff in one. If I had to wear a hat, it should have a brim. Yellow dresses—not my favorite color. Oh well, grin and bear it; I would have a new dress to wear, at least.

I have never been a bridesmaid,' I said to Joyce. 'It should be fun. Glamorous even. But Ralph! Annabelle's betrothed—hardly the answer to a maiden's prayer.' Ralph was apparently well-meaning, but tactless and hot-tempered, on a short fuse.

'He rubs everyone the wrong way, including me. But I won't have to live near them, thank God. Annabelle and Ralph are moving to the naval air station at Pensacola, Florida.'

'Maybe Annabelle will see a flamingo!' Joyce, she was so nice! Always bonny and blithe.

'Pensacola is a long way from Charleston.'

'South Carolina! I have heard there are some beautiful old graveyards there, and a wonderful Gothic church—Lutheran, I think. I'm sure you will like living in Charleston.'

'Yes, I'm sure I will.'

Annabelle's letter continued to be full of surprises:

Kate, please be kind to Ralph. I love him so much. Until I met him, I was not a happy teenager. You know how miserable things are at home; and I wasn't comfortable at school either. I

Chapter Nine: *Pretty Flamingo*

did not have that refuge, as you did, of books and a boyfriend. I didn't enjoy high school at all, wasn't a good student, didn't do well, and graduated only by the skin of my teeth. My one happy year was when I was drum majorette at Sherwood Junior High. It was the only time in my life when I felt really pretty.

At school, I couldn't make friends easily, though I had some. Two of my girlfriends were acting rather strangely to each other, and less so, to me. Later, I realized one of them was a Lesbian.

(*What is a Lesbian?* I wondered.)

It was a miracle that I met Ralph. I loved him right away. He took me seriously in a way no one ever did before. I became aware that I am actually attractive, with long, shiny auburn hair—it's nearly waist-length now, since Mother relented and let me grow it (she says I look like a Quaker)—and I have a firm athletic body that wears sports clothes well.

There were other sailors from Millington who wanted to date me, but I preferred Ralph. There was this one boy who tried to talk me out of marrying Ralph. He was the first one to French-kiss me, and I was shocked by the experience. Has that ever happened to you?

(No comment.)

Do you remember my ex-boyfriend, Ronny Sopwith? I heard that he dropped me because I would not spread my legs. That's a coarse way to say it, but it's exactly how I was told. I don't know what the world is coming to. He even said I wasn't normal. But I know I am normal. And if one day I should have to be interned, as other people have been who were normal too, at least it would be a quiet life—if not safe in the bosom of a happy family, then safe in a padded cell. A quiet life in Bedlam, or some such place, where I can dream my dreams, form my philosophies, and think my thoughts.

Well, now I was shocked. Her vocabulary seemed to have exceeded mine! Annabelle had never spoken to me so frankly before. She rarely confided in me. We were not actually friends.

She must be overwrought, I thought. Annabelle could be a gloomy gus, but this was far worse than usual. *I wonder what is wrong?* I thought, alarmed. *Maybe she has wedding-bell blues?* No, I did not really believe it. 'Marriage' was what we believed in as providing the perfect life for a Southern girl: respectability, a rise in position, a new title, a new name, new destiny.

Could things be worse than they were when I was at home? I wondered.

The letter was not finished. It wended its way to a startling conclusion:

Things got worse after you left, Kate. Mother was suffering so bad. Daddy slammed her up against the wall, and hit her with everything, including his rifle butt. On nights when he was out getting drunk, she tried to hide from him before he came home. Sometimes she slept in the attic, or went over to her friend, Dorothy's, for the night. On mild evenings when the weather was good, she slept outside under a bush. If she isn't well-hidden when Daddy comes home, he makes her pay.

Mother rigged up some kind of bed in the attic to get a few hours sleep; after all, she has to go to work every day. And she figured out how to pull the attic stairs up behind her to disguise where she was, though it must have been nearly impossible. Then after the stairs, the attic door panel has to be heaved into place. It weighs a ton. I don't know where she gets the strength.

Until I leave home next month, I have the responsibility to protect myself and my brothers. I can't believe Daddy would harm a hair on their heads, but who knows what a madman will do? He's like Dr. Jekyll and Mr. Hyde. The next morning, he swears he doesn't remember anything.

Sherry stayed a lot with friends before she went to Florida. Who can blame her? One night after Mother was already asleep in the attic, Duane and Alun woke up and started play-

Chapter Nine: *Pretty Flamingo*

ing with Daddy's gun, which was left laying around. I found them with the rifle, took it away from them, put them to bed; and then went to sleep draped over the gun so as to keep them from messing with it again.

When Daddy came home and found me asleep on top of his rifle, he whipped me. I ran away with Sherry, but it couldn't last long. There was nowhere to go. Sherry caved in first, and went home. She told Daddy and Mother where I was. They brought me home, and I was whipped again. I should be so happy now, but sometimes I feel like I am losing my mind. Ralph saved my life by asking me to marry him. And Daddy called him a 'damn Yankee!' Well, it's to be expected. At least he didn't call Ralph a papist!

Sherry has been sorely missed (even though she is usually such a pain). She knows how to sweeten Daddy up.

Please come home soon. I need to hear the voice of reason.
Love always,
Annabelle

Voice of Reason? Me? I didn't know which end was up. The situation sounded dire; I had forgotten how bad it could be. The memory of pain is mercifully short, as long as it doesn't come back.

Daddy had not always been like he was in 1966. I remembered when we adored him: he was handsome, had bags of charm, was intelligent and sensitive. There had been a day when he was ambitious and hard-working, had conquered the business world he lived in, was loved and admired. And he had a wicked sense of humor, was hysterically funny (sometimes at Annabelle's expense). I felt that I got my license to be witty from him. Oh, how I missed that man, the Adam Bamber I had known as a child, before the drink.

I wished I did not have to go home—it was like opening a can of worms—but I couldn't cut Annabelle's wedding, now could I? And Mother was expecting me to help her with the aftermath. But I must consider very carefully whether I wanted to risk having a wedding in Memphis in December, with all the attendant grief. Wouldn't it be more sensible to elope to Charleston, and marry Terry there?

There was still some time left to decide—Terry and I couldn't tie the knot before late December at the earliest. And then, a new life as a Navy wife would begin. I looked forward to it as a queen to her coronation. What color would my bridesmaids wear? Pink? 'Think pink.' Mother would want red, because the wedding day would fall just after Christmas, and it was her favorite color; but, in my opinion, you can't wear red to a wedding: Tennessee is not the Indian subcontinent.

As I finished reading Annabelle's letter, Mario and Sherry returned from yet another 'photography' session. Gad. They looked like a bridal pair. So happy. Weren't they a sight for sore eyes? Mario, with his thick head of wavy hair, that formed a widow's peak at his forehead. He was not so very tall—about five feet, nine inches. Sherry's dark hair and small stature seemed a perfect compliment to his. They made a beautiful couple; so I angled the camera and snapped a picture of them—the only decent photograph I ever made. My eyesight was just not good enough for such frivolous hobbies, and film was expensive!

Meanwhile, back at Miami-Dade Junior College, the next thing I knew, Mario's art class had painted Sherry's body all over as an exotic, psychedelic flower (or was it a butterfly?) while she crouched on a small flat pedestal in his studio. She resembled that famous 'feathers' picture of Cher on the cover of *Time* magazine. What a shock I had when I saw Cheryl Lynn Bamber there, a naked, deep-bosomed nymph wearing only a smile and a G-string, swirls of bright body paint covering her from head to toe. I was responsible for Sherry's conduct in Miami. Clearly, I was losing control. And what if Sherry became asphyxiated from paint, like that poor girl in *Goldfinger*? I could not imagine what Mother would say.

'What will Mother say?' I asked her.

'Oh, she'll probably just laugh.' Sherry knew a different mother than I did. 'Mother has a sense of humor.'

Chapter Nine: *Pretty Flamingo*

Does she?

'Sherry,' I shook a warning finger, 'Hell will freeze over before Mother approves.'

Recently, I asked Sherry to describe the experience for me, her initial trip to Florida, the year she turned from girl into model. She was delighted to comply. Sherry loves an audience.

To write authentically of an era that occurred practically in my childhood when I was little more than a silly gadabout, I needed to pick at Sherry's memories of the summer of '66. *I hardy knew where I was at the time—so caught up in the fairy-tale of being in love with Terry Muszyka.*

Sherry had the gift of the gab from an early age, and could talk convincingly on almost any subject. She remembered Mario very well, though she has known many men since then—some people never forget anything (and she never forgets a slight, believe me!).

Sherry recounted, 'It was a very exciting summer, quite out of the ordinary for me. I remember Mario as being Spanish, handsome, a gentleman.'

'I'll say.' It was shameful, but I had been feeling positively lustful, as I scribbled about him—it didn't matter how long ago and far away it had been. His memory roused something in me; that was when I had learned to love an exotic side of life that was missing in plain, down-home Tennessee with all that banjo-strumming, Sunday-go-to-meeting, fried okra, yellow squash, hoe-downs and hayrides.

'He was your boyfriend,' continued Sherry, 'and he did not try to compromise me.'

'Very creditable,' I murmured '. . . um ... was he still my boyfriend?' I was surprised.

'Yeah, I think so. Haven't you noticed how you never let go of anyone until you've got the next one?'

'Oh, gee ... is that so.' Am I so selfish?

'I was thrilled,' related Sherry, 'that Mario wanted me to pose for him. It came naturally to pose for a camera. I didn't know I was attractive, much less, "beautiful"— no one had ever told me. I just had a feeling I could charm people into doing what I wanted, and I did!'

'Yes, you did.' Sherry could have the pants right off you, and the money out of your pockets in no time at all. Sherry's sparkle was as bright as the North Star.

'I loved cameras from babyhood,' Sherry continued, ' ... used to pose for Mother when just out of the bath, wrapped in a towel. Mother adored my panache. You and Annabelle would run away screaming if she pointed the camera at you.'

'Yes,' I agreed. 'I didn't like to be photographed.'

Sherry smiled. 'Mario had a good camera—a Canon F-1, I think. I had not seen such a wonderful apparatus before. He showed me how to adjust it, bless his heart. It was a lesson put to good use when I got my own camera, at graduation.'

'I didn't want to learn about photography,' I said. 'I thought if I ever once started, I wouldn't be able to stop.'

'It is addicting. I've thousands of pictures; but I'll keep 'em, even if I have to use them for wallpaper.

'Well anyway, while you were at work, Kitty, Mario and I did some shots at the beach—head and shoulders in front of a palm tree. The contrast between my young, sweet face, and the rough bark of the coconut palm was fascinating; I had never noticed textures before. Later, he snapped you in the same pose, remember?'

I remembered, but it didn't move me; in that photograph, I resembled an ordinary teenager, nothing special. Sherry, in hers, looked like a worldly-wise twenty-year-old. And though she claims she wasn't aware of her beauty, her smile in the photograph said she knew.

Sherry had a rich brunette beauty, so true in every color graduation—I could never match it. The only one of us who was as beautiful as Sherry, was Mother. Those two left Annabelle and me in the shade. No contest. Mario made so many pictures of Sherry and few of me during July, but I did not feel jealous or slighted. I was walking steadily towards my castle in the air.

'Please go on,' I prompted Sherry.

Chapter Nine: *Pretty Flamingo*

She did (ad infinitum).

'There was a sprinkle of freckles on my nose: the sun popped them out. I couldn't believe it was really me in the picture—there was this beautiful girl there. Who was that? I was detached somehow, could not accept that it could be true. Even now, when I see pictures of myself, it's like I'm looking at somebody else. Meeting Mario was the best luck I ever had.'

'Mother and Daddy did not give us compliments,' I observed. 'People believed it would spoil children, to give them compliments.'

'I know,' she agreed. 'Usually they did quite the opposite. I'm sure you remember that Annabelle and I were drum majorettes in the Sherwood Junior High school band?'

'Yes. I was jealous.'

'We loved it. We looked stunning in our uniforms, but nobody ever said so.'

'Yes, I can still recall the sensation the two of you caused when you marched down Main Street in the Christmas parade.'

Sherry giggled. 'It was so much fun! It made us special, and we needed that. Do you remember how pretty the costumes were? Black velvet, embroidered with green sequins. And green-sequined tiaras! Annabelle was the most athletic girl! Do you remember she could do the splits, and bend over backwards, double? And turn somersaults, and twirl that baton like mad! She had a cute little body, right up to the time of her first pregnancy, when she, sadly, allowed herself to eat everything in sight, even things she really did not want. She said she was eating for two, and gloried in it.'

'It was another attempt,' I reflected, 'to be special.' Annabelle was the first, actually the only, to give my parents grandchildren.

Sherry wasn't finished with the drum majorettes.

'Right from the time Annabelle and I were majorettes at thirteen and fourteen, we had "figures"! We did not have the straight-up-and-down bodies of the other girls in our corps—we already had womanly figures, with breasts. The others had children's bodies; we had "developed" figures, curves. Those other girls never looked so good in their costumes as we did! Theirs had to be padded, while ours had natural contours.'

Gosh, how can you remember all that? I was thinking. Ancient history. I could 'rib' her a little. 'Sherry, what about the grapefruit diets you went on, hoping your prominent breasts would disappear? What about the tomato and egg diets you tried, attempting to look as boyish as your peers?'

She said, 'It wasn't so pleasant to have large breasts at a young age, because boys ogled you, and made crude jokes.'

Sherry clearly relished her memories of the innocent sixties, the last days of her childhood, before she had to tackle the stresses of marriage and womanhood. I was getting a good interview. How much of it I could use, I didn't know. But I let her rattle on.

'Mario,' Sherry rolled the name over her tongue, 'made a shot of me on the beach, lying on my side, head propped in my hands—the blue sea and sky, the background to my bikini-clad body.'

I raised my eyebrows. 'You had a bikini? I don't remember that.'

'Mother didn't know I had one. I bought it with the money I earned at Crystal's Hamburgers in Memphis. Daddy knew about the bikini, but he didn't tell! I loved Daddy. I needed his love. I would have clung to his coattails, no matter where he went, or what he did. I do not blame him in the same way you do. Daddy lived a hard life—poverty-stricken childhood, number twelve of fourteen children born to an Indian woman who was not demonstrative, the Depression, semi-starvation, the CCC camps, feet frozen in the snow during the Battle of the Bulge in World War II ...'

'How,' I marveled, 'could you have dared to wear a bikini in 1966, at seventeen? Only Bridget Bardot was wearing bikinis then. You floozy!'

She giggled again, an infectious laugh, and pointing her pretty, well-manicured finger in my direction said accusingly, 'You matron.'

Touché.

Chapter Nine: *Pretty Flamingo*

'I still wouldn't wear one,' I retorted, very much on my dignity. The very thought made me cringe.

'Well, you should. You don't know what you're missing. There is a marvelous freedom …' Her eyes glazed over. I happened to know that Sherry had once shown up at the door of her new boyfriend's house, naked underneath her full-length fur coat. She got a new car out of that escapade.

The conversation about bikinis put me in mind of my friend and bikini-enthusiast, Delores Delaney, that I later knew in Virginia Beach. Delores was 'stacked.' Men used to stop in their tracks as Delores sauntered down Virginia Beach in her white bikini. She was totally aware of the chaos she caused, and didn't care.

When Delores crossed the sandy little beach side street to buy a hamburger and Pepsi from the beach grill, she left a few fender-benders in her wake. Delores only laughed and tossed her mane of hair. 'Call the police,' she would say.

My boyfriend of the time, a man who had a penchant for nicknames, dubbed Delores 'the Amazon.' He wasn't far from right; Delores was accomplished at judo. There was a big fad for physical fitness just then, and lots encouragement for women to learn to defend themselves though it wasn't 'feminine.' Everyone had been inspired by 'Kung Fu Fighting' [82] and other martial arts movies, songs, and exhibitions. The incidence of rape had gone way up, according to statistics. When I was cornered by a rapist in 1975, I wished to heaven that I had learned judo.

I thought Delores Delaney was amazing, not only because she could defend herself, but also because of her different value system. She was only six years younger than me, but she seemed to have the idea that it was all right to flaunt her sex appeal. Where did she learn that from? Didn't they teach girls the same morality in Virginia, as they did in Tennessee?

I learned from Delores, *if you've got it, flaunt it.* She showed me how to pick up men by giving them a special look.

---

[82] 'Kung Fu Fighting,' performed by Carl Douglas, 1974.

A Quiet Life in Bedlam

I tried it one time with considerable success, and then didn't have the nerve to do it again.

Delores was truly a blond bombshell; and being of German descent, had that robust Teutonic figure and honey-colored skin. She worked as a desk clerk at the Holiday Inn on Northampton Boulevard in Virginia Beach. Many traveling salesmen propositioned her, but Delores' flashing, sea green eyes could pin to the wall any fresh fellow who went too far.

Delores was not one to suffer fools gladly. I shrieked with horror, or delight, each time she told me another story of the effect she had on men. The attention she got wasn't all flattering. There was this odd man who lived across the street from her, who did obscene things in his picture window whenever Delores came out into her front yard. She said she'd like to kill that man, but she didn't.

At nineteen, Delores (when I met her, in 1972), was already a divorced woman. Her young husband had come back from Vietnam a drug addict. Delores' dramatic experiences in young adulthood were almost beyond my comprehension. I guess it's not surprising that she converted to Catholicism and became a nun.

Another astonishing thing about Delores was, in her job as desk clerk at the Holiday Inn, if a customer presented her with a credit card that subsequently proved to be bogus— which Delores quickly found out about by checking her fraud-list— she calmly, coolly, right in front of the guy, took out a pair of scissors, cut up the expired/stolen credit card, and handed it back in small pieces. Then she asked for cash. He that plays with cats must expect to be scratched.

With an effort, I hauled myself back into the present, away from Delores and the lessons I had learned from her, to Sherry and her recollections of golden days. I had been writing furiously on my steno-pad in shorthand. (I learned shorthand 'after the telephone company,' when I trained as a secretary.)

'So,' resumed Sherry, 'the resulting pictures from the sessions with Mario …'

'Are you still on about that?'

Chapter Nine: *Pretty Flamingo*

Alas, Sherry's insatiable ego had been a principle characteristic, ever since she discovered how strikingly beautiful she was. (But I still love her to death.)

'... looked like something from *Seventeen* magazine. I was so proud.' Sherry preened herself.

'The experience proved to be a turning point in my life. I have been an eager model and photographer ever since.'

'You are a maniac with a camera,' I commented. 'I don't like to get around you when you've got one in your hand. You would snap me scratching my bottom.'

'I make *good* pictures! I want to get Life on record.'

'Oh, pooh,' I said. 'Some things are not worth recording. Didn't Mario sell some of the photographs of you to a sports magazine?'

'He did, yes.' Sherry chortled. 'He sold several. And one portrait was destined for a record sleeve—Raymond LeFevre, I think. No, it was Paul Mauriat: *Blooming Hits,* 1968.'

Hells Bells. 'No!' I couldn't take it. My one claim to fame ...

'Cool down, Kate. That was my only cover. I would have liked to do more ... I had to go back to school in September. And after that, I married. But for all of July 1966, I was a photographer's model,' she said wistfully, 'and you and I lived the good life. I wish it could have lasted longer.

'There was a red-belled hibiscus bush growing in your yard; I picked the flowers and tucked them behind my ears. The flowers were crimson, like passion. I felt as exotic as a South Seas princess. I knew that was the way I wanted to live, in a tropical climate. I suffer from chilblains.

'When I moved to the Navy base in Spain after my marriage, I felt perfectly at home.'

'You and John were stationed at Rota, Spain, weren't you?'

'Yes. Spain was fabulous. I loved Spanish food, Spanish music, the flamenco. Dancing the flamenco caused me to develop varicose veins in my legs, more's the pity; but I had them stripped out.'

'The varicose veins? Really?'

A Quiet Life in Bedlam

'It was you, Kate,' again, she pointed her finger, 'who brought us into the world of the Navy. For good or ill, we all married sailors who brought tremendous changes into our lives. I met John Henderson on the beach one day while you and Mario were working. John and I were instantly attracted to each other. John was older, so I thought he was right for me. I felt "older" already, though still a teenager. Life at home with Mother and Daddy, seemed to make me grown-up and wise in ways that some of my friends certainly were not.'

'It's true,' I said. 'Before I was nineteen, I knew a lot about sorrow and despair.'

'John and I got married in June of 1968. Strangely, I knew hours before the wedding—maybe even as much as two days—that it was all wrong, that we should not marry. But I couldn't cancel the wedding; seemingly huge, unstoppable forces were already in motion. Wedding guests were on their way from long distances. The food was ordered. The flowers were arranged. You were flying in from Florida. The bridesmaids were primed ... in high fashion. Do you remember, there were eight bridesmaids, dressed in a rainbow of pastel colors, Oleg Cassini designs. You were one of them of course, dressed in green silk, and you had your hair up in a chignon. You were pencil-thin. You'd been taking diet pills.'

Thank God for diet pills, I thought. *They are illegal now; but at least I had them when I was young.* 'Those were the days, Sherry,' I concurred. 'Annabelle and I gave you a cuckoo clock as a wedding present. It seemed appropriate.'

She let that pass.

'So we married.' Sherry was thoughtful. 'It was done. But I had hope. John was so blond, tall and handsome, quite a catch. He had a promising career in the Navy. John was a deep sea diver, skilled and brave. He was like a fish when he swam. And he was slippery—that's something I didn't know until later. But at nineteen, in June of 1968, I was so needy for love, so needy for someone to care about me—it just had to work out. I was willing to do my part. But that's another story.'

'Yes, and I'm only allowed 120,000 words.'

Chapter Nine: *Pretty Flamingo*

Sherry was amused. She didn't let anybody put limits on her.

'In a way,' said Sherry, 'my adult life began when I visited you and Mario in Coral Gables. I became accustomed to the freedom, to making decisions. I got a job waitressing at a nearby restaurant, and made some money for school clothes and senior pictures. The customers were so nice to me—good tippers.

'You and I used to go to the Laundromat. As the warm sheets came out of the dryer, we folded them up by taking the crisp, squared ends into our hands and dancing the minuet, as we glided towards each other for the fold—voluminous clean sheets in hand and laughing like fools.'

'I remember it fondly, Sherry. We were young. And so innocent. Both of us.'

'God, yes.' Sherry sighed, then she rallied. 'I'm still young!'

'So you are. And still beautiful.'

'Can you remember, Kitty, when I went to Key West with Mario to meet his parents? You did not go, for some reason.'

'I wanted to go—I was longing to meet his parents—but Terry was coming down from Charleston to give me an engagement ring.'

'That was a good reason!'

'A very good reason; I thought I would die for joy.'

'Well one day, on a trip to Key West, Mario and I, and his twin sister, sailed on a boat, and went deep-sea fishing. We caught a swordfish. What a struggle we had to land it! It was blue, really blue! It was huge, and cold and slippery. Then we sailed to an island, and grilled our catch right on the beach; but the sharks came to eat the leftovers, and we couldn't swim anymore.' Sherry pouted. She remembered it like yesterday.

On July 4th, Terry Muszyka brought me a diamond ring, and we became officially engaged. It was no problem though— Mario and I were really and truly friends; he did not resent the fact that I was promised to marry someone else. He had another beautiful girl to claim his attention, Sherry; in the event, Mario was really good-humored about my perfidy.

'While I was visiting you that summer ...' Sherry wasn't quite finished.

Yes, Sherry?

'Are you still here?' My sleepy eyes popped open.

'Well, you haven't driven me to the airport yet. While I was visiting that summer, in 1966, Mario grew a beard. It was dark and curly. He was very attractive, very handsome. I admired your taste in men, was sorry you didn't marry him. He was a good guy. I felt very safe with him, never threatened in any way. I liked him.'

His eyes adored you ...

'I liked him too.'

'Why didn't you marry him?'

'It's too complicated ...'

CHAPTER TEN:
Welcome Aboard

Summer was an endless season as July and August of 1966 sweltered and passed. Only the ocean breeze saved me from heat stroke. The humidity was so enervating that I wanted to cast aside all reservations of modesty, strip off my already scanty clothes, and walk forever in the altogether, out on the beach.

I thought with nostalgia of the mellow ripeness of autumn in Tennessee; of slushing my feet through great mounds of colored leaves, the pitter-patter of raindrops in puddles, or alternatively (if there was a drought) throwing myself onto the dry grassy ground and gazing skyward to the azure blue heavens. Soon the wild Canada geese would fly in formation overhead, following the Mississippi River to their winter nesting grounds further south; I wanted to see that. As undeniably lovely as South Florida was, it could be a bore without the rotation of four seasons, the Dance to the Music of Time.

It was only a year since I had moved away. The one year seemed like two years: I had experienced so much, learned so much, but also suffered. 'Womanhood' was not all it was cracked up to be. Thus far, true happiness and satisfaction with life eluded me.

In Coral Gables, I kept to my usual routines, walked back and forth to work everyday, and in the cool, cool, cool of the mornings under the pine trees and palm trees, I dreamed of being married in white, though I was aware it would be hypocritical. It brought me down to Earth to discover that some weirdo had been stalking me around Coral Gables; it had been going on for a month, perhaps two. The man had been trailing me as I walked to work in the mornings, and following me quite closely, almost up to the front door, as I strolled home each night.

I was blissfully unaware of the stalker, however, lost cloud-cuckoo land as I was, and did not actually realize anyone was following me until several of the neighbors told me they had observed a man doing just that. *Yipes!*

I didn't want to believe it—how could it be? until I caught the creep peering in through my windows a few times. There was something 'wacko' in his eyes that distinguished him from other peeping toms of Coral Gables: something unsymmetrical about his eyes, as if they belonged in two different faces. I well remembered reading, in *The Franchise Affair,* by Josephine Tey, that unsymmetrical eyes marked a killer, or at least a 'plausible lyer.'

The situation made me nervous, rattled; there was no one to ask for help; and for the first time in my life, I had trouble sleeping. I took to carrying around a steel-tipped umbrella for warding off any attacker, should one materialize out of the evening's shroud. It was comforting to know that Sherry or Joyce would normally be home at five-thirty, or six o'clock, when I arrived.

During the long year of my transition from teenager to twenty-year-old, I had slowly become aware of the feminist movement, or Women's Liberation as it was called, and their radical ideas about women being equal to men: that women could pursue careers; that women, like men, should be allowed to have multiple sex partners and 'do it' just for the animal pleasure of it (that was a shocker); that women could acknowledge they enjoyed sex; that marriage should no longer be seen

Chapter Ten: *Welcome Aboard*

as the sacred institution of 'love, honor, and obey' it had been from time immemorial. Women should refuse to obey; but, in my family, we didn't have a tradition of obeying the men anyhow.

I thought the feminists were mad (as everyone else did), and didn't pay them more attention than I would have given to a newspaper advertisement for a trapeze artist in the Ringling Bros. Barnum and Bailey circus. Women's Lib was ridiculous, in my opinion: I did not feel oppressed, just lonely.

If anyone had hinted to me that *I* was liberated, ahead of my time in having accepted for myself a sexual freedom that was still more or less forbidden; and that I should continue to expand my life, stay single, pursue a career, establish a bank account, buy a house, escape from narrow attitudes and sexist slavery, I would have hollered my head off and asserted, 'No, I want to get married!' The trouble was that I did not want to accept responsibility for my life; it hadn't occurred to me that I should.

Nevertheless, I wasn't so sentimental, as Annabelle was, that I would decline to apply for birth control pills (as Annabelle refused to do, and got pregnant on her wedding night). I had to find out how to handle a marriage before I could coddle a squalling brat. My little brothers had been sweet of course, and I enjoyed mothering them, but I could hand them back to their real mother whenever she came home from work.

A Navy wife would live far from her family; there would be no extra pair of hands to share the responsibility for an infant. I wanted to enjoy being young for a time, though my mother never had that privilege—she gave birth to me at nineteen. But that was in the Old Days.

I had conflicting feelings about motherhood, reservations about pregnancy. My mother, grandmother, and aunts had spoiled the whole idea for me—the secrecy, the embarrassment, the snide remarks, the shame—as if the making of a baby were actually wrong and should be avoided: the idea in Christianity that children were conceived in sin—these things left a strong impression.

In addition, I did not want to be trapped for nine months in an ungainly, unsightly pregnant body. The telephone company did not allow for morning sickness. You had to go to work even if you threw up on the switchboard. Another real fear was the birth pains women were said to experience. Every month since I was thirteen, I had suffered the most gruesome period pain. It left me with a kind of horror about giving birth, with more of the same agony to live through, only worse. The doctor had told me early on that menstrual cramps were just a simulation of natural birth pains. *And* maternity dresses were hideous.

It had been Terry Muszyka himself who informed me about the various contraception methods available to married people: diaphragms, rubbers, and spermicides. (Birth control pills were a very recent phenomenon.) Terry was well informed. The men in the Navy were actually given sex education! How droll. I had had to absorb a shock, however, and feign nonchalance, when Terry informed me of the existence of VD (which he called 'the clap'). We had talked about these things during the weekend we became engaged.

Terry also told me about ... ah ... dare I name it? Self-stimulation. But dire warnings in childhood from my mother about what would happen if I touched my genitals would not allow me that diversion without the most intense shame, guilt and self-recrimination.

Sherry and I needed to get home for Annabelle's wedding, and that would be the end of Sherry's idyll. Sometimes her energy had a manic quality to it, and I wasn't exactly sorry she was leaving. Besides, I didn't want to have to be the one to tell her about 'clap.'

'How are we gonna get home?' Sherry asked me.

'The Greyhound bus,' was my answer.

'Should I ask Mario to take us?' Sherry's finger was in her mouth, giving the impression of a pout.

In a rare moment of stubbornness, I said, 'No. That would be taking advantage.' I didn't want to be beholden to Mario. 'Don't ask him,' I said.

Chapter Ten: *Welcome Aboard*

'Oh, I don't think he'd mind.' Sherry got a glint in her eye; her smile gleamed. *Cherchez la femme.* Uh oh.

The Greyhound bus seemed the only possible conveyance when one considered that cotton, not moolah, lined our empty pockets. But the next day, in a magnanimous gesture, Mario agreed to drive Sherry and me home to Tennessee for Annabelle's wedding.

'Thank you!' I said, pecking Mario on the cheek. 'What a relief not to take the Greyhound bus! Poor as I am,' I complained, 'Greyhound made me pay a rental fee last time, for a *pillow* on a trip to Tennessee! And the "pillow fee" had to be *repaid* at each stage of the journey. Usury and greed, in my opinion. Highway robbery.' To add insult to injury, the Greyhound stations were dirty and uncomfortable inside. The cafeteria food was expensive and of poor quality, and there were unsavory types hanging about in the restrooms. It was only sheer unadulterated need that would make me do it again.

'Air travel,' was a concept unknown to twenty-year-old single working women, in 1966. And there weren't any trains, except for freight trains. Freight trains made me think of, *'Trailers for sale or rent, rooms to let fifty cents; no phone, no pool, no pets, I ain't got no cigarettes ...'* [83] King of the Road. I got through many a lunch hour at the telephone company listening to that, on the jukebox.

It was actually Sherry who convinced Mario to drive us home. *I knew it,* I thought. That Sherry—no shame when it came to asking favors of men. Well, we could offer to pay for the gasoline. Should we offer anything else?

If you could have seen Sherry as she was at seventeen and a half! She had the tender charm of a young Mary Tyler Moore playing 'Miss Dorothy' in *Thoroughly Modern Millie* (1967), a favorite film of mine. They resembled each other closely. It was uncanny to see Sherry/Mary up there simpering on the wide Technicolor screen in *Millie.* 'Miss Dorothy' could get anything she wanted, and so could Sherry.

---

[83] 'King of the Road', a smash hit sung by Roger Miller, 1965.

Dangerous Sherry—few inclinations to deceive showing on the surface of her still waters—but ruthless as Beatrice Lillie's 'Mrs. Meers' in the same film *Millie*; with the disarming personality that (nevertheless) intended to nail you for everything she could get out of you, empty your wallet down to the last sou. And Sherry thought she had the right! She believed the world owed her something—especially the world's men. It was because Daddy didn't want her. Sherry was the *third* baby girl, alas; Daddy had a 'Henry the Eighth' complex. Why did people always want boys?

Uncle Landon, Daddy's older brother, had to get Daddy drunk, then steer him to the Baptist Hospital to pick up the post-partum Mother and the infant Sherry. It was reported that Daddy said to Uncle Landon, 'I don't want Brenda back if all she can produce is girls.' Poor Mother. At the time, no one knew that it really wasn't her fault.

Uncle Landon adored Sherry: she had the same sense of gaiety, the *joie de vivre,* a similar attitude of being on the way to a party somewhere. Even Daddy liked Sherry better by and by, and she became his favorite child. Sherry could tease Daddy, she could tame him; she could charm him, she could tune in on his sensitivity like nobody else.

We did not often get pocket money, and Uncle Landon seemed to understand that even daughters needed small change to buy jaw breakers occasionally. Uncle Landon was an easy touch, but said he wanted us to 'earn' the money he would eventually give us. Then he'd think up some fantastic scheme for defrauding our parents (a practical joke), and we'd see how far we could get with it, of a Sunday afternoon, before giving up the cause as lost and collapsing in a heap of laughter and petticoats on the living room floor—75 rpm phonograph records cascading down the spindle as *Peter and the Wolf* reached its conclusion.

After dinner, it was fiddle-and-bango time with the uncles, cousins, and Daddy playing wild renditions of *'Orange Blossom Special,'* and *'Bonaparte's Retreat' (*which we called 'On A Partridge Tree'). Annabelle, Sherry and I pretended it was

Chapter Ten: *Welcome Aboard*

Lawrence Welk, partnered up, and pressing five-year-old Duane into service, danced like marionettes.

I can still remember when 'Unca Landon' used to sit three-year-old Sherry on his knee and say, 'I will give you a quarter if you can say *star*.'

Dutifully, Sherry would repeat, 'tar.' Unca Landon would laugh delightedly.

'Star,' intoned Unca Landon once again, beaming like Santa Claus.

'Tar,' repeated Sherry, grinning broadly.

Sherry got the quarter anyway, as she knew she would; but she would have done anything for Uncle Landon, as we all would. That was why it was so sad when he went and cheated Daddy, his younger brother, in business, just at the time when Daddy was the most vulnerable. Uncle Landon was a building contractor, and he contracted to remodel our house. We lived for six months without a wall on the west side, while Uncle Landon fooled around with 'more important' business matters, and left us to the winter weather unshielded.

I don't blame Uncle Landon anymore; Daddy made a lot of his own trouble.

Our uncle Landon had the knack for inspiring confidence even in those with the best reasons for distrusting him. He intended to do right by people, but invariably was controlled, as often happens to good people who do bad things, by the passions of the mind: greed, lust, anger, and vanity. Nevertheless, he was successful in ways that Daddy could never have dreamed of.

Landon was my favorite among my father's brothers. He had a smile like the Cheshire Cat. I could feel the genuine warmth pouring off of him, and was drawn to such effusive love as he represented. Later on, it transpired that Landon was manic-depressive, and mistreated his family almost as much as Daddy mistreated us.

When Sherry, Mario and I got home to Memphis for the wedding, my mother was in a fluster and a flurry. Nevertheless, she welcomed Mario with as much hospitality as she was capable of, and that was plenty. You should have seen the coconut cream pie and the chocolate meringue pie! (You should have eaten them.)

Well, wouldn't you know it—Mother and Mario loved each other at first sight. The vision of the two of them, beaming at each other, plucked at my heartstrings. They made a charming couple of complimentary height and coloring—they could have been brother and sister. Oddly, they both had a widow's peak in their dark hairlines. It was like two souls meeting again, after many past lifetimes together.

My mother was *not* charmed to hear that I planned to marry in December—there was so little time to prepare adequately. Most of the responsibility would be hers. And the expense! Mother actually hinted that I should elope, but I was determined to have a church wedding, in front of God and witnesses. A person only gets married once: every bride should have her day.

'Don't you want me to get married?' I asked her.

She rolled her eyes, imploring heaven. 'I don't want all our friends and family to have to buy a wedding present again so soon,' was all she said. I was being inconsiderate.

It turned out that Mother was indignant for Mario's sake, because I had jilted him. She coolly inquired, 'Why would you marry Terry Muszyka, career Navy man, a person you don't even know, a man we have not met, when Mario Fiqueroa could be had, almost for the asking?'

I deliberately misunderstood her. 'Me, ask him? You must be joking, Mother.'

'Don't you see that Mario is still in love with you?' Mother was patient, trying to explain the ABC's to a daughter who lacked the gumption of a billy goat.

"Still in love?" I said. *Still in love?* 'If he is in love with me, he *should* have asked me to marry him! *That* is the natural order of things! But he didn't.'

She looked at me. I flounced.

'Anyway, he's divorced,' I said.

She turned away. End of discussion.

Chapter Ten: *Welcome Aboard*

There was nothing I could do. I had already made up my mind, and would marry Terry Muszyka in December, short of Apolcalyse Now.

Mother seemed never to have guessed I had been Mario's mistress for a time. I suppose I carried off the part of innocent virgin quite well. Anyway, Mother was, herself, in some ways innocent—she probably did not understand the word 'mistress' except in a Shakespearian connection.

Mario and Mother remained friends until her death in 1973. I have in my possession a sterling silver charm bracelet that Mario presented to my mother on her birthday. On one side of the pendant disk charm, which is central to the bracelet, Mother's three initials are engraved, *BKB*; and on the other side, it reads *'Love, Mario.'* Charm bracelets were popular in the late 1960s. I received a silver charm from Annabelle after serving as bridesmaid in her wedding; and when I turned twenty-one, Mother gave me a silver 'rocking-chair' charm; she said with a smile, 'Old rocking-chair's got you.'

I didn't think that was funny. I didn't like that rocking-chair charm. The silver 'rockers' kept snagging at my stockings.

Mario did not stay for the wedding, but drove home to Miami on the 5th of August, before the wedding rehearsal began. The wedding day arrived with thunderstorms—but that was supposed to bring good luck, along with the tin cans and odd shoes we would tie to the honeymoon car. Annabelle and Ralph wouldn't really have a honeymoon, just a night or two at the Holiday Inn. Then, they were off to the naval air station at Pensacola.

During the wedding week, my family floated on a cloud of *bon homie* such as I hadn't seen in years. The house was *en fête*. Mother had had a marvelous time designing and sewing the dresses, preparing the food, and arranging the details *par excellence*. Daddy was tearful as he walked Annabelle down the aisle; he was just the same, maudlin, tearful, later that year in December, at my own wedding. *Sniff, sniff.* We got a nice surprise that he cared that much about us.

Ralph's New Hampshire relatives descended en masse and began to make trouble immediately. Their family and our family were like chalk and cheese. Ralph's mother especially, seemed to have the New Englander's contempt for the Southerner. But their attendance put the lie to the story that Catholics could not be present in a Protestant wedding.

At one point, just before the ceremony, Annabelle became so exasperated with her new mother-in-law's interference that she snapped at her; whereupon Mother took Annabelle into another room and slapped her hard upon the face for being so disrespectful to 'an adult.'

Annabelle was shocked, to say the least. Wasn't *she* an adult?

There certainly is a mystique about being a bride. Annabelle's was the perfect wedding, like every girl dreams of. When she threw her plastic bouquet from the church balcony, Sherry caught it. Though I wasn't there for Luci B. Johnson's wedding, held on the same day at the Shrine of the Immaculate Conception in Washington, D.C., I'm sure it couldn't have been any more impressive than our little Memphis one at Park Avenue Cumberland Presbyterian Church. Luci B. Johnson might have had real flowers, though.

Mother was adamant we hire plastic flowers for Annabelle's wedding, because real flowers would have been crippling to our budget, and they wouldn't have lasted long, in the summer heat. Anyway, 'plastic' was stylish, she said. Poppycock.

They didn't look too bad, the plastic flowers; but it was the principle of the thing.

Mother relented enough to allow a real orchid as the centerpiece of the bouquet, so that Annabelle could have it later as the traditional 'orchid corsage' every bride should wear pinned to her going-away suit.

The best picture we have of Mother was taken at the moment of the bouquet-tossing. The photographer, my cousin Glenn, snapped the picture from the top of the stairs where Annabelle was standing, her bouquet in mid-toss. Glenn caught

Chapter Ten: *Welcome Aboard*

Mother's bright eyes and exquisite head looking up to the flying bouquet, her index finger resting against her cheek, wonder and pride in her face, witness to her daughter's rite of passage.

Annabelle, a tomboy, had not cared for dolls, but she owned a magnificent 'bride doll' in full wedding finery, with the prettiest gauzy veil I'd ever seen. That bride doll was Annabelle's touchstone, her point of sanity, serenity, stability in an unstable household, and it represented a goal she knew she could attain. Annabelle was not ambitious; she was entirely untroubled by imagination, straightforward, down-to-Earth, hardworking, and so direct that people thought she was temperamental.

When Annabelle was only four years old (before seatbelts), she stood upright in the backseat of our Studebaker car as we drove along to the Pink Palace on a summer's day, humming the Wedding March. Suddenly she announced, 'I want to get married and have children.' Daddy slammed on the breaks; Annabelle went flying.

I don't care for her children, but at least she has some.

With Annabelle, it was 'what-you-see-is-what-you-get.' Not so with Sherry and me. We were proud, theatrical, ambitious, lazy, spendthrift; and Sherry, at least, was temperamental, though she hid it well. She seemed to be the personification of 'happy extrovert,' and danced like a fairy through her life.

The best picture we have of Annabelle was taken as she and Ralph fled down the church steps enduring the shower of rice pelted on them by Ralph's brothers and sisters. Annabelle was smiling. There is no other picture in existence of Annabelle smiling. She won't smile because of her crooked teeth. But my cousin Glenn, the photographer, caught her in an unguarded moment.

So Annabelle was married, the pinnacle achieved. The one thing I thought of as amusing about Annie's new status was when she acted so smug and superior towards me, as if she had 'grown up.' Overnight Annabelle had acquired status. She had become mature and respectable, a matron, like 16-year-old Lydia Bennet when she eloped with that odious Mr. Wickham in *Pride and Prejudice;* then said to her eldest sister: 'Ah, Jane, I take your place now, and you must go lower, because I am a married woman!'

When we were together, Annabelle bridled and posed as if she possessed a secret knowledge of 'marital relationships' that I did not have. Well I figured, what she knew was probably from reading. Mother had presented Annabelle with a book, *Ideal Marriage, Its Psychology and Technique,* written in 1926, by Dr. Th. H. Van de Velde. I wasn't allowed to look at the book, unmarried and unconsecrated as I was; but I sneaked a peek. It was fascinating reading. There was a whole new vocabulary. We had not been taught to call a spade a spade, or a penis a penis.

After I married, during that first year when Terry was at sea, I was desperate to know more about 'sex'; and got hold of *A Man With A Maid,* by Anonymous, an early work of Victorian pornography. I found it much more interesting and informative than that other old chestnut, *Ideal Marriage;* at least in the first half-book *(A Man With A Maid).* The second half turned my stomach, rather. Sickmaking. I never told anyone, not even Terry, that I read *A Man With a Maid.* My reputation would have been in ruins. I still have the book hidden somewhere in the house. I wouldn't even let the garbage men find out that I read such a book.

The wedding-of-the-year over, I boarded a plane and flew home to Coral Gables: 'Katharine's First Flight.' *Ahh.* No Greyhound bus, hurrah! I had had the good fortune to be in contact with my married friend, Sally Hedges, who worked for American Airlines. Sally, bless her heart, arranged for me what was called a 'youth fare' on American Airlines, and I flew to Miami International Airport in style, gazing out the porthole and saw (believe it or not):

Flows and flows of angel hair
And ice cream castles in the air
And feather canyons everywhere

Chapter Ten: *Welcome Aboard*

I've looked at clouds that way ... [84]

It took me years before I discovered that *Both Sides Now,* written by Joni Mitchell, (the verse just quoted) was about teenage disillusion. I thought it was about First Flight. Oh well, live and learn. For me, travel by air was the Discovery of the Age. It was as delicious as flying in dreams.

The pretty American Airlines' cabin stewardess said to me, 'Welcome aboard, miss,' and handed me a pillow. For free!

Stewardess! That was a glamorous job—'coffee, tea, or me,' as they used to say ... but no, wait, stewardesses were not allowed to get married, were they? Fudge. *And* they had to rise into the air wearing straight skirts, high heels, a French twist and a pillbox hat—darned inconvenient. And they couldn't wear glasses, drat. It wasn't a job for me. But how exciting, to think of being an air hostess and traveling the world. Gosh.

I arrived at Miami International Airport on Cloud Nine, only to be met by Mario with the tragic news that Tommy, Joyce's boyfriend, had been killed in a motorcycle accident on the very same day he received his draft notice. It set a person wondering about fate, about destiny. Was 'predestination' the same thing as fate? There had been endless arguments at church over predestination. Apparently, some people were damned from the moment they were born, while some were predestined for Paradise.

I did not believe in Predestination. What use would it be to try to live a virtuous life?

Anyway, Tommy's sudden death was an omen, I was sure, but I could not interpret it. I went straight to the bungalow, gave notice to my landlord, packed my things, arranged to have my household goods shipped to Memphis on the Greyhound Bus, asked Southern Bell for a transfer back to Memphis, and within a few days bid farewell to Miami, never to return. (Sad,

---

[84] Lyrics to 'Both Sides Now,' sung memorably by Judy Collins in 1968. Written by Joni Mitchell.

but true. I never set foot there again, although I wished to, often enough.)

Before I got away, Mario drove me down the Keys to meet his parents, Mario, Sr., and Carmen Fiqueroa: that made me feel 'legitimate,' and not a State Secret. Mr. and Mrs. Fiqueroa were perfect poppets; they would have made excellent parents-in-law. We were in touch with each other for years, until their deaths in the late 1980s. I adored them.

I did not say goodbye to Joyce, because I couldn't find her. Someone said she was in Hialeah at her mother's house. I never found out. I don't know what happened to her, and we didn't stay in touch. I was in a desperate hurry to escape the lonely, empty bungalow and the terror of my very own personal stalker. What is it about me that attracts crazy people?

Mario drove me to the airport through the soft darkness of the Miami night. We had the windows rolled down. My arm hung out. I felt again the delight of seeing palm trees lit up with pastel-colored lights. Mario was solemn but tender. I hated leaving him, but it was something I had to do.

He gave me a farewell present, and it turned out to be a bottle of *'Je Reviens'* perfume by Worth, a scent I still like. *Je Reviens* was popular at the time, along with *White Shoulders, Chanel No. 5, Chantilly,* and *Taboo.* But what Mario could mean by it, I did not know. The name, *Je Reviens.* I had heard people discuss *Je Reviens* at work. Was there anything symbolic in the name? Did it constitute a promise? And if so, on which side? Later on, at my leisure, while Terry was deployed to Vietnam for ten months, I learned the legend of *Je Reviens,* 'I will return':

'Je reviens en trois jours, ne te laves pas,' was reputed to be the beginning of a dispatch sent from Napoleon to Josephine: the *billet doux* read, 'I will return in three days, do not bathe.' Odd, that. I'll never understand the French. Do they like body odors?

My American Airlines 'youth fare' ticket home to Memphis was a 'standby' for a flight leaving in the middle of the night. I dressed as comfortably as I could for the trip, but was

Chapter Ten: *Welcome Aboard*

loaded down with hand baggage. I was excited, and thrilled with my prospects; I hardly noticed the fifty pounds of hand luggage as I manhandled it around the airport, waiting what seemed an eternity for my call to board. I boarded at one in the morning on September 1, 1966; thereafter, my life took a different turning.

It was a blunder to go back home—not as bad as a blunderbuss, but a blunder just the same; it shot me into a negative sphere—995 Walthal Circle, Memphis, Tennessee. I hated leaving Miami—it had been a wonderful place to live; but really, I was all alone there except for Mario, and I couldn't say he was mine anymore. Memphis was where my few remaining friends and vast numbers of family were situated, and I wanted everyone of them, *everyone,* to see me married. I was proud of Terry, and intended to show him off.

Labor Day came a few days later; and with it, another trip to the airport to pick up Terry, who arrived from Charleston to meet my parents. They loved him immediately. Mother was mildly astonished that I could do so well. Terry came back at Thanksgiving, and the next time I saw him was the day before our wedding.

Settled again in Memphis, I telephoned various friends to tell them of my plans for December, only to find they were married with children, and not interested in me anymore. I had already been away from home too long. People can be so fickle! Even Roger Douglass had married, on the rebound so his grandmother, Belle, said, to a dark-haired girl that was the image of me. Imagine that! Will wonders never cease? 'Granny,' as I called Belle, had been tremendously disappointed that Roger and I had not married, and she didn't particularly like Roger's new wife.

Roger's grandfather offered to sell me a five-year-old Buick at a reasonable price. I took a loan at the bank—my first—and bought it. But that was later on, after I had to suffer a Memphis winter, catching the bus in the ice, rain, and snow. Did I really like four seasons? I was changing my mind.

A Quiet Life in Bedlam

Terry returned to Charleston following his Labor Day visit to Memphis. Our household reverted to its usual uneasy, brooding atmosphere: I had noticed the miasma immediately upon stepping in the door upon my arrival from Miami a week earlier. Gloom and Doom.

If I'd had any sense, I'd 'ave left for Charleston immediately, but I didn't. I was intent on having my wedding my way, even though it would cost me dearly, in more than money. My philosophy was, 'Ya do things right, or ya do things right: no compromises.' A wedding in church could not be dissolved; a courthouse wedding was 'hole in corner,' and perpetrated only by divorced people.

By mail, Terry and I made all the wedding plans. I had to apply for the marriage license alone, as Terry could not get leave until just before the wedding. I bought the wedding rings and had them engraved. I went to see good old Dr. Kirkendall, our family doctor, for pre-marital counseling and contraceptives, but needn't have bothered. The good doctor found it impossible to tell me the things I needed to know, and as it turned out, I didn't really need the contraceptives at all.

The next problem arose when Mother insisted on taking apart Annabelle's wedding dress, and remaking it for me. Annabelle pitched a fit, and who can blame her? Annabelle had planned on having the dress embalmed and hanging in her closet forever, perhaps composing a museum around it, with all the wedding accoutrements and memorabilia in a glass case. She did get the dress back after my wedding. What use did I have for it?

But all of our arguments for the cult of the bride, and against vivisection of the dress, were to no avail—we were pitted against a strong woman, a stalwart woman who could be punished all night by her drunken, nearly psychotic husband, and then get up the next morning and go to work.

The four months that passed from September to my wedding day in December were little short of excruciating. Every single day was wretched, miserable, distressing, disturbing, boring, confining, with little constructive activity. For me it

Chapter Ten: *Welcome Aboard*

was just *stayin' alive, stayin' alive.* It was a hellish existence, watching Mother suffer, not being able to do anything about it. On any number of nights when Daddy was rumbling around, threatening Mother with his gun, I heard him say, 'Shoot the bitch, I'll shoot the bitch.'

I was terrified, but there was nothing I could do. A smart girl doesn't run away from home unless she is being threatened herself. I did not want to live in a cardboard box on the street; and though technically I could support myself, there were greater issues at stake.

I couldn't tell you how Mother found time to sew four dresses and complete the wedding arrangements. She was the bravest woman I ever knew. Mother had decided on red velvet sheath-dresses with long fitted sleeves and boat necks for the bridesmaids, and red satin pillbox hats, with bouquets of holly balls holding small red candles.

Though Mother had been svelte in yellow watered silk for Annabelle's wedding, she was bingeing on food again, and gaining weight rapidly. Her constant worry was what would *she* wear for the ceremony. She ended up wearing white, which was a 'no-no': only the bride wears white to a wedding. Mother looked almost like a different woman from the one who was hostess at Annabelle's wedding in August.

Early in December, I wrote out the formal wedding invitations in my copperplate handwriting, and paid the numerous bills associated with 'a small wedding.' Several times, I wondered, *Why didn't I elope?* I went to work, come hell or high water; that had to be done, despite whatever winter weather the skies could throw at me. I opened wedding presents. My day would come.

My mother's boss gave me a place setting of *Repousse* sterling silver made by S. Kirk & Sons, Inc., silversmiths. I suppose it was lovely, tooled with embossed summer flowers— daisies, chrysanthemums, bluebells, an orchid—but I didn't like it. It was too modern for me. I wanted traditional things, baroque, if possible. Mother would not allow me to change the pattern for something else. Jacqueline Kennedy was known to favor *Repousse,* so it should be good enough for the likes of me.

Another of the gifts proved to be quite a surprise. It was a book entitled *Welcome Aboard, a Service Manual for the Naval Officer's Wife.*[85] *Welcome Aboard* was given to me by the daughter of the dreaded Mr. Smythe, our child-molester neighbor. Doris Smythe was a naval officer's wife, and she gave me the book to help with the coming transition. Henceforth, I would be 'married to the Navy.' Doris already knew what I didn't know—that I was in for a culture shock. A significant chapter of *Welcome Aboard* was titled, 'Your place in the Navy.' Good Lord. My place in the Navy? Did I know what I was doing?

I definitely didn't.

---

[85] *Welcome Aboard, A Naval Institute Publication,* by Florence Ridgely Johnson, 1956.

CHAPTER ELEVEN:
Lovers of the World, Unite

Christmas that year (as in every year) was a horror, because Daddy was at his worst during the holidays. Our home became a loony bin from which no inmate could escape unscathed. I could not *wait* to be married. That was my *deus ex machina.* I could only thank God that I had found a gentle, passive man to love me, and who, I was sure, would never lift a finger to hurt me.

Then I began to have doubts. Could men really be trusted? Would Terry hit me? (As it later fell out, Sherry *did* marry a man who hit her. And worse than that, Sherry's husband, John, roughly grabbed her breasts each time he wanted to show her who was boss.)

As my wedding day approached, I found I was terrified at the prospect of marriage to a virtual stranger. What did I know about Terry, really? I had not met his parents. They disapproved of his marriage to a Southern girl. Mr. and Mrs. Muszyka were not acquainted with any Southerners, apart from the migrant farm workers that arrived in hordes during the summer months to pick the fruit. Terry's parents apparently thought Southerners were little better than gypsies.

Terry tried to explain his mother's attitude: 'My mother is the town librarian.'

A Quiet Life in Bedlam

'A librarian!' Normally, I like librarians—should have been one myself.

'Wait a minute,' Terry said. 'She read *The Grapes of Wrath*. Mother thinks you resemble a character in a John Steinbeck novel.'

'*The Pearl*?' I suggested modestly.

'No, not exactly.'

'An Okie?'

'Yes.' Terry flashed me a rueful smile. 'I can't convince her otherwise. I love my mother, but I had to get away from her, lead my own life. Sometimes I think she expects me to be her lapdog.'

(Puzzlement) 'But, doesn't she have a husband?' There I was, greener than grass, didn't have an older brother, hadn't a clue about that special relationship between mother and son.

Terry gave me an uncomfortable look, then remarked, 'Mother is a strict Christian Scientist, and has some funny ideas about things …'

'Christian Scientist?' That was a new one.

' … suffice it to say that's why I moved to California, then joined the Navy to see the world.' He grinned. 'And I found you, in Florida. Among flocks of flamingos.' (Yes, I had been 'flocked,' but how did *he* know about it?)

'Thank goodness,' I said, truly grateful to the Highest on High.

Terry sighed, 'And, Bangor, Michigan, is a quiet town, too quiet for me. There are less than a thousand people living there, few of them young. My parents like it, though.'

I shrugged. There wasn't anything I could do about a mother who was attached to her son. I hadn't come so far in my education as to know about Oedipal complexes, or the doctrines of the Church of Christ, Scientist. My mother had liked Roger Douglass, loved Mario, adored Terry. I wasn't familiar with 'mother-in-law' trouble. I couldn't see what was coming, faster than a speeding bullet.

Needless to say, Terry's parents wouldn't be attending our wedding. Their prejudice ran very deep. Nor would Terry's

Chapter Eleven: *Lovers of the World, Unite*

brother, Roy, two years younger, who was serving in the Marine Corps. He had been unable to get leave, and was ready to ship out for Vietnam. Terry's family representatives would be a pair of uncles driving in from Indiana and Oklahoma. The two uncles and their wives had difficulty in reaching Tennessee, were delayed, and arrived just before the ceremony. I liked them immediately: Uncle Chet and Aunt Flora, Uncle Roy and Aunt Diana. Perfect poppets. Could Terry's mother be that bad?

The winter weather that year was severe. An early storm blanketed the long, elliptical Mississippi River valley in a frosty rim of ice and snow, and all around us, people were snowed in, left without electricity or telephones.

It was a curious thing, but the great floods of the Mississippi River, and the tornadoes that tore through the surrounding low-lying areas of Arkansas and Mississippi, and even the snows that fell steadily throughout the winter only a little further north and west, almost never touched the inviolate Memphis, situated as it was on the Chickasaw Bluffs, in an advantageous position that has withstood siege. But after Christmas, following an otherwise mild march of seasons, our big Bluff City had been coated in a killing cloak of sparkling, beautiful, prism-filled ice by a freak winter storm, and Memphis had been transformed into something primeval and unspoiled.

Mother, who had wanted to hold the wedding on December 31st, tried to warn me that people would not be willing to go out into the elements on December 30th, then out again for New Year's Eve, the next night; but I was pig-headed about it: I wanted my wedding to be a separate event from New Year's Eve. A bride is a bride is a bride. Up 'til that time, there hadn't been a party in my honor in my life. I would have it my way, except for whatever interference from Mother I could not prevent.

Our friends, kin, and acquaintances must, indeed, have been too shocked by Old Man Winter to venture out of doors, because the attendance at the ceremony proved to be minimal. Terry's relatives from Indiana brought the news that his mother had slipped on the ice at her kitchen door and broken her leg. This was doubly unfortunate, because Mrs. Muszyka was over sixty years old, and already lame from a childhood bout with polio.

Though it spoiled our honeymoon plans, Terry and I agreed with the aunts and uncles to travel to Michigan next day with Uncle Roy and Aunt Diana, and visit Mrs. Muszyka in hospital: we thought it was the right thing to do.

Edith Muszyka's broken bone was being set at the hospital in Southfield, Michigan, even though it was against her religious beliefs to accept traditional medical treatment for her maladies: Christian Scientists trust in God to heal them through prayer and God's grace. In the case of a broken femur, however, Mrs. Muszyka listened to reason, and allowed an ambulance to drive her to the hospital.

Early in the morning of my wedding day, I sat on the front steps of our home looking out over the startling, blinding, ice-covered landscape. Children ran wild out of school; the air crackled and popped with electricity, and sound carried through the air greatly magnified. Tiny brown birds pecked about, looking for treats, and the young (the really young) were having the times of their lives, breaking limbs (with few regrets) as they slid around on the glassy surfaces, shouting for joy, and snapping off ice sickles to suck.

On real winter days in the South—like the day I speak of so nostalgically—when the dark green magnolia leaves are coated by Jack Frost, life seems to stop for a bit, breathe in, breathe out, and sing, *'On a clear day, rise and look around you, and you'll see who you are ...'* [86] (Oh, I wish.) Jumbled thoughts take on a bell-like clarity, and the pressure of modern life eases off a bit, because you can't get out, even to buy bourbon.

---

[86] *'On a Clear Day You Can See Forever'*, the song, was from the eponymous 1965 Broadway musical. Music, Burton Lane; lyrics and story, Alan J. Lerner, loosely based on the book, *Berkeley Square,* by John L. Balderston, 1929; it concerns a woman who has ESP, and has been reincarnated. *With thanks to google.com.*

Chapter Eleven: *Lovers of the World, Unite*

The winter wonderland was a fascinating scene, but I took no comfort in it; I cried all day. Daddy ambled in and out of my bedroom, asking over and over, 'Katharine, why are you crying?' But I couldn't answer. It wasn't something I could articulate.

'It's supposed to be the happiest day of your life, hon,' he said, bewildered.

Sighing heavily, I answered, 'I'll be glad when it's over.'

It made everything worse that Terry and I had decided to observe the Southern tradition, and not set eyes on each other until the wedding ceremony that evening. In retrospect, it seemed a waste of very precious time.

'Daddy,' I asked, 'why do Southerners get married in the evening? Is it so they can go to bed straight away?'

Daddy looked shocked, so I didn't say more along those lines. Evening weddings were just customary, that's all.

Abruptly changing the subject, Daddy remarked, 'Your mother and I eloped. We married at the courthouse in Bahalia, Mississippi, on Friday, March the 13th, 1945. Our car broke down, and we had to push it two miles in the rain to our honeymoon cottage. And a black cat ran over our path.'

I raised my eyebrows. I knew that what he said was true, had heard it all before. Granddaddy and Grandmother were hot on their trails, and would have stopped the marriage if they could. That was because Adam Bamber was 'no account,' according to my grandmother.

An even better story that Daddy told occasionally, was about how he had met my mother in the first place: 'I found Brenda sitting on a rock in the woods,' he would say, or 'in an enchanted garden,' or 'dancing 'round a Maypole,' or 'sitting on a stump'—depending on how his imagination ran on the day he was relating the tale. When Daddy had a twinkle in his eye, what he said amounted to a tall story. It wouldn't be wise to put any faith in it.

'She looked so sweet,' he said sweetly, 'and helpless, sitting there in the moonlight (or the sunlight, or the storm), that I couldn't resist the impulse to make her mine.' Ahh. The line from a hundred country music songs, '*make her mine.*' But Mother was neither helpless nor sweet. Women were still supposed to be the 'weaker sex' then, though such an idea never, ever occurred to my grandmother, and not very often to my mother. We kids didn't find out the genuine version of the fateful meeting, but it certainly was true that our parents married on Friday the 13th, and a black cat ran in front of their path. I had many times counted up the months carefully to be sure I was conceived in wedlock. It seemed likely that I was. (Whew.)

So on the day, the day that should have been my day, I kept to my room, and sobbed and sobbed. My face got redder and redder. For me it was a dreadful day, like waiting for a sentence of doom.

Purdah was hell; Mother just stayed away from me. My future as a married woman yawned like the entrance to the fiery furnace. Even though I remembered my Bible lesson about Shadrach, Meshach, and Abednego, and how they were saved by simple faith, I was so afraid. I did not know what to expect! How could I understand what it meant to wed a man who would constantly be coming and going, spending short weeks or weekends with me sometimes, then leaving me to my own devices—devices and desires.

A Navy wife, I was to find, lived her life in pockets of time. Whenever her sailor was at home, she was alive. And the rest of the days, hours, minutes, was … a holding pattern . . what to do with the time? Dear Lord, what to do with the time? '*Somewhere beyond the sea, she's there waiting for me …*' [87] And so I would always be, waiting, waiting for Terry.

That was when, as the religionists say, one called upon one's 'inner resources.' I didn't have any inner resources. Loneliness was my enemy, but I hadn't really grasped that married life could be a lonely life. Mother and Daddy had hardly been separated a day in twenty-two years. It was the same, with Grandmother and Granddaddy. They had not been

---

[87] *La Mer*, Charles Trenet, 1945.

Chapter Eleven: *Lovers of the World, Unite*

separated ten minutes in forty-odd years, though Granddaddy sneaked off occasionally to listen to baseball games on the electric radio, down at the general store.

A few days earlier, before Terry flew in for the nuptials, a telegram had arrived, stating that in less than two weeks from the wedding day, he had to report to his new ship at Mayport, near Jacksonville, Florida. The USS Bigelow DD-942, a destroyer of the Forrest Sherman type, was scheduled to depart for Vietnam in January 1967.

It would be such a short honeymoon! And yet, I realized it was wartime.

Mother sympathized. 'Blame it on the war,' she said, and gave me a wintry smile. She remembered very well when Daddy was away in the World War. His letters had been few and far between; and when received, were hardly legible, the copy mud-spattered. Those crinkled pages were precious to her. She took pains to hide them from her own mother's prying eyes, slipping them behind loose wallpaper in her bedroom.

'He'll come home,' I stated positively, as if I were trying to convince myself, then pulled a face.

And where should I live in the meantime? I wondered. Even at my tender age, I had come to value domestic tranquility above other states of mind. 'No. I definitely cannot live with Mother and Daddy,' I reflected quietly. Another 'exit act' was in the offing. I was becoming experienced in one thing, at least.

Mother's attention was already on making biscuits as I muttered to myself, 'A quiet life in Bedlam, or some such place …' as my sister, Annabelle, once said … 'Yes, siree Bob! I'll have to skeedaddle out of here again.' But plans must be laid.

'Just listen to that Memphis drawl creeping back into your speech again!' I chastised myself. 'Cut it out. It's not a bit cute.' Gad. I sounded like such a honky. My supervisor in the Miami business office had brought it to my attention that a Southern drawl was not all professional. I believed her. Some people (Yankees) thought an accent sounded ignorant.

'What did you say?' Mother asked.

'Nothin', mama.'

'Well, can you help me with the milk gravy?'
'I'm no hand at makin' gravy, mama.'
'Alright, get out of the way, then.'
'Yes ma'am.'
I beat it, fast.

The deep personal loneliness I had felt since the break-up with Roger Douglass promised to be a permanent feature of my life. Terry would be away on his tour of duty for ten months—it could be longer. The Vietnam conflict was rapidly escalating. Terry was not a naval officer, but a sonar technician second-class, an enlisted man. There was a deep divide between officers and men, and subsequently, officer's wives and enlisted men's wives. Of course, I wasn't aware of this. The traditions of the Navy, and the social and welfare systems applying to dependents, were mysterious entities that I would come to know and hate.

After his fifteenth trip to my room, I said finally to Daddy, 'I'm scared.' He put his arm around me, squeezed me, and replied, 'Honey, you don't have to go through with it if you don't want to.' He must have understood my sadness, because he cried all the way down the aisle of the church as he escorted me to my husband and the marriage vows.

You wouldn't know I was unhappy from looking at the pictures. Terry and I are both beaming like cherubs. We made an attractive couple, seemingly fair set for a long and happy life together. Terry and the groomsmen were dashing in their black, rented tuxedos. Terry's shoes were spit-shined. He wore Navy-issue glasses that lent him a boyish air, naïve, artless as an Eagle scout; but he was much more worldly than I. Terry was young, and fit; even so, he had inherited a tendency to gain weight. He strove to discipline himself hard when it came to food.

Annabelle and Sherry were my matron of honor and maid of honor, and my friend Martha Boston was my third supporter. Martha made me shriek, because she seemed to have the absurd idea that I was some kind of blithe spirit, impulsively running off to Miami, spending my life barefoot on the

Chapter Eleven: *Lovers of the World, Unite*

beach roasting pigs, and then coming home with a handsome husband; while she had lived such a boring life, dutiful, gray and uneventful, studying nursing, looking after elderly parents, with hardly any fun to speak of. She didn't even know how to dance the Watusi! (Of course, Hard-shell Baptists, like Martha, were against dancing, but she envied me my gaiety.)

When I protested it wasn't true, that I wasn't 'a gay adventuress,' she produced packets of merry letters hinting at the goings-on in Miami. The letters were mine all right, written evidence in blue fountain-pen ink on vellum paper, sent by post from the wilds of Southern Florida, where they had, yes, flamingos! And alligators. And palmetto palms. And palmetto bugs, ugh. Mold, mildew, the Fountain of Youth, athelete's foot, Latin lovers, the Everglades, and beaches without an end. Amen.

The stamps on my letters told a tale, with the image of an egret on one, a heron on another, and a crocodile on a third. But still, Martha had to be exaggerating. I didn't come back with Fred Astaire or a millionaire! A color photograph fell out of one letter. What was it? Oh, there I was, wearing short-shorts (they had cuffs), sitting at the bitter end of a diving board in Miami, the pool lights reflecting all around me—it was nighttime, shortly after I moved there, over a year ago. I was only nineteen!

The wedding had gone smoothly. The only disappointing thing was that Mother and Daddy had refused to let me be married in the Episcopal Church ('Romans!' Daddy said, teasing me), and insisted that the ceremony must be performed in our family Cumberland Presbyterian church, where my grandfather had been pastor. How boring. No chance to repeat the beloved words from the Book of Common Prayer, '*I will have this man to my wedded husband, to live together after God's ordinance in the holy estate of Matrimony, to obey him, to serve him, love, honor, and keep him in sickness and in health, and, for-*

saking all others, keep only unto him, so long as we both shall live.' [88]

And Terry did not say, *'With this ring, I thee wed, with my body I thee worship, and with all my worldly goods, I do endow ...'* Holy words are like incantations—they would have set the seal on it, somehow.

Instead of glorying in the occasion and queening it as 'December Bride,' I did a turn as 'Lady Bountiful,' skipping around, seeing to the comfort of the guests, smiling and flashing my wedding ring to all and sundry, serving more punch than the church secretary did, and stuffing candy-coated almonds down my brothers' faces.

'Open, sesame!' I said to Alun, and his mouth fell open like a baby bird's beak. Poke. Swallow. 'Umm,' said Alun. *Sim sim sala bim!* What a fine thing to have brothers.

It was a nice reception in its way. I remember seeing Mother put her arms around Terry, and Daddy drying his tears and smiling beatifically. Yes, I was married, but I wasn't secure. I didn't think it was enough to give the wedding guests only cake and punch. But that was what they got. Such is a Southern wedding. The 'reception' was just a reception. The wedding cake, however, was without equal. I ate enough sugar icing to keep me going all night long.

It would have been a fine thing had I known (not that it would have done any good) about the traditions of Greek weddings, and Italian weddings, and Jewish weddings, where everyone stuffs envelopes full of money into the hands of the bride and groom, then sits down to a traditional dinner, and dances afterwards. That kind of wedding would have been far more exciting, far more memorable. Once, I attended a Greek wedding, and we danced the famous Greek circle dance, the *Kaslamaniano,* at the reception; and the young Greek bucks stood 'round, watching my breasts bounce up and down as we kicked our joyous way around the floor. Everyone was laugh-

---

[88] *Book of Common Prayer,* 1946.

Chapter Eleven: *Lovers of the World, Unite*

ing about it afterwards; so much unwonted attention as I received was unnerving, but thrilling.

Annabelle, Sherry and Martha had pooled their resources to buy me a cuckoo clock as wedding present. I was delighted. A cuckoo clock fitted right in with my view of life. My mother gave me a chic wedding ensemble for going-away. The suit was designed in two pieces, with a drop-waisted dress of winter tweed, and a tailored tweed jacket that had brown, green, black and cream speckles in it. The suit was gold-chain belted, and had a green knit dress-top sewn to the knee-length skirt. I loved that suit, but the orchard corsage did not sit well on it somehow.

'Pink orchid, against tweed?' I questioned Annabelle.

'Umm hummm.' She had pins in her mouth.

'Well, it is tradition.' I was still reluctant.

'Be brave,' she encouraged me.

'There must be some special meaning ...' I encouraged her to spit it out. Annabelle made a cult of 'tradition.' She must know why ...

'I suppose so ...' she offered.

'... in wearing an orchid taken from one's bouquet—similar to the "something borrowed, something blue," custom, I guess ...' I said.

'Yes. And here you are asking for bad luck by not wearing a blue garter! You'd better watch out.'

'It kept falling off. It was embarrassing! You know, it tears me up if anyone even sees my bra strap, and a garter, well ...' I unpinned the orchid. 'Phooey!' I stuck my finger, then had to suck it.

'That was elegant.'

'Indeed.'

'You must wear the orchid,' said Annabelle. 'We can stick it in some Kool-Aid and dye it raspberry. Raspberry would look better with your suit.'

To Annabelle's amusement, I warbled, '*A white sport coat, and a pink carnation ...* ' but she had that 'school marm' look about her. Annabelle could be severe.

'Entirely inappropriate,' she said scornfully. Annabelle was 'Miss Etiquette of 1966.' 'Miss Prim and Proper.' So I pinned the orchid on her. 'That's better,' I said, admiring my handiwork.

'Thank you,' she nodded. 'But Mother won't like it. It was the only "real" flower she ordered.'

Married just four months, Annabelle was already pregnant. Hmm. Mysteries. She was supposed to be taking birth control pills. What happened? Had there been a slip-up? 'I don't want to take birth control pills,' she answered my unspoken thought. 'They don't agree with me.'

'Well, it's your funeral,' I commented.

Annabelle huffed off. She felt very sentimental about her pregnancy; and Ralph was more than glad to prove his virility.

I wore brown winter pumps with my going-away suit, and a string of cultured pearls, my gift from Terry. I received from Daddy— glory be!—the revolutionary, brand-new, Carmen electric curlers. Those curlers were the Miracle of the Ages. With regard to women, there has never been a better invention, except perhaps for pantyhose, and birth control pills.

Terry and I had our wedding dinner, the two of us alone, at the noncommissioned officers' club near the naval air station. I don't know how Terry wangled that privilege, but it was a lovely end to the nuptials. There were several courses, and I tried to observe carefully, as he chose the proper knife, fork and spoon. I had never before negotiated my way through a formal dinner with four courses! But I managed it very well.

I was allowed to drink wine with dinner, and discovered I could consume much more food than usual with a couple of glasses of good wine below the belt. I also drank (before the meal for cocktails), half a 'Harvey Wallbanger,' and after the meal, a 'Velvet Hammer.' It was the height of sophistication. One could not taste the alcohol! One was hardly aware that one was being wicked! As long as it wasn't whiskey, I was sure it wouldn't make me drunk.

When I went to the ladies' room to 'freshen up,' I sat down on the commode, and thought with alarm, *I can't feel my body!*

Chapter Eleven: *Lovers of the World, Unite*

I was numb all over, a zombie nearly (or zombress), and my blithe spirit seemed to be circling around, up by the ceiling lights somewhere.

It seemed more difficult to raise myself from the commode seat, than to climb in a barrel up Niagra Falls. I was in a stupor from which I could not fight free; but so in love, it hardly mattered. My feet were not touching the ground in any case. I had Terry to guide me through the pitfalls of life, didn't I?

Though he drank a lot at the wedding dinner, Terry didn't usually do that: beer was his tipple, his having been born to a half-Czech, half-Polish father, so close to Anheuser-Busch country.

Back at the dinner table by hook and by crook, after clawing my way through a jungle of wavy tables, dizzy chairs, and leering noncommissioned officers (feeling decidedly non-graceful), I asked for some black coffee in hopes that the life's blood would return to my face and hands. Terry seemed amused at the rickety way I was teetering around on my clicking high-heeled shoes. 'Come and sit down, wife,' he said in a jocular tone. He drank one last Singapore Sling before we departed, and eventually we retired to our hotel room, happy and exhausted. What a day! Now, for the main event.

As I have noted, during our courtship, Terry and I had shared much mutual affection and many loving caresses, but we never had sexual intercourse. I did make a half-hearted attempt to seduce him on the night before the wedding, when we were having a 'last date' after the rehearsal dinner. We went to the drive-in movie, and though it wasn't the ideal place, I was *ready*.

Terry, who seemed tempted, said, 'No, Kate. Let's not spoil it. Only twenty-four hours to go! That's not long. Then it will be legal.' (In other words, not sinful.)

'Okay.' So I waited. The cat was not actually in the bag, yet.

The film at the drive-in movie that night was *What's New Pussycat*. It was interesting if risqué—funny, of course, and

A Quiet Life in Bedlam

Tom Jones sang the title song. Everyone was mad about Tom Jones.

Later, I heard that *What's New Pussycat?* was a 'sex comedy.' Sex comedy? Blimey. Was there such a genré? (Don't let my mother hear about it.) I think the reason people liked *What's New Pussycat* was because they were flaunting traditional values by seeing it. One wanted to be rebellious, and seen to be rebellious. *I* liked *The Pink Panther* better. I loved that song, 'Meglio Stasera'*: 'If you're ever going to kiss me, it had better be tonight, while the mandolins are playing and stars are bright ... '* [89] I can still hum it.

Then, at last, we came to our honeymoon suite, got undressed and in bed together. I anxiously anticipated Terry's first embrace. As at the end of a long journey, I was to know lovemaking without fear, without guilt, legally entitled, a married woman not a fornicator.

I must have been too eager. Terry could not consummate the marriage. He didn't seem concerned about it, and rolled over onto his side of the bed, falling asleep instantly. There was this strange, horrid 'gripping' feeling around my heart and in my stomach, like I was experiencing indigestion or a heart attack. I was burning inside. Charcoal was consuming my innards. These physical sensations were new to me, and not at all what I expected on my wedding night.

To say the least, I felt hurt and rejected. It never occurred to me that alcohol might have had something to do with the débâcle. I tried to think where I could go, what I could do to get away from Terry. If he could reject me, I could reject him. I did not want to be in the same bed with him, nor in the same room.

Is that all there is? I thought wildly. Mario must have been more of a libertine than I gave him credit for. By my reckoning, Terry and I should have been canoodling all night. Upon

---

[89] 'Meglio Stasera' ('It Had Better Be Tonight') from the 1963 film, *The Pink Panther,* directed and co-written by Blake Edwards; music by Henry Mancini, English lyrics by Johnny Mercer.

Chapter Eleven: *Lovers of the World, Unite*

reflection, I was really shocked. Terry didn't want me? What about all of those 'Tarzan' stories I had heard from other married women, about how their newly-wed husbands behaved on their wedding night, bounding out from the bathroom dressed only in a towel, if that, with their member fully erect and ready to make children? Then with a cry pouncing on them like a Green Beret in training, only to roll on into forever?

This was the reality. I was alone and awake on my wedding night. What a disappointment!

'Lovers of the world, unite.'

Lovers of the world unite.
You alone know what is right.
People all should feel this way,
Needing someone everyday ... [90]

Oh God! The only other room in our suite was a large, cold and clinically white-tiled bathroom. It looked like a morgue, but I guess it was just an ordinary bathroom. I took the pillow from my side of the bed, and the extra blanket, and removed myself to the bathtub, where I spent the night trying to sleep, utterly miserable. That was the bed I made, and so I must lie in it. 'Shucks.'

Terry didn't notice the 'token separation' I had made until early morning, when he expressed surprise at finding me curled up in the bathtub. 'What on Earth are you doing?'

He held out a hand to me.

'I don't know,' I answered, almost crying. I was very cramped and cold. I didn't feel bridal at all. Pulling me out of the bathtub, Terry administered a few kisses and hugs, and I began to feel better. At least I could relish the fact that I was married, a person called Mrs. Muszyka, a respectable woman, part of a pair, potential mistress of my own household, bearer of a golden wedding ring.

---

[90] Lyrics from, 'Lovers of the World Unite,' by David & Jonathan, 1966.

A Quiet Life in Bedlam

As Terry and I made our way downstairs to breakfast in the hotel restaurant, all the people we met along the way smiled at us, some even beaming and nodding 'Congratulations.' We were so obviously newly-weds, with confetti in our hair. I liked the attention, and I believe Terry did, too. 'Good morning,' he said to the left. 'Good morning,' he nodded to the right. I tried to assume the dignified facial expression of 'wife,' but I was smiling all over myself. Terry always, from the first day, looked like 'husband.'

My first full day of matrimony to Terry Muszyka was spent driving through the snow, ice, and freezing rain of January, to Michigan—which is pretty near the North Pole as far as I know. I couldn't recall noticing Michigan on the map, but I was sure it wasn't in Canada. As we drove along, we were singing, *'North to Alaska, we're going north, the rush is on ...'* [91] Terry had a good baritone voice, and could match me note for note.

Terry and I made each other laugh; we enjoyed talking to each other, and sharing ideas. He liked my spontaneity—Terry had a propensity to impulsiveness, too. We were able to express ourselves freely to each other. It was delightful. He was my equal. I had hit the jackpot. *The Millionaire* had knocked on my door.[92]

Terry's aunt and uncle were kindness itself, and pretended not to notice when Terry and I were smooching in the back seat. We tried to be discreet by hiding behind the travel bag that held their wedding glad rags (a tuxedo and formal gown), but I suspect they knew what was going on. Everybody loves a lover. Anyway, Uncle Roy was quite busy, grappling with the car in extreme weather conditions—he was the best driver in the world. (And he didn't swear like Daddy did.)

Uncle Roy had actual 'snow tires' on his wheels, with metal studs in them! The tires looked like whirling maces as they whipped up the snow. I had never seen such. Daddy had

---

[91] 'North to Alaska,' by Johnny Horton, 1959.
[92] *The Millionaire,* hit 1950s television series staring Marvin Miller.

Chapter Eleven: *Lovers of the World, Unite*

always used chains on his tires in sub-zero weather. Well, live and learn. What other secrets did Northerners know?

In Indiana, all roads led to Indianapolis; and there we were, on January 1, 1967. We paused for dinner and ordered breaded pork tenderloins, a food specialty in those parts. The people of Indianapolis called themselves, apparently, 'Hoosiers.' Why, I couldn't say; I was so busy at the time, thinking, imagining, and learning to spell 'Muszyka' backwards and forwards and upside down. I did consider whether there could be in existence an edition of *Who's Hoosiers* somewhere, in a library, perhaps. No. 'Don't make bad jokes,' I giggled to myself. 'Silly me.'

What interested me most about Indiana were the black, horse-drawn buggies one observed moving slowly, painfully it seemed, along the roads. Uncle Roy had to watch himself when overtaking, so as not to run down the good people of the Amish and Mennonite communities as they clopped their way along to church. Suddenly, they were just *there*. Uncle Roy did not blow his car horn at the vehicles. He and Aunt Diana lived in Ligonier, Indiana, in Noble County, not very far away. They were used to running up on horse-drawn carriages, as they loomed out of a snowy dream world.

Oh, and another thing, the windows of the Amish houses had no blinds or curtains on them. That was odd. The house windows stared back at me like vacant eyes. It was unsettling. I remember 'salt box' type structures, seemingly uninhabited, sitting on frosty farmland. There was scarcely any time to make a study, but the women wore their hair in tight little buns at the backs of their heads. The hair bun was covered over by a tiny, neatly pleated, hand-stitched thin white cap; and the men wore collarless shirts.

The sight of these 'Plain People,' eschewing the material world, struck a cord. I had known of no other plain people, save for my own grandmother, Zadie Kerr. Her family-oriented living style, her complete lack of ornamentation, wearing such simple homemade garments and relying on farming for subsistence, plus maintaining a semblance of devout religious faith, contributed to her looking more artless and pious than she really was. Other people thought she just wanted to be 'different.' (It wouldn't be surprising.) In our family, Grandmother Kerr was the original 'original.' What she had, of course, and Granddaddy too, was the Puritan Work Ethic. Sadly, I have not inherited the trait; I work only to survive.

Grandmother was wishy-washy about her religious beliefs though. One day she was a Methodist, the next, a Presbyterian, and she certainly flirted with the Church of Christ when it seemed expedient to do so. At other times, she behaved like the Devil's own imp. Once when she was mad at Granddaddy, she waited for a full moon, blacked her face with charcoal, dressed in a white sheet with the eyes cut out; and just as Granddaddy was good and asleep, snoring loudly, she set up a howling and banging all around the house, that scared the living daylights out of him.

We arrived at Terry's hometown, Bangor, Michigan, too late at night to visit Mrs. Muszyka in hospital. It was a cold coming we had of it: we met Terry's father, Terrence, a taciturn, heavy-set, second-generation Pole, and former chef de cuisine at a hotel in Chicago, at the screen door of the little cottage. Terry's father did not give me a fatherly peck, didn't even shake my hand; and the entire time we were there, he called me 'Ducks,' or 'Mrs. Muszyka'; and never once, in all the time I knew him, did he address me by my given name, or even a variation of it.

We shuffled in, and were made to take off our shoes. That was the custom in the North, to disrobe before you were let into the house. The 'mud room,' I think they called that little annex. Having no house slippers, I had to walk around in my stocking feet the whole time. I didn't like it.

Terry had mentioned before we arrived, 'My dad is ten years younger than my mother.'

That's very odd, I thought. I had never heard of such a thing. Mother had said, 'The man should always be *older.*' I must observe Terry's father closely, I thought. 'A rare speci-

Chapter Eleven: *Lovers of the World, Unite*

men.' Does it give him a complex to be younger than his wife? But I did not say these things to Terry.

When it was necessary for me to speak to Mr. Muszyka, I called out, 'Mr. Muszyka,' as politely as I could, and he would answer in a put-on voice, 'You called my name …'

It was disconcerting. And there was other clowning around which seemed undignified. Really, I didn't know what to make of him. Thinking back on it, I can't believe Terrence Muszyka meant to be unfriendly—he was probably just shy. Then too, he must have been nonplussed by my arrival at his door wearing traditional winter attire instead of appearing in the cut-off dungarees, pig-tails, and bare, dirty, tape-worm-riddled feet of a runaway from Appalachia. Or, an Okie.

Alas, there was no spare bed for Terry and me to sleep in, but Mr. Muszyka made up the living room couch for us, then retired to his own double bed in his own bedroom without saying goodnight. Mr. Muszyka must have needed that double bed more than we did, because he never even offered (though we would have politely declined) to let us have it for the week of the visit.

Terry and I were still young—Mr. Muszyka was not, and he weighed 325 pounds: a more rotund individual, I had never met. Terry had mentioned that his father was portly, but it was not an adequate description. Terrence Muszyka was monumental. During my visit, he did silly, gauche things, perhaps from embarrassment, and pirouetted around on very small feet in a supercilious way, like an elephant dancing in a tutu.

I wish I could say that our sleeping couch was a hide-a-bed, but it wasn't; it was just a couch, and an old musty one at that. It was flat, hard, lumpy, and about three-quarter-bed- width in size. The color was gray-blue, and it was that old kind of couch where a spring lets down the back of it, to form a flat bed like the Romans would use for banquets.

The sheets were well mended, and smelling of pine needles—which I have yet to figure out. Had the faded, snowy-white sheets been stored in pine straw instead of lavender? Well, I was happy if I could just sleep with Terry. I wanted to cuddle up against him like a kitten. We had only a few nights together before he would leave for Jacksonville to assume his duties at Mayport Naval Station.

Terry must have felt inhibited by being in his mother's house, or sleeping in an open room, or by our Spartan bedding accommodations, I don't know, but the marriage was not consummated on the second night, either. I felt a bit queer. How could I have been so badly misled by the society around me, as to think there was something mysterious about marriage? What I was experiencing was just a close friendship between two people who preferred to stay together—was that the right interpretation? And was it normal? Who could I ask? I felt confused and dismayed.

Next day, we made our duty call to Edith Muszyka at Southaven Hospital. She requested that each of us hold one of her snowy-white hands. There was something she wanted to say. Mrs. Muszyka displayed quiet tears, and began to tell Terry (as if I were not in the room) how sorry she was that he had made this unfortunate marriage to a Southern girl. She said:

'I can only hope that such a mésalliance has not ruined all I have done to ensure that my brother Chet, your uncle who is childless, will leave his money to you when he dies. It is right and just that he should do so; he has no son of his own. I have groomed you since childhood to be your Uncle Chet's heir. Chet has always said that he would leave his money to the San Diego Zoo; but I cannot believe that—not when he has such a fine nephew as you are, my boy. Not when the money should stay in the family, instead of thrown away.'

Terry did not say anything. He knew his mother had hoped that he would marry one of the Christian Science daughters, but he'd never had any intention of doing such a thing. Terry observed the spirit of religion, but not the letter. And he wasn't expecting to inherit anything from Uncle Chet. Terry would make his own way. His unspoken question was, 'Is she attempting to punish me by making this speech?'

Chapter Eleven: *Lovers of the World, Unite*

Terry was inclined to take a modern, progressive, even unconventional approach to life, keenly aware of modern trends, while his mother's style was practical, down-to-Earth, and simple. Survival, not experimentation, was her watchword. She was sentimental, and obviously emotionally attached to the past. She liked to be around familiar places and people, and loved the security, safety and predictability of all she knew in southwestern Michigan.

Terry liked newness and excitement, and the thrill of the chase. He tended to be rebellious, as I did, and was more or less indifferent to traditions of the past. He liked disappearing over the next hill to see what was there. He wasn't going to stay at home and be her altar boy, any more than I would stay at home and be my mother's handmaiden (not that she wanted that).

What miracle had produced Terry? I wondered. (What fluke had produced me?)

I was aghast at Edith Muszyka's remarks: firstly, because of her inference that Terry had made an 'unsuitable marriage'; and secondly, because she totally ignored me—I might not have been standing beside her at all, though we kept contact by holding hands. I had little sympathy for her. She was just a cold stranger. I carefully removed my paw from hers and withdrew to the hall. I was listening at the door, however.

Terry's mother went on to say, while allowing a quiet sob to escape occasionally, that Terry must consider, even though he was married, that his mother should always come first in his concerns and affections—one could always find another wife, but one could not get another mother.

How true! I thought. I would have ordered another one years ago.

Edith Muszyka was a first class drama queen. I was on the verge of crying myself. *Blubb.* I walked back into the hospital room, so as to defend myself if necessary.

The woman continued, 'Don't forget that your mother must always come first in your finances, too, Terry, because I have this disability, and have needed the financial help of others all

A Quiet Life in Bedlam

my life. My brothers have been generous, bless them, but really, I have no one to care for me but you, my dear. Don't let me down, son.'

In the silence that ensued, I pointed out, 'You have another son,' but I was ignored.

My mother had not dealt in 'guilt trips' and emotional blackmail. I couldn't believe my ears. Could a mother manipulate her son in that way? Was this an Alfred Hitchcock movie? In my swollen, bursting heart, and hating her with all my might, I was screaming, 'What about your husband? Doesn't he support you?' But apparently, he didn't.

Terrence Muszyka was a mountain of flesh who swung himself ponderously around the house, accomplishing little. He tired easily, was continually grabbing beers out of the refrigerator, was uncouth, possibly unwashed, and unable to get a job or do much else. He cracked corny jokes, used odd, squeaky voices like Donald Duck, and tried to amuse by practical jokes; but underneath his buffoonery was, I suspected, the enormous melancholy of the enormously fat.

I realized then and there an important thing I had not given my mother credit for. She had not deliberately set out to make me feel guilty about anything. If I had done wrong by her standards, I got punished, but the 'guilt trip' angle of motherhood was not her style. Even to my young eyes it seemed a very potent weapon.

Terry still did not say anything, though his blue eyes were open wide. He patted his mother's hand, looked at me with sympathy, then walked out the door to smoke a cigarette. I was so railed; I could not trust myself to speak. This was only the second day of my marriage, for God's sake! I had never in my life believed I could be so disillusioned only forty-eight hours after getting hitched. Certainly, I could not say that heaven had descended.

(There seemed to be three people in my marriage, alas.)

I wish you could have seen Edith Muszyka, as she lay there clutching Terry's hand. She had a beautiful, delicately white complexion, soft, wavy, silvery-white hair, china-blue eyes as

Chapter Eleven: *Lovers of the World, Unite*

round as grapes, and a perfectly innocent expression. She looked a picture of health and betrayed motherhood.

Mrs. Muszyka, née Chatsworth, a Daughter of the American Revolution, no less, planned to go back to work at Bangor Library as soon as her broken bone healed: well enough. She earned a modest salary; that was a plus. She had a husband; that was an advantage, and she had another son, a strapping boy. Edith had kind, concerned brothers. Terry earned very little money as an enlisted man, and would do well to support himself and me. Didn't she understand that?

Mrs. Muszyka continued a speech that obviously had been planned to the last detail. Speaking quietly, gently, as if she were addressing a backward child, Edith said: 'Terry, please do not stop the allotment checks that you send me each month. I depend on that money. Katharine is young and healthy; she could go to work.' At last she turned to me: 'Heaven forbid that you should get pregnant. You're not pregnant, are you?'

'No, ma'am.' I believe I had gone puce by that juncture, but I definitely wasn't pregnant. I sputtered and gagged. 'No,' I said again.

Fume, fume. Fidget, fidget.

Edith came to her last caveat. She wanted Terry to promise that he would retain his mother as sole beneficiary of his Navy life insurance policy, because if he should be killed in Vietnam, as so many young Americans had been, 'Kate,' she said, looking mournfully at me, 'can begin again, make a new life for herself—marry again. But I, your devoted mother, would have no one, and nothing, to fall back on.'

Insult to injury. *May I suggest euthanasia, ma'am?*

Really, I could hear the theme from *Dragnet* pealing in my ears. Edith Muszyka neglected to mention the annuity she received from her decreased brother's life insurance policy. The eldest Chatsworth, James, had been killed during World War II. That brother, a martyr, a saint, was newly married with a pregnant wife when he died in the Battle of the Bulge, in 1944. Nevertheless, his life insurance premium went to his sister,

Edith, and not to his wife and child. I wonder how that happened?

There in that hospital room, on New Year's Day 1967, Mrs. Terrence Muszyka, wife of twenty-five years to a man whom she despised, begged and pleaded with her fine son, Terry, in front of his new wife, Katharine, to provide for her, his mother—to be a partner in her life, to not abandon her, to be someone who ranked before *moi*, the young Mrs. Muszyka, when it came to all the essentials. (Except, perhaps, sex ... now I am being cheeky.) She cried 'poor-mouth' better than anyone I've ever seen. What a nerve!

'At least it's a change from last year,' I reflected, 'when I was walking around airports at the New Year.' Count your blessings, Kate.

She asked me to call her 'Ma': sweet of her.

I had spoken but little during the visit. I was speechless. I was numb. Could this scene be just your everyday family life? What sort of family had I married into? Were they all koo-koo?

After I got over feeling numb, I was dumbfounded. I was incensed! I hated Mrs. Muszyka from that moment, and never forgave her. Even my own mother had seldom treated me as cavalierly as that. Terry had no explanation for his mother's behavior, and would not say what he would do about the named beneficiary of the life insurance policy. But it seemed clear that his mother's attempt at domination must have been what he was escaping from when he joined the Navy.

We stayed a few days in Michigan while I boiled, trying to come to terms with all these terrible shocks. I kept waiting for Mr. Muszyka to ask me to call him 'Papa,' but he never did.

CHAPTER TWELVE:
Sing No Sad Songs for Me

The setting of the Muszyka cottage in Bangor was pretty, if rural—a large fenced-in lot filled with fruit trees, on the mitten of Michigan they called home. But it was a dull place, nothing interesting about it at all. The one semi-exciting event was an auction on Saturday night. I had never been to an auction, and was enchanted by all those old moldy things, pulled out of people's attics. There was a rocking chair similar to John F. Kennedy's. I wanted so badly to bid, but had no money. Gosh! Antiques. (What a concept.) I would buy some when I was prosperous—I made a silent vow.

One night, Terry and I opened up a lapful of wedding presents from the family and friends. Many of the presents were handmade. There were two feather pillows, embroidered pillowslips, an embroidered linen tablecloth, egg cozies, blankets, domestic things. It was touching. One of the gifts was a tin 'bun warmer.' But I had never heard of such a thing. It had to be explained to me.

On another night, we made a trip with Terry's cousin into Kalamazoo, and attended a supper-dance. The band was playing *I've Got a Gal in Kalamazoo* ...

A Quiet Life in Bedlam

A, B, C, D, E, F, G, H,
I've got a gal in Kalamazoo
Don't want to boast, but I know she's the toast of Kalama-
   zoo,
zoo, zoo, zoo, zoo, zoo ... [93]

I wanted to dance, but Terry wouldn't, he didn't like to dance, so I tried the jitterbug with his cousin.

I had a ball! I threw my head back and laughed like a maniac.

The cousin was a clever dancer, even though he was over thirty.

Terry was good-humored about my perfidy. But I just had to ask ...

I said, 'Why didn't you tell me before we got married?'

'Tell you what?'

'That you don't like to dance.'

'Does it matter?'

'No, not really ...'

We rode the famous train, 'City of New Orleans,' out of Chicago —*'rockin', rollin', ridin' all along the way; halfway down to Memphis Town, many miles away* —where we continued our honeymoon. I hummed to myself Malvina Reynold's *Morningtown Ride* as we waited. I will never forget the cold bleakness of the Chicago rail yard at five o'clock in the morning. It was like being in a scene from *Doctor Zhivago*, without the fur coat.

As we sat close together and talked, Terry and I discovered the intensity in our relationship. We had deep discussions that may have revealed too much, too soon. During the few days of our honeymoon, we probed each other's innermost thoughts and feelings. We made plans, set goals. We discussed fears and ambitions. Somehow, we understood each other on a deep

---

[93] 'I've Got a Gal in Kalamazoo,' written for Orchestra Wives, 1942. Lyrics, Mack Gordon; Music, Harry Warren.

Chapter Twelve: *Sing No Sad Songs for Me*

level.[94] The one forbidden topic was sex. He did tell me that he was not a virgin. Well, that made two of us, but I was very careful not to mention 'Mario.'

While riding on the train, I had lots of time to think. Darling Terry, in sleep as beautiful as a child, looked so vulnerable that my heart went out to him over and over. The vision of him tugged at my feelings so compellingly that my eyes misted over. I decided I must be wrong about what was expected from a husband. The failure in our marital relations had to be ... what? Misunderstandings? Irrational impulses on my part? Lack of desire on his? Who was responsible for what?

'There must be something I don't know, that is vital,' I mused. I needed to talk to a proficient, find out what was normal. An older married friend would be just the ticket—but whom? Martha Boston wasn't getting married until March; and anyway, she was three months younger than me. But as a registered nurse, she must know *something*. Could I dare to ask her some pertinent questions? It would be humiliating, but I could steel myself. For my sanity, the problem had to be solved.

Or could I somehow get up the courage to speak to a doctor about the difficulty? A woman doctor would have been perfect, but in 1967, women doctors were thin on the ground. 'If only I could talk to Terry about it!' But I was too inhibited, too afraid. The man should always take the lead in such matters.

What was it that he didn't like about his initiation into manhood? I wondered. *And who was she?*

Back again in Memphis at the end of our honeymoon, Terry and I found that we were able to talk about many things, art, music, books, theatre, and religion. 'Are you a Christian Scientist?' I wanted to know.

'I used to be, but I'm not now.'

'Is it okay, then, if we be Episcopalian? That's the Anglican Church.'

'That's fine with me,' he said.

---

[94] A note of appreciation to Wizards@star.iq.com. for their Quick Compatibility Report services.

'I am religious, you see. And if we have children …'

'Yes, of course, it's important to have a faith.'

'Okay, that's settled, then.'

I told Terry things about myself that I had never mentioned to anybody else in the world. Sometimes we could understand each other without the need for words. Terry was my Renaissance man. It was thrilling—my joy knew no bounds. I would try not to fret. But if we didn't have sexual relations, how would we have children? I had never believed in the Virgin Birth.

As we dreamed our dreams, Terry and I touched in the psychic realms, but not so much physically, other than a minimal amount—holding each other close, keeping warm, sitting wrapped around each other like contortionists in front of the TV set. Several times, I was ready to scream with sexual tension and frustration (a Harvey Wallbanger would have been quite in order), but kept my pain a secret. How could I tell him I wanted sex when he didn't? The man was the instigator, the initiator; the woman should not seem too eager, and would do well to keep passive (but available). Passivity, however, was not in my nature.

Terry reported for duty to Mayport, Florida, within a few days of our return to Memphis, and I went shopping for marriage manuals. I thought 'orgasm' and 'organza' were the same thing, not knowing what either one was. And 'organism'; did that fit in there somewhere? What about 'organ?'

Once, I knew a woman who said to me, 'Would you like to see a picture of my husband's organ?'

All innocence, I answered, 'Yes.' With a mischievous smile, she presented to me an impressive color photograph of her husband's antique pipe organ, an instrument on which he played regularly some of my favorite religious music, Bach's *Jesu, Joy of Man's Desiring (Jesus bleibet meine Freude)*, among other things. She said, by way of explanation, 'I show this, instead of pictures of my grandchildren.'

'Your husband's organ?'

I realized afterwards that the lady was teasing me.

Chapter Twelve: *Sing No Sad Songs for Me*

Meanwhile, back at the bookstore searching for marriage manuals (and hugely embarrassed to be caught in the act), I displayed for the benefit of the sales clerk my wedding ring. 'You see?' I said. It seemed necessary to exhibit lawful entitlement to the secrets of conjugal life. The shop assistant was nonplussed, I could tell that.

Would you believe, there weren't any 'marriage manuals' available at that bookstore. The clerk had directed me to the section marked 'Hygiene.' No luck. What could I do? The first 'sex manuals'—though I would have croaked before I called them that—entered mainstream United States culture a couple of years later, in about 1969 or '70. *Everything You Always Wanted to Know About Sex* (*but were afraid to ask),* by David Rubin, MD, comes to mind (it was a toothsome morsel); but by that time, I was on the road to perdition, thinking, dreaming of other men, my need for physical love consuming me.

When I got to Jacksonville in April, I donned my dark glasses and went searching through the 'adult' bookstores down by the Navy base. There I found *The Story of O,* by Pauline Réage. It was totally horrible; I could not read it. The 'characters' were behaving like animals, or worse. Human beings actually engaged in a practice called 'bondage'? In my opinion, it was sick; and it was surprising to find such an obscenity on the shelves; the censors were very heavy-handed in those days. *The Story of O* must have been smuggled in from Europe by some nasty person, some reprobate; but even D. H. Lawrence's (comparatively blameless) novels were unavailable to the American public before about 1960.

It would have helped, had I known about *Lady Chatterley's Lover.* Then, at least, I would have had the comfort of knowing I wasn't the only one who couldn't live solely for the enjoyment of the mind. Copies of *Lady Chatterley's Lover* were scare as hen's teeth in 1967, and I didn't discover a volume until years after my personal crisis. (That was just as well, because I didn't actually read Lawrence until I was middle-aged.

Such genius was beyond me when I was still so inexperienced in the ways of the world.)

Before I left Memphis, I tried to talk with my family physician about a condition I didn't even know existed: impotence, but the good doctor was no more forthcoming with information than he had been at my initial consultation in November.

Dr. Kirkendall said to me, 'You are probably putting too much emphasis on what is meant to be a very small part of the married state.'

I quietly blushed. God bless him, Dr. Kirkendall did seem to be full of outdated notions and Victorian ideas. He'd probably been brought up like that. Dr. K. flew the flag for conventional morality high. Doctors, in those days, had a responsibility to guide young people in adopting the proper values, morals, and practices of the society around them. He tried it with me, but I was a hard egg to crack. (For years, I suspected that I was surrounded by a parcel-full of hypocrites. And I was.)

At last, the doctor said heavily, 'Whatever your husband wants to do—that's normal.'

Grim, I thought. If I hadn't been so delighted to be married, I'd have been downright discontented.

So Terry met his departing ship in Jacksonville, and I moved back in, temporarily I hoped, with my parents. Our home situation was as dreadful as ever, but January whizzed by, and then it was February.

I went to the movies a lot, seeing Lynn Redgrave in *Georgy Girl.* It took my breath away: it was a shocking story, and proposed ideas which were incredible to me, about giving birth to unwanted babies, marriages that were over quickly, unions between people with large age differences, and the abandonment of innocent children. But that was nothing to *Blowup,* a British-Italian art film, with Vanessa Redgrave and David Hemmings. *Blowup* was even more futuristic, and incomprehensible—too arty-farty for me. The film featured full-frontal nudity and sexual conduct that was not romantic, attractive or appropriate. I

Chapter Twelve: *Sing No Sad Songs for Me*

was certainly getting my education! *Whatever happened to the X-rating?* I wondered.

I also saw the horror sensation of the year, *The Shuttered Room,* with Carol Lynley and Gig Young. Though the film was well received by critics, it upset me rather a lot, and I determined not to see any more movies of that genre. Creepy gothic horror, that sets the teeth on edge and starts a train of fearful imaginings, is not the medium for me. I get sucked right into the action and atmosphere, and fix my attention to a degree that I am 'in there' with the plot. That is not pleasant, unless the film in question happens to be a British costume drama (which I love). I could well imagine myself as say, Trollope's Lady Glencora Palliser; I would be more than happy to let someone cinch in my waist.

Tired of movies, and thinking to give my mother a present (she wanted me to pay room and board again), I bought tickets for the two of us to see Neil Simon's first play, *Come Blow Your Horn,* which was very popular at the time, and had won some important awards. *Come Blow Your Horn* seemed to express the attitude that sex was fun and did not require marriage. The dialogue reflected rather well some of the new social situations of the 1960s, and was perhaps, improper, the concept of 'playboy after dark' brought well to the fore.

Mother and I also went to see the musical play, *A Funny Thing Happened on the Way to the Forum,* which turned out to be a bawdy, wild comedy based loosely on the farces of the Roman playwright, Plautus. I liked that one; Mother didn't. Mother walked out on one of the plays: 'Dirty and disgusting,' was what she said; and blessed me out about the other: 'Debauched,' was her final word on the subject.

I hadn't realized Mother possessed such a varied vocabulary! Gosh. I knew she was reactionary, but I was trembling from her censure. It seemed suddenly she decided I needed to be protected. She even suggested I should have permission from my husband to view such licentious productions (I was still underage); and she wondered whose daughter I was! The way Mother looked at me caused electrical currents to flash through my body. *Scorpios are not to be trifled with,* I thought. That's a 'home truth' you should always remember, in case you ever run into one.

I did not want to be on bad terms with my mother (though it was a constant struggle to swallow my pride and knuckle under), so I formed a plan to win her over, make her love me, even appreciate me, smile and say 'thank you' for once.

At the time, 'channel rings' were very fashionable, and I knew my mother wanted one. What she really wanted was a diamond channel ring, but that cost the Earth; so instead, I bought her a gold ring with five tiny birthstones in it—one for each of her children: a diamond, a blue sapphire, a ruby, an emerald, and an aquamarine. It was a beautiful ring; she *was* very pleased with it, and wore it all her life.

February 14th, Valentine's Day, was an especially sentimental time for my father, because he had proposed to Mother on that day. Daddy therefore had a good excuse to begin drinking heavily along about the second week in February. His family had no choice but to put up with it as the winter weather was miserable, and it was difficult to get about.

I had requested a work transfer to Jacksonville, but it hadn't come through yet. I still spent all my days at the telephone business office, as the customers tried to come to grips with my unusual name (poor them). There wasn't a single customer who had ever heard the name 'Muszyka' before. We didn't have any Poles in the South, apparently.

Upon pressing a button to answer a call, I would say, 'Mrs. Muszyka, may I help you?' And the customer would answer, 'Mrs. Swaztika, *Mrs. Swaztika,* what kind of name is that?'

They also called me Mrs. Musakk, Mrs. Muskrat, Mrs. Sedaka, Mrs. Musketeer, Mrs. Juicykar, Mrs. Boozika, and Mrs. Floozie. I would have laughed, but I wasn't supposed to laugh at the customers.

On Valentine's Day evening, I was pasting up valentines in our living room with my brothers and sister, Sherry, and trying hard to ignore the miserable moans coming from behind the locked door of my parents' bedroom. Suddenly there was a

Chapter Twelve: *Sing No Sad Songs for Me*

knock on our front door, just beyond where I was standing. The door wasn't locked, and whoever was out there, friend or foe, had only to come right in.

Proud of my new married status, and in Mother's absence adopting a pose as lady of the manor, I swept to the door, trailing my full-length, plaid-wool skirt. (I noticed a similar skirt on Mia Farrow when I went to the cinema and saw *Rosemary's Baby* a couple of years later.) I opened the door to see who it was.

At first glance the stranger seemed to be an ordinary drunk, and looked oddly like someone we had seen our father carousing with. What he actually was, was a murderer. He was insane, and had just butchered his wife and children while they lay in their beds. I can only think, from knowing subsequent events, that he had come to kill us as well; but somehow, I saw a threat in his eye, and slammed the door in his face, just as he said, 'Lady,' and reached for my arm.

I had a sure conviction we were in mortal danger. Why? Undoubtedly, too many horror movies. But in an instant, the door was well-closed and locked. Were we safe? With the blood pounding in my ears, I leaned hard against the door, my back to it, expecting any moment to feel the Devil's own knife blade come through the door and into my back. Why did I feel this terror? It seemed unreasonable.

Quickly regaining my senses, I ordered my sister to draw all the curtains, and my brothers to make sure every door, every window, was locked. 'Hurry!' We were safe; the stranger did not try to come in; but he did get into another house in the neighborhood. Fortunately, the family was not at home, and the man was arrested, next day by the police.

During the months of separation from Terry, I regularly found my nerves on edge, and ended up taking Valium. Somehow, I did not have the confidence or peace of mind that should have been mine in abundance. To calm myself, I bought a belated trousseau of wonderful clothes that I enjoyed wearing. I could see that I was pretty, and it was a great comfort.

In March my childhood friend, Martha Boston, married in a blaze of glory at the Park Avenue Baptist Church. Her wedding dress was the most beautiful I had seen, and put mine to shame. I asked her where she got it, and she said she borrowed it. 'Will wonders never cease!' I exclaimed. 'All you had to do was crook your finger, to get the most beautiful dress in the world? Veil and all?'

'Veil and all.' Martha tried to look modest.

'Maybe Baptists do have some advantages over Presbyterians,' I considered.

Life as I knew it was still a mystery, even at almost twenty-one. 'Perhaps I should find a soothsayer, and have my horoscope done,' I reflected. There was an idea! Just as soon as I was out of Mother's house ... she would never understand ... would think I was going to the devil.

'I'm a *Leo,*' Martha contributed, just to make things more confusing.

Martha Boston married a Southern Bell Telephone 'frame' man, Richard Braveheart, and they lived happily ever after, giving birth to two little telephone repairmen. Martha's and Richard's was the kind of marriage I really wanted (at the time), but in reality, it probably would have bored me to death.

Terry and I corresponded regularly. I didn't know where he was, except 'Vietnam,' and sent my letters to the Fleet Post Office in New York. That was how the mail was always handled when ships were on deployment.

I was still very much in love with Terry—indeed, I stayed so right up until the end. I was eager to receive his letters—elated, over-the-moon—in which cramped, lined spaces, he continually expressed his affection for me. All things considered, I was a lucky girl. Why did I feel fear niggling at the back of my brain?

Terry wrote virtually nothing about the war. His letters were censored. We saw plenty of news reports about the Vietnam conflict on television; it was the most televised war ever. The intense coverage led to mass protest, civil disobedience,

Chapter Twelve: *Sing No Sad Songs for Me*

and even rioting. I knew that the nation was seething with frustration, but all of it seemed unreal, and I felt untouched.

Curious about it, what Terry could be experiencing, and having little knowledge of armed conflict, except for the War Between the States, which I was an expert on, I said to my father:

'I don't know much about history ... well, I know all about the Roman Empire, which I find fascinating; and I can recite the names of the kings and queens of England, right down from Alfred the Great, to Elizabeth—yes, mercy, I'm an Anglophile—but modern history has never interested me, particularly.'

'Well, it should,' Daddy said. 'That's what you were born into.'

'I do know, however,' I remarked, unaware that I sounded pompous, 'that history, in general, is the history of war, and more war. It seems to be a warring old world, Daddy. Can you tell me a little bit about World War Two?'

'WW II?'

'Enlighten me.'

'Enlighten you?' He grinned. 'Awright, I will,' he drawled, 'but first I'd like to sing a little song ...'

Uh, oh. 'Okay.'

Tuning his guitar, he sang lustily: *'Blue moon of Kentucky, keep on shining. Shine on the one that's gone and proved untrue ...'* [95]

Yes, Lord, another one of those disillusioned, down and dusty country-music ditties: depressing. I rolled my eyes. 'Can't you sing "Rock Around the Clock"?'

'Naw.'

Daddy sang every song to Mother, and 'Rock Around the Clock' wouldn't do Mother any honor, so he wouldn't sing it. I don't doubt he knew the words.

My father was a notorious wag and practical joker, but sometimes I could get him to be serious. On this occasion, it

---

[95] 'Blue Moon of Kentucky,' words and music by Bill Monroe, 1946.

took a couple straight shots of Jim Beam, and he had to sing to me—warbling, picking at his guitar, and blowing on a harmonica he had propped up with a clothes hanger around his neck—but eventually I got him to tell me about the part of World War II he had been in; though he had to finish playing *Guitar Boogie* first.

'What was it like?' I asked Daddy again. He had that far away look in his eyes.

'Well, Kate, I was twenty-one years old, and had been through boot camp. I was sent in a troupe ship across the Atlantic to my battalion, the 44th Combat Engineers, which was already involved in heavy fighting in France.

'The 44th Combat Engineers needed a brave man—but not necessarily a foolhardy one—to man a machine gun nest at the front of the battle lines. As a boy, I had had some practice with a rifle at home on the farm, taking pot-shots at squirrels whenever there was ammunition for hunting; and this small experience was considered sufficient to warrant my new position atop the machine gun nest.'

I was making notes, scribbling furiously: ... *might need this information some day,* I was thinking.

'I was in four major battles,' Daddy said proudly. 'I'll show you my discharge papers so you can get the details from that. It was an honorable discharge, of course. I was no hero like Audie Murphy, but I did my part.'

I smiled at him. He could be so winning when he wanted to.

'I just tried to do my duty,' he said, 'and hoped one day to go home. I really wanted to see your mother again. She wasn't your mother then; I should say not! We weren't married.'

'But you knew her, didn't you, Daddy?'

'Yes, I knew her. I found her sitting there in the sunlight on a stone in the forest, but it was starting to rain ...'

'Okay, Dad, I know all about that. Tell me about the War.'

'I got some good conduct medals, some battle ribbons—four battle stars—that sort of thing. Like every soldier gets, who fights overseas.'

Chapter Twelve: *Sing No Sad Songs for Me*

'Did you ever think you were going to die, Daddy?'

'No! Hell no! I had too much to live for. My parents were waiting for me to come home. And I had a girlfriend, your mother. I also had my brothers and sisters that I loved to pieces. I still love them, so much. Yes, I wanted to get home again.'

'Weren't your brothers in the war?'

'My brother Lawrence had flat feet, so he was exempted, and Leo had many small children to provide for, so he didn't have to go. Landon was in the Army Air Force, and Travis was in the Navy. Letters took a long time getting to us, so I didn't know about Travis being missing in the Pacific, or that Landon was shot down over the English Channel.'

'Is that how we got Aunt Mildred?'

'Yes, of course, you know that. She came from a fishing village in Essex.'

'Were you in a foxhole?'

'Well, yes—I was in every damned place that provided some shelter. But mostly, I stayed on the machine gun nest.'

Daddy's chest began to swell, and taking a swig of the whiskey, he added, 'I was a good hand with that big gun. It was a .30-caliber, water-cooled machine gun, and shot 500 rounds a minute. When I was on the gun, I could smell the fear in those Krauts, who were only a few hundred yards away.'

Then grunting, he finished his thought, 'I could smell the rotten cabbage they ate, which is how those bastards got their names. I've never been able to stomach sauerkraut since. I used to like it when I was a kid.

'Dirty rotten Germans, they killed a lot of my friends. But I gave our boys plenty of cover when I was in the nest. I was a damned good shot, real accurate ... accounted for a few Krauts.'

Somewhat shocked by his attitude, and comprehending little of the suffering that comes with total war, I said solemnly, 'You knew that you had killed men?' It sounded accusing.

'Well, hell, Kate, what do you think we went there for, a picnic? They were out to kill us. We just won it by the skin of our teeth, anyway. There ain't any fine sentiments, like obeying the Ten Commandments, when you're in a war.'

'Yes, I know, Daddy, but weren't you afraid someone might kill you?'

'I never thought about it. I couldn't think about it. I was too busy staying alive.'

'Did you get enough food?'

'Well, no, but then, I never had enough food in my life up to that time. I didn't know the difference.'

'Did you get a bath once in a while?'

'I was in combat a year, and I never, in all that time, had a bath.'

Teasing, I said, 'There must have been quite a smell in the trenches!'

'Yes, daughter, there was the stink of death.' He was not joking.

'Tell me more, Daddy.' I was sober now, remembering Terry, thinking, *Where is he?* And wondering, how would it be with him. Later, we got news that one of the USS Bigelow's gun mounts was fired upon by the Vietcong: it exploded, and killed eight men. I did not know for a long time if Terry was among the dead.

'Well,' Daddy said, 'we wore hand-grenades all around our waists, hanging on our belts. We were top-heavy because of the ammunition strapped to our chests and around our mid-sections. We couldn't move about very fast, but then we didn't have any place to go. I'd say we were a walking menace to ourselves, as well as the Hun!

'We called the hand-grenades *pineapples*, because of the shape. You've probably heard the expression before. I could throw a "pineapple" a hundred yards into the German front lines, and I always knew when it hit, by the bodies I saw fly up into the air ...'

'Great Jehovah, how gruesome!' I shrieked. 'You never felt sorry that you were killing men, young men like yourself?' I just had to ask, though I am not a pacifist.

Chapter Twelve: *Sing No Sad Songs for Me*

'For God's sake, *Katrina*, what a lot of nonsense! Don't you understand that they were Germans? That they were *the Enemy*? That they wanted to kill *us*? Hell, they weren't human, anyway. They ate babies for breakfast.'

'No. I suppose it doesn't do, to humanize the enemy. Hmm. So, were you there until the end of the war?'

'No.'

'How did you extricate yourself?' Daddy didn't upbraid me for being flippant. The conversation would have been entirely different, more formal, if it had been conducted with my mother.

'There was no extricatin' to it, Kate. My feet froze in the snow, during the Battle of the Bulge. It happened to a lot of men. The heaviest fighting was in late December of '44. That's when I was taken out of it. The Army evacuated me to a mobile Army hospital, where I was treated for a severe case of frostbite.

'I got a letter from your mother right at that time, and it gave me heart. God knows how the letter found its way to me. The mobile hospital was right in the middle of the fighting.

'At one point, the doctors weren't sure if they could let me go without amputating my feet. That's the only time I would have been worried, except that I was too ill to think about anything. And, I was lucky. The medics managed to restore my circulation, no gangrene set in, and they left me for a few days … for observation, so they said. But I have a theory that what saved me from amputation was the bloody Germans.'

'The Germans?' Extraordinary. 'How so?'

'About the time that I was physically at my worst point, the Krauts began moving in on the Army hospital. The decision was made to suspend all surgical activity, except for real emergency cases, and get on the road away from advancing lines, out of harm's way.

'So the mobilized hospital vans moved a few miles away, and set up again, only to be surprised to find themselves in the midst of the German counter-offensive; and then the Allied counter-attack followed that. We went flying out of there, the white crosses on our wagons not proof against the metal whizzing all around us. Finally, we reached a shelter of sorts under the walls of an abbey full of Roman Catholic monks. We could hear them singing in plainsong.'

'You can spin a yarn, Daddy.'

'It's no yarn. There was heavy artillery all around us. I could hear the bombing, waking or sleeping. I got used to the sound after a while, and couldn't sleep when the air wasn't dense with reverberations. Sometimes, the booming was far away; and then, all at once, it would be so close that we wore our helmets right in our cots.

'After one more move to get away from the advancing Germans, I was sent to a regular hospital in Paris, that had real beds, not cots, and where I got really good care from the prettiest damned French nurses you ever saw. There was this one redhead—she was about eighteen—who was a mighty fine lookin' woman, and I fell in love …'

Daddy's eyes rolled up into his head, and I had to pinch him to bring him back to Earth.

'What's that supposed to mean?' I queried, scalp bristling, loyalty to my mother paramount, all 'objectivity' flown away.

'Well, Kate,' he countered, 'you know I never could resist a pretty woman. You can't blame me for having eyes in my head, especially as I almost didn't have any feet.'

(Wearily) 'No, Daddy.'

'It was too much of a shock,' he said, 'to go from the battlefield to Paris. A madness comes over a man when he re-enters the civilized world. You do silly things, say silly things.'

'Um humm?'

'Every soldier falls in love with his nurse—still, all I could think of was the girl I left back home in Tennessee.'

'Aww …' Pacified, I let him go ahead and get drunk.

One night, as I walked home from the bus stop at Park and Highland, I could hear sirens. *What's up?* I wondered idly. I didn't like walking alone in the dark at 11:00 p.m., but at least it was a nice quiet evening in early spring. It was strangely

Chapter Twelve: *Sing No Sad Songs for Me*

warm for March. The moon was a creamy orb sailing through the cloudy night sky.

I kept myself company by reciting my favorite narrative poem, *The Highwayman*, by Alfred Noyes:

The moon was a ghostly galleon tossed upon cloudy seas
The road was a ribbon of moonlight over the purple moor,
and the highwayman came riding, riding, riding ...

Oh! The romance in *The Highwayman*, it thrilled me to pieces.

As I neared Walthal Circle, I realized with a shock that there were fire engines encircling my parents' house. *What on Earth?* I ran.

In the front yard were my sisters, Annabelle and Sherry; they were crying. Alun and Duane, small, cold, and shivering, clutched at my sisters' arms. *What in heck?* I jumped back as a fire hose swung in my direction. I held on to the trunk of the mimosa tree, and shivered as the old seedpods rattled over my head. 'This must be a nightmare,' I said, to no one in particular.

Annabelle's husband, Ralph, appeared from nowhere, a faint smile on his face.

What are they doing here? I thought. *Is he on leave?*

Ralph looked, for all the world, as if he were enjoying himself. Well, he had told us, hadn't he: 'Someday, I want to be a fireman.' Apparently, he was getting some practical experience. Lordy, he had an axe in his hand.

'What happened?' I asked him. No answer.

I couldn't see Mother or Daddy, couldn't think what was wrong. There were no flames. I tried to get some answers from my sisters. Sherry was babbling about Daddy being drunk. Annabelle was stony-faced. She left the boys with Sherry for a minute, and told me the situation:

'Daddy was drinking. He went to sleep on the living room couch with a cigarette in his mouth. Somehow the draperies caught fire, and the blaze spread quickly from the living room curtains to the bedroom where Alun and Duane were asleep in their twin beds. I yanked the two boys from their covers just as the flaming bedroom curtains came down on them.'

'Jesus Christ,' I exclaimed. Annabelle's eyebrows shot up.

'You might well say that,' she answered. Annabelle had never heard me talk like that before; it was tantamount to swearing, something we had been warned strictly against.

Annabelle had saved the lives of my brothers by inches. The bedroom section of the house was badly damaged, but no one was injured, not even Daddy. He had wandered off to bed hardly knowing anything had happened. Then he had passed out.

No doubt about it, it was back to the business of getting myself moved to Florida. Why was I delaying? Was it because I did not look forward to eating TV-dinners and chicken pot-pies again? Mother only made pot roasts, anyway. A person can eat only so many pot roasts in one week.

Was it because I didn't want to be lonely? 'There are worse things,' I reflected, but actually, there weren't too many worse things.

Again, I packed up, loaded up. The quantity of my possessions seemed to be increasing. Gad. What about that simple life the San Francisco Flower Children were touting? Did such a state of euphoria exist in reality? I doubted it. And would I be comfortable, crashing in somebody's pad to spend the cold night on a bad sofa after smoking too much pot and drinking too many Bloody Marys? 'Nah, hardly likely.'

No, I'd never be able to sleep without having a bath first. And so far, I hadn't learned how to smoke anything—much less, marijuana. And I was skeptical about the 'easy road' that life in the Haight-Ashbury district seemed to imply. Nope. I wasn't an anarchist. I wanted my own home; I wanted to be settled.

'Free love.' Would I like that?

'Shut yore mouth,' I heard our maid, Honey Bunch say in her deep, rich voice. 'Huh. How did she know what I was thinking about?' Honeybunch had eyes in the back of her head.

Chapter Twelve: *Sing No Sad Songs for Me*

Well, I was more amenable to the suggestion of 'free love' than I ever had been, though I still cringed at the word 'promiscuity,' which was how 'free love' was interpreted during the reign of 'counterculture.' I looked it up in the dictionary: 'free love—the free union of adults; seen as legitimate relations, which should be respected by all third parties whether they are emotional or sexual.' Pooh. 'Free love' would never be respectable or accepted in the U.S.A., I was sure. Too, 'civil libertarian' for my stomach.

But did I really need all this stuff? My possessions. Well, the clothes, I had to have. Okay, and the records and books, yes, definitely. And my English china—it was Adams' *Singapore Bird*. I would never give that up: 'til death, do us part.

The jewelry? No, I wouldn't give that up. The bric-a-brac? What for? It didn't weigh much. My silver tableware was quite heavy. Could I sell that back to the pawnshop? The Norwegian *Rose* pattern, service for four. It was classy. And my crystal goblets—the pattern name was *Antonia*—terribly Roman, like me.

It was satisfying to see that marriage to the Navy had brought a certain amount of prosperity. I liked to own things. What about my framed oil paintings—I could sell those. People said my style was 'Grandma Moses,' but I wasn't flattered. I would keep the landscape I painted in Coral Gables, though. It held such memories. Well, what about the torso Mario had created? Was it appropriate for me to keep it? I still felt slightly embarrassed by it. 'Well, nobody has to know.'

My final decision: 'I need everything.'

Terry had warned me that the Navy applied a strict weight limit to the shipping of household goods. You got more tons, the higher you went in rank or rating. We were still pretty low on the totem pole, though Terry was rising fast. But I didn't have to worry about 'weight' this time; the Navy would not be moving me.

I bought a second-hand Buick from Roger Douglass's grandfather, who sold it to me at a very good price. Needing a traveling companion, I adopted a half-dachsund puppy at the dog pound, and wormed him.

Still unsure, I recruited Sherry for the trip. Then, we left Memphis late in March when the crocuses were popping up. As we pulled out of the driveway, Sherry and I sang what we knew of Peter, Paul and Mary's, *'Take me for a ride, take me for a ride, take me for a ride in your car, car.'* [96] Mother and Daddy waved from the door.

We were merry. We were excited! We were radical. A new adventure lay before us. What fun to discover new places! I had never been to Jacksonville.

---

[96] 'Car-Car' song lyrics, 1966, by Peter, Paul and Mary.

CHAPTER THIRTEEN:
On the Beach

The automobile trip to my new home in Jacksonville was uneventful. The car thermostat zonked out in Alabama, but the garage mechanics who fixed it were very accommodating. Sherry and I both knew how to smile at them.

Arriving in Jacksonville after a routine journey—I followed the maps all the way, all by myself, while Sherry took care of the dog—we stayed for a few nights with a girl named Monica and her three-year-old son. Monica's husband was also aboard the Bigelow, and we were both young, unsure, insecure, inexperienced, and trying to cope without a husband or a family during the long months of a period of 'war' duty. Neither of us had knowledge of our privileges and obligations, those special ones that life as a Navy wife could bestow.

Monica and I were strangers to each other, and only met because Terry arranged for me to stay with her until I found an apartment. The one thing I liked about Monica was that she had hanging on the wall a fine pair of temple rubbings from Angkor Wat in Cambodia (formerly French Indochina). The temple rubbings portrayed the myth of a maiden so pure, that she was able to fly away on a magic carpet, when threatened by a mischievous gargoyle-like monkey god. It was a fascinating picture. It provoked in me an even greater urge to travel.

A Quiet Life in Bedlam

Terry was sitting somewhere out in the South China Sea. It was so strange. The sun I looked up to was the same orb he saw each day. It was the same azure blue sky. But I could not reach him in time or space.

'We are here on the same planet ... Terry and me,' I said, unbelieving.

Monica was sitting beside me on the porch, smoking a Lucky Strike. 'Yeah,' she said, 'sometimes it seems as if I am not even married to Floyd, my husband. He has been in Vietnam twice, and he's not even twenty-four.'

Monica was small and dark, with a long nose and a thin body. How she gave birth to that sweet little blond boy of hers was anybody's guess.

Taking our farewell of Monica, Sherry and I drove out to Jacksonville Beach, and easily found a furnished, ground-floor apartment right on the oceanfront. The location had the advantage of being cheap (it was *then*; I bet it's astronomical now), and close to Mayport, the Base where my ship would come in.

My transfer to the Jacksonville Beach office of the telephone company was a long time coming, but all was in order at last; and, bingo, I was established as a resident of Florida once more. I began working immediately, answering queries and complaints, and got called 'Mrs. Barmitzvah' for my pains (among other epithets). If I spelled my name once, I spelled it nine hundred times. As much as I had disliked my maiden name 'Bamber' as a handle, it had been far, far better; but I wouldn't go back to being 'maiden' for anything. 'Marriage' gave me independence that I liked. I was free to come and go as I pleased. Though money was tight, I had enough of it. Barely.

The five women I worked with at the telephone business office, all handsome and middle-aged, proved to be eccentric in the extreme. Office intrigues such as they got up to were something new for me. In other telephone offices, we had been far too heavily supervised for such shenanigans to succeed. But whatever the old biddies did to me, said to me, I knew I was young with my whole life ahead of me, while *they* were march-

Chapter Thirteen: *On the Beach*

ing towards old age and death. There was one of them, who must have been over forty, that wore a lot of make-up, and I said, 'What bad taste! She is far too old for makeup.'

There was another one, Marge, who hailed from Charleston, South Carolina. Marge had a Southern drawl so thick you could slice it with a knife and butter your bread at breakfast. (So much for elocution.) I liked Marge. She was kind to me. She admired my hand-embroidered cardigan sweaters: that was a winning strategy. I was proud of my handiwork.

I started to become acquainted with life as a Navy dependant, and, to my dismay, found out what it was like to be discriminated against, white skin or no; the tables had turned rather neatly for someone who grew up in the racially segregated South. It was a bitter pill to swallow, that I found myself in the category of 'second-class citizen' because my husband was an enlisted man, as opposed to being an officer. In my deepest heart, I had always thought I was as good as anybody else.

I discovered that trying to make friends with my neighbors was impossible, because they were mostly officers' wives—their husbands were away at sea, too—and I was not their social equal. It was a very hard lesson to learn. In fact, it was too hard, and I never did learn it—to take that one step back, bow my head, and be truly humble. My unwillingness to acquiesce to the Navy class system eventually brought disaster a couple of years down the road. I wonder now, why did I have to be so stubborn? Why wasn't Terry enough?

In the budding beginnings of my acquaintanceship with these new neighbors—conversations over the fence, that sort of thing—I had been delighted that these young wives, and I, apparently had so much in common. We were the same age, had a similar education, similar backgrounds. But then the inevitable question would come up, 'What does your husband do?'

When I answered, innocent as a babe, but also proud, 'My husband is a Sonar Technician, Second Class,' a designation that shouted *enlisted man*, these women literally turned their backs on me. They made no further attempt to be polite, or even civil.

I was crushed. I thought, *What am I going to do for companionship while Terry is away?* It had never been a problem for me to make friends. Few people could resist my gregarious nature; folks seemed to like my forthright ebullience, my outspoken honesty. Though it took me a few years to realize how attractive I was, I always felt a flame within me: even at my lowest ebb, I was never less than a firefly glowing through the deep Southern dark.

Nevertheless, I was a dolt, that was clear. 'Why didn't I realize what an upscale neighborhood I was moving into?' I commented to Sherry, who was busy making friends with every good-looking, unattached male in the neighborhood. She just grinned, and bopped on out the door, chanting, *'Chantilly lace and a pretty face, and a ponytail hanging down; a wiggle in her walk and a giggle in her talk, makes the world go round, round, round ... '* [97]

'You hussy,' I said, but she ignored me.

Terry had warned me that life in the Navy would be more difficult than it would be in civilian circles, but in point of fact, I felt dazed and daunted. It was only Jacksonville Beach, for Christ's sake, where North Florida's hippies hung out. And they looked poor, not psychedelic. They seemed lazy, not subversive. They were not counter-revolutionary—they were pathetic. And, those 'free love' Jax Beach hippies moved back to Jacksonville, don't 'cha know, when the rents went up in summer. 'Mama and Papa' would take care of their cigarette requirements.

I snapped my fingers; so much for non-conformity, 'alternative society,' contempt for money, and work. Hippies just didn't want to grow up. 'There's no free ride, sweetie,' I mouthed to them as they lounged around on street corners.

---

[97] Lyrics to 'Chantilly Lace,' by The Big Bopper (J.P. Richardson), 1958.

Chapter Thirteen: *On the Beach*

I definitely lacked compassion for Flower Children. In my opinion, they were wasting their lives. Some of them were wasting their minds, too. There was a man who said, 'If you remember the 1960s, then you weren't there.' All I can say is, poor them. But some people don't want to be awake.

But why did those junior officers' wives have to get so exclusive with me? I couldn't understand it. Yes, there was a rule about officers not fraternizing with enlisted men, but who had transferred the husband's rank onto the wife's sweet shoulders? I ask you.

One night I was sitting in the Laundromat, trying to pass the time somehow until my clothes were dry. *BORING!* rocketed through my brain. *GET ME OUT OF HERE!* I thought wildly.

'Distract yourself,' I said to myself. I began to tap my feet to the inner music:

Counting flowers on the wall, that don't bother me at all,
Playing solitaire 'til dawn with a deck of fifty-one,
Smoking cigarettes and watching Captain Kangaroo,
Now don't tell me I've nothin' to do. [98]

Oh these sad daily pursuits. Isolation. Alienation. What sort of life is this? *I need a challenge*, I thought. *A challenge, hmm ... what can I tackle next?*

I read a magazine, *Cosmopolitan*. I had discovered *Cosmo* the moment I hit Jacksonville, and was rather fascinated by the 'cleavage' on the front cover. Since when did women dare to show their bosoms to such an advantage? This wasn't the 1950s, for Pete's sake. It wasn't the reign of Charles II, either! My understanding was that Space Age fashions did not allow for breasts. I'd had to flatten mine down by using a special bra.

Well, if breasts were back in fashion, the bankrupt 'falsie' manufacturers would be happy! Good for them. And so would I; I didn't like hiding my breasts.

---

[98] 'Counting Flowers on the Wall,' the Statler Brothers, 1965.

A Quiet Life in Bedlam

Whatever happened to the Unisex concept? I thought. 'Is it still valid?' I asked the pages of *Cosmopolitan.*

According to *Cosmo,* Unisex was on its way out; women wanted to be feminine again—feminine, but equal. Helen Gurley Brown, *Cosmopolitan's* editor, had the last word on everything. 'Hurray!' I had never believed in Unisex, but it takes me a few years to adjust to almost any fashion change. By the time I do adjust, something else comes along. You couldn't guess how many times I refused to stop wearing my pointed-toe, steel-tipped stilettos when shoes became low-heeled and boxy.

I was only just beginning to consider Unisex in 1967. My body was slim as a willow after taking diet pills. I stopped taking the pills though, because I noticed they made me more nervous than I already was. (And they were *so* expensive.) I absolutely couldn't drink coffee, the Great American beverage, when using diet pills; it made me jump through the roof. The Vitamin B shots the doctor gave me helped my nerves a lot—I was strong as a horse, even if I did look like a baby doll. I could lift my own weight.

Ankle-length skirts were the fashion news in *Cosmo*; but those maxi-length dresses were not too popular, except among the ultra-fashionable, or the flower-power people. I nearly croaked when I saw models in the magazine wearing short skirts (or shorts) teamed with long coats. It was brazen. And those new ruffled culottes by Mary Quaint that had been introduced in the spring, were nothing I would ever wear—not in this life.

'Are you kidding?' I said to Helen Gurley Brown. She did not respond, but she never wore them, either.

Still sitting in the Laundromat after all that fashion contemplation and the adjustment of my sensibilities, I listened to my transistor radio, but didn't care for the popular music that was getting more psychedelic and acid everyday. 'Oh, stop the blaring,' I complained to the little silver thing, and switched it off, no longer diverted by reading magazines and listening to music. My tedium was complete. There was nothing to do.

Chapter Thirteen: *On the Beach*

Then I took a chance, and struck up a conversation with the girl sitting near me. I was wary, but she looked harmless enough. We talked for forty-five minutes before she got around to asking my husband's rank. As soon as I replied to her question, her smile died, her eyes turned to ice, and surveying me coolly, she collected her laundry and left. One would have thought I had been presuming upon royalty. I was suddenly a nonentity.

I was floored! I got my challenge in spades. Somehow, some way, I had to solve this problem. The solution eluded me for many months.

On another day, I visited an old school chum who was living in Navy Housing 'aboard' the Base. I was so thrilled and excited to find a friend from home, and driving to Mayport, I turned into the Officers' housing area. Cruising down the narrow street, I was almost to my friend's house when I was stopped by the Shore Patrol. The uniformed man, who looked at me severely, informed me that I was in 'Officers' Country'; and then he escorted me to a 'neutral' part of the Base. I was so mad, that my eyebrows seemed to catch fire and singe; there was this burning sensation around the crown of my head. Electrocution couldn't feel much different, I was sure.

I got permission from the Shore Patrol officer to make a phone call to my friend, Nancy, who drove to meet me in her station wagon. The unexpected trip was an inconvenience for Nancy, because she had several small children. Cool as a cucumber, she escorted me, the pariah, to her allotted Navy bungalow in Officer's Country. I felt utterly humiliated. It did not take many of these incidents before I suspected that I was paying for all the sins ever committed in many lifetimes.

Well, next time, if there was a next time, I would know: in Officers' Country, all the street names began with an 'O'—Oglethorpe, Oliver, Ostracism, Ophelia, Orangutang, Outrage; and in Enlisted Man's Country, all the streets were named with an 'E'—England Street, Eagle Street, Elderberry Lane, Ebony Court, Elephant Avenue, Evangeline, etc. Talk about a 'dichotomy!' ('Dichotomy' was a new word I learned while being introduced to Navy traditions.)

Upon very brief reflection, I resolved that the *only* way I would allow Terry to make a career of the Navy was if he became an officer. Life as a second-class citizen did not appeal to me. I hadn't been born black, and I wasn't going to be treated like one. Hadn't my portrait been on a record sleeve? Wasn't my name listed in the National Honor Society? Hadn't I been chosen to sing first alto in the Tennessee All-State Chorus? Wasn't I the first-born? Hadn't I been inducted into the National Thespian Society—a lifetime membership?

I wasn't going to spend the rest of my natural life being treated in this unfair, inhumane way. I might have been a dog! Mixed breed, of course.

Speaking of mongrels, my little pound puppy was growing apace, and made a good companion, but he became rather neurotic because I left him alone too much. That puppy, whose name was Pretzel, chewed up countless shoes and many record albums, but somehow, I abstained from strangling him, understanding all too well his need for someone to pet him, love him, talk to him—show he was needed. The only time I really got angry, was when I woke up at three o'clock in the morning of a working day to find electrical sparks flying all around my bed, because the puppy had been chewing on the cord of my alarm clock.

And what of my contemporaries, the enlisted men's wives, those sad neglected ones? If there were some of them enjoying life, I didn't notice it. Unfortunately for myself—rather left out in the cold, a stranger in a strange land—the enlisted men's wives, for the most part, did not make suitable friends either. Many of the poor darlings were uneducated, disorganized, economically challenged (to say the least), and burdened down with passels of scruffy children.

Left alone for months on end, some of the enlisted wives were clearly adulterous. I remember Monica, for example, who had moved in next door to me in the upstairs apartment across on the other side of a wire fence and through the lawn full of

Chapter Thirteen: *On the Beach*

Bermuda grass and sand spurs. Monica hadn't been living there many weeks before I noticed that her four-year-old son was spending a lot of time alone, outdoors in the sunshine, the rain, whatever. He was red, sniveling, hungry and lonely. My heart went out to him.

I asked him, 'Where is your mother?'
'She's in the house.'
'Isn't it time for lunch?'
'I can't get in.'
'Why not?'
'Because the screen door is locked.'
'Why is it locked?'
'Mother has a friend in there.'
A friend? Was Monica able to find friends?

The friend was a man, and he came to visit Monica nearly every day. Her poor little boy; I can't remember his name at all.

In addition to the 'enlisted wives' who lived in rented apartments near me, there seemed to be an unusual number of rough, unhappy women living in Navy Housing aboard the base. I met some of these women by attending various 'enlisted wives' functions. *By no means do I ever want to live in Government Quarters,* I thought, *low rent or not!* In my opinion, government housing was a ghetto. Though it wasn't easy to grow grass in that part of Florida, their yards were just sand pits or dust bowls. And everything in Navy Housing was so functional, humdrum, and exceptionally basic.

The enlisted wives had to live on practically nothing, but because the Navy 'gave' them shelter (for a small fee, deducted directly from their husbands' pay), and reduced prices at the commissary, it was thought that they had enough.

I know I'll be flayed alive for saying this, but I could see why the officers' wives did not have anything to do with them—though I wouldn't have admitted to it under the basest torture! I wouldn't either, if I had any choice. Finally, I found a few acceptable friends, thank God, in the right 'class.' I realize now that I was a terrible snob, as ignorant in my own way, as the officers' wives were in theirs. Well, well, live and learn.

The two or three 'enlisted' wives I became friendly with were beautiful, clever, well-educated, and as sleek as Siamese cats. I learned a lot from them. We had some jolly times together. One woman was actually from Michigan! She accepted me as her equal. I was so glad.

Still, whether we were officers' wives or enlisted men's wives, we were on a par in our loneliness and boredom, our lack of something constructive to do. Work, even the satisfying kind, consumed only forty hours. Our husbands were away fighting a war—would be for months, and when the men came home, they would be in port for only a short time; and then, away to sea they would go again.

Sailors are a pack of wayfaring wanderers, if you ask me.

The war in Vietnam was at its height. There was nothing we could do but grin and bear it, and count down the months like prisoners hoping for a commuted sentence. *'Those were the days, my friends, we thought they'd never end. We'd sing and dance forever and a day ... '* [99]

'Lord have mercy on us all,' intoned the priest on Sunday mornings at Jacksonville Beach's Episcopal Church. I agreed with him. Lord have mercy.

So, we were a society of women—never a promising situation, and in this case as explosive as a powder keg. Adultery was rampant. It knew no class barriers. Some of the people I met tried to tell me that I might as well expect my husband to be unfaithful while he was away, rationalizing (as they did to cover their own behavior) that *all* Navy men (or at least 99 percent) were regularly unfaithful to their wives when abroad, and that it was just something I would have to accept.

I couldn't accept it.

The idea of an adulterous husband, that these ladies tried to foster upon me, did not in itself upset me, because I knew very

---

[99] Russian folk song, 'Those Were the Days,' sung gloriously in English by the Welsh singer, Mary Hopkin, on Apple Records, 1968.

Chapter Thirteen: *On the Beach*

well that Terry didn't have a particular interest in sex, so I couldn't imagine him romancing a stranger in Saigon. But it did hurt to hear that everyone in Mayport *expected* him to do just that, and would have considered him to be quite abnormal if he didn't. It was that ancient and ugly 'double-standard' rearing its repulsive head again. Sigh. (Has the world ever been without a double standard?) And it was *women* who were pushing it, promoting scurrilous gossip.

'Shame on them,' I said. 'Fish wives.' I was not convinced by these spurious arguments. I searched my vocabulary for suitable epithets to use on them.

I had too much time alone to think, became more introspective than I'd ever been; and eventually, the idea presented itself that perhaps it was only 'me' that Terry found undesirable. 'Is there something wrong with me?' was the inevitable question. Certainly the few people I had broached the subject to, seemed to think I was some kind of freak for wanting to have sexual intercourse with my husband (including my mother). 'As the years go by,' my mother said, 'you get enough of that.'

Lordy, lordy, can that be true? *Show me.*

The months passed with an agonizing slowness, and the loneliness became an illness. I needed a human companion in life. A dog wasn't good enough. How do you talk to a dog? Walking the miles of the open, sandy Jacksonville Beach absorbed some of my energy, but there was still too much time alone, sitting in my apartment, even though I was away working five days a week. The Navy put out a great deal of helpful information for just such poor ignorant *péons* as me, but I did not realize this, and would not have known where to look for the information, had I been aware of its existence.

There was a good 'support system' among the officers' wives, so I heard, but it did not seem to exist among the 'enlisted' wives. My charming 'service' manual, *Welcome Aboard,* stated, and I quote, 'Your friends will be primarily other Navy people and you will find them perfectly magnificent. They are friendly and helpful, thoughtful and kind and loyal to such a marked degree that you will enjoy the finest of

A Quiet Life in Bedlam

friendships. They will give you all the help you need and more advice than you want.'[100] Well, you can see why I was disillusioned. The support system broke down, before it got to me.

I had only one chance to be on good terms with the 'Bigelow' junior officers' wives, and I blew it. I invited four of them to tea. Unluckily for me, and my 'outspokenness,' there had just been some sort of March Through Mississippi and Alabama by Dr. Martin Luther King, Jesse Jackson, Jesse James, George Wallace, and the Multitudes, et. al., after a long period of Civil Rights activism, with hundreds of riots and many other violent incidents taking place in the Southern States and across the land. It had been the worst summer for racial disturbance in United States history, and Southerners were fed up.

Even 'Americans' were tired of it, and worried to death. Where would it all end? We still remembered John Kennedy's death. Malcolm X of the Black Panthers had been killed in 1965. The Black Panther Party, led by Huey P. Newton and Bobby Seale, was still fomenting revolution even without Malcolm X, espousing extreme ideologies—Marxist-Leninist-Maoistic, far-left, radical (Communistic) measures to cure the ills of American society. Nothing short of revolution would do for the Black Panthers. The kind of violence they were advocating made every white person, and many blacks, tremble in their boots.

The folk rock group Buffalo Springfield sang:

What a field day for the heat
A thousand people in the street
Singing songs and carrying signs
Mostly say, hooray for our side ... [101]

I still had not learned how to throw off my racist attitudes, and stop being so opinionated—a bigot, plain and simple—one of the clearest signs of ignorance, I regret to say. I had heard

---

[100] *Welcome Aboard, A Naval Institute Publication,* by Florence Ridgely Johnson, 1956, preface ix.
[101] Song 'For What It's Worth', by Buffalo Springfield, 1967.

Chapter Thirteen: *On the Beach*

rumors and gossip concerning 'irregularities' in the moral conduct of the demonstrators, rioters, and marchers (et al) in Alabama.

Paranoia strikes deep
Into your life it will creep
It starts when you're always afraid ... [102]

I repeated the rumors and gossip to these ladies, thinking they would be sympathetic. The outrageous 'side-of-the-road' stories I told were probably ridiculous (and sounded so, even to my own ears), and I shouldn't have done it.

Stop children, what's that sound
Everybody look what's going down ... [103]

Again, they turned their backs on me. I guess most of them were from the North.

My face is burning with shame right now, as I remember it. Live and learn, live and don't learn.

I decided to become the ideal housewife, tried to get interested in all the 'domestic' things. 'Maybe that would give my life meaning,' was my hope. I knew, even then, that I was not the domestic type, but it was worth a try. I bought a deluxe vacuum cleaner on a monthly payback plan. It was difficult to keep sand out of the house—we were always tracking it in.

I bought a Singer Sewing machine and sewed some clothes. My best effort was a kind of Florida 'playsuit' in a wild Hawaiian pattern. The playsuit even had a built-in bra. I looked adorable in that playsuit, though Sherry laughed at me. 'Ukulele lady,' she called me.

I bought a whopping great electric fan at JCPenney. It chopped the air day and night, but the heat was oppressive. I drank so much Coca Cola that I realized I was getting addicted

---

[102] 'For What It's Worth.'
[103] Ibid.

to it. Jacksonville Beach was Florida, yes, and I loved Florida, but it wasn't the paradise that Miami had been. I missed Miami and Mario. I missed the innate Spanishness of it all.

A trip to St. Augustine in August helped to soothe the savage beast of loneliness. St. Augustine certainly had that Old World, Español flavor. Founded by Spain in 1565, it was the mythical location of Juan Ponce de León's Fountain of Youth, and the oldest continuously settled city established by Europeans in the continental United States. The Spanish colonial style architecture suited some deep need in me for the strange and exotic, and I could play 'pretend' while touring the nineteenth century mansions built by rich industrialists like the Vanderbilts.

Back home again, I painted my kitchen, scrubbed and cleaned until the apartment was like a hospital. I bought Emily Post and studied etiquette. I went shopping for my first simple furniture. I learned how to use a Sears catalogue. But I felt that life would not begin again until Terry returned home. I read *A Man With A Maid* in secret, though it only added fuel to the fire within.

I had never been so miserable in my life, but it didn't occur to me to go home to Memphis. I just stayed in Jacksonville and waited. It seemed clear that to be a successful Navy wife, I needed a certain philosophic turn of mind. I didn't have it. Who could be a philosopher at twenty-one? Not me. A life's philosophy needs time to age, assimilate, agitate, ferment, and percolate. That would take me until at least age forty, maybe even fifty.

It seemed a good time to hone my body. The girls on the beach were wearing skimpier clothes. I wanted to get rid of my round, soft, baby tummy that Mother had said would go away when I grew up, but didn't. I lifted weights, jogged. I took a 'lifetime membership' in a health club (of all the dumb things). I had never looked better in my life. My beautiful clothes fitted like a dream. Gazing in the mirror, I pronounced myself to be gorgeous—gorgeous, and twenty-one. But, so what? Gorgeous, twenty-one and alone. *Sigh.* Solitude was for nuns.

Chapter Thirteen: *On the Beach*

Sherry didn't help; she was always out on dates. 'What about John?' I asked her.

'Oh,' she said, 'he's on duty in Spain right now.'

'Spain?!'

'Yes. Rota, Spain. The USS Canopus AS-34, a submarine tender. John wants to be a Navy Seal. He's like a fish in the water. (He's pretty slippery out of it, too.) We will get married next summer, probably in June. John has promised to bring me some Spanish lace for my veil.' Her eyes shone.

That shut me up. Her life was already well planned. (She would use her beauty to get whatever she wanted. In fact, that strategy never failed her until she began to age. And by the time her looks were fading, Sherry was so convinced that she was beautiful, she wouldn't believe it that she wasn't, though the evidence was all around her, in her crumbling life.)

'What a waste,' was all I could say to my perfect reflection in the cheval glass. Somehow, I hadn't planned things properly. Time had gone by, and I had found out that officers' wives usually met their young husbands in college. 'What a bummer!' I said. 'Missed that boat. Why didn't somebody tell me *long* ago the facts of life?'

It's a good thing nobody told me 1967 was supposedly the 'Summer of Love.' I couldn't possibly have appreciated it. I had only contempt for the hippies and their bohemian ways; however, I adored the music from *Hair, the American Tribal Love-Rock Musical,* and was longing to see it off-Broadway, in New York. When I did finally see it, a year or so later, I had a few shocks. It didn't seem that I would ever get used to looking at nude bodies. I was such a prude! But prude only means prudent, doesn't it?

I spent my time alone trying to get control of my emotions, attempting to come to terms with my situation, telling myself how lucky I was that I did not have to live at home in Memphis any more. 'Home,' of course, wasn't as bad as what Anne, Jennifer, and Neely had had to suffer in Jacqueline Susann's novel, *The Valley of the Dolls;* but I needed, as they did, worse than the sky needed the sun, worse than the beach needed the sea, someone to love me.

As my head hit the pillow at night, Paul Anka, that darling boy, sang to me alone from somewhere deep in the heart of the clock radio:

> *Someone, yes, someone to love,*
> *Someone to kiss, someone to hold*
> *At a moment like this.*
> *I prayed so hard to the heavens above*
> *That I might find someone to love.* [104]

'Nighty-night, Sherry,' I whispered.

'G'night, big sister,' she said.

Then we repeated in unison, 'Don't let the bedbugs bite.' It was tradition.

Sherry chuckled. She was home with me for once, but tomorrow, she would leave for Memphis. That 'old gray dog,' the Greyhound bus, was going to sling her out of Florida one more time.

October came. The squadron steamed into port. It was the most thrilling experience of my life when I stood on the Mayport Destroyer Piers, and watched my ship sail in over the horizon and into the bay. The squadron had returned home. To think! Here they were, after so long. They did exist after all.

It would not be an exaggeration to say that I was delirious with happiness. I jumped up and down, and clapped my hands, and laughed so much that the other women must have thought I was loony; and I was! It's the world's wonder that I didn't fall off the pier into the Atlantic green froth, foam, flotsam, and jetsam.

All hands were on deck, standing in stiff rows. They were dressed in their white summer uniforms, with 'Dixie-Cup' hats jaunty at just the right angle. I was not the only happy wife on

---

[104] 'Lonely Boy,' words and music by Paul Anka and Joe Dowell, recorded 1959.

Chapter Thirteen: *On the Beach*

that October day. It was magnificent to see the proud United States Navy come sailing, in their glory, to their homeport. Hurrah! Rah! Rah! Rah!

They disembarked. In their summer uniforms, sailors had a kind of flirtatious, reckless look that other uniformed men did not have. They were irresistible. I was wearing such a wonderful navy blue knit suit, with a low-waisted, box-pleat skirt, that I actually got compliments from those shrews who had shunned me before. I tossed my head and turned my attention to my loved one. He resembled a Nordic god, his eyes blazing like a torch, his blond hair shining like the sun on spring day in Scandinavia. We were a fetching couple, a dynamic duo, and he was my better half.

I brought Terry home, for the first time to our *own* home, and the two of us spent hours sitting on our bed telling each other about the months we had spent apart. We did not make love; we were too excited for that.

I was lost in the wonder of it all, and to do anything other than gaze into the eyes of my beloved, feel his presence, inhale his scent, was quite unnecessary and beside the point. I was in paradise just having him in near proximity.

'Shall I unpack now?' Terry broke the spell.

I clapped my hands. 'Yes, please.'

He had exquisite taste, and his presents were always the best he could afford. He brought home wonderful, exotic things—a hand-carved camphorwood chest, bronze figures, temple bells, Chinese lamps, a full stereo system with enormous tape deck and the latest in stereophonic record players.

That late October was better than Christmas had ever been. There were gifts for his mother and my mother. There was jewelry—I remember a string of black pearls from Tonga. There were Japanese tea sets, carved figures from Bali, incense and peppermint—magical, mystical things: even a silk kimono.

I was impressed. This was 'bounty.'

'I love you,' he said, and I knew he meant it. I would have thrown myself on him like a tigress, but the moment was too holy, too precious. Those days with him were golden days. I

A Quiet Life in Bedlam

didn't have so many of them as you might think—the Golden Days. Even though the ships of the squadron were in their homeport, they were still on full alert, and Terry had to stand duty every second night, it was called 'Blue and Gold duty'; then he was away for twenty-four hours at a time.

In addition to the 'losses' I suffered through Blue and Gold Duty, the Bigelow was steaming in and out on operations weekly. Really, that ship was more out than it was in. I couldn't take a lie detector test and say that we lived together—we didn't. Terry lived on the ship, and I lived at the apartment. It was not the way I had expected life to be.

Once, when Terry was out at sea, I went to see an astrologer. I needed to know the future, and asked to have my horoscope done. She said, 'You will likely spend your life in institutions.' I did not understand that at all. What did she mean, 'institutions'? Like the madhouse, or a prison, or a hospital? I was confused and upset.

'Why do you say that, miss, that I will spend my life in institutions?'

'Your sun, in Taurus, lies in the Twelfth House.'

'The twelfth house?'

'Yes, the Twelfth House is the House of Secrets, Dreams, and Self-Undoing. It is also the house of institutions, the subconscious mind, secret fears, the past, solitude, confinement, secret enemies, and those who wish to harm you or work against you.

'But with the Sun in the Twelfth House, and also Mercury in conjunction, you will probably realize your dreams through institutions, and win more friends than you will lose. But beware of secret love affairs.'

'Secret love affairs?' *You can't mean it,* I thought. *I'm all done with that illegal stuff.* 'What a puzzlement.' When she saw the question in my eyes, the astrologer said, 'A sudden separation may work to your advantage, because you will have some exciting events ...'

'Don't talk about separations,' I interrupted her. That subject was anathema.

Chapter Thirteen: *On the Beach*

'You will always attract love to you, though,' the gypsy continued, 'and if you are alone, it will be because you want to be.'

What?! Alone. 'That is the very last thing I want to be.' Crikey, one conundrum after another. This Age of Aquarius with its constant 'enlightenment' and chopping and changing, would not let a body be. 'That's enough for today,' I said as politely as I could. I wanted to get out of there.

'And you will have one very true and rewarding relationship.' That was the astrologer's last word on the subject.

Well, that was something. The marriage to Terry was surely *it*. The One.

The whole encounter was upsetting to me, and I felt threatened by her predictions. I said to her, 'Why do you do this, practice fortune telling?'

'It is a way to serve,' she said.

I wondered about those words for a long time, 'It is a way to serve.' *Hmmm.*

I took my leave of the astrologer, and seizing the day, I asked the telephone business office for a leave of absence. I wanted to be with Terry every available moment. Who knew what the future would bring? 'Take your happiness while you can,' I told myself. 'Tomorrow may never come.' I was beginning to discover that I was a fatalist. Could people who were religious be fatalists, too?

I had begun taking contraceptive pills in September on the off-chance …

Because I really thought …

Alas, there were few 'chances.' I was more thwarted than I had ever been.

Terry and I decided to take a better apartment, and a bigger one became available nearby. This time, it was an upstairs apartment with a large sun terrace. The apartment had lately been quitted by an Officer's wife; it must be a plum. It had two bedrooms, and was carpeted wall to wall. There was a strip kitchen, and a Florida room. I moved us in there while Terry stood duty. It was in that apartment that Terry taught me how to cook.

I began growing roses on my sun porch, planting them in great tubs of earth, without any water drainage holes. Well, no one had told me the water had to drain out. I was really surprised when those roses mildewed and died.

In December, Terry got leave, and we knew it was our duty to visit the family. I wasn't looking forward to seeing my parents-in-law again, but I could face up to it. Terry would be at my side.

Within a few days of Terry's getting leave of absence, we left for Memphis. We would spend Christmas there, and celebrate our first wedding anniversary. Imagine, that out of a year, we had lived together only about two months. I was not the sort of woman, however, 'that thought the United States Government was offering her a personal affront each time her husband had to stay aboard ship overnight for duty.' [105] No.

At least at the beginning, I had that necessary spark of adventure in my soul; so if I had wanted to do it, I could have made my life attached to the Navy, into something exotic and delightful, developing a serious case of 'Channel Fever,' accepting the advantages and disadvantages, the good with the bad.

But it could not be. I was already well on the way to becoming neurotic.

---

[105] *Welcome Aboard,* Frances Ridgely Johnson, p. viii, preface.

CHAPTER FOURTEEN:
He's Not There

On our trip north for Christmas vacation, we stopped in at the farm of my uncle and aunt in Georgia, and left them my little dog, Pretzel. He was just too destructive, and I couldn't handle the grief I felt over the loss of shoes and records and books. I didn't ask my aunt and uncle if they would take the dog—I just assumed they would because they had a farm.

It took me long years to realize how callous and selfish I was, leaving another hungry mouth in their barnyard. About ten years later, I remembered to ask my aunt, 'What happened to the dog?' and she said, 'He run off.' 'Oh,' was all I could say.

Alas, the domestic situation at my parents' house in Memphis was more dreadful than before, if that was possible; or maybe I had just forgotten the intensity of the strife, the resultant disharmony among my brothers and sisters, and the hopelessness I felt when I speculated whether any marriage could be truly happy. Christmas was worse than I could ever imagine it could be. Ours was not a pleasant visit.

Our wedding anniversary dinner was an unmitigated disaster; Daddy's mean drunkenness was nearly unbearable. Mother did the best she could to shield us from the worst of it. She gave me a wonderful present of a cream-colored silk party blouse that was covered in hand-sewn pearl sequins. I had lost so much weight that the blouse hung on me; but I remember that blouse and the one time I wore it, because I have a photograph of Terry and me dancing together, and I am kissing him passionately.

In the picture, my hair is short and curly—gosh, I didn't remember that! What happened? Oh, yes. Now, I know. To save money, I had put a home permanent in my hair. But I took so long over the processing, that my hair burned up.

'Eeek, a freak from Battle Creek!' I cried: that bit of childhood doggerel came to mind. I made a beeline to the beautician to get the frizzy hair cut off. I wasn't happy about cutting my hair, but what else could I do? Otherwise it was life to the tune of *The Monster Mash:*

> *I was working in the lab late one night*
> *When my eyes beheld an eerie sight*
> *For my monster from his slab began to rise*
> *And suddenly to my surprise*
> *He did the mash*
> *He did the monster mash*
> *It was a graveyard smash.* [106]

In days gone by, I had had a phobia about cutting my hair. The reason was that my mother insisted on cutting it, against my will, over and over; and on occasions, she tied me to the chair while I screamed bloody murder. She cut my hair off and administered a permanent wave, whether I liked it or not. I was disempowered. It was like Samson and Delilah, and I wasn't Delilah.

For weeks afterwards, I would moan, 'Ruined, ruined,' each time I caught my reflection in the mirror. Cutting my hair became an experience of trauma, and I would not do it unless forced.

---

[106] Lyrics from, 'The Monster Mash', 1962 novelty song by Bobby 'Boris' Pickett and the Crypt Kickers.

Chapter Fourteen: *He's Not There*

Terry had a big surprise when he saw me with that short, dark, curly hair as I came aboard the Bigelow to fetch him for his leave of absence. But he liked it. Never hard to please, Terry liked everything. Then I felt better about it, too.

To see the effect, I tried setting my wiglet on top of my short hairdo, but it looked as if I had an elaborate bird's nest on my head.

It caught on in a flash
It was the monster mash ... [107]

I gave my wiglet away to a friend who needed it more than I did.

Terry did not make love to me after the anniversary party, or at any time during our stay in Memphis. We slept at Annabelle's house: she and Ralph had many times regretted the sentimental reasons that caused them to buy a home right next door to Mother and Daddy. Eventually, Annabelle and her family had to flee in the middle of the night—I kid you not—to Ralph's folks in New Hampshire, from the frying pan into the fire, in my opinion (Ralph's mother was a tartar), because of my parents' problems threatening to overwhelm them.

Talk about troubled spirits—Annabelle and Ralph's house was haunted. Yes, indeedy. If I had ever doubted the existence of the supernatural, I received a hair-raising confirmation. I got a visit from a ghost; it raised the hackles on my neck.

True to the cliché, the air turned suddenly cold as I was sitting up in bed reading. I had a lot of restless energy because Terry didn't want to make love. 'I'm not in the mood,' he said. 'It's a strange house, with thin walls, and someone might hear us.' Well, they would certainly hear me, if Terry ever dared to put the hand of desire on my body.

I could understand his anxiety, in a way. My father, who made free with both houses, had a habit of staggering in and

---

[107] Ibid.

out of the bedrooms at will; there were no locks on the doors. He smelled liked a distillery.

Daddy would say, 'Well, hell, Kate, I only got out with my scalp, anyway.' He was still 'on' about the war. 'We've already finished that discussion, Daddy,' I said, and he went away.

During that holiday visit, Terry did have good reasons for his abstinence, but eventually, his reasons ran out. In retrospect, it is shocking to think I could have loved him so much, and then in the end, did not love him at all. Not one iota. Not one jot.

So, it was one o'clock in the morning, and I was reading. Terry was asleep. Our bed was situated so that, as I sat there propped up against the post, I could look down the corridor of the bedroom wing of the house. Annabelle had not mentioned the ghost, though she knew of it very well. She was always the first one to notice supernatural goings-on.

As I looked, a light that flickered like a candle-flame began moving down the hall from Annabelle's bedroom. The light stopped at my door, which stood open. It flickered there for a full five minutes while I sat in bed, stupefied, wondering if I were dreaming.

The light flickered out for a second then moved along the hall towards the living area. The light was about five feet off the floor—a short ghost.

Then, there was this appalling banging coming from the dining room. It was a small house, and any noise carried. Everyone jumped out of bed, and ran into the living room to see what was going on. We wondered if Daddy was making a ruckus.

On the scene, it appeared that all the table linen had been pulled out of the buffet drawers. The silver plate had been knocked off the top of the buffet where it had reposed in the dust for many months. (Annabelle was not a good housekeeper.) But most surprising of all, there was a glass pane

Chapter Fourteen: *He's Not There*

knocked out of the large mahogany china cabinet. Spooky! It was like being in a scene from *The Amazing Mr. Blunden*.[108]

'Annabelle,' I said, 'I wonder what you have done to attract a poltergeist?'

'Lord only knows. Such things have happened before.'

'Really?!' I was shocked, but I could be stalwart. Big, strong Terry was standing beside me in his shorts. He was fully alert, ready to douse the fire or do whatever else was necessary. If nothing else, he could hold my hand.

'I think,' Annabelle said to us, 'that I am over-sensitive, perhaps what they call "clairvoyant." And I have had some dreams that seem to be about past lives …'

Really! 'You're not the lone ranger,' I said. 'I'll have to tell you sometime, about mine …'

Annabelle would not let me finish. 'One of my dreams was so awful! It seemed to be a memory of how I died, when shipped to America as a slave or an indentured servant. I was in the hold of a ship, manacled to the bulkhead. I was shackled together with other people. I was so afraid. Some of them died, and the bodies were taken away periodically. We didn't get enough water, or enough food …' Annabelle looked as if she would cry.

'Weird!' I interrupted her. 'That's worse than any dream I've had.'

'It upset me. It goes against everything we were taught in Christianity, only one life, and heaven, and …'

'Gee, I'm sorry I interrupted you,' I said. 'Tell me more! I'm really interested.' The concept of 'past lives' was something I knew I should not investigate, but was compelled to, somehow.

'Another time, please,' Annabelle answered. 'I need to get this mess cleared up first. The children …'

'Of course.' I was disappointed, but there was a danger to the babies with all that broken glass laying around. Ralph was

---

[108] *The Amazing Mr. Blunden,* popular British film from 1972, taken from Antonia Barber's novel, *The Ghosts.*

standing duty at the fire department, so he was not on hand to help. We wished he were. With his fiery, energetic, no-nonsense nature, he would have had everything back in order in a jiffy. The only risk with Ralph, was that he wouldn't believe in the ghost, and would say, 'All of you have gone bananas.'

Yes, we have no bananas ...

The morning came, and over a late breakfast, Annabelle related what to her, was the most horrifying incident that had occurred in the house. There was no more time for 'past lives' that day—we had *a whole lotta shakin' goin' on* in the lives we were living. And that was, supposedly, the reason why people did not regularly remember their past lives: it would only be confusing and frightening, and distract the reincarnated soul from the present life's lessons and issues, to know about 'the past' and possibly get bogged down in it.

Recalling past lives would not help anyone live a better life, except in certain instances, where a lesson well learned need not be repeated. Indeed, it might hinder to remember a past life in a case where someone had been important, or of high status, in the past, but was no longer that, in the present lifetime. There would be unwarranted pride and vanity to overcome; troubles upon troubles, trials and tribulations.

'It was on an ordinary day in broad daylight,' Annabelle related. 'I was standing at the kitchen sink, washing dishes. I have a sensitive nose, and suddenly became aware of the scent of cheap perfume in the kitchen. I looked around to see if one of the kids had gotten into something, but nothing was out of place. I went back to washing dishes.'

I shuddered involuntarily. 'Go on,' I said.

'Presently, I had the distinct feeling that someone was standing at my elbow.'

I gasped. I didn't like the idea of body-less spirits gliding around. Could it be true?

'Looking down at myself,' Annabelle continued, 'I observed involuntary goose flesh rising on my arm. I said, "Who is it?" No reply. And again, "Who's there?" Still no answer.

Chapter Fourteen: *He's Not There*

But I was sure there was someone. The smell of perfume had not gone away.'

I was thunderstruck. It was the first time I had heard of such sensitivity in our family. 'Most unusual,' I said, and began to think furiously. I did not want the same 'gift,' the Sixth Sense—no, no, not at all. And I really did not want to know that there were apparitions that walked in ordinary houses. One would expect such phenomena in, say, the North of England, or, in the *House Of The Seven Gables,* but not in Tennessee at the corner of Radford Road and Walthal Circle, in the little house that had been lately occupied by the kindly Mr. and Mrs. Webb; and Mr. Webb was a Mason! It didn't figure. How had he left a ghost behind?

The climax of Annabelle's story had not been reached, however: Annabelle, her composure stretched very thin, continued washing the dishes. Something soft bumped into her. Shocked, Annabelle stood her ground. The thing bumped her again. Annie fled out the back door of her house, and ran lickety-split to Mother's house next door, where her two small children were visiting their grandmother.

'I did not return home until Ralph came back from work later in the day,' she finished.

'Who can blame you? I wouldn't have come back at all.'

That did it. I could not *wait* to get out of that house! My imagination ran wild. I expected a spectre to appear before me at any moment (and not the James Bond kind), and ghostly voices to address me. I could not bear the thought of preternatural forces around me. My blood turned cold. It was like being electrocuted again. I wasn't having any part of this extrasensory thing. Terry and I left Annabelle's house on January 3, 1968, and never visited her again until she and Ralph had been living for some time in Laconia, New Hampshire, near Ralph's parents.

I remember nothing about our further visit, to Mr. and Mrs. Muszyka's home in Michigan, except that Terry gave his mother a Japanese tea set that I wanted very much. Our Christmas vacation had been dominated by the incidents in

A Quiet Life in Bedlam

Memphis, and the visit to Mr. and Mrs. Muszyka eclipsed by Annabelle's ghosts.

My sister and her husband left their home in Memphis by a pre-arranged secret plan that was made with great ingenuity, not to escape the ghosts, but to escape Mother and Daddy (especially Daddy) who would certainly have laid a heavy 'guilt and duty' trip on them. Daddy was by that time like a weight carried around on Annabelle's young back, and Mother was pathetic in her need for help in her terrible troubles. She lived only a few more years after Annabelle, Ralph, and their children were gone. Mother never saw her grandchildren again.

By the time Terry and I returned to Jacksonville after our 'holiday,' I was very preoccupied with feelings of sexual frustration. It hurt, it really hurt me each time I turned to him for lovemaking, and he turned away. After a while, I was too humiliated to make any more advances to him, or to try to get him to read more of the chapters from the marriage manual I had bought.

Sometimes, in sheer disgust, I made up the extra bed in the spare bedroom to sleep in, in token of my feelings of rejection and physical separation from my husband. It was probably the worst thing that could have happened to me in my own marriage, other than physical cruelty like beating, for example.

Terry actually seemed relieved on the nights I chose to sleep in the spare room; apparently, he had never, in all his life, known his own parents to sleep in the same room, in the same bed. Mrs. Muszyka's little cot had been hidden from us when we visited there. I was bewildered by the whole situation. Why did this have to happen to me?

It seemed that Terry and I did not have much of an opportunity to work out our problems; we saw very little of each other. I don't believe he knew we had a problem. The 'full alert' situation with the military at Mayport continued throughout the winter on the Bigelow and the other ships of the squadron. They left on maneuvers almost every day.

1968 was the year of the heaviest fighting in Indochina—the peak of the Vietnam conflict (which eventually included

Chapter Fourteen: *He's Not There*

Cambodia and Laos), with the Tet Offensive beginning in January, to everyone's shock and dismay. It was easy to wonder if Terry's squadron was practicing for another stint in some war-torn area. Who knew? The 'blue and gold' duty shifts held, day in and day out, as before. I hardly felt like a wife at all. I had been warned, by that awesome book *Welcome Aboard*, 'Keep your complaints to yourself.' So I knew the score.

Florence Ridgely Johnson, an Officer's Lady, the author of *Welcome Aboard*, must have been a trooper and a brilliant woman—she wrote a service manual that is must reading for every Navy wife, no matter what their station (in life). She covered every contingency: 'Traveling with Children,' 'What Furniture Should I Take,' 'If My Husband Is Missing or a Prisoner of War,' 'In Accident or Emergency,' 'Naval Social Usage,' 'How to Enjoy Your Husband's Sea Duty,' etc. etc. etc. For comfort, information, reassurance, or if I needed to scream, I consulted Florence's well-thumbed pages many times. She said, 'You share, equally with your husband, the responsibility to the Navy. This means accepting the bad with the good, without criticism or complaint, and doing the best you can ...' [109] Oh, God.

'Okay, I can hack it for now,' I confirmed to the ethers; and I said the same thing to Terry when he was at home.

When Terry was off duty, we sang together in the Jacksonville Beach Community Chorus, and made some non-Navy friends. Those new friends were lovely; I didn't have to be conscious of rank. They happened to be 'telephone company,' so it was still 'all in the family.' They were 'older' people—around forty; and I found out I got along very well with older people as long as they weren't Mother and Daddy.

We had traded in the Buick, and bought a Volkswagen Beetle, a car I never expected to have in my life. I felt like Tinker Bell driving around in a flower pod! It took some time to learn to maneuver the darn thing—the feel of the Beetle was

---

[109] *Welcome Aboard*, p. 251.

A Quiet Life in Bedlam

other-worldly, compared to the Buick—but it was very practical, and good on gas. That blue Volkswagen Beetle was the first 'new' car I ever had.

The Bug was a manual shift car; I had never driven one of those. I was bothered, boggled, bogged down and bewildered by the manual transmission. At eighteen, I had failed my driving test on a manual car, and only passed when trying again in an automatic. I said to Terry, 'Manual, you must be kidding!' But he would have it that way. It could be that Volkswagen did not manufacture an automatic transmission 1968, I can't remember.

Anyway, the high seatbacks in the new VW were another problem for me. I am short waisted; and though tall, when sitting down in a car seat, my long legs don't come into the equation, as regards the height of the driver's torso. If you, for example, looked in through the dashboard window, you would probably see just the top of my head, and my eyes, but little more. In this new '68 model VW, as a safety factor the head rests were contoured into the top of the seat, so there was no break; the result was a broad head rest so comprehensive that a small person couldn't see over or around it when trying to change lanes. The driver's vision was about as good as if he had three heads and no neck.

I ended up having two mishaps (or, we could call them 'accidents') in the VW Beetle. I quickly came to hate that car. I hated it even worse when, one time while Terry was at sea, I changed lanes downtown in Jacksonville, and lo and behold, the lady behind me changed lanes too, resulting in a little fender-bender where her headlight was broken, but there was no damage to my car, thankfully. Because I felt so inadequate in the VW, I jumped out of my car and said to the lady driver, 'Oh, I'm sorry; it must have been my fault.' Well, I was only twenty-two. I didn't know you shouldn't say such things. I fell into a trap.

She nailed me to the wall. Nearly a year later, I was notified by letter from a lawyer that the lady was suing me for $20,000, because I had caused her to have a nervous break-

Chapter Fourteen: *He's Not There*

down! So she claimed, due to my carelessness in changing lanes and crushing her headlight.

It was a lesson in physics, two objects not being able to occupy the same space at the same time. In 1968, $20,000 was a *huge* fortune. I had never been so shocked in my life. Where was I going to get $20,000? Could I sell my soul to the Devil? I knew she was just taking advantage of the situation, taking advantage of me, but what could I do? The travesty of justice happened right about the beginning of the half-century trend that followed, where so many Americans became 'victims,' and sued others for perceived wrongs, asking whatever they thought they could get, in money and property, and in karma that they will surely have to pay, in the fullness of time.

In early 1968, *I* was the real victim. I nearly had a nervous breakdown myself. It was terrible to think of the injustice of it all. It made me doubt the essential goodness of mankind. When Terry came home, he put the situation into perspective for me, spoke with our insurance company, found a lawyer, and helped me with the court case. The lawsuit was settled out of court, with the neurotic woman receiving her filthy lucre ($20,000) from my insurance company. Sometimes if I drink a lot, I can forget about it.

When Terry was at home, life was gay; we laughed, we played like children, we listened to lots of wonderful music. Propped up on bolsters at opposite ends of the sofa, toes entwined, we listened to the insistent rhythms of 'She's Not There,' [110] as the Zombies sang:

Please don't bother tryin' to find her
She's not there.
Well let me tell you 'bout the way she looked
The way she'd act, and the color of her hair
Her voice was soft and cool,
Her eyes were clear and bright,
But she's not there.

---

[110] *She's Not There*, the Zombies, (Rod Argent) 1964.

A Quiet Life in Bedlam

The music was pumpin'. I could just picture the Zombies in their tight pants—I'd seen them perform on *Hullabaloo* in 1965. The Zombies were Englishness in all its glory, with their peg-legs, winklepickers, neat round collars, clipped vowels, dropped 'r's,' and clean, pale faces. I loved it.

On long winter evenings, Terry taught me how to play chess. He taught me how to cook. He surprised me with his expertise at both.

One day he said, 'Shall I show you how to make Swedish pancakes?'

'Ja, visst!' said I.

The pancakes were yummy, and quite different from the ones my mother made. Terry's pancakes were lighter, flatter, broader, and had more eggs in them.

When I was washing up the dishes afterwards, Terry said, 'You need a Polish carpet.'

'A what?'

'A Polish carpet. That means, some newspaper under your feet. The floor's getting wet.'

'What we need is a dishwasher,' I retorted. That was the new American gadget.

'Fat chance,' Terry responded. 'You're in the Navy now.'

And so I was; 'Ja visst,' I said.

Actually, I was delighted with the new vocabulary I was learning from Terry. One's existence can be dull without words and expressions like: bogie, boot, bow, brass-hat, brig, bulkhead, chit, 'cut of his jib,' ditty box, galley and gangway, to name a few. Terry used Polish and Swedish words too, due to his heritage. For example, when we went out into the winter wind, he suggested, 'You should wear a *babushka*.'

'Does *babushka* have anything to do with *baboon*?' I teased him. 'What about *babble*? Bubble?' Bother.

I believe Terry liked to swagger a bit with his foreign words.

He taught me many useful things, like how to treat fungus between the toes (athlete's foot), how to make a necklace out

Chapter Fourteen: *He's Not There*

of my sharks' teeth collection; how to dry my back with a terrycloth towel by flinging the towel around me like a cape and then, towel to back, rubbing myself like a bear against a tree. The 'toweling' movement was executed something like, doing the Twist.

I still dry my back that way. And I often think of him.

In further lessons of practicality, Terry taught me how to wrap a long electrical cord around my forearm and upper arm in a neat loop before putting it away; he taught me how to change a fuse in the fuse box. 'Magic! Lights, action, camera!' he said, as the darkened house began to blaze with light.

'Most useful,' I nodded sagely.

He taught me how to move our special chandelier from house to house, by doing the rewiring myself. He taught me how to use a screwdriver in ways I never thought possible (and some of them were made of orange juice).

Yes, bless his heart, he taught me how to cook, but I already had a good instinct for cooking. I liked the color, the texture, the smell, the taste of food well prepared. Both my mother and my grandmother had been excellent cooks. Terry and I loved good food, and we spent some happy hours preparing meals and consuming them, together with a bottle of Chianti wine. Then we used the Chianti wine bottles as candlesticks, and I was so unsophisticated as to think my new candlesticks were stylish.

Terry bought me a washing machine, my very first, and had it installed in a shed outside the apartment. I have never had a better gift to this day, though I remember well when my second husband (more fool him) laughed in derision at the suggestion that a washing machine could make a good anniversary present.

Terry taught me how to launder, starch, and press his summer uniforms. That was a process! Luckily, spray starch had been introduced onto the commercial market, so the work proved not to be as onerous as it might have been. I had to beware of scorching, however. Both of us were glad when it was time for the winter 'blues' to be donned near Christmas-time, but in Florida, winter lasted an extremely short season. The whites were in use during most months of the year, and there was little relief from starching and scorching until the Navy allowed the white uniforms to be made from a sort of synthetic fabric—it may have been Dacron or some other early polyester material.

And Terry told me (the dear), that it was *not* morally reprehensible to use Bactine on minor wounds and scratches!—instead of isopropyl alcohol and mercurochrome, as my mother and grandmother would have it; and that it really wasn't necessary for scratched children (or anyone else) to suffer the sting of antiseptic. I had a hard time getting used to that idea. My mother had said, 'The suffering is to remind you not to do it again.'

Ja, vel. Yes, Mother. 'I suppose your teachings will continue to control me until I die.' After some years, I went back to using isopropyl alcohol and iodine on my cuts and scratches, which I had in plenty, because of my rose garden. One can only assume that I like to suffer. Else, I wouldn't grow roses.

While I had the extra time away from my job, I took some classes at the university. I was (sort of) working towards an associate's degree. But it didn't occur to me that someday, some way, I would really do it. I had begun to believe my mother's teaching that pretty girls did not need a college education. It was a relief in a way, not to think of studying—it was such a lot of work to write term papers, take examinations, etc. Why bother? That said, I will always be grateful to the teacher in Jacksonville (a man) who taught me how to type and take dictation. He was an old fussbudget though, an old maid in pants.

During that winter of 1967–1968, I still felt keenly the miracle of finding a husband, marrying, and beginning in earnest my adult life; and on nights when he was at home, I lay very still, listening to the sound of his breathing and feeling his male presence, the warmth and companionship of his body. The beating of his regular heart was somehow a safe and reas-

Chapter Fourteen: *He's Not There*

suring accompaniment to the wuthering of the wind and the roar of the sea.

It was announced in late February of 1968 that the ship would leave for maneuvers in the Mediterranean on Sunday, April 26th, my twenty-second birthday. I became increasingly more nervous and distraught as the fatal day approached. The dread of Terry's departure had its wicked way with me, and I fell to pieces. Oh, I was sick, just *sick.* The psychological pain went out over me physically—I found a lump in my breast that subsequently proved to be benign. 'Think of it, twenty-two and a lump.' I was hysterical.

Terry said, 'Don't take on, so. It's only something physical. We can see it through together.' But I was not comforted. 'You are going away,' I reminded him. But there was nothing he could do about it.

The day Terry left, I could not even pretend to be brave. I'm afraid I caused rather a scene at the docks, and the only time I was able to stop crying for weeks was that same departure day, when I was still numb from the shock. I rushed out to Atlantic Beach, a nice quiet place where I had been thinking of taking a house, and stood there scanning the horizon.

I watched while all my hopes sailed away. The fleet of destroyers and their escorts steamed up the Florida coastline on their way to begin a tour of duty in the warm Mediterranean waters. I could actually see Terry's ship moving away over the horizon from where I stood in the sand, and wished with all my heart that I could give away the next six months of my life, so that it would be about time for him to come home again. Then I would be happy. I watched the sea for so long that my eyes turned sea green.

A trip to the Mediterranean was just what the doctor ordered for war-weary men—it would be a welcome change from the Far East, to which they would undoubtedly sail again one day; and I should have been glad for those officers and men of the U.S.S. Bigelow. Men joined the Navy because they wanted to see the world, and see it, they would. And they would see the sea: *we*

A Quiet Life in Bedlam

saw the Atlantic and the Pacific, but the Pacific isn't terrific, and the Atlantic isn't what it's cracked up to be ...[111]

Many of the wives, especially the officers' wives, had arranged to 'follow' the ship to Europe. What larks! They made a party out of it and went roving around the Mediterranean from one wonderful port to another, hoping to meet up with their husbands. And sometimes, they did. Gibraltar, Monaco, Italy, Greece, Crete, Cyprus, the works.

They, as I, had the choice of following the ship on a limited income, or being separated from our better halves for a very long period. Well, to be separated was what I had come to expect. Did I want to go to Europe? Yes, of course. But how could I? It might have been the moon.

'Water from the moon,'[112] was a trip to Europe on no money. Impossible. Nevertheless, I bought a travel book called *Europe on $5.00 a Day;* and technically speaking, I could have done it (though probably, it would have been 'Europe on $3.00 a day')—but I did not need that kind of uprootedness, that instability, a sort of 'displaced person' syndrome, mobility without a cause, which would certainly have finished my marriage once and for all. How would I resist it when an Italian pinched my bottom?

Terry had said to me, 'It won't be long. I'll be back. I'll send you as much money as I can.' And he did. Poor Terry had to forego a tour to Pompeii, and a trip to Florence with the rest of the crew, because he sent all his money to me, and he had enough small change left only for cigarettes and chewing gum. He was a good man.

I never asked him whether he was still sending an allotment of money to his mother, but he probably was.

I stopped taking my birth control pills. 'What do I need them for?' I asked myself. Those contraceptive pills were wonderful for my complexion though; I never got a single zit or

---

[111] 'We Saw the Sea,' written by Irving Berlin for the 1936 movie, *Follow the Fleet,* with Fred Astaire.

[112] *Water from the moon*, meaning, 'anything impossible'; expression taken from the 13th century Persian poet, Rumi.

Chapter Fourteen: *He's Not There*

or pimple or blackhead while I was using them. They plumped up my breasts a little, too. But everything cost money, and I had to pare down my expenses wherever I could. *Am I being reckless?* I wondered. I should give this matter the consideration it deserved.

'Now, let me think …' I tapped my brain. 'Contraceptives are to stop conception.' That's logical. 'No husband, no conception.' That followed. 'But, what if …' No, there will be no what ifs. 'I will never, ever have an affair.' No, never ever. And that's final.

'The last thing I need is a baby,' I reasoned. 'I can hardly take care of myself.'

All things considered, I could take it for granted that I wouldn't get pregnant. But just in case, I went to the Navy doctor to get fitted for a diaphragm. Think of that. A diaphragm. How very grown-up and sophisticated I had become. 'The next trick is to find out how to insert the darn thing.' The diaphragm proved to be very fiddly.

The Navy doctor said to me, 'You will still need some spermicide. I will give you a prescription.'

'Spermicide?' I didn't like the sound of that. Was it anything to do with regicide, fratricide, insecticide or homicide?

'It's to kill the sperm,' confirmed the doctor.

So, for better or worse, I stopped taking the little round pink pills that popped out daily from a disc. I was firm about the decision: some people were suspicious of the side effects attributed to contraceptive pills, but not me. I dealt in the realm of practical realities.

'The pill' had been very convenient. I learned to manipulate the dosage so that I didn't have any 'period' when Terry was at home. And the contraceptive pills had stopped, seemingly for good, the awful, stabbing pains of the abdominal cramps that I got with each recurrence of the menses—that was nothing short of a miracle. Though the telephone company was full of women, the institution did not have any understanding (or sympathy) for women's problems, and insisted I come to work, even if I were at death's door, which I often was.

A Quiet Life in Bedlam

The leave of absence from Ma Bell had been wonderful; but now that Terry was gone, I wanted to go back to work. I had no use for leisure time. Wouldn't you know it, the telephone company was on strike. On strike! That was bad timing.

I just had to wait, then; wait until: 1) the strike was over. 2) there was an opening for a service representative in either Jacksonville Beach, or Jacksonville. I certainly did not want to drive into Jacksonville, across that high bridge span over the Saint John's River, but I would do whatever I had to do. I needed the money, among other things. Of course I couldn't go to Europe. It was just a dream.

I volunteered to be a strikebreaker and help man the switchboards during the strike. I didn't feel guilty—I did not like the union and their pushy methods.

The strike was over in May, and I was taken on in the Jacksonville business office downtown. I had to pay to park! Raspberries. The city of Jacksonville was a different world altogether from the environment at the lazy, hazy, crazy Jax Beach business office; and I found I had lost my 'cushy billet.' I also lost my identity, because I became just one of a hundred service representatives instead of only six, and we did not get any 'live' customers cruising into the office, barefooted, in baggies—it was just telephone contact with the faceless multitudes.

But I did not regret the leave of absence I took, nor the precious days I spent with Terry. Those few months were my only 'married time' late in 1967, and early in 1968.

My close supervisor at the Jacksonville office, Beverly, was strict, but fair—even humane, and though I seemed to be constantly on the verge of a nervous breakdown, she put up with my nervousness, skittishness, scattiness, jumpiness, crying jags, very well. But things gradually got worse for me.

I had always been able to sleep. In fact, sleep was my greatest escape from everyday life. When problems were overwhelming, I looked forward to the darkness and the balm of sleep. A friend gave me some sleeping pills—they might have been *Seconals*—and then ... ah, sleep. That sense of

Chapter Fourteen: *He's Not There*

weightlessness stole over me, and I surrendered to the darkness. But there were nightmares. I couldn't tolerate that! There was something about the dreams that was too real, something I could not escape from, a danger that terrified me. What was it?

Seconals are barbiturates (so they say), and I felt dreadfully hung over the next morning. I didn't like that fog I was in each day. It felt worse than with an alcohol hangover, and I couldn't eat an onion sandwich as an antidote.

No. I couldn't take those little red capsules. At least I had had a little trial before I asked the doctor for a prescription. No. I had to find another way to sleep. Would cherry brandy work? Everyone kept talking about cherry brandy.

'What I wouldn't give for peace of mind,' I mused. 'That brings the best sleep.' But inner peace eluded me. Someone gave me a small slim volume of Kahlil Gibran's *The Prophet*, and I scoffed it up like a starving man.

The Navy system of medical care was not one that suited me. It was like the 'cattle call,' and we had to wait and wait in lines for everything. Each visit to the clinic brought out a different doctor from his hiding place, one I could not develop any relationship of trust and understanding with, as someone young and unsure needs so much, because it was always some new young doctor who did not specialize in women's illnesses.

I also had the feeling that Navy doctors treated only the symptoms, and not the cause. I did not know whom to turn to for medical help. The first time I got a vaginal infection, I was sure that I had the clap. Stories abounded about what you could pick up from commode seats. My skin in the 'private places' was burning up, and I could hardly walk. No one had ever told me that women could get a rash on their bottom.

I was panic-stricken. In the end, I went to see a private doctor, a specialist, in Jacksonville, and liked his manner very much. He joked with me, treated me like a human being, and put me at my ease in a most delightful way, considering the horror one feels about having to put one's legs up into stirrups, and show one's holy of holies to anyone who may be looking.

After the examination, I dressed, and followed a nurse into the doctor's office. The doctor looked up at me over his reading glasses, and said, 'Yes?' Then, 'Oh, Mrs. Muszyka. I didn't recognize you with your clothes on!'

I giggled. I got medicine for 'my problem,' reassurance that recurrences of *candida albicans* were normal in mature women; and that was that. But you have no idea how much the whole thing scared me. How would I have explained to Terry that I had the clap?

I was still depressed and getting attacks of nerves. It had become more socially acceptable to see a psychiatrist: I simply had to do it. There seemed no other way to cope with the despondency, despair, melancholia, and even paranoia that struck me down time and again. Though in the past I had had my complexes, I always presented a picture of self-confidence and trust in my fellow man. I had never really been afraid, not even when I had reason to be. My mother's fine example of how to be an independent woman had done its work on me.

But now I was terrified of everyone and everything. I wouldn't come out of the house, except to go to work or to the doctor, and my record of showing up at either establishment was not too good. But then, on the other hand, I was so afraid to be at home alone. I jumped with every creak of the house. I was petrified every moment that someone would break in and rape me. Sigmund Freud or any of his disciples would have made short work of that—they could have figured out my ailment in two seconds. Half a second. A nanosecond.

My supervisor at work, Beverly, and my landlady who lived downstairs from me, Mrs. Davis, seemed to be persecuting me. That I was alarmed by the gentle Mrs. Davis, shows how sick I was. She must have been as mellow as the Earth.

Mrs. Davis was about thirty-five, had several small children, and wafted around in the house and garden wearing a full peignoir set, like some ethereal spirit. But she asked too many personal questions that were really none of her business. I took umbrage at her interest in my background. I didn't want to talk about it. I was trying to leave old sorrows behind. And I didn't

Chapter Fourteen: *He's Not There*

want anyone else to snub me because of my association with the Navy. In those days, signs in the neighborhood front yards used to say, 'Sailors and dogs, keep off the grass.'

In June, I moved from my old apartment to escape Mrs. Davis. I was sure she was stealing the *Playboy* magazines from my mailbox. I found a wonderful duplex on Sea Horse Avenue in Atlantic Beach, right where I wanted to be. The house was just one block from the ocean, and had a private path that led down to the eternal sandy beach. My house was located not far from the Mayport Naval Station, and that meant I didn't have to drive like a bat out of hell to get to the base on time when Terry was to be picked up. It was my new goal to stop being late for appointments.

I did face a challenge over furniture—I had so little of my own. The duplex was unfurnished, with hardwood floors. It meant I had to buy some serious pieces, like a sofa, a coffee table, and bedroom furniture. A Turkish carpet would be nice. That would set me back! What could I do for money? I wasn't prepared to sleep on the floor, even to get away from Mrs. Davis.

'Aha,' I said. 'I'll cash in my AT&T stocks.' And that was what I did. Too bad they split only six months later, garnering a fortune for other shareowners, but I had to have the money for furniture when I needed it—and also to pay my psychiatrist. It cost fifty dollars an hour, an exorbitant sum; my telephone company insurance would not pay for it.

In the end, I bought a mahogany buffet that I needed like a hole in the head, a round dining table with captain's chairs, an oak bedroom suite in the Spanish style, a Turkey carpet, a tweed loveseat sofa that did not let down into a bed, and an oak school clock that rang the hours. I was more than satisfied. I had incurred my first 'furniture' debts. There would be more, of course.

I could not escape from my job, alas, but I'm afraid I was something less than a model employee. Some days, just to be able to go to work, I had to see a doctor to get a shot of tran-

A Quiet Life in Bedlam

quilizer in my rump to calm me down enough so that I could sit at my desk all day.

'Why a shot in my bottom?' I asked the doctor. He replied, 'It works faster.'

I was so tense when I got the shot that it could have been a bullet penetrating my skin for all I knew. I always trusted doctors, and never questioned what they were giving me. It may have been Demerol shots I got. Whatever it was, it helped a lot.

The move to a new house in Atlantic Beach was a positive one, if expensive. I got away from all those depressing Navy wives, to a quiet residential neighborhood where I found loyal friends who were very supportive—and they are still my friends to this day, God bless them. We have baked turkey together on Thanksgiving many times, in many different cities.

One of these new neighbors was a Mrs. McDaniel, a divorcée, who lived across the street. This Mrs. McDaniel had a gentleman caller who sometimes stayed the night. I knew it for sure, because his car sat in front of the house all night long, especially on weekends. I was scandalized, because I still didn't know, ignoramus that I was, that it wasn't against the law or a sin against God to take a lover. '*Stupido,*' I can say now and laugh. A few years later, Mrs. McDaniel and her lover married, so then it was all right.

Sherry was always good company, but she had gone home long since, and was merrily planning her wedding. During her engagement, Sherry worked as a secretary for a lawyer in Memphis, and he chased her around the desk a lot, but she made hay out of it, acquiring money and position. Then Sherry gave it all up to marry and move to Spain where her husband, John, was stationed with the Navy.

Sherry's wedding was on June 1. I flew to Memphis, and joined a huge family party, people coming in from all directions, corners, and recesses to see Sherry be married. She was very popular. As I look at my bridesmaid picture from the wedding, I can see that I was stick-thin in my high-waisted green silk column dress; and now that I am remembering it, I wonder how much dextroamphetamines, i.e., diet pills, had to do with

Chapter Fourteen: *He's Not There*

do with my nervous problems. But at the time, no one warned of side effects, and Benzedrine, Dexedrine and their ilk, were the best thing ever to happen to dieters.

I always used to congratulate myself that I did not get hooked on diet pills, and did not suffer some of the health consequences that others did; I never abused them, and used only one per day; but now that I look back and remember what a wreck I was, I wonder ...

The only peculiar thing that happened in connection with Sherry's wedding was, when I was driving home from the Jacksonville airport, late at night, on the expressway leading from town to Jacksonville Beach, some unknown man chased me in his car, and nearly ran me off the road.

I was frightened to death, and had to resolve then and there that I wanted to live and not die in a car crash, as apparently I had the opportunity to do. I kept control of the car, and control of myself, and finally got the bastard off my tail. It was the fastest I had ever driven. I did some running in and out of the little lanes of Neptune Beach, and was amazed at how coolly I handled it. Could I, after all, be a Bond girl?

When I got to my duplex on Sea Horse Avenue in Atlantic Beach, I fell into the bed so exhausted that I slept for once.

CHAPTER FIFTEEN:
Rose Garden

I wanted another dog, so I went down to the dog pound and adopted a beagle puppy. It was so tiny and vulnerable. I had to work long days, so I really should not have taken on the responsibility of an infant, but I had to have something to love. My mother had told me that it was of the utmost importance to worm a puppy right away, that the parasites could be dangerous to humans. So I wormed the little guy that night. When I got up the next morning at six o'clock to prepare for work, the puppy was dead.

'Oh, dear heavenly father,' I moaned, stricken. I had to 're-port out' from work, because I could not pull myself together. It was so terrible. I cried and cried. Why me, Lord?

The earth in my yard was made up of sand and clay. Floridians were suffering from a major drought, and I simply could not dig an adequate hole for a grave. My tears were flowing so fast that the shovel handle was slippery from the run-off. In the end, I gave up and buried the poor mite in the trashcan; but I wrapped him well in a handmade quilt from my grandmother. That was the best I could do for the puppy, other than bless his tiny soul.

I was still taking too many of different kinds of pills, and seeing a psychiatrist, Dr. Cheshire. Yes, Dr. Cheshire's name

Chapter Fifteen: *Rose Garden*

was the same as the famous smiling cat; I smile as I think of it. Dr. Cheshire was a Freudian, and as is their practice, he had me recline full length on his leather sofa for our sessions.

Each time I drove down the boulevard for an appointment with Dr. Cheshire, I was tearful and rebellious about having to go and tell the doctor my problems; but it did me good, and before long, I had at least two of my friends, a man and a woman, going there for therapy, too. Hah. The man friend, whose name was Tom, used to say, 'I'm goin' to see that Cheshire cat today.' The implied humor put a different spin on the whole experience.

Dr. Cheshire was a very interesting man, though I cannot remember much of what he said. Like many Freudians, he let me do the talking.

There I was, lying full-length on the leather sofa, a pillow under my head. The sofa was brown, and well worn, but it had a dignity about it, and was very masculine, as was the doctor himself. I trusted him, and that was a start.

Dr. Cheshire said to me, 'Tell me about your mother.'

I gave him an earful.

'Tell me about your father.'

I gave him another earful.

'Now tell me what is *really* bothering you.'

Only fools and horses lie to their doctors, so I let him have it between the eyes. The admission was one I thought I would never make to a living soul. My pride nearly strangled me to death as I said, 'My husband does not make love to me.'

'No?' He seemed surprised.

'No,' I confirmed. Poor me. Up to my elbows in shit. There I was, a beautiful woman, and what did I have to show for it? (Mama didn't say there'd be days like this.)

'Why not?' asked Dr. Cheshire.

'I don't know,' I answered tearfully. 'Perhaps I am not desirable.'

'I can assure you, you are desirable,' said the perceptive doctor.

Thank you, Lord. Anyway, every woman is the same in the dark, he might have said; I had heard that before.

'Then why?!' I asked him. 'Perhaps I am not loveable.'

'That remains to be seen. Has he some medical problem?'

'I don't think so. He hasn't seen a doctor.'

'Does he want a platonic relationship?'

'Platonic relationship—what's that?'

'That you two should be good friends and live together in marriage, but not engage in sexual relations.'

'Are there relationships like that on the Earth?'

'I assure you, there are. It's perfectly respectable, though not usual.'

'Well, that wasn't what I wanted at all. I thought that every man wanted sex. This whole thing is so bizarre. I am only twenty-two. You have to tell me what is normal, and what isn't. I don't know who to talk to.'

'How old is your husband?'

'Twenty-five.'

'He should be at the height of his prowess ... something is not right, but I couldn't say what it is yet. We'll have to talk about it some more.' He looked at his wristwatch. 'Time's up for today, I'm afraid.'

In a way, I was relieved.

There was a pause while his brows knitted. He was perturbed about something.

'I believe I need to talk to your husband as well.'

'You can't. He's at sea. Won't be back 'til October.'

'The Navy?'

'Yes.'

'Hmmm.'

'But there are more problems.'

He nodded his head. 'I can believe that. I'll see you next Saturday.'

So we came to the end of that first fateful hour, and I paid him the fifty dollars. It seemed a huge sum, but I knew I had to

Chapter Fifteen: *Rose Garden*

have help, or I would end up at the funny farm. *They're coming to take you away, ho ho he he ha ha, to the funny farm ...* [113]

Full of self-pity, I thought, *There isn't even anyone around to commit me, though I am practically barking.*

I suppose Dr. Cheshire himself could have committed me, but he made no move to do so, and he seemed to have every hope that one day I could function as a true wife to my true, functional husband.

In that year of enlightenment, 1968, I hadn't the slightest idea that we had manic-depressives in our family. It was kept a state secret, in much the same way that pregnancy among females (even the legal kind) had been. Or maybe we did not know how to put a name to it. In any case, mental disturbances were shameful, dreadful, not to be spoken of.

I always knew something was wrong with my family, but I thought if I left them, and never went back, their crotchety dispositions would not catch up to me. There was a big discussion in the late 1960s about 'nature' and 'nurture'—it may have been Dr. Spock who started it—and it was generally believed that babies were born a blank sheet, and that nurture was far more important to the eventual development of the child, than nature, or heredity.

It was possible to blame one's parents for everything.

We certainly had alcoholics in the family, and I was the daughter of one. In later years, people came to conclusions about what the children of alcoholics had to cope with in the way of personality defects and character weaknesses, but I knew nothing of that. *Whatever was wrong with me was my own fault*—of that I was sure.

It was rather nice to have that bearded, bespeckled fellow, Dr. Cheshire, absorb all of my problems; and what was best of all, Dr. Cheshire did not censor me. He did not judge me. So refreshing! I had such a fear of being criticized. It seemed as if my whole life had been spent being judged and criticized by

---

[113] 'They're Coming To Take Me Away Ha-Haaa!' By Jerry Samuels, *One-Hit Wonder*, 1966.

A Quiet Life in Bedlam

people who did not use my standards, did not share my values, could not see into my wild and serious heart, did not know *me*.

I began to get my checkered past into perspective, and found out that I had an interest in psychology and the psychological processes. I began to study psychology after checking out a few books from the library. I also liked sociology. It explained a lot of the mysteries concerning humankind.

Next, I was into anthropology. The 'ologies' were fascinating, but anthropology turned my stomach with any in-depth study of it. I did not like to immerse myself in primitive cultures where rats nestled in the rafters and were called 'ancestors,' where children were pot-bellied with indigenous parasites and hunger, where women went about bare-breasted and wearing only thongs, and hunters met visitors with poisonous spears at the ready and green snot hanging a foot from their nostrils. I was no scientist, and eventually took a degree in arts.

In the autumn of 1968, just before Terry came home, I announced to Dr. Cheshire that I had psychoanalyzed myself, and found that I was both likeable *and* lovable! Eureka! It seems I had been in doubt about both qualities, though he never had, whew.

This insight I had, about being *likeable* and *lovable* (tra la), came to me suddenly one day as I sat in the dentist's chair, affected by laughing gas. That was some good stuff, laughing gas (nitrous oxide, used as an anesthetic), and I always wanted it used when I was at the dental clinic—it was the only time I was able to leave my mental processes behind— until the sad day that I threw up my lunch all over the dentist. After that, I had to do like other people, and get needled.

Dr. Cheshire was delighted, of course, that I was *likeable* and *lovable*. I had come far. It appeared, even to myself, that I had made great progress. I was ready to go out and tell the world. But Dr. Cheshire did not agree with me that I was in a position to give up the therapy. 'Things are just getting interesting,' he said.

I smiled.

Chapter Fifteen: *Rose Garden*

'I reckon it will take about two years to induce a cure,' he mentioned absently. He was obviously serious, but then he winked at me. I had to go home and look up that word 'induce' in the dictionary.

It was a fascinating process, being psychoanalysed. I could be as emotional as I liked, express all my inadequacies, get things off my chest that had been sitting there for years, and go through the loops of every conundrum ever produced by my fevered brain. I could relate and discuss my weird dreams. All I had to pay for the privilege was fifty dollars an hour. It was cheap at the price.

Dr. Cheshire discovered, through a graphic dream I had one early morning immediately before my session, that I was terrified of the pain associated with having babies, and then the responsibility that came afterwards. Hmm. Imagine that. Why? I would never have guessed it in a million years. Didn't every woman want to have children?

'Am I normal?' I asked again. I needed a great deal of reassurance.

Dr. Cheshire thought that a session with my husband would be beneficial, when Terry finally came home. I wasn't sure I wanted that. I was afraid I would become hysterical, or that Terry would say I was imagining the whole thing. Perhaps I *was* imagining the whole thing.

I took a parting shot. *'Life is just one damned thing after another, and then you die,'* I quipped, but I was smiling. So was he. Dear Dr. Cheshire.

In fairness to the doctor, I had to admit that I was still suffering from paranoia. At one point during the terrible summer of 1968, I slept with a butcher knife under my pillow, Terry's loaded Luger pistol in the bureau drawer, and empty tin cans strung together on the jalousie windows and on the front door, as a security alarm. Oh, I was a nervous wreck. So I reluctantly agreed to continue the therapy sessions for a while, and did continue until Terry came home.

During the summer of 1968, I knew little of Woodstock— *'An Aquarian Exposition'*—or anything else that could be

A Quiet Life in Bedlam

called happy and carefree, like rock 'n roll music. I probably had never heard of the big names that were legendary to Woodstock, like Janis Joplin, Jimi Hendrix, Joni Mitchell. It was later, much later, that I learned to appreciate them—probably after Janis and Jimi were dead.

There were some lighter moments that year. I joined the Christ Episcopal Church on San Juan Drive in Ponte Vedra Beach because I liked the architecture—the Episcopal Church in Jacksonville Beach was too modern—and there I met the crème de la crème of northeastern Florida society.

The Reverend Mr. Juhan, unfailingly humble, wise and gentle, led his flock of millionaires through the rituals of Episcopalians as if he didn't know what they were and who they were. I was delighted to be around people who oozed such confidence and joy in life—and with good reason. They were loaded. What was even better was that they had the indefinable essence known as 'class.' I was impressed. I knew innately that I could watch them, learn from them how to move, how to walk, how to talk, what to talk about, how to dress, how to hold a fork. In Ponte Vedra Beach, no one thought to ask me if I was connected with the Navy; that was a winning strategy. I was ready to be friends.

One of the parishioners at Christ Episcopal Church was a Mr. Frederick Clarkson. He befriended me at once, and took me home with him on several Sundays for lunch. Before lunch, we were served medium dry sherry by his housekeeper.

Mr. Clarkson must have been around seventy years old—old enough to be my grandfather. I trusted him. He lived in his mansion alone. He was a widower, but he had servants in the house.

Mr. Clarkson's dining room doors opened right onto the magnificent Ponte Vedra Beach; his view of the sea was unimpeded. Mr. Clarkson had beautiful paintings on the walls, and Chippendale furniture. That house was everything I could like in a well-appointed home. There was a marble fireplace. There was a crystal chandelier. Would I ever have such lovely things?

Chapter Fifteen: *Rose Garden*

I enjoyed Mr. Clarkson's attention. He clearly considered me to be attractive. It was my first experience of sherry, and I found that, upon drinking just the one small goblet, I lit up, became animated, talkative, and ever-so-slightly uninhibited, smiling hugely and laughing gaily.

Imagine my surprise when, one Sunday after we had been acquainted about two months, Mr. Clarkson began wanting to touch me. I moved as gracefully as I could out of his reach, but he pursued me. We made a few circuits of the dining table, and then, at my wits' end, I bolted out the French doors and into the deep sand of the beach. Not minding the sandspurs, I kicked off my high-heel shoes and ran for my car while that old satyr chased me. I escaped, and Mr. Clarkson made it up to me later on, when he gave me the money I needed to attend my mother's funeral.

Mother and Daddy picked that summer to visit me. They drove all the way from Memphis to Jacksonville in one long day. It must have been a difficult trip; and they brought my brothers along, too.

My family stayed one night as welcome company, but then Daddy got up to his old tricks, drinking, and abusing us, and Mother. I had run away from that scene of domestic violence, and wouldn't have it following me to my own home. I wasn't going to put up with it. So, at about 10:00 p.m. on a Saturday night, I turned them all out of my house, and left them to drive back to Memphis. It was really Daddy I was talking to when I said in no uncertain terms: 'Get out of my house.'

But of course, Daddy had no other place to stay the night, and Mother always loved him, cared for him, even when he behaved like a beast. So if Daddy was leaving, and he was, then she was leaving, too.

They were traveling with very little money—Daddy had not worked in so long—and they couldn't afford to put up at a hotel. Naturally, Daddy was in no condition to drive. He was drunk as a skunk. My mother, who was weary and sick at heart, drove all night long to get them back to Memphis, and into their own house, where they could at least be unhappy behind closed doors.

My poor brothers: in adulthood, they struggled with emotional problems, serious physical ailments, and their own alcohol abuse. It has wrecked their lives, and has one of them living on the streets in Nashville. I can do little to help them. Alun has lived with me at times, but few can tolerate a chronic alcoholic, one who loses control and blacks out, except perhaps the staff at a private sanitarium.

As regards my behavior towards my mother during her lifetime, this incident of kicking them out of my house at night is the only one I am sorry for. It was not fair. How she must have suffered driving back through the darkness to Memphis! She was never any worse to me, than any other mother was to the young of my generation. Nevertheless, I have not been able to conquer my resentment—I was such a good child. Why couldn't she just love me?

Once, when I was in high school, I said to Mother, 'You owe me …'

She slapped me hard on the face and replied, 'I do not owe you anything.'

And another time, Mother said, half in fun—long before Lynn Anderson made the line famous—*'I beg your pardon, I never promised you a rose garden.'* [114] There is no rebuttal to that. As she pointed out to me occasionally, her life, on a farm in the 1930s and '40s, had been far harder than mine had been.

The summer and autumn of 1968 proved to be an active hurricane season. Several tropical cyclones formed in the Atlantic basin. The initial big blow was Hurricane Abby. In June, we got the news that Hurricane Abby would hit Jacksonville. It was my first experience of a real hurricane, and I was scared to death.

Why, oh, why did Terry have to be gone? The Navy had a lot to answer for! How would I see it through? I did not have

---

[114] '(I Never Promised You A) Rose Garden', written by Joe South, 1970.

Chapter Fifteen: *Rose Garden*

the pioneer spirit—I only wanted to be left in peace without new challenges, protected from anything that would upset my life more than it had been.

Fortunately, Jacksonville was spared the worst of the hurricane. Abby had reduced slightly in force before it passed us by, and we got only the tail winds. That was bad enough however, for a first experience.

I did not want to go to work on the day the storm hit, because I had to drive across that high bridge that spanned the Saint John's River. I knew it would be blowing worse than a gale up there, and I did not want to tackle the steel span in my minuscule VW. But I had no choice. The telephone company demanded (commanded) that we come to work, and said no excuses would be accepted. Telephone 'traffic' was always heavier in bad weather. People who were nervous just had to talk to somebody, Lord.

It is easy to guess what happened to me. My little Bug was nearly blown off the bridge in 75 mile an hour winds. The gusts actually picked my car up, and set it over into the next driving lane. Well, at least the hurricane did not set me into the river! It could have; it's been known to happen. That wouldn't have been a pretty death. I suppose the telephone company would never have known what happened to me.

I got to work alive, shaken but not stirred. Hurricane Abby dumped many inches of rain on Florida, and we needed all of it. There was a considerable lessening of the drought conditions after the hurricane passed by.

Terry's ship arrived home at last, and I was overjoyed as usual. To meet the ship, I wore this wonderful iridescent striped, belted trench coat that had wide lapels. I had very little on underneath it. The trench coat was short, like a miniskirt, and worn with a kind of Mary Jane shoe. I looked like a doll baby in it, but the colors were the most flamboyant I had chosen to date. I felt so beautiful and desirable. I thought I might 'flash' him when we got home. In the event, I didn't have the nerve.

A Quiet Life in Bedlam

Terry liked my fashion sense, and later allowed me to buy civilian clothes for him. I kept him colorful, in silk ties, plaid sport coats, striped pants, pink shirts. He got a paisley print handkerchief for his breast pocket. The way he looked, when decked out, could gladden any woman's heart. There were many who envied me.

Terry was open-minded, tolerant, impartial. He admired equality and originality. He would never knowingly put limits on anyone, least of all me. Any reasonable request of mine was granted. I wanted to see *Barbarella*,[115] even though it got bad reviews. This 'erotic' science fiction film, which was being shown at the theater on the naval station, was known to be naughty, far out, over-the-top, 'camp' to an extreme. It was taking a chance to be seen outside the theater. I donned my sunglasses.

Jane Fonda, in her role as *Barbarella,* a character based on an 'adult' comic strip by Jean-Claude Forest, was so sexy that she caused my eyeballs to fall out of my head, nearly. Breasts and bottom exposed? (So Space Age fashions did allow for breasts!) Striptease, at zero gravity? That was quite a feat.

I don't know how she had the balls to go to Hanoi afterwards.[116]

'Striptease' had always been a dirty word for me; in the 1960s, it was universally accepted that striptease was something tacky, even sleazy. But Jane Fonda, in her ingenuousness, made it into something almost respectable, and very erotic. That one scene made the movie into something worth seeing, as long as it was only the once. Terry seemed to think the film was inventive, original, quite all right in his opinion—could be viewed by consenting adults, and he seemed to understand the jokes.

Barbarella, Queen of the Galaxy (as it was known in Europe), included much sexual innuendo, which mostly went

---

[115] *Barbarella,* 1968 film, directed by Roger Vadim.
[116] Jane Fonda, famously in opposition to the Vietnam War in 1972, made an allegedly treasonable trip to Hanoi in North Vietnam where she denounced the United States for being involved in the extended conflict.

Chapter Fifteen: *Rose Garden*

over my head; and the dialogue was delivered tongue-in-cheek, a dramatic method I didn't really understand. I wondered what was going on about half of the time. I didn't like the film. The French could keep it. It was weird. But Terry and I could be zany and eccentric together, and we just laughed it off afterwards.

Alas, no sooner had Terry's squadron safely returned from the 'Med,' than another hurricane moved in our direction. This time it was Hurricane Gladys, and it was a bugger, causing the most damage of that hurricane season.

The storm reached landfall at Homosassa, Florida, on October 19th, then began its northeasterly drift across the Florida peninsula, heading straight for Jacksonville. The Navy ships sitting in the Mayport basin were ordered to steam out to sea as a safety precaution. Ships and boats sitting in port were vulnerable, having no choice but to take the battering that the storm offered. If the squadron ran for it, out into the Atlantic, beyond reach of the hurricane, it had a much better chance of avoiding a stint in dry docks. Nobody wanted the dry docks. That cost the Navy time and money.

I was highly annoyed when the squadron was suddenly ordered out to sea again. They'd only just gotten back, for Christ's sake. I wanted my husband's loving arms to protect me, I wanted him stay with me, pet me, and keep me from feeling the terror I had felt during the wretched Hurricane Abby, which was a recent memory.

What a bummer that I should be left alone again! This was a real grievance.

And would Terry really be safe, out at sea during a hurricane? It didn't figure somehow. Damn the Navy. It was making my life a misery. 'I swear and declare!' I stomped around.

I had read an advertisement in the newspaper about a litter of dachshund puppies that were available for twenty-five dollars a piece, and decided to get one. Then I could put my attention on the dog, be more concerned about that little red-brown baby than about myself. The puppy was precious, and we sat it out together. The hurricane came in like gangbusters and I listened as the wind tried to blow the house down. The jalousies did blow out; I didn't care. I didn't scream. The cherry brandy was very, very good.

The puppy cried for its mother; I never left him for a moment until Terry came home again. 'There, there,' I said to the little bloke, and stroked him till he was nearly purring. We comforted each other.

When the danger was over, the squadron sailed back into port, and Terry and I tried to get re-acquainted with each other. He brought me *Joy* perfume, and a garnet cluster ring. Married life in the Navy *could* be a constant honeymoon, or a constant trial by torture, depending on which way a body wanted to look at it. I saw only the losses and disadvantages, unfortunately.

When we at last had a chance to talk, I told Terry about the sort of summer I had had, and asked him if he would agree to a few sessions with Dr. Cheshire. But Terry could not agree to see the psychiatrist. With a wrinkle on his brow, he said, 'If the Navy became aware of any such therapy/doctor appointments, it would be entered into my permanent record, and could become a detriment to my career.'

I believe he had already made up his mind, though I didn't know it, to be a 'lifer' in the Navy. Terry had a natural ability to work within well-ordered institutions. And he exuded such a positive, enthusiastic outlook, that no one, least of all a psychiatrist, could come to any conclusions that he shirked any aspect of a normal life at all. Terry seemed to enter into everything headlong. Though he was outwardly calm and off-hand, he had enough vision and energy to conquer unseen worlds. I understand now that he had genius quality, but I didn't see it then.

November came, and Terry and I went to the polls to elect a new president. It was my first chance to vote, as I had not been of age in 1964. President Johnson had decided not to run for a second term, his policies in Vietnam being such a topic for dissent, violence, and division in the nation. Hubert H. Humphrey, Johnson's vice president, was the Democratic nominee.

Chapter Fifteen: *Rose Garden*

Terry and I voted for Richard M. Nixon. To conservative people, as we both essentially were, Hubert H. Humphrey came across as a rabid socialist liberal, and we Tennesseans were having none of it. Michigan went for Humphrey, though.

Terry, my own dear husband, proved to be a 'loose cannon,' politically speaking. He happened to mention that he voted Democratic in 1964, for Lyndon Johnson and Hubert Humphrey. I was shocked at his admission. Could this be the man I married, a 'closet' liberal? We did occasionally disagree on political and social issues, but it was not a great problem. I could live with a Democrat, if that was what he wanted to be.

By the late autumn of 1968, Terry had advanced to the rank of first class petty officer (E-6). My nearest and dearest had *three* chevrons on his sleeve! Glory be! Sailors made rank quickly in wartime. He had been in the Navy for less than five years. That was very quick advancement. He seemed to have a bright future in the Navy—it was as plain as gold buttons on a blue uniform. The higher Terry went, the more money he would make, and we were still living on very little.

I never really understood what work Terry was doing on the ship. It was all 'Greek' to me. With his typical breezy humor, Terry said, 'I'm a sonar technician. I work with "blips"; that's a little joke.'

I beamed at him. Whatever he said was fine with me. But I wanted him to be an officer. It wasn't impossible, but it was unlikely. SONAR was an acronym for 'sound navigation and ranging,' and was used to detect other vessels, most especially submarines. Sonar could also be used for navigation, and to communicate with other ships. It was understandably useful and important during a time of war.

Terry was looking thoughtful. 'As an alternative to a career in the Navy,' he said, 'I could work as a civilian in the field of electronics. It's the coming thing. We only have to move to a place where there is a large Civil Service, and …'

'Electronics? What on Earth does that mean?' Electronics was a discipline I did not understand at all. *Better the devil you know,* I thought. The devil I knew, being the Navy.

A Quiet Life in Bedlam

I never did find out what 'electronics' meant.

So there we were, discussing the possibility of Terry's getting out of the Navy. He was coming to the end of his enlistment, and had to make a decision. Terry had had to enlist for six years to be allowed to take something so specialized as sonar technician training. He had no idea what he might 'strike out' for if he left the Navy at that particular time.

There was a mild recession in 1968, and jobs were scarce. Interest rates were very high. As a Navy couple, we were not too bothered by the national economy, didn't notice the recession much, being as we were, cushioned by Uncle Sam. But the prospect of separation with the service frightened Terry. (And I'll tell you in secret, that it frightened me, too.)

Terry wanted to experience *life*. He dreaded being trapped in an existence where he was limited in any way. He sort of liked tucking me away at home, serenely (as he hoped) keeping house, and waiting for the return of Terrence Muszyka, the conquering hero: with lots of fruit preserves made, and cooked meals prepared, and completed sewing projects to show for my industry. Fat chance of that; I wanted some excitement, too. I would rather work, and pay somebody to do all those boring things.

Terry liked the Navy; he was a disciplined sort of a fellow and felt at ease with the seafaring life. He needed constant challenges and goals to stimulate him. The Navy certainly provided plenty of that. And the plain fact was that Terry was advancing rapidly. In two years, he could possibly become a chief petty officer. *Such echelons of power!* I thought. Oh my. 'Are chiefs' wives treated with respect?' I asked him.

'How should I know? Possibly.' He grinned his toothy, bright, happy-as-a lark grin. He was irresistible. Darling Terry.

My antipathy towards the Navy was as nothing to my fear of being cast economically adrift upon the financial waters, and I accepted it easily when Terry elected to stay in the Navy. We were offered a large reenlistment bonus, about two-thousand dollars. Riches!

Chapter Fifteen: *Rose Garden*

'What shall we do with all the money (supposing we get it)?' I asked him. I didn't think there was that much money in the whole world; I couldn't think of saving it. No. I was ready to spend it all at once.

Terry was prompt with his answer. He had already thought about it. 'Well,' he said, 'why don't we take a driving trip around the U.S.A.? Though we'll have to wait until I reenlist and am allowed to take a month's leave.'

'Sounds divine,' I fluttered, and it was settled, more or less. Still, I had a knot in my stomach. Could I really stand it, to stay in the Navy?

I could accept a vacation traveling around the U.S.A. with Terry, better than I could consider 'taking Europe' by storm, with other Navy wives. Having to fend almost entirely for myself in a foreign country did not appeal to me. There were all those 'furren' languages to worry about, and the foreign currencies to manipulate. I had heard that you could have thousands of Italian *lire* in your billfold, and still have nothing. The only kind of money I understood was green American dollars. And the only foreign language I knew was Latin. How useful would that be?

Terry was due for two years of *shore duty*—he was awaiting orders. We would get to live together in one place for two whole years—but where? That was the question. We could be sent north to Newfoundland, where we would need wool underwear, or south to the bikinis of San Juan, Puerto Rico—from the ridiculous to the sublime, one could say.

We could be sent to the Canal Zone in Panama, or Guantanamo Bay, Cuba. The possibilities were staggering to a little hick like me. Terry somehow was never sent to any place on the West Coast or in the Pacific. Hawaii would have been nice, but nobody suggested that. Drat.

Terry did have something to say about his choice of stations for shore duty, though ultimately, the Navy would decide. He had always wanted to be a teacher, and considered it a positive sign when, in the spring of 1969, the Navy offered him a position as Sonar Instructor at the naval station in Key West, Florida.

Terry wanted to accept the post in Key West; but he waited to get my agreement first. He sent me a wire from the ship, which was on maneuvers somewhere in the Caribbean. A letter followed. It read, 'Accepting the appointment means that I have to re-enlist for six years, according to the Navy rules which govern such things.'

I had mixed emotions about it. I wasn't too sure I wanted to live in Key West. It seemed that life on such a small island would be a boring and confining existence. *There can't be much to do to keep busy,* I thought, *in a place that is only eight miles long and four miles wide.*

Terry wrote: 'We are now at a good liberty port, San Juan. Would you like some maracas?'

Maracas? What on Earth would I do with maracas?

I suspected a place in the sun might lack challenge, and creative and constructive energy. Would I want to sleep all day? I thought Key West might be as boring as life without a husband, though, of course Terry would be there day and night, except when he had twenty-four hours of duty to stand.

A house with a husband in it—just think! I can hack it, I said.

I surmised that Key West as a destination was a heck of a lot better than Guantanamo Bay, Cuba, which was our other real option. At Guantanamo, one would be confined strictly to the Naval Base. Upon reflection, I discovered a morbid fear of being trapped in such a limited space as Guantanamo Bay with those superior, hoity-toity, toffy-nosed officers' wives; therefore, I vetoed *that* suggestion.

Terry didn't take me seriously. He wrote again. 'The advantage of Guantanamo Bay would be, we would save a lot of money, there not being any place to spend it. And with regard to the heat, there is always a sea breeze. There is lots of leisure time, and not much standing of duty.'

Swell. *Save money?* I thought. *Who wants to do that?* You only live twice (once in Tennessee, and once in Florida). The

Chapter Fifteen: *Rose Garden*

heat? What did he mean? Wouldn't we get air conditioning? What about the food? Would it be only black beans, rice, and picadillo? Would I be able to buy American dry goods, make biscuits and cook hominy grits for breakfast? Would there be any Bisquick?

Terry wrote back. 'I'm certain you can get what you need at the Navy Commissary, the Navy Exchange, etc.' That was reassuring.

I looked up 'Guantanamo Bay' in my *Welcome Aboard* book. 'Aha.' The 'disadvantage' of living in the tropics, so the author said, would be that we would have to leave most of our precious household goods in Government or commercial storage while we were away: because mildew and mold would ruin fabrics, books and leather goods; dampness would rot draperies, cause rust on typewriters, sewing machines, coat hangers, and even pins and needles; and the salt air would ruin my silver. I wasn't much 'into' sacrificing anything that I loved. 'No go,' I said.

We would get to keep Pretzel, though. Thank the Lord for that.

In Guantanamo, Terry further explained, 'It won't be necessary to wear clothes, because of the intense heat and humidity; so that would be a savings. Less wear and tear. Suits and dresses in Gitmo are almost unheard of. We would wear shorts and bathing suits most of the time.'

Oh, dear. What would I do with all my beautiful clothes? I was dismayed. I looked so adorable in my little high-waisted dresses and Mary Jane shoes. And I looked bad in a bathing suit. I didn't have the boyish figure it required.

'It would be an excellent opportunity to learn Spanish,' Terry's letter continued. 'The recreational facilities are said to be excellent,' but this was an advantage I could not pin my hopes on—I hated exercise, especially in the heat. The only kind of recreation I had in mind was not available to me, and I had no wish whatsoever to learn Spanish; those days were gone.

A Quiet Life in Bedlam

So the vote was in: Guantanamo Bay lost, hands down. It was a trap, and I wasn't falling into it. I believe I would have run mad at the prospect of two years in Gitmo.

'In Key West,' I mused, rereading Terry's letter, 'one is confined to the island, with possibly irregular trips to the mainland.' Hmmm. 'But Key West is full of atmosphere and island culture, and there are plenty of ways to keep busy just sightseeing, snorkeling, swimming and the like.'

Could I work at the telephone company in Key West? I wondered. I lived my life under the great umbrella of American Telephone and Telegraph, and might apply for a transfer, if there was a telephone business office there. Terry lived his life under the great peacoat of the United States Navy, and would get his transfer come hell or high water. *Wouldn't it be sublime,* I thought, *if we could combine life in both institutions to the one small island in the sun? We might grow to like it.* I smiled with the hope of someone who never stopped believing.

Institutions. That word struck me later. The astrologer said … No, that can't be what she meant … I wonder what she meant?

I checked with my supervisor at Southern Bell. I was in luck—Key West still maintained its own little telephone business office, though one day in the not too distant future, it would be integrated with the South Miami office and closed down. *Oh, we'll be transferred by then. Not to worry,* I thought.

Another dilemma, as I saw it, was that in Key West, I would be forced to live in Navy Housing—how morbid. The very air that I breathed would be Navy air. Puke. Ah well, I was not feeling well enough to face beginning a new life outside of the Navy, no matter how much I loathed it. So I told Terry to accept the posting to Key West. He was delighted to do so.

At least he would be home. 'Excelsior!' He would be home everyday. 'Hallelujah!' He would stand duty only once in a while. 'Terrific!' Rah, rah, rah. Oom, pah pah.

Chapter Fifteen: *Rose Garden*

Terry accepted the job, and sent me a telegram from the ship, which was as usual, at sea on maneuvers, along with a check for $1,500, most of his bonus for extending the enlistment. I was overwhelmed; I had never seen so much money in my own little hand. I decided that the Navy provided a certain measure of security after all. I could dig it.

After signing his reenlistment papers, Terry arrived home expecting us to leave immediately on our trip around the U.S. I was astonished; I wasn't packed. I hadn't really believed that we would have the chance for something like that. But I packed in a hurry.

My sweet neighbor, Jill, agreed to keep Pretzel for us, and we left Atlantic Beach on April 24, 1969.

I was wearing gorgeous new sunglasses and looked as pretty as a Florida peach. I was even bronzed a little from the incessant sun.

Terry was owl-like in his Navy sunglasses, which were not stylish, but he made me love him all the more for taking control, and getting us out of there, out of Jacksonville. I was not sorry to leave. I remember only sorrow.

We made short work of the drive west to New Orleans. I celebrated my twenty-third birthday in the French Quarter, a strange place if ever there was one. I liked the architecture though—the French colonial style was very appealing.

Everything, in New Orleans, was described by the tourist brochures as being 'French Creole,' though the term 'Creole' actually indicates the mixed heritage of the people who settled the Gulf Coast, including Spanish, Italian, African, French, and Native American.

The French Quarter itself was a sleazy neighborhood even then, with genuine strippers in abundance, but I liked the Dixieland jazz, and the Cajun cooking—boiled crayfish, seafood gumbo, jambalaya, pralines.

I admired very much the wrought iron railings and lacy details on the buildings in the French Quarter. We walked the streets to look at everything, and found house facades that seemed as if they were covered in a film of lace. The deciduous trees were decked in a cape of Spanish moss.

We ended our walk at a grotesque cemetery, where all the tombs were built above ground to avoid getting moisture in them. There was an odor there ... what was it? Could there be vampires about? Terry laughed at me. I felt uneasy, and we walked back to the heart of the French Quarter, probably in the nick of time.

The house structures I liked best in Louisiana were the ones built in the 1700s. The crafters of those Creole houses implemented traditions from the Spanish, the French, the Caribbean islands, and many other parts of the world. The houses were built in their own particular style to provide comfort in the hot, humid, rainy, stormy, mosquito-infested climate, and featured large porticos, or porches, covered by wide hipped roofs.

I don't know why I like architecture so much; I have never studied it.

New Orleans was built up straddling the Mississippi River, laying over a swamp. The wood-framed French Creole dwellings were built east-west facing to take advantage of prevailing breezes, and used the wide porches as passageways between the rooms. There were no interior hallways, and the living quarters were generally on the second floor to give protection from flooding, thievery, piracy, insects, and to provide working quarters for the servants.

It was in the French Quarter that Terry pointed out to me couples, made up of two men, who were engaged in a liaison with each other, lovers, so Terry said, and I found it difficult to believe him. As the sun set, we could see the various pairs back-lighted in the same way a tree might be, or a statue. It was rather a shock to find out that there were 'other' kinds of love relationships between consenting adults. I hadn't the inkling of a paling. Deary me ... was there still more to learn?

In New Orleans, Terry and I drank intoxicating, delicious, rum-fruit juice drinks, and then toddled back to the hotel to curl up together in a real bed. A genuine bed would not be

Chapter Fifteen: *Rose Garden*

something we had access to every night. We had to save our money for gasoline.

Though I didn't feel quite comfortable there, New Orleans impressed me with its multicultural, multilingual atmosphere—the city patois was so special that I had trouble understanding it sometimes. The people slurred their words and dropped their r's. It seemed similar to the older Southern American English sometimes referred to as the Tidewater Accent, or the 'English of the coastal Deep South.' I had heard it once before when I visited Terry in Charleston, South Carolina, during a period when he had been away at sonar school.

We kept driving west, and hit all the states between Louisiana and California. We slept in sleeping bags or cabins at camping sites, cooked on open gas or charcoal grills, and occasionally stayed in a hotel so that we could get really clean and warm. I had such problems with my contact lenses! They fogged up each morning when I washed them under the cold-water taps in the campsite bathrooms. It was so irritating not to be able to see.

We visited Carlsbad Caverns in New Mexico, to view the fantastic limestone configurations, and watched as thousands of bats flew into the caves at early morning. We drove through the Painted Desert in northern Arizona, and marveled at the brightly colored landscape.

We skirted Death Valley in California. I felt a bit nervous about the implications of the name. I was very familiar with the history of the area, as regards the pioneers who died there while trying to cross. It made me shudder to think of death from hunger and thirst. I remembered, too, the story of a musician who had to dump out his grand piano into the sandy waste in order to lighten his load enough to keep going.

Whenever we needed money, Terry just stopped at a military installation and collected his pay. He seemed to always have some money coming to him. When we got to the San Diego area, we drove through Palm Springs, spotted Bob Hope, and celebrated by eating dates stuffed with walnuts and honey. In Orange County, we sat in the middle of our hotel bed and ate tacos and tostadas from Taco Bell. I had never before tasted Mexican food. It was scrumptious.

California was a different world to any I had known. It was cold in Los Angeles in May, and I nearly froze my bottom off. On the freeways, Terry drove like a maniac, matching the wild driving style of the other Angelinos. I was scared speechless. Did I know this man? He even had a manic gleam in his eye!

We visited Disneyland (what a dream!) and Knott's Berry Farm. We ate our way through both of them and were beginning to put on weight. We tracked down Terry's Uncle Chet and his new wife, Aunt Marian, who lived in Santa Ana. They took us wine tasting at a former Spanish monastery. I was no success at tasting wine, becoming tipsy when only inhaling the fumes; but Terry was jolly, expansive, and mellow. It seemed a mystery why I could tolerate a little hard alcohol—rum, for example—but not any wine spirits whatsoever.

Uncle Chet made it very clear that his money was still going to the San Diego Zoo. Terry and I raised our eyebrows and glanced at each other. Did we look like gold diggers? We were offered free tickets to the zoo, but unfortunately, we didn't take time to go. We should have.

Terry and I saw the swallows come back to San Juan Capistrano. We had to wait a long time for that, but it was worth it. The mission itself was lovely, with boganvillia tumbling over the walls, and there was the scent of many fragrant flowers in the air. It was all rather romantic, as much as the song would have it to be: '*When the swallows come back to Capistrano, that's the day I pray you'll come back to me ...*'[117]

In Los Angeles, we went to a topless go-go club, and I was hit right between the eyes by young California girls walking around waiting on tables, without any clothes on! Whatever next? Well, it was other blond, beautiful, naked girls dancing on small tables while the men (and some women) watched their nubile bodies bounce up and down. My eyes were riveted on

---

[117] 'When the Swallows Come Back to Capistrano,' written by Leon René, and sung by many sentimental old fools.

Chapter Fifteen: *Rose Garden*

them. Had they no shame? I was aghast, but in some perverse way, I liked it.

The drinks were expensive, but I guess the customers got more than the alcohol. We were required to order drinks, which were watered down, because that was the way the club made its money.

Terry said, glancing at me sideways, 'This scene is just par for the course, for a sailor.'

'What?' I said. 'You mean you do this, go to bars and watch dancing girls, when you are away from home?' But I think he was kidding me. Even at twenty-six, after five years in the service, he looked as innocent as a cherub.

But then, I almost slapped Terry's hand when he handed one of the girls a five-dollar bill to tuck into the strap of her G-string. The dancer already had a number of dollar bills hanging out, and some tens as well. For me, that place was literally like sitting in Sodom and Gomorrah, but I wouldn't have missed it for the world. The experience was priceless. I've never seen anything like it since. From that day on, I knew what it was like to flaunt sexuality in the flesh, and not just on the silver screen or in a secret bedroom.

California had a different topography to what I had seen before in the East. All those brown, rolling, seemingly burnt hills, the lack of deciduous trees, and then the startling cliffs and crashing ocean waves of the Pacific Coast Highway. Everything in Southern California looked 'toasted,' one could say, while Northern California was as blue-green as the evergreen forests caused it to be.

A highlight of California was Yosemite Valley, with its extravagant waterfalls, racing rivers, otherworldly beauty, black bears that raided picnic tables, and scenic trails for hiking and horse riding. I rode a mare for the first time, and got my bottom thoroughly bruised. At least I was able to get control over my libido for once.

San Francisco was another wonder of the western world, with its perpendicular streets, beeping streetcars, luscious seafood, quaint architecture, and crowds of laid-back, California

Dreamin'-type people. Terry and I were standing on a busy street corner in Chinatown, watching for White Slavers on a weekday in May. And there, catty-cornered across the broad avenue, I saw Ralph, Annabelle's husband. But how could it be Ralph? Ralph was safely tucked up in New Hampshire with his wife, children, and his dream job in the fire department. Wasn't he?

But I was sure it was Ralph. I said to Terry, 'There's Ralph!' and with my usual 'fools rush in where angels fear to tread' impetuousity, I rushed across that busy street, tapped the man on the shoulder and said, 'Ralph?'

The man turned, and in absolute astonishment replied, 'Kate? Terry? What are you doing here?'

'What are *you* doing here?' we chimed in. It was just one of those things. Ralph didn't know we would be there—we didn't know he would be there. He was serving his yearly stint as a Navy Reservist.

Terry and I drove back East by way of the middle Western states. We saw the stark bleakness of Utah, the heat haze in Las Vegas, the majesty of the Grand Canyon; we dodged a tornado in Kansas, made a pit stop in Chicago, crossed the Mississippi River, and then visited Terry's parents in Michigan. And so, from there back to northern Florida. We had traveled approximately 8,000 miles on about $800. It was the most fun I had ever had in my young life. I felt so close to Terry, so very close.

CHAPTER SIXTEEN:
Key West

As we returned to Jacksonville from our month's journey, pudgy, and very well satisfied with life, the Navy packers arrived to load us up and get our household on its way to Key West. Terry would fly directly from his farewells on the USS Bigelow, to Instructor Training in Norfolk, Virginia, though he was already officially transferred to Key West.

'Goodbye, Kate,' Terry said, and he kissed me. 'See you in Key West.' I had had him to myself for a month, but it was over. 'Goodbye, darling.'

I moved myself, and Pretzel, to Key West, taking in my car whatever was necessary to survive three months without the main man. Traveling down from Miami was a dream of sailing through a tropical paradise, with everything that implies, and nothing but the turquoise sea on both sides of me. A person could go skinny-dipping from a coral reef, and never see another soul. On the right of me was the Gulf of Mexico, on the left, the Atlantic Ocean. U.S. 1, the Overseas Highway, was just a raised-up coral and limestone platform sitting at barely more than sea level.

I spotted turtles, sharks, blue herons, a flamingo or two. At a place I stopped to rest on Big Pine Key, I sighted the mysterious roseate spoonbill, a rare bird. I came close to running over a Key deer, and narrowly avoided a turtle that was crawling across the road.

I was so happy as I drove along Key Largo to Tavernier Key, then Plantation Key, Islamorada, ever more southerly and westerly, Long Key, Marathon, Bahia Honda, Big Pine Key, Summerland Key, Sugarloaf Key, and Boca Chica, where there was a Naval Air Station. I crossed Stock Island in a whoosh. Then, suddenly, there I was, entering Key West.

'Which way to go, Lord, which way to go?' My head was swiveling left and right. I could choose S. Roosevelt Boulevard or N. Roosevelt Boulevard.

I chose South, and knew pretty quickly that I had made a mistake. South Roosevelt took me past the mangrove swamps, salt marshes, and some uninhabitable areas; and surprise! I found the airport. That knowledge would come in handy one day.

Eventually, I turned my car around, drove down North Roosevelt Boulevard, and so into town. Whoopee, Key West on a summer's day. The perfume of oleander was heavy in the air. I stopped to eat dinner, and reached Mallory Square just as the sky over the Gulf of Mexico turned coral pink streaked with crimson, then heliotrope.

There in that impossibly beautiful setting, I tasted my first slice of Key lime pie. Now I am an eternal devoté. There is Key lime pie, and there is Key Lime Pie. Only the real thing will do. It is made with key limes and condensed, sweetened milk.

It was necessary to put most of what Terry and I owned into storage. Our shippers arranged that easily. Then I set about trying to find some place to live. The island had such a small land area and was already crowded, even without the Navy. There was an acute shortage of places to live. It was a real problem. Pretzel didn't like living in the car. Neither did I. The heat was a hovering thing, a miasma like *The Blob*.[118]

---

[118] *The Blob*. A sci-fi/horror film from 1958, with Steve McQueen.

Chapter Sixteen: *Key West*

It was too expensive to keep living in a hotel. There was several months' waiting list to get into Navy Housing, but that was all right with me! I wasn't anxious to live there, anyway. I could fend for myself, I thought. And I had an ace in the hole—Mario's parents lived in Key West.

I viewed a few apartments (very few), and a couple of bungalows. The rentals cost the Earth, plus they were dirty and full of roaches. I could not see, for the life of me, how I would fit in my furniture, pitiful though it was, and made no decision to rent during that first week. There wouldn't even have been anything to look at, if it had been The Season—wintertime—when all the rich Yankees came down in droves to bathe in the warm, healing waters of the Caribbean Sea.

'What can I do, Lord? What can I do?' I pulled my hair. 'Where, oh where can I set my mahogany buffet?' I loved that mahogany buffet better than my life.

You'll never guess who took me in, and gave me a roof over my head while I waited for Terry to come back from his training in Norfolk: yes, of course, Mr. and Mrs. Fiqueroa, Mario's parents. I swallowed my pride and telephoned them, asking for their charity. Mario, Sr., directed me to 1302 White Street, Key West, Florida, and I arrived with alacrity. I already knew every street in Key West like the back of my hand.

How good and kind they were to me! And how Spanish! How decidedly 'Old World' they were. *Señor and Señora* Fiqueroa. 'Make yourself at home,' they said, embracing me warmly. And I did.

Carmen and Mario, Sr., consistently spoke Spanish to each other, and to Mario, who was also in residence there with his new and pregnant wife, Leigh, who was from West Virginia (of all places).

It was just a small upstairs apartment, about a hundred square meters, and the Fiqueroas were real, true friends to take me in like that. I don't know what I would have done without them.

The apartment had only the two bedrooms, and those were both already fully occupied. So I slept in my muumuu, on the

A Quiet Life in Bedlam

couch in the living room, not at all afraid or shy to do so. I was so grateful to find a home, and to be with people whom I could love and trust. If anybody ever needed love, it was me, and the Fiqueroa family lavished affection upon me. What a joy to live with them! But it was a little bit cramped.

Señora Fiqueroa made me try all the Cuban foods, like fried plantains, and picadillo (Cuban beef hash). For dessert there was caramel pudding or *boniatillo,* sweet potato pudding.

Mario Jr., my ex-lover, was his old genial self, and Leigh, his wife, was pleasant. It took her a little while to realize what Mario and I had been to each other, and she didn't become jealous until after her baby daughter was born. Of course, Leigh had no reason whatsoever to be jealous of me. The situation between Mario and myself was completely changed.

I don't believe Mr. and Mrs. Fiqueroa ever did realize how close I had been to their son, unless perhaps they knew and didn't allude to it. Those old darlings were very perceptive. It never ceases to amaze me how Latins accept the weaknesses and peccadilloes of ordinary people, people who do wrong by their lights, but don't hurt anyone else in the process. (Every sin will be paid for in the end, though, after umpteen years in Purgatory; but they would let God take care of that.)

Mom and Pop Fiqueroa had met my sister, of course, when Mario brought us both down the Keys to visit his parents; and they may have known that Mario visited my home in Tennessee. Mario could have spoken of his admiration for my mother, I just don't know. We didn't talk about it. *But I would like to know if they know,* I thought to myself time and again. They would have made such excellent parents-in-law!

Ah well, heck, I thought, *I guess it doesn't matter anymore. Mario and I are both married. Our fates are sealed.* I glanced at him. Mario saw me thinking my thoughts, thinking, thinking, and he smiled that secret smile. I blushed vermilion, and forcibly made myself 'forget' him, even though he was so close I could smell his cologne.

Three months later, Terry finally arrived in Key West from Norfolk, Virginia. Another reunion!

Chapter Sixteen: *Key West*

Pretzel and I picked him up at the Key West Airport. 'How did it go at Instructor School?' I asked him.

'Plain sailing,' he replied. He was jaunty. I loved the look of him, his way of moving and standing, and throwing his head back to laugh. Terry and I were young in the same way as each other. We were of the same generation. We had similar wishes and expectations, similar attitudes to life. We were like bookends.

By that time, I had gotten us moved into a new concrete-block house about twenty-five miles up the Florida Keys from Key West. The house was located on a tiny island called Summerland Key. Summerland Key was just as rural as can be; I was lucky to get telephone service, and there was no mail delivery, so I had to have a post office box, down in Key West.

There was no fresh water on Summerland Key, and that too, had to be piped in from Key West. Key West had for years piped its water in from Miami, but the city had recently installed a saline rinsing plant that processed the plentiful local salt water into fresh water.

A real difficulty with the rental house on Summerland Key was the concrete block construction that did not allow for the installation of central air conditioning! The atmosphere inside the block house was like an oven you could bake pizza in, and I suspended all other activities to drive down the Keys to the new Sears store in Key West. Sears was the only department store on the island, but you could get everything there that one would expect to find at any Sears, even if they had to catalogue-order it for you.

I purchased two new air conditioners, one large, for the living room, and one small, for the bedroom, just to keep from roasting in my juices. The whopping great fan that chop-chopped the air, the one I used in Jacksonville, could not cope with the heat of the Florida Keys. But it did help spread the cool air from the air conditioners around the house a little bit.

I like pictures, and have always had a lot of them. There were a number of pictures that I would hang or die. Well, try hammering a nail, or a picture hanger, into a solid concrete wall! Even King Kong couldn't do it. Really, I think they overdo concrete structures in Florida. Concrete and terrazzo, that's all you see in the new constructions.

I never did solve the problem of hanging my pictures, and the paintings sat stacked up on the floor during my tenure on Summerland Key. Our rental house was actually available to buy, and we could have bought it, but I never even dreamed of such a thing. Key West was temporary—only two years.

Summerland Key was one of the 'Lower Florida Keys.' Some geologists claimed that the Florida Keys were just an extension of the Appalachian Mountain Range, but that seemed far-fetched. 'Why?' I asked Terry. He had studied up. 'Because of their physical characteristics,' he said.

'What is similar about a mountain and a coral island?' I asked.

'The keys have a deep foundation of fossil coral layered with *oolite,* or egg-shaped limestone granules, as do the Appalachian Mountains and other areas in North America; and the islands have a northward alignment into the Gulf of Mexico.'

No kidding. I hadn't noticed that at all.

The Keys were endlessly fascinating, not least for their varieties of flora and fauna, and their northward alignment that seemed westerly.

My little Summerland Key was a coral island with a lot of palmetto scrub, mangroves, and other tropical vegetation; and depending on the weather patterns, I saw grouper fish and rock lobsters, or baby sharks (not too dangerous), swimming about in the salt water canal behind my house. Once, a young alligator visited me, and I made the mistake of feeding him. It did not take many days before the alligator tried to take my arm away along with the share of the raw meat I was giving him. It seems as if, in my lifetime, I have created more monsters than Dr. Frankenstein. I love animals, but alligators will be henceforth excluded from my list.

I was rather worried about Communist Cuba being go close to where I lived in the Florida Keys. Key West is much closer

Chapter Sixteen: *Key West*

to Havana than it is to Miami, and it was like sitting on a hornet's nest, in my opinion.

The Cold War was still on, in full force, and the movie producers kept churning out those James Bond films. I knew, because I read it, that James Bond had had some adventures in the Caribbean, the location for the Ian Fleming novel, *Live and Let Die.*

Castro, I thought, *could be in league with someone like Mr. Big. Or even SMERSH!* It's not that I believed there was a real Mr. Big or SMERSH, but the James Bond intrigues had infected us all, and I could well imagine similar wicked goings-on in those mysterious islands where nothing was what it seemed to be. The Cold War was the Cold War, and everyone was aware of it.

What should I do if Castro tried to invade? How would I save Pretzel from being, at best, killed, or at worst, eaten for dinner by the enemy? It sounds ridiculous, but this was actually a concern of mine. I had read reports of how the Japanese had killed all the dogs in the occupied Singapore of 1942. Were the Communist Cubans any better? Would they use Pretzel to make picadillo?

One night as I was sleeping, I had my first out-of-body experience. Seemingly unafraid, I flew, straight as a slow bullet, across the Florida Straits to Cuba. The night air was so balmy, the stars twinkled in an inky black sky, and fish jumped in the abundant waters. I could just see the lights of Havana, when fear suddenly took me over, and instantly, I found myself awake and back in my body. It wasn't just a dream ...

We didn't actually live on Summerland Key for very long. Navy housing became available in January of 1970, and after we looked at the proffered Navy house, we decided to take it. Terry's rank of First Class Petty Officer entitled him to a good house, and the townhouse-type structure, which was on the end of a building of four such, was just what the doctor ordered. It had become tedious, as well as costly, to drive up and down the Keys to Key West—Summerland Key, Cudjoew Key, Sugarloaf Key, Saddlebunch Key, Shark Key, Boca Chica. The heat was hot. My car was not air-conditioned.

While Terry and I lived on Summerland Key, in the autumn of 1969, there came a little 'blow' that threatened to develop into a hurricane. Terry was home with me, and he proved himself to be a good hand at weathering storms. It was creepy, but the deadly coral snakes and water moccasins that thrived so well in the Florida Keys, came up to high ground from the low places, in anticipation of the flood waters that their primeval instincts knew was coming.

High ground meant *my* patio and *my* yard! It was pretty scary, like something out of Rod Sterling's *The Twilight Zone*. At one point, there were snakes lying all over my yard of one kind or another, coral snakes, water moccasins and the like, and my little dachshund, Pretzel, killed a snake that attempted to enter our house through the sliding glass door.

The storm wasn't too bad that time—it just lasted a couple of days—and we got through it with the help of my only neighbors, a delightful Missouri family called 'The Shaws,' who brought us food and water when we didn't have any.

Mr. and Mrs. Shaw had seven children! Mrs. Shaw told me frankly, and almost immediately, that she finally had to stop having intercourse with her husband because of so many children; they just couldn't afford anymore. The constant and frequent births were really a bone of contention between Mr. and Mrs. Shaw at the time, but many years later, when the family had moved back to Missouri, they wrote to me and said, 'It took us a few years, but we finally found out that it is only *the children* that matter!'

Blimey. 'As we grew older,' continued Mrs. Shaw's letter, 'we realized that our children meant more to us than anything else; and we are so glad God has given us so many.' It was an interesting lesson for me. I had the impression from Mother and Grandmother that children didn't mean a great deal, could be done without—were practically a nuisance.

Mrs. Shaw thought that it was very sad, and also very amusing, that all *her* husband could think about was sex, sex,

Chapter Sixteen: *Key West*

sex, while *my* husband couldn't even be persuaded to consummate the marriage. As it fell out, Terry's return to me from Norfolk, as exciting as it was, did nothing to change our relationship, or solve 'the problem.' Though on a daily basis we got along beautifully and found ourselves to be the best of friends, there was no physical relationship to pacify me. A platonic marriage was not what I was born for! My feeling was that the situation could not be ignored any longer, as Terry was wont to do.

I tried to talk it out with Terry. I tried to get him to go to a doctor. He refused.

I began to worry that I was unbalanced. Secretly I suspected there was something wrong with me that I needed physical love so much, while Terry felt little need for more than modest affectionate gestures. I began to be confused. I still didn't know: what, exactly, was normal to a marriage? Was I expecting too much? At that point in time, September of 1969, I had been married for less than three years.

My inner being was in turmoil. I could not get Terry to talk about what he felt. He was in a constant position of having to defend himself. We did not fight, except for my occasional temper tantrums. Terry wasn't a lover, but he wasn't a fighter either. I kept probing him in the manner I had learned from the psychiatrist, Dr. Cheshire.

Eventually, Terry was ready to talk about it. Poor man, I wouldn't give him any peace. He said, 'When I was about four years old, my mother caught me masturbating. Mother punished me so severely, and shamed me so thoroughly, that I thought my penis was an appendage that should be ignored, or cut off, or disregarded as much as was humanly possible. Anyway, something nasty.'

I was sitting there with my mouth open, able only too well, to imagine the scene, and what it had done to him.

Terry said, 'She made me feel like a very wicked child indeed. In a subtle way, my mother continued to punish me throughout my childhood for the one incident and other similar misdeeds, which I know now was just a child's natural exploration of his own body.'

'How sad,' I said. But I knew that my mother had behaved in much the same way to me, and my sisters. 'Do not touch yourself! Touching yourself will make you blind, or crazy, or sterile ...' and all those other ridiculous things parents used to tell their children.

'My mother took every opportunity,' Terry continued his story, 'to point out to me my own father's inadequacies, and persisted in verbally comparing me to my dad—at great disadvantage, of course. Then she would go to the other extreme, and I would become the apple of her eye, the darling of her life, the child she never expected to have. (She was over forty when she had me.) And always, always, her theme was duty—duty and loyalty to *Mother*.'

How I wished Dr. Cheshire were there to hear it. But I had left him behind in Jacksonville.

'My mother was jealous of the girls I dated. She accused me of promiscuity, though there was no foundation for this. She showed openly her lack of regard for my father—sometimes it degenerated into plain contempt.'

After the two children were born, Terry and his brother, Roy, the couple never again slept in the same bed, or the same bedroom, and Edith informed her husband that she had produced children only to secure the family inheritance from her brother, Chet, who had no children.

Then, as the boys grew up, Mrs. Muszyka began to devote her life to the library where she worked, and to the Christian Science Church that she attended. Edith insisted that only Christian Science could save Terry from turning out like his ignorant father, and she began to demand that Terry accompany her to all the Christian Science meetings. Terry was the only one attending who was under the age of fifty. He finally had the courage to leave for California, where he lived until he joined the Navy.

At last we came to an agreement that Terry should see a doctor. There were no civilian psychiatrists in Key West, and a

Chapter Sixteen: *Key West*

Navy one was quite out of the question. So Terry went to the urologist at the Navy Hospital. Would you believe it, there *was* something physically wrong with Terry. It had to do with swollen tubes in his testicles, something similar to a varicose vein. In addition Terry's sperm count was very low, and he was advised that he could not father children, except possibly through artificial insemination—but the chances didn't look good, even for that.

And so, after years of suffering, we found the reason why our marriage had not been consummated in the usual way. With great difficulty, I accepted the fact that I would not bear children. Even for a woman who doesn't especially want children, it is hard to face that, the end of all hope. The trouble is, whenever you can't have something, you want it all the more.

The doctors operated on Terry to correct the tubular condition. Terry was in the hospital for three weeks. He was advised not to engage in sexual activities for a least a month, maybe two months. Terry never touched me again after that. He had a legitimate medical excuse; he didn't have to pretend anymore. The surgery provided the wedge that Terry needed to avoid, permanently, intimate physical contact.

Somehow, I accepted it, and life went on. I got used to having a platonic marriage, and I must say that in every other respect, Terry and I were really happy together. And once I stopped letting sexual frustrations color our relationship, we began to have fun, just being young together. The next year I remember as the happiest in my life. I called it 'the days of my roses.'

We adopted another dog from Mr. and Mrs. Shaw, whose dachshund bitch had had puppies fathered by Pretzel. What a nice surprise! Puppies! Of course I had to have the boy black and tan. We called him Anheuser.

I had gone back to work at the telephone company shortly after Terry returned from Norfolk. The office was right downtown, off Mallory Square, near the Hemingway House on Whitehead Street. The Hemingway House seemed to be full of cats. Hemingway had loved cats, and left his own to the city when he died. Some of Hemingway's cats were polydactyl, having many toes, and they had beautiful colors and markings.

I found a man, a Conch (native to Key West), living in a houseboat not far from the downtown area, and he had a boatful of Siamese cats. Those cats were so sleek and graceful—and smart! They represented every shade and variety of the Siamese breed. They were purebred but had no pedigree papers.

On a whim I said to the man, an old salt, 'I want one of your cats. Would you sell me one?'

He looked at me, winked, and then gravely said, 'I don't sell my children, but I will give you one.' Oh, for joy! I needed a child that did not require too much out of me. It so happened that one of his cats had queened about two months before, and he gave me a beautiful seal point Siamese kitten called Kahlua. I had that wonderful baby for fourteen years before she passed on. And she made many people happy with her pretty kittens, which were seal point, chocolate point, lilac point, and other flavors.

I had started on diet pills again after finding a private doctor in Key West who would prescribe them, and the capsules pepped me up to an extent that I practically had to run around the city block at every lunch hour, just to use some of the excess energy I had. That was how I found Hemingway House and the boat full of Siamese cats. Soon, I went back and adopted another seal point, name of Drambuie. It was just the thin edge of the wedge, using Siamese cats as surrogate children, and I never gave up keeping them, not even until now.

Terry took my diet pills, too, as we both had put on weight while traveling in the summer. Terry liked the effect the diet pills had on him. He was able to do everything better and faster. I still did not fully understand the true extent of the change diet pills worked on individuals, and neither did Terry, but we had enough sense not to use them on weekends. Then we could eat what we wanted, and lounge around, without being affected or inhibited by the drug.

Chapter Sixteen: *Key West*

I remember that we were both very upset when artificial sweeteners manufactured with cyclamates were taken off the market. Those were so good in iced tea. But the scientists said that cyclamates caused cancer when given in humongous doses to rats. Nevertheless, we bought up all the packages of 'Sweet and Low' we could find.

While we lived on Summerland Key, Terry and I caught rock lobsters for dinner in our own back yard; we enjoyed sun and sand, and picnics, and bicycling. After we moved into Key West, Terry bought a moped, and scooted around town in the same wild way he had driven the car in Los Angeles. One time at an intersection, he hit an oil slick and did a loop-de-loop.

We danced a little (very little), and I remember with laughter the time Terry expressed puzzlement over the lyrics of 'Joy to the World,' sung by Three Dog Night:

Joy to the world
All the boys and girls
Joy to the fishes in the deep blue sea
Joy to you and me!' [119]

'*Joy to the world* is for Christmas,' he said. 'Isn't it?'
Poor, naïve Terry.
Sing out!
'Jeremiah was a bull frog
He was a good friend of mine ... [120]

Joy to the World was for Christmas, before that magical year of 1970–71, when Terry and I were like kids romping together over the confines of that playground known as Key West, Florida. I am not ashamed to say that I knew joy. Thank the Lord we were sent there; it was our last happy time together as friends.

---

[119] 'Joy to the World,' Three Dog Night, 1971.
[120] *Ibid.*

A Quiet Life in Bedlam

We celebrated two Christmases in Key West. There were no live cut trees available to buy because of the dryness of the climate and the heat, so we bought our first artificial Christmas tree at the Navy Exchange, along with enough red, green and blue ornaments to fill it. And we bought a beautiful Italian Nativity scene that I still treasure.

It was early in 1970 that we moved to Government Housing in Key West, at 1515-F Trout Court, in Sigsbee Park overlooking 'Paradise Bay.' It wasn't so bad, after all! We didn't have to pay much to live there, and utilities were furnished. There were orchids growing in my back yard, and the milky scent of frangipani was in the air. Key West seemed a paradise, and I was enjoying my life there immensely. The relaxed, sporty, resort-area style of living was just right for somebody who needed to be distracted.

Our Navy house was centrally air-conditioned, so my two new window air conditioners went into storage. It was a pity, but instead of having regrets, I counted my blessings, which were many. I left the telephone company on a temporary 'leave of absence,' but didn't go back until years later. I wanted to be free! But freedom does have its costs.

The Key West Conchs were a very foreign and exotic people, in my opinion, bawdy, merry, uninhibited, relaxed about everything. They are Americans, of course, but you'd hardly know it. They have something of the Creole about them, and something of the buccaneer.

The native Key Westers are called 'Conchs,' for the beautiful pink seashell that holds a large edible snail. The conch meat is used to make soup, or chowder. The shell itself has been used for thousands of years, to blow a mournful signal, and to communicate with, across distances. One could think of it as the first megaphone.

Many original residents of the Keys were immigrants from the Bahamas, and were of European descent. And those descendants of Europeans had been holding the fort, and holding court, for about two hundred years. Key West did not secede during the Civil War, and was the most southerly outpost of the

Chapter Sixteen: *Key West*

Union. The Union soldiers used the Old Martello Tower to defend Key West against the Confederates. The Martello Fort had been standing there since the British built several of them in the eighteenth century.

But later on, in 1982, after I was already long gone, Key West briefly 'seceded' from the United States, and called itself the Conch Republic, raising their own blue banner! There was some sort of squabble over the U.S. Border Patrol blocking cars from entering and leaving Key West after the Mariel boatlift in Cuba of April 1982. The Mayor then dubbed himself 'Prime Minister,' and applied for foreign aid! The Conchs are just *like that.* Crazy.

The Conchs I knew were very, very stubborn, and didn't want to change anything about the way they lived or believed or thought. Sometimes, I got so exasperated with them, because they wouldn't recognize the year as 1970, late in the twentieth century! It was wasting one's breath even to make a suggestion. I would say, 'Why do you do it thus and so?' and they would maintain, 'Because we have done it that way for over one hundred years.' 'Oh.' And that was the end of the matter.

Key Westers also called themselves 'Wreckers,' because of all the shipwrecks they had had the pickings from in the eighteenth and nineteenth centuries, making Key West a very rich city by about 1900. When a shipwreck was sighted, the whole city turned out to harvest the ship's cargo. If any of the wrecked ship's crew got in the way, they didn't live for long. And rumor had it (and sometimes, recorded fact) that Key Westers lured Spanish ships to the dangerous coral reefs with hurricane lanterns, then reaped family fortunes in gold doubloons, solid gold and silver bars, emeralds, and priceless artifacts. And they were merciless if anyone tried to stop them.

Terry and I had our turn on the Conch Train, and gradually became accustomed to the very rare circumstances we were living in. We were both intoxicated by Key West, and decided to buy a new Volkswagen fastback, cherry red. (The car color went well with the sunset.) It was blissful to get rid of the Bug.

A Quiet Life in Bedlam

I felt like a rich woman driving around in that VW fastback. It had leather seats and air conditioning.

Terry and I enrolled as students at the brand new Florida Keys Community College. What a great time we had! We made many friends. Skirts were so short by 1971 that the co-eds exposed their entire length of leg. If they had been wearing shorts, it would have been decent to show so much leg, but we were not allowed to wear shorts to school.

Some of the professors were distressed because the girls wore little, or next to nothing, underneath their short skirts. It was very hard to ignore a naked bottom, legs slightly parted, sitting right in front of you in the classroom! I remember one co-ed who came to class wearing bikini panties with tiny satin bows sewn all over them. The professor teaching the class noticed them at once, which was the point. Girls will be girls, I guess. Terry and I had a marvelous interlude at Florida Keys Community College, and he took his Associate's Degree.

After a semester at college honing my secretarial skills, I looked for a job. I hadn't the slightest wish to go back to the telephone company. When you are young and beautiful and a secretary, it is easy to get a job.

First, I worked for the director of the new hospital being built in Key West. Our slapped-together offices were sitting on a construction site, and the place was full of workers who leered at me each time I had to cross the vast coral waste to visit the 'ladies' room.' That was bad enough, but then my boss, the hospital director, was not happy with my shorthand and typing, and I felt that I had to resign. Life was too short to work for a perfectionist.

Next, I worked for a brilliant young criminal attorney who later became a criminal himself: drug smuggling, so they said, but I don't believe it. Anyway, the man did some time in prison, but that was later on. While I worked for him, my working life was the very best I have ever known. No boss was ever better to work for than he was. 'Manny' was a real Conch, with all the peculiarities of mannerism that implies. He could

Chapter Sixteen: *Key West*

get me to do anything he wanted, even take good shorthand, by simply smiling at me.

The one time I could have been taken by the police for drunk driving, was after an evening out with Manny and his other secretary (with whom he was having an affair, I suspect). We drank Mai-tais before having any dinner, at a bar that was covered with some early form of thick clear laminate, or Perspex; and under the clear, slightly yellowing plastic bar top was an exact model of all the islands of the Florida Keys, strung out in their special pattern of coral reef, and traveling the length of the bar. It was very atmospheric. Tennessee Williams and Ernest Hemingway drank there.

I can remember that while I worked for Manny there was a sensational case of an eighteen-year-old who was arrested for possession of marijuana, and he was sent to prison for years. It was shocking and sad. The laws were much more severe then than they became later on.

After that job ended, I worked for the Monroe County Circuit Court Judge, Ignatius Lester. Alas, the unhappy judge shot himself in the head with a .45-caliber revolver. That job ended. So then I worked for a court reporter, Charo Skagen, another Conch. Charo was as happy and easy going as the rest of the Key Westers, and that job was great fun, too. Working as a secretary in Key West did not give me preparation to face the real working world, and that's the truth. What a dream it was, to be treated like a valuable human being.

Charo Skagen was the most spiritually advanced person I had ever met. She believed in reincarnation. I had never actually met anyone who believed in reincarnation other than myself; most people would have called me blasphemous and bound for Hell, for even mentioning 'reincarnation' as something to be taken seriously.

Charo and her husband, Gene, were Theosophists, and we talked for hours about esoteric things and the mysteries of life and death. Charo spoke of the Ocean of Love and Mercy, which is the true form of God Almighty, and not, as I believed, the Great Jehovah of our traditional Christian upbringing. She spoke of spiritual masters who guide us through life, and of the Law of Karma.

Charo Skagen was the first one to verify my belief that domestic animals have souls, and do advance through the ages to become higher forms of life, even human beings. She told me so much about spiritual principles, concepts, religious philosophy and metaphysics, that I was reeling from the shock—I couldn't take it all in.

Charo said to me, 'Every religion has a portion of truth. Every religion leads back to the Godhead—it just has its own ways of getting there. "Time" doesn't come into it at all.' Indeed, experiencing the torpor of the tropics can induce a lightheaded feeling of just wanting to float in green water under crystal blue skies, and consign all other 'important matters' to those who have nothing better to do. Then dream, while you let the centuries go by.

Gene Skagen taught me how to 'contemplate,' or 'meditate,' and though I had some difficulties in locating my spiritual 'eye,' which sits just above the bridge of the nose between the two physical eyes, I eventually found it, and with practice, learned how to still my overactive mind. Later on, I forgot how to do it, though. 'The Music That Went Round and Round and Comes Out Here,' in my head, refused to stop. It was just one of those things.

Terry was with me on some of these metaphysical marathons, but he did not take it as seriously as I did. He could believe anything that was well presented, but he reserved his own opinions and judgments, letting the information gurgle around inside him until he digested it. Then, he would say what he believed. But he never stopped me from doing anything I wanted to do.

Charo and Gene lived in one of those wonderful wooden 'gingerbread' houses that were originally built on the island in late Victorian times, and their house had been faithfully restored to the last fillister and filigree. Charo's land deed dated back through her parents, grandparents and great-grandparents to the Kings of Spain. But she had married just an ordinary

Chapter Sixteen: *Key West*

American guy, a Floridian, and though they were happy together, they had no children.

I remember as I sat in suspense, hearing Charo and Gene tell the story of when he had been demobbed, after the Second World War, and Charo used all the money she had to get from Key West to San Diego where Gene would disembark from the Pacific Theatre. Then, she and Gene had to work at small jobs right across the nation, to get themselves home again. There were times when they could just manage a tank of gasoline, but had no food to eat. They lived on love.

Terry, too, modern man though he was, was as enthusiastic as I about Charo's house and the other 'gingerbread' architecture on the island. Gingerbread architecture is reminiscent of the Queen Anne style, and includes gables, towers (the widow's walk), porches upstairs and downstairs, false overhangs, decorative wooden panels, columns, and spindlework. It was overdone, overblown, and like the icing on the cake of Key West.

Terry was doing very well in the Navy. He had won all sorts of awards and commendations for his work as sonar instructor. I encouraged him to do everything possible to advance to the rank of commissioned officer. I wanted to be the wife of one of those rare birds.

Terry was too old at twenty-six to become an unlimited duty commissioned officer. But he was eligible to be a limited duty officer, by way of advancing to warrant officer, and lieutenant (j.g.). And that's exactly what he did. Terry skipped chief petty officer and ensign entirely. It was a heady progression for someone as ambitious for my husband as I was.

I was the power behind the throne. Terry would have been perfectly content to become a Chief. He did not feel the pressure of rank and social status the way I did. Terry was a 'behind the scenes' sort of guy, and never had any intention of becoming a 'star'; but with my prompting (a regular stage mother) Terry began the testing required to gain his commission.

He passed the tests with very high scores. He had enough recommendations from his senior officers, who were enthusiastic about his chances, and he had the education required. The interviews went well. The committee interviewed Terry and me together, and warned us that the divorce rate was higher for Warrant Officers than for any other group in the Navy. We looked at each other, exchanged smiles, and chose to ignore the warning. *Not us,* we thought.

Finally all the data was submitted to the Department of the Navy. There were more than five thousand applicants nationwide, and only nine hundred would be chosen. Terry Muszyka was chosen. I have not known a prouder moment in my life than when I, Katharine, his wife, had the honor of fastening on Terry's bars in the official ceremony.

There is an 8 x 10 photograph of us both looking tanned, toothy and gorgeous in white clothes. It was like an initiation. Long after Terry and I were divorced, when a prospective employer asked me, 'What would you say was the proudest moment of your life?' I stated without hesitation that it was that moment, when Terry became a warrant officer in Key West. It was the pinnacle of my life. Then came The Fall.

But for that moment in time I was so happy for my husband and for myself; a great goal had been reached and surpassed. Life developed a whole new set of complications, however.

Though my heart was bursting with pride for my husband, who looked splendid in tropical white officer's uniform, involuntarily I began to notice other men, especially those flashy, smooth-talking lawyers who worked around my old boss, Manny. They began to look attractive to me.

No longer was I so blinded by my husband's light that other men proved insignificant by comparison. I had truly never had eyes for anyone but Terry. But now I did. I didn't know what to do with these new and unworthy feelings, so I tried to ignore them. I had everything I wanted, didn't I? People kept talking about being 'oversexed,' and 'undersexed.' Well, which one was I?

Chapter Sixteen: *Key West*

Overnight, Terry and I became friends with the junior officers and their wives. This was fine, and what I had always wanted, and we began to socialize. Terry was marvelous in mixed company, and I discovered that at a social gathering, I had a certain charm and attraction for both sexes. I couldn't believe it.

It was that quirk of mine, which I was in the process of discovering, that I tended to be either terribly reserved in company, or madly outspoken; and I noticed with wonder that I left people breathless wherever I went. I believe I actually liked to shock people, to put on a show. Perhaps it was for the attention. I certainly was not a natural clown. Terry was simply amused, glad that I was having so much fun. He really wanted the best for me.

Now I have to tell the truth; blame me if you will. I felt a little contemptuous towards those officers' wives for suddenly finding me acceptable as a social acquaintance when only two weeks before, I had been beyond the pale, socially speaking—absolute pariah, judging from the disgraceful way I was treated. Shame on them!

I prayed to God that I would have the grace *never* to pull rank on anybody the way they had done to me. I was bitter. Yes, I was. And it got me into trouble later on. If I have ever given the impression in this document that I am an angel, I think I should say now that it isn't true. I can be the devil in disguise.

As I became acquainted with my peers, the junior officers' wives, I found that they were, for the most part, pretty shallow individuals, and really—surprise, surprise—as insecure as I was. But it was nice to have new friends. I really liked people, the social give-and-take, new ideas, conversation, and I wanted to have a wide variety of friends. Becoming an officer's wife did put me in the way of meeting attractive people, and developing my social instincts, ones that have served me well through the years.

The junior officers' wives became more 'human' with time, but the senior officers' wives continued to remain Queen

A Quiet Life in Bedlam

Crabs, carrying their husbands' rank around on their shoulders, dictating what was acceptable, and what was not. They were the doyennes of our little society.

I had new responsibilities as a warrant officer's wife; and I was rapidly given to understand that the success of my husband's career depended very much on my ability to perform certain social functions. I found that I felt really inhibited at the afternoon 'teas,' where a false word from little me would result in one of the following: an expression of mild shock, a delicately-raised eyebrow, or a disdainful look down the nose. I found that I still smoldered with resentment towards these sanctimonious hypocrites.

So just before I left Terry for the last time, less than a year later, I went to an afternoon 'tea,' and when the Captain's wife asked me, in front of the other ladies, what I intended to do to keep busy while the ship was gone to Vietnam, I replied, with a level gaze, 'Well, I've heard that the topless go-go dancers around here make a lot of money, and have a lot of fun. I think I'll find a job like that. They say you don't have to be experienced!'

The captain's wife dropped her teacup.

CHAPTER SEVENTEEN:
Love Is a Dark Horse

I like to think that everything would have been all right if Terry and I could have stayed on in Key West. It is easy to delude oneself.

Our lives in the Florida Keys had a structure, a light-heartedness, no worries, no complications. How lucky we were. Though I enjoyed working, I did not have to work for us to make ends meet. Our living expenses were very low. I was able to buy some good furniture for the first time. I bought carpets in blue and gold, the Navy officer colors.

Terry had no choice but to accept the proffered transfer to Norfolk, Virginia: the Navy could not, of course, allow a former enlisted man to remain in a location where his associates had worked with him as an enlisted man—it just wouldn't do! Respect for an officer had to be maintained.

I'm afraid I gave Terry a bad time about the transfer. I railed against going to Norfolk. 'It's only going to be more sea duty anyway,' I wailed. 'You will never be at home!' A period of sea duty lasted five years.

'Nevertheless, Kate, I need you there.'

'Why not let me stay on in Key West, Terry, where I have made a life for myself, where I have friends?' I reasoned. 'Key West is the only place I have ever been happy!'

A Quiet Life in Bedlam

'Would you be happy without me?' he asked.

'I ... I don't know.'

'You couldn't live in Navy housing. You'd have to find an apartment.'

I didn't listen. 'If I have to be alone for the next five years, it might as well be in Key West where I have things to do,' I argued. I dug in my heels. I did not want to accept the change.

Poor Terry. He was torn. I know he sympathized. But Terry never laid down strict rules about anything. I could do what I wanted.

I felt sure that Norfolk, Virginia, would be just another emotional prison like Jacksonville had been—nothing but long periods of loneliness and depression for me. The prospect of more sea duty seemed like the pit before the void. I didn't know if I could face it.

I had visited Norfolk once when Terry was going to Instructors' School there. After the first two days, I said, 'I have never seen a more ugly, dreary, and depressing place—and such grim people, the Virginians!' They were more uptight than Tennesseans! Heavens, I was a real Florida girl by that time. Give me the sun, the sand, Spanish cooking, and hibiscus in my hair! I was too free a spirit to be caught in the net of the Navy.

Terry could not take my arguments seriously. He knew how I loved him, how easy we were together, how right, how we reveled in his times at home with the pets and me. 'You will adjust,' he said.

But I was adamant. 'I won't move north,' I said. But I did. The practical realities presented themselves. I could never manage without Terry, and it was my 'duty' to be waiting when he came home. The Navy life became our prison; but it had been very much my decision that Terry should stay 'in.' I had no one to blame but myself.

Terry traveled to Newport, Rhode Island, in June 1971, for Officer Indoctrination School, where he graduated first in his class. I have always had an intense need to collect honors, and

Chapter Seventeen: *Love Is a Dark Horse*

for Terry to collect them instead was just as good. Vicarious pleasures can give their tiny 'highs.'

I made the trip to Newport to see Terry graduate, and once again, I was presented with a new world, the world of New England. It was September, and already, the autumn had come creeping in. The nights were cooler, the days had a mellow warmth. For the first time, I heard a fox scream in the night. What a wild, uninhibited scream it was! I jumped straight up in the air, even though seconds before I had been sound asleep.

In Rhode Island, there were different smells in the air, wood, salt, fish, and sweat. The architecture was different, but very attractive. The saltbox houses, clapboard buildings with medium-pitched roofs, seemed to hint at the conservative nature of the people, who looked at me suspiciously because I was wearing my Florida clothes.

During the three months Terry was away at school, I moved our household to Norfolk, found a new house in Virginia Beach, bought it, moved in, furnished it, and resigned myself to life as a Navy grass widow. Or so I thought. Actually, my marriage ended when we left Key West, for it was never the same after that.

My old dread of loneliness returned, and with it, the despair of knowing that I would spend the rest of my life waiting for arrivals and departures, for Terry was now truly a career Navy man. He was an officer, and there wouldn't be much shore duty available for a man in his line of work. And sadly, there weren't any blond babies to distract me, occupy my time. Not that I wanted any. Who would help me take care of them? My dogs and cats would have to be enough.

It was during the first stretch of living in my new Virginia home, and while I was feeling so desolate and desperate, that I got myself into a little trouble. I thought it would help me both morally and financially if I went back to work. Never a good money manager, I had spent too much on buying the new house. I found out that I loved to decorate, and I got a little bit carried away. The house was *beautiful*, but I didn't have any money to do anything else with. I was what they called 'house poor.'

A doctor in Norfolk hired me as his office manager. I behaved like a real idiot, a goose. I developed an immediate crush on Dr. Winterstine. He was magnetic, charismatic, as a Scorpio can be. I came to work early just to catch a glimpse of him. I left work late, on the chance that I could be alone with him for a few minutes. I could not see myself doing all these silly things, but I followed him around like a hungry puppy just panting for a dog biscuit.

I was dying of love for Dr. Winterstine, or maybe it was lust, and it did not take him long to get the message. What an idiot I was.

Dr. Winterstine was a Jewish man. He was happily married—had been for years. Naturally, he was older than I. He was *handsome*—oh my! And there was something rugged about him, something so positive and masculine. I was wildly attracted to him. I just could not help myself.

Well, Dr. Winterstine rightly decided that he had to do something about this lovesick calf, me, before the situation disrupted the office staff. Dr. Winterstine called me into his private office one evening, just before time to go home. As usual, I was staying late. What else did I have to do?

Now, I know you won't believe I did this. I can't believe I did it. I cringe even as I think of it. Had I no shame? I said to Dr. Winterstine, 'You look so tired. Would you like me to massage your shoulders?'

So, he sat down in his big leather chair, and I did just that, massaged his shoulders. I just wanted to touch him, you see. I didn't know it would lead to anything more—I swear it. I just wasn't thinking clearly, and anyway, I was still quite naïve about the ways of the wicked world regarding the interaction between men and women.

I knew he knew I was married. He knew I knew he was married. I thought that protected us both. Up to that moment, I had not considered having an affair. I was just so lonely. I wanted desperately to be close to a man.

Chapter Seventeen: *Love Is a Dark Horse*

Okay, I was really stupid. But I learned my lesson, and it was Dr. Winterstine who taught it to me. Before I knew what was happening, he sprang from his chair and pinned me against the wall like the wolf with Red Riding Hood. It scared me half to death. Then, quite deliberately, Dr. Winterstine placed his hand on my breast.

I believe I could have fallen unconscious from shock, but I was electrified. All I could think of to say, was, 'Dr. Winterstine, I am married.' (Miss Lily-White-Shoes is speaking, pay attention.)

He looked at me in all seriousness, and said, 'So am I.'

We were at a stand off. He had not removed his hand.

I stammered, 'Why are you doing this?'

He said, 'Isn't this what you wanted?'

I replied, 'I don't know what I want, but please let me go.'

So he did. I left the office then, and never came back as an employee. But I see him from time to time on a professional basis—he, as my doctor, eye, ear, nose, throat, nothing from the neck down; I, as his patient. Neither of us has ever referred to the incident again.

But, I can tell you, and this is the truth—that it's a lucky thing I have been healthy, and not visited his office too often, because the sparks still fly each time he touches me.

Well, you can see how it was with me, though I am not trying to justify my actions. I was desperate for a man; but my 'faculties' had lost their powers of discrimination. I was a ripe plum ready to fall off the tree. Everything in pants began to look good to me.

One day a young, charming electrician came by the house to finish putting in some electrical sockets and the protective plates that should be screwed in over them. There was still a lot of work to be done to my house; the new subdivision was not quite finished. The electrician kept talking about 'female' plugs, and 'male' plugs, and I thought I would swoon. I asked him to leave, saying I had a migraine headache. He smiled a very delicious smile and said, 'All right, ma'am, but I'll come back anytime you're ready.'

A Quiet Life in Bedlam

Oh God, get out of here, I thought to myself as I closed the door on him.

Terry was away more than he was at home; so he did not notice that anything was wrong with me. Or if he did, he thought I was just being 'emotional' again; Terry knew I had some weaknesses, though he treated me as if he worshipped the ground I walked on. Terry did not seem emotional at all. Anyway, I couldn't tell it if he was. I believe he was sensitive, though I chose to ignore it at the time.

I couldn't settle to anything. Being an officer's wife wasn't making me happy. Norfolk was just a big, wide-open Navy town, and I was not exposed to the other wives as much as I had been in Jacksonville, or in Key West. But I found out that officers and their wives were just human after all, just regular people, really.

Though Terry's new status as an officer had given me back my pride, *my* new status as an officer's *wife* involved me more than ever before in the Navy life that I so thoroughly despised. I was caught in a net, but the free spirit in me was not allowed to expire.

An officer's wife has duties and obligations. An officer's wife is a conformist. An officer's wife does, however, get to sit at the captain's table. I liked it, but how often was the ship in port? Not much. The rest of the time, it was TV dinners at home alone.

I hated the Navy as the author of my misery, but mostly, I hated it because it took Terry away from me. Even though I am a great deal older and wiser (but not wrinkled), I don't know if I could handle the situation any better now than I did then. Basic character does not change.

Needless to say, I was not adjusting at all to the tremendous changes wrought in my life only from the mere facts of changing states and climates. The Virginia way of life was entirely different from that in Florida, and suffered by comparison. Virginians were proving to be very stuffy people, and they did not react well to the outrageous things that I loved to say, simply for shock value and attention, as I have mentioned.

Chapter Seventeen: *Love Is a Dark Horse*

I tried another job, taking on a position as legal secretary to four attorneys in Norfolk. I thought such a position would be a natural for me, as I had enjoyed every minute of working within the legal profession in Key West.

There were several other secretaries attached to the firm. These women were veritable harpies. They had nothing but contempt for the Navy in general, and thought, almost put into words, the opinion that Navy wives were the lowest of the low, scum of the Earth, whether officer's or enlisted. That was a shock. Was I not entitled to some respect?

'Officers' wives are two a penny,' stated the youngest of the firm's secretaries. The oldest secretary wouldn't even deign to speak to me. Why does life play these tricks on us?

The secretaries were catty and spiteful during the whole time I was working there. They went through new secretaries like typewriter paper. This kind of cold and mean treatment, coming as it did at such a vulnerable time, did not help my emotional stability, or ease my difficulties at all. May they burn in Hell for it! That was the only time I thought about murdering someone. But I didn't know how to dispose of the body.

There weren't any attractive men in the law firm, thank goodness, so I wasn't tempted in that way. The two senior partners were elderly brothers. The elder of the elderly brothers held the position of Norfolk divorce commissioner, and he (his name was Theodore) had probably been practicing law for forty years.

Teddy had a reputation for putting his hands on his secretaries, and for harassing and sexually abusing divorcées who came to his office seeking the granting of their divorces, which only old randy Teddy, as the divorce commissioner, could do. I don't know how he got away with it, but there was certainly still a stigma attached to the word *divorcée,* and Teddy took advantage of the world's cynicism to gain his own ends.

Needless to say, no one told *me* about this man's moral conduct, or warned me to beware—which would have been a kind gesture, but was not forthcoming from anyone in the place—not even from Andrew, Teddy's respectable brother.

The other secretaries were only too eager to observe what would happen to me! Well, it happened pretty quickly. Old Teddy chased me around his desk a few times (Teddy had to be 75, if he was a *day*), and at other times, he played little tricks on me, to maneuver me into positions where he could take advantage of my person. I heard stories that he did the same kinds of things to his respectable women clients, the city's divorcées. Old Teddy was a real menace! He must have been evil.

The last straw was one day when Teddy called me around to *his* side of the desk, which was tightly wedged in a corner. He politely asked me to hold steady a pole lamp for him, while he found the electrical plug, and put it into the socket. The socket proved to be somewhere underneath my skirt. Apparently. For that is where he went with his hand and the cord, ostensibly to plug it in. I kicked him over, bloodying his curious old yellow nose.

I went to see the other brother, Andrew, and told him that I would have to resign for 'personal reasons.' That wasn't good enough for Andrew, who was shrewd old dog—as careful and thorough an attorney as ever lived. But Andrew did not delve too deeply into the situation—he probably knew what had happened. The firm had been losing a lot of secretaries. I was just one in a long line.

To save the day, Andrew suggested that perhaps I would like to work for the two junior partners, Norman and Ed, who were pleasant-looking men, if somewhat effeminate; they needed an extra secretary, too. That suited me; I really needed to keep the job. But then I walked unannounced into one of the junior partners' offices, and found the two junior partners reclining on the sofa together; it wasn't just a friendly afternoon nap.

Pulling myself together and trying to take an adult view of other peoples' peccadilloes, I stayed on at the firm until the two junior partners were arrested for fraud, convicted, and sent to Sing Sing, or some such place. Actually, I was only too glad

Chapter Seventeen: *Love Is a Dark Horse*

to leave those wicked witches, the secretaries, behind. They had had a fine time tearing me apart. What, you may ask, had I done in all my innocent life to deserve these calamities? You may well ask that. I could not possibly give a reply.[121]

On April 30, 1972, Terry and I were at home hosting a party for friends when the telephone rang. It wasn't a particularly ominous ringing—just an ordinary Bell Telephone ring-ring like telephones always do. But it was the death knell of our marriage. Terry's executive officer had called to give him notice that their ship, the USS Biddle, a guided missile cruiser of the Belknap Class, would be leaving within twenty-four hours, on an unscheduled, emergency trip to Vietnam. This sudden sailing would relieve a sister ship that had been shelled by enemy crossfire, and suffered heavy damages, including casualties. It would be the Biddle's second deployment to Vietnam.

You can understand how surprised I was, because the war in Vietnam was nearly over, or so I thought. I don't believe I was really paying attention to the war news at that point in time. What did it matter, anyway?

Though I knew it had to happen sometime, another long cruise, it was still a great shock to me. For such a thing to happen so suddenly! 'Oh, no!' was the first thing out of my mouth. Terry took it all philosophically.

The USS Biddle was expected to be deployed until Christmas. The Navy doesn't go to Southeast Asia just for a short cruise. What a change in both of our lives! Well, I guess it was better than waiting out the agony of a scheduled departure, which would have come sooner or later. It took me many years and a lot more experience before I learned to live just for today.

When Terry left, that was the end of an era, the end of our marriage though of course, he didn't know it, and I certainly

---

[121] A direct quotation from the BBC dramatization of *House of Cards;* as spoken by Ian Richardson playing the British prime minister, Francis Urquhart. Adapted for television by Andrew Davies from the political thriller novel by Michael Dobbs, 1990.

didn't plan it that way. I did know, without a doubt, that I would have an affair while Terry was away. I would actively look for it. I couldn't remain celibate any more, not even to obey the Ten Commandments. I dusted off my diaphragm.

Still, I tried to control myself. I had the sinking feeling that I would become a nymphomaniac. I read Irving Wallace's *The Nympho and Other Maniacs*, and got seriously worried. In desperation, I went to consult a private psychologist in an attempt to get help. Poor, dear Dr. Cheshire had gotten into his bathtub in Jacksonville, with some electrical wires around his wrists, and electrocuted himself. I was so sorry. He was a very good man and an excellent doctor.

This new psychologist was very interested in my case, and allowed himself the opinion that Terry was probably a latent homosexual. (He wasn't.) The doctor insisted that he would have to see my husband when he came back from Vietnam—if the marriage was to be saved.

I wasn't sure that I wanted the marriage to be saved. I was almost beyond that. I wasn't sure that I wanted Terry to come home. Sometimes I wished that he would be killed, so that the problem would neatly resolve itself. I almost got my wish. The USS Biddle suffered a combined attack, on the night of July 19th, by North Vietnamese MiGs and gunboats. The Biddle returned five-inch gunfire at the gunboats, which sped away, and simultaneously the Biddle shot down two MiGs with Terrier missiles. The Biddle was apparently the first ship since World War Two to put up a barrage of fire against an enemy.

But I knew nothing of this until long after. I was fighting my own battle against a kind of insanity. I told the doctor how I longed for a lover. It's all right to say such things to a psychologist, they're used to hearing it, and they won't jump you. The doctor stated quite frankly, 'I fully expect you to fall into the arms of the first available man who pays you any attention. So be careful who you smile at.'

Was that a license to steal? I felt a little sting when he said it, as if the rubber band had snapped, and I was free of the obligation of my marriage. As yet, however, I did not know this

Chapter Seventeen: *Love Is a Dark Horse*

consciously—it was 'back there' somewhere, like a nervous little spot at the outer limits of my brain.

The first available man who paid me any attention was Vincent Scandellari. I had first met Vincent in the office of the sales agent where I bought my house on Banbury Court in Virginia Beach, about eight months previously.

Vincent was the site building superintendent for his brother, Cæsar Scandellari, the owner of the development. It was all new houses, at least a hundred. Working also at the development was Cæsar and Vincent's younger brother, Luca. The three Scandellaris had yet another brother, Sandy, living in town, and their over-protective mother, Paula. Their father, Dominic, the brains of the outfit, had been dead for a couple of years. A simple man, Papa Scandellari was a hard-worker and a saver. He was an immigrant from Sicily, and came to America for opportunity. He made his own way, and did very well.

Before Pop died, he set up his two eldest sons, Sandy and Cæsar, in the construction business. Pop himself was a bricklayer, but he made his sons into General Contractors. Sandy and Cæsar in turn, and according to Sicilian custom, were to employ the two younger sons until they matured, and then set them up in their own businesses. 'One hand washes the other,' is the way they explained it.

There were several reasons why things did not work out the way Pop planned it. First of all, Vincent and Luca had been so spoiled as the younger children, that Vincent did not want to accept any responsibility, and Luca was too busy being a 'playboy.' In addition, the world had changed a lot from Pop's day: an oath given was not a bond anymore; businessmen were more cut-throat; brothers didn't care a speck about brothers, having had some bad experiences with same.

The older ones, at least, had their own large families to think of, and then too, there was a drastic change in the business climate before Pop died, with a lot of builders going bankrupt. There had been too much speculation, with houses being built that were not sold. So there came a day when Vincent and

Luca were on their own, not having been trained for anything but to be on the administrative end of a construction site.

My relationships with the Scandellaris have been so complicated, and so strange over these last several years, that I don't know quite how to begin. Vincent was looking for love, too. His relationship with his family had been rather stormy for a decade. In 1964, when he was 30, he had made a marriage that 'the family' did not approve of. There had been a subsequent fall from grace, and an estrangement that had lasted several years—lasted, in fact, until Vincent left his first wife, an alcoholic, in another city, in a sanitarium, in 1970. Vincent then came home to Virginia to be with his critically ill father, who died within the month.

In the spring of 1972, when I began noticing Vincent, he was thirty-seven, almost thirty-eight—in his prime. I had just turned twenty-six. Both of us were in that borderland, a shadowland, where soon we would cross over into middle age. (I knew it was coming.) Was youth giving us one last chance?

Vincent had been watching me for some time; that is the way of the Scandellaris, never getting too close, they watch and wait, and look for an opportunity to press an advantage.

It had seemed rather curious that everywhere I went, *that man,* Mr. Scandellari, would turn up, and I would see his dark eyes peering at me from behind the palm fronds in a restaurant, or from behind the wheel of his car, in a drive-in, or even just out around my house, where he appeared to be working on other, unfinished new houses; but really he was watching me. I did not have a presentiment of evil intent, felt no danger. Vincent must have known I was restless.

The Scandellaris as a family are long, lean, and aquiline—except for Cæsar, who is rather heavy-set like his mother's side of the family. The 'boys' each have a curious, characteristic walk, or gait, which I can only assume was unconsciously copied from their father. How it would have helped me to understand 'them,' if I had known 'him'!

The Scandellaris walk with their legs kept very stiff, and their torsos bent slightly forward from the waist—rather like a

Chapter Seventeen: *Love Is a Dark Horse*

proud rooster about to go into its mating dance; but they are sexy, and very virile. Not one of them is in any way unattractive. (Alas.)

They all, with the possible exception of Sandy who is an aesthete, have this obsession with being 'manly'; and the funny thing is, for all their efforts to be manly, they are each ever so slightly prissy, like a nest full of Virgos, which they are not. They're Scorpios to a man, except for Vincent. I should really have known to be careful.

The Scandellaris are very proud, and they are arrogant to the point of it being laughable. And the personality quirk that is the most peculiar of all, is that they don't like women. Yes, it is true. They don't like women; oh, they know how to use them—but strictly as sex objects. The Scandellari men do not value women as people; they don't expect the fair sex to have any brains. The Scandellaris just want a pretty woman to hang on their elbow and look delicate. Decorative, you know, Edwardian. Vincent was like that too, but I believe that at least he came to value me.

Vincent loves to poke fun when I intimate that I think I might have some intelligence. He'll say, 'You look peculiar when you're thinking … you don't look like yourself.' Or he'll say, 'Some people are not made to do certain things, Kitty. With you, it's thinking you should avoid … every time I catch you thinking, it scares me; you look like you're about to become a stroke victim.' Hah, hah, hah, very funny, Vincent boy.

And, the rake; he won't leave it at condescending remarks like that. When I tried to get him to take it seriously that I was writing a book, he said, 'I have the perfect title for a book for you, kid: *One Million Excuses Why I Can't Do Anything,* or alternatively, *100 Thousand Reasons Why I'm Always Right.*' Well, I guess that is the character I presented to him when we first knew each other. I presume he came to know me better, later.

Vincent thinks it is hilarious (and it is) that I adore having a formal portrait of myself made each year. It documents my metamorphosis. Vincent told me recently, 'The next time we have a picture made of you, we'll get you sitting at your desk with your eyes crossed, your head propped on your arm, and one finger to your cranium in the vicinity of the brain; and we will title the portrait, "The Thought".'

Male Chauvinist Pig, Vincent Scandellari.

Well, you see what I have to put up with; his brothers are just as bad. One time, they all became hysterical, just because I remarked that I needed to 'gather my wits.'

But anyway, they don't like women; they are terribly suspicious. And, so far as I can tell, they don't like other Italians, or Blacks, or Jews, or Greeks, or Arabs, or Chinese, etc., etc. Once, when I complained to Vincent, 'The Scandellaris don't like me!' Vincent answered in his indolent way, 'They don't like anybody, not just you.' 'Oh,' I said, 'that makes me feel better!'

Sandy and Cæsar apparently don't even like their wives—talk to either one of them for a few minutes, and you'll see what I mean. Very disparaging. Any opinions their wives have are completely discounted. It is a male supremacy world for them. After thinking about it a lot, I have come to the conclusion that the reason the Scandalleris don't like women is because their own mother is so despicable; and they initially learned to relate to women by relating to her. Does this sound reasonable? Have I got the situation scoped out?

I suppose there are as many brothers who hate each other as love each other; are strangers under their skins. This seems to be the case with the Scandellari brothers, but I can't be sure. They treat each other coldly. I have seen Vincent and Cæsar deliberately avoid each other on a chance meeting in a restaurant. They, the four of them, relate to one another as if they were cousins, perhaps, but not brothers. It is very odd. Perhaps it is the age difference. Sandy and Cæsar are ten and nine years respectively older than Vincent, and Vincent is nine years older than Luca. They're almost from different generations.

Vincent is the only true romantic of the four, and has been consistently taken advantage of by his hard-as-nails brothers. He has let them get away with it, of course. Vincent just lives

Chapter Seventeen: *Love Is a Dark Horse*

every day on a wave of dreams and feelings, hardly coming down to Earth where we mere mortals are doomed to live. If you have ever heard of the Astral Plane, that is where Vincent lives.

Vincent regrets that his romantic nature has kept him from making a success out of his life. Really, he is just too soft to survive; and I suspect that, deep down inside himself, it is Vincent who loves his mother best, and Vincent who really does like women, though he would never admit it.

Once, when Vincent was feeling especially dreamy, he wrote this note to me:

We need more romantic people in the world,
But, if we had more, there wouldn't be any work done
Everyone would just sit around and dream all day
Like I do.
I've been thinking about the types of people who
Make up the world, and I believe they may be
Grouped as artists, musicians, mathematicians,
Lovers, fighters, and plain, ordinary, hard-working people
Who are more dead than alive.
What I mean to say is, that those who pursue work,
And only work as a means to an end, died long ago;
They just forgot to lie down.
I'm glad I'm not one of those, even if
I have to be poor all my life.

Chances are he will be. I didn't realize until years later, that Vincent had written a poem; it came to me phrased as prose.

Then, apropros of nothing, he'd say, 'I don't know why the Russians want us (the U.S.A.). Nobody here wants to work.' That was in the days of the USSR.

Or, he'll say, 'Kid, you've got a screw loose.'
'Why ever would you say that, Vincent?'
No answer.

The Scandellari family hails from New York City, though they have all been in Virginia for twenty-five years. But each still carries that rude, tough, cheeky, street-sounding New York City accent which makes one know immediately that they don't belong in Virginia. And they don't; they belong to Europe, for that's what they are, Europeans to a man—the Latin kind—even though they were born in the U.S.A. It's the way they were raised. Both parents were born in Sicily, and continued the old ways with their children.

I believe that Paula Scandellari took some pains with Sandy and Cæsar. She was young then. She made them 'mind' her; she forced them to eat a balanced diet, whether they wanted to or not. She supervised their activities. But with Vincent, coming as he did in her mid-life, she just let him grow up like a weed, doing what he pleased. He played hooky from school more often than not, going where he wanted to go.

Vincent used to take the subway, all by himself, downtown to Manhattan when he was only six years old. He wasn't afraid. He wanted to go the movies, or to the 'midway,' or to any place he wanted to go, eating what he wanted to eat—and Paula allowed the same freedom to Luca. Vincent can't even write a decent hand, but he reads voraciously.

The two youngest boys, Vincent and Luca, became spoiled, and eventually, their doting mother, Paula, prepared *three* meals each night for her three men remaining at home—Papa, Vincent, and little Luca—the menu depending on what they each said they had in mind to eat, for lunch or supper. As a result of this preferential treatment, Vincent eats only steak, potatoes, and corn—oh, yes, and copious quantities of pasta. They think their mother is a saint, but I don't see it that way. She just made life hard for two other unnamed women, and that might have been her intention.

I cannot deny that there were some strong points in the family life of the Scandellaris. It certainly was a triumph of parenthood that the boys never questioned who they were—their identity, their masculinity, or the fact that their parents loved them.

They grew up with this insane sense of humor that causes them to laugh at other peoples' discomfort. Once I coerced

Chapter Seventeen: *Love Is a Dark Horse*

Vincent into taking me to the ballet. He was reluctant because he said that people who saw him would call him a 'closet gay.' He would have been acutely miserable at the ballet, which was *The Nutcracker,* but some poor fellow fell down the auditorium steps in the dark, right in front of us. Vincent laughed his head off, and he wouldn't stop laughing. It was a horselaugh, too. I was so embarrassed!

Vincent accelerates the car if he sees a pedestrian in his path! I believe the clue to his behavior is that he's a typical New Yorker. Vincent proudly told the story of his cousin who drove out to a pick-it-yourself field of vegetables, picked a car-trunk load, and then, concealing it from the farmer, paid only for a bucket full of vegetables he placed in full view on the front seat! It was slowly borne in on my consciousness after some years had gone by, that the Scandellaris think it is honorable to be dishonorable.

And there's another thing that is not logical about the Scandellaris. They have a peculiar habit of sticking everything with a 'gender.' Do the Italians in Italy do that? Ballet is 'feminine'; therefore, it is for Women and Gays! Or so Vincent says. I love the ballet.

Cars and work are masculine. Housework is feminine, and only done by women. You get the idea. Vincent, in particular, has a habit of labeling every aspect of life with 'male,' or 'female.' Any woman who dares cross Vincent's imaginary line (and be successful in business, for example) is masculine, and not at all attractive to him.

Any man who engages in certain activities that Vincent has designated as being 'feminine,' he immediately labels as a 'closet gay.' If anyone counted up Vincent's accusations, I think we would find there a lot of closet gays in the world.

Any woman who becomes dominating, instead of manipulating, is out of character to Vincent. Any man he meets who appears to be affable and mild-mannered, Vincent says probably goes home at night and kicks his wife around—and throws his children up against the wall!

A Quiet Life in Bedlam

I know all this sounds ridiculous, and maybe Vincent is pulling my leg, but I cannot convince him that he is hopelessly old-fashioned. He carries this mental attitude into every aspect of his life. Witness the following scene in a restaurant where we went to have dinner:

Vincent sees bread, and the breadbasket, as feminine. I make the statement after years of watching Vincent as he approaches the bread basket with two hands, eyebrows raised, a look of intense concentration on his face, an expectant look around his eyes. Like a guilty boy, Vincent 'peeks' underneath the linen napkin to see what's in there; it is precisely the expression he would wear if caught looking under a woman's skirt!

After the meal, he'll say to me, 'Why does a meal make you happy, Kate? Most women want jewels and furs.'

'I want jewels and furs, too, Vincent.'

'That don't cut no ice. Yuk, yuk, yuk.'

Vincent's personality is so interesting and complicated! He fascinates me. His brothers are no less so. They fascinate me, too. For a person of my sensitivities, these years' long association with them has been like an emotional roller coaster ride. In addition to that, my mind plays a game (a losing battle) of trying to dissect them and find out what makes them tick. They hold me spellbound.

The Scandellaris make me think of ferrets, dark of visage, dark of purpose, heavy brows straight over hazel or brown eyes—the eyes set close on either side of the long nose. A melancholy, brooding sort of family, their eyes look like still pools of limpid, dark water whose calm, passive reflection belies the strong currents beneath—they're all desperately passionate. Cæsar and Luca have eyes that can take on a wily look. Sandy perpetually wears a bland expression, and Vincent's eyes are large and soulful.

They have black, wavy hair, thick at the back and sides, and a little thinner on top, at least in Vincent's case. He has,

Chapter Seventeen: *Love Is a Dark Horse*

lamentably, a receding hairline. When he was younger, Vincent had enough hair on the top of his head to stuff a mattress with. He wore it combed to the back, with 'ducktails.' The other three Scandellaris still have full heads of hair, but are going a little grey around the temples, which makes them look more sexy than ever.

The Scandellaris have what I would call 'fatal attraction.' Impossible to resist, they dazzle the unsuspecting innocent with worldly allure and a patina of riches that do not really exist. Oh yes, they used to have some money. 'The Old Man,' Papa Scandellari, made plenty of money for them, and left them quite a legacy. But the money is all gone now. According to Vincent, after Pop died, Paula Vannelli gave away the bulk of the fortune to her two favorite sons—Vincent wasn't one of them—who lost it in bad business deals.

Sometimes I doubt if there ever was any money.

Vincent Scandellari's motto is 'Walk softly, and carry a big wallet.' Well, the same could be said for each of the four brothers. Money and power are what turn the Scandellari family on. Perhaps I need someone to dissect me and find out what attracts me to this mad Scandellari family. Am I self-destructive? Do I like to live dangerously?

That eternal cynic, Vincent, says that I ignite a spark in crazy people, who are irresistibly drawn to me like the moth to the flame, and that the same is true in a lesser way as regards eccentrics, eclectics, recluses, college professors, Scandellaris—anyone who has bats in the belfry. He's probably right. Certainly my life is a testament to it.

(I do think he's very hard on me, though.)

Though I know I had met him before, the first time I can recall setting eyes on Vincent Scandellari was just after I moved into my new house. I marched down to his construction office, fully militant, and gave him hell for not finishing off my house properly. There were a lot of important things left undone: the toilets didn't have seats, the yard was a sea of mud, the windows were jamming, and the kitchen did not have all the proper fixtures. It was real, important stuff! I demanded action or recompense!

I was, at that point, a woman alone and did not want to be taken advantage of. I was mad. Becoming angry always upsets me. When I get upset, I always cry; so, as soon as I was finished with my tirade, I promptly burst into tears.

Vincent never forgot me after that. In, fact, he claims it was love at first sight. I remember he laughed a kind of low, throaty, 'Yuk, yuk, yuk.'

I turned and ran.

CHAPTER EIGHTEEN:
The Planets Collide

Astrologically speaking, an eclipse must have hit my planets in July of 1972. I became acquainted with—positively enmeshed in the lives of several people who have changed the whole course of my existence. And I met them all in that same month.

First of all, there were the four Scandellaris: Vincent, Cæsar, Sandy and Luca. Then there were two female friends who stayed around to be bridesmaids when I finally married Vincent several years later. Their names were Delores and Lynette. I have already mentioned the blond bombshell, Delores Delaney, the one who cut up customers' bogus credit cards, right in front of their faces, behind the front desk at the Holiday Inn. Lynette Mckinnon was a fascinating creature too, with raven hair, the antithesis of Delores. Lynette could not be contained by anybody's rules, and had her own code of ethics.

I was looking for a job in May of 1972, and not having much luck finding one. I was feeling too emotional, too vulnerable, too sensitive, to be good for much. Being fired from Dr. Winterstine's office had gone down hard on me. What a blow to my pride!

There was a Holiday Inn on Northampton Boulevard, just down the road from where I lived, and I decided to take a job there as restaurant hostess until a secretarial job became available. I was not too interested at that point in working for the telephone company. It was so tedious, so boring behind those four gray walls; I would go demented.

I wanted excitement and challenges, something to engage me fully. The telephone company's automated work fossilized me, stifled me, and made me nearly suicidal. I would have to need a job desperately before I would go back to work there.

The restaurant hostess job was fun; I began it in June. For the whole month of June, it seemed as if I were ushering the Scandellari brothers in and out of the restaurant, in and out the attached bar, as well as various ones of their construction crew, who were working on the new houses around about my own. They all seemed to be rolling in money—as indeed they were. Times were good in their business. They were very merry, and certainly chauvinistic towards me and my coworkers.

The new houses, at Lake Edward, were selling like hotcakes at only 7% interest on a Veterans' Administration loan. That was considered a good interest rate for a thirty-year loan. Or you could get a Federal Housing Authority loan for the same interest rate, with a small down payment. The F.H.A. was actually giving divorced women loans! Imagine that.

Because the men recognized me as one of the new homeowners, already safely tied to a V.A. mortgage, they indulged themselves by making me squirm with a little good-natured teasing. I did not mind a bit, I was happy to be noticed. I could tell they thought I was attractive. I liked it. It gave me a sense of power.

The mini-skirts I wore to work were really short, and since I never could be sure if my underwear was showing, I took to wearing panties with satin ribbons threaded all through them, like that girl I knew at Florida Keys Community College who had the professors all in a tizzy. Nevertheless, it was disconcerting that I was inspected so closely with the men's eyes. Aspects of my body and shape were remarked upon. Gee. But I didn't know enough to be insulted. I just tried to roll with the punches, and come up with suitable retorts when I could get a word in edgeways. As far as I could see, it was good, clean

Chapter Eighteen: *The Planets Collide*

fun—they meant no harm. A feminist would have killed them, but there weren't so many feminists working around bars in 1972.

'Hostessing' paid only the minimum wage, which was very little. It didn't take me long to find out that the girls who worked in the bar were making really good tips—sometimes as much as fifty dollars a night, or even more. Cæsar Scandellari, enjoying his role as magnanimous baron, regularly left a fifty dollar tip, which was divided by the two girls who worked in the bar. The bargirls were so busy serving drinks and snacks to the construction crew of the 'Lake Edward' project, that they needed help.

Within a few days, it was agreed with the hotel manager that I would become the third girl working in the bar, helping out the bartender, Arlene, and the barmaid, a cute little brunette named Debbie. The only thing I was nervous about was wearing the bar uniform, which seemed to me rather racy, and consisted of a pullover knit striped cotton shirt, 'hot pants' (short-shorts), and knee-high white boots. And we wore suntan colored pantyhose, of course.

I didn't know it then, but the bar girls came in for a lot of lowbrow remarks and pinches that they simply ignored or were impervious to; and they heard all the gossip. It was a risky life. Women who worked in a bar were considered fair game; but at first, I thought it was just an ordinary job, like any other.

Tackling the task with my usual courage, I was not afraid, did very well with serving the drinks—except I couldn't tell the difference between Scotch and water, and bourbon and water—and mystified the customers with my seeming lack of comprehension for their suggestive remarks. I had never before been exposed to such a ribald crowd. Even Navy enlisted men were more circumspect than that!

Everyone in the Holiday Inn was talking about the Scandellaris—the way the money fairly flowed out of their pockets, and into the pockets of everyone who worked for them. The rumor was rife that the youngest Scandellari, Luca, was looking to find a girl and get married, and it had all the Inn clerks in a flutter, hoping he would look their way. Few realized that Italian Catholics could marry only another Catholic, preferably Italian, and non-Catholics were permanently off the list.

This was all very interesting. There was a pizzazz about life at the Holiday Inn that was very appealing to poor lonely me. I began to observe the Scandellaris closely. Cæsar Scandellari was all but worshipped by the crowd as the author of their prosperity. He seemed to absorb the flattery like a sponge, then pour it out again as charm and hospitality.

Cæsar was said to be looking for a mistress, Luca for a wife. No one said whether Vincent was looking for anything. Sandy, the eldest brother, frequented the place but little, and he was solidly married with umpteen children.

I did not consider myself to be a candidate for any proposals, because at that time I still thought of myself as Mrs. Muszyka, Officer's wife; in fact, I used my 'married status' to fend off unwonted advances. That worked for a while, but the men, the customers, got bolder and bolder with their remarks as time went on and they found out that I did not know any smart rejoinders to make to their obscenities, as Arlene and Debbie obviously did.

Cæsar, Vincent, and Luca Scandellari always conducted themselves as gentlemen towards me. I blessed them for it. I got no trouble at all from them. But the sub-contractors, the plumbers, electricians, painters, bricklayers, who came in with them, men with small minds, enjoyed their little games that they played at my expense, sometimes nearly embarrassing me to death. I was still my mother's well-brought-up girl, in spite of everything that had happened.

Cæsar and Luca, though they did not insult me themselves, let the others have their fun—their attitude being that a barmaid had to expect such treatment. Vincent, on the other hand, was careful to defend me, or to deflect whatever remarks he could for my sake, and he probably let himself in for some good-natured ribbing and raised eyebrows, which implied, 'I know what *you're* up to!' But Vincent shrugged it off, and went on sipping his little glass of wine. I never saw Vincent

Chapter Eighteen: *The Planets Collide*

swallow any of the hard liquor, as the other men did in large quantities. It was a constant party at the Holiday Inn.

Vincent and I smiled at each other a few times, over a period of weeks. He would say, 'Kitty, bring me a Brandy Alexander.'

I was honored to do so.

As though through a fog, I would hear the others say, 'Here, kitty, kitty!'

Vincent got up enough nerve to ask me out for a drink. I felt a jolt. Did he know I was looking for something, someone? Though, of course, I denied it to myself, over and over. *'I'm married, I'm married.'*

But then, like a real retard, and as if I did not feel worthy to let him spend any money on me, I answered him, 'I have plenty of things to drink at home. Why don't you come there when I get off work tonight; you know where I live.' I guess it was the old, 'Why don't you come and see me sometime.' Gad. Had I no shame?

It was a Saturday, July 1st. Strictly speaking, Holiday Inn employees were not allowed to date the customers, but no one observed the rule, and anyway, I could hardly consider myself to be going on a 'date.' I was a married woman; I still wore my wedding rings on my fingers everyday.

How was I to know that it's understood, that if a married woman asks a single man over for a drink, she is automatically asking him to take her to bed? I should have known, though. I was such a dumb bunny. And yet, I wasn't stupid. It must have been a subconscious surrender, or simply complete non-chutzpah. Woe is me. Whatever else happened is totally my own fault. My life changed from that moment.

So, it was July 1st, five days before Vincent's thirty-eighth birthday. He told me he was thirty-four. That was the first lie. He told me he wasn't married. That was the second lie. Vincent was still married to his first wife, Cathy, though he did not like to think about it, and refused to acknowledge it, even when cornered. He had not seen, or communicated with her, for over four years. Vincent lied about it, but he said it was because he never, in fact, felt that he was married to Cathy at all.

'Extraordinary. How can you say that?' I asked him.

'We ran away together in an act of rebellion against my family. I started dating her in 1964, when she was working for my brother as bookkeeper. Cathy was divorced with two small children.

'My family seemed to be horrified as a romance developed between us. My mother told Cæsar to fire Cathy, and he did.'

'No!' I exclaimed.

'Yes. Cæsar fired Cathy from her job, leaving her with no income, and two small children to feed.'

Cæsar was always doing what his mother told him to do, the fool. Vincent, a genuinely sympathetic, and tenderhearted man, felt as if the debacle had somehow been his fault. He felt sorry for Cathy, and he continued to date her, and to lend a little financial support whenever she needed it.

'My mother was not satisfied. She gave me an ultimatum: "Stop seeing Cathy, or move your things out of this house".'

Naturally, Vincent moved out; it was as predictable as the day following the night. Then Vincent didn't have anywhere to live. It seemed convenient for the two wronged parties to live together; so they did. Vincent moved in with Cathy and her two boys.

'I was twenty-nine, and I should have been able to make my own decisions, but my family was dead-set against the match, and they began to persecute me more. My mother told me to break it off, or I would be fired from my job. But I wouldn't stop—my mother only made me more determined—so Cæsar fired me.'

'This is too incredible,' I wrung my hands. But it was all too true.

The relationship between Vincent and Cathy probably would not have resulted in marriage, as the two were basically incompatible, *if* the Scandellaris had just let it alone. But they wouldn't. The situation became very tense. The Scandellaris

Chapter Eighteen: *The Planets Collide*

had such an intensity, that you could feel them glowering at you, clear across town.

By that time, it was midsummer, July, and Mr. and Mrs. Scandellari were leaving, as they always did, for their summer home in Long Island, New York. The birthday message the parents left for their son, Vincent, who turned thirty on July 6, 1964, was 'Break it off, or never come home again.' Well, Vincent married Cathy. A blind man could see it coming.

Up until that July, Vincent and Cathy had just talked about marrying in a casual way, with no definite plans made. But with Vincent's domestic situation coming to a head within the two months of summer, after which his parents would return from New York, it was decided that if the two were to marry, it might as well be done immediately. At least there wouldn't be any family Mafia cars on their tail!

Vincent and Cathy drove to Elizabeth City, North Carolina, in late July, and got married at one of those 'get-hitched-quick' places that some states have on the border.

Vincent told me, 'We were married by a man who said he was a minister, but he looked like the janitor to me—a janitor just making an extra buck by performing marriage ceremonies. The couple waiting behind us in line were the witnesses.'

'Oh, my God.'

The gentle monologue went on: 'I regretted it immediately, but it was too late. I realized I hadn't wanted to get married at all. I felt like some sort of an outcast, running out of town to get married, and not having anyone there who knew us and would wish us well. Real Italian weddings are so very different from that.'

Vincent was so upset that, 'As we drove to Richmond for our honeymoon, we were involved in a head-on collision with another car.'

'Oh, Lord!' I said.

'That car had been special to me. It was a new, white T-Bird convertible. It was a total wreck.'

Cathy Scandellari spent their wedding night in a hospital, and Vincent stayed at the Holiday Inn. Cathy was not really hurt, but, 'She had had a love affair going on with doctors and hospitals for years. I just wasn't clued into it yet.'

Cathy was a secret alcoholic, and to cover up her drinking bouts, hangovers, lack of appetite, and general ill-health caused by the heavy drinking, she claimed to be sick with any sort of ill-defined malady that would carry her secret into another day.

'I had no idea that Cathy was an alcoholic. I hardly drank at all; I was not from a hard-drinking family, so I didn't recognize the signs.

'Before we were married, Cathy seemed light-hearted, happy, and bubbled with gaiety.'

Vincent wished a little of her spontaneity would rub off on him—he tended to be shy, even reserved. In the beginning of their friendship, Cathy had seemed to offer the happy companionship that he longed for, and hoped would make a marriage. But now that the marriage was made, Cathy seemed to remain in a perpetual state of depression, and began to get sloppy about her drinking, not bothering to hide it.

'Cathy seemed to stay chronically ill,' he said, 'and it slowly dawned on me just what the real trouble might be. I didn't know what to do. I couldn't look to my family for help. They had ostracized me.'

There is little so intriguing as the confessions of a reticent, and sometimes he let things drop that revealed more than he intended. I was listening to him tell me my fate, but I would not believe.

'I think the whole unhappy situation came about because I felt an overwhelming urge to rebel against my family who had always made decisions for me, and in general, tried to run my life. It was the day that the worm turned.'

The marriage of Vincent and Cathy was a disaster right from the beginning. The situation was made worse by Mrs. Scandellari refusing to receive Cathy; in fact, the whole family treated Cathy as if she did not exist. They would invite Vincent to come home for dinner, or the Christmas holidays, or any other occasion, and not extend the invitation to his wife.

Chapter Eighteen: *The Planets Collide*

Cathy drank more and more, though Vincent did everything he could to make life easy and comfortable for her. At one point, Cathy said to Vincent, 'I am so miserable that I want to kill myself.'

In an effort to do something constructive, Vincent took Cathy to her home in Memphis, Tennessee (good God, we're back to Memphis again!), so that she could be near her relatives. Vincent got a job driving a truck to try and support her. While he was out working, Cathy was out drinking.

'She became more and more sloppy, and dirty,' he said, 'and abusive, and after a while, she seemed to be mentally ill. I used to go looking for her after her drinking bouts, and find her collapsed in the alleyways and gutters of the darker side of Memphis. I felt that I had no choice but to put Cathy in a sanitarium, then I came back home to a cool reception by my family.'

His father died, leaving everyone bereft. It was decided to let bygones be bygones, and Cæsar took Vincent on as superintendent of his new project, Lake Edward. Then against all odds, he met me.

So on Saturday, July 1st, Vincent came to my house for a drink, and I felt very nervous and excited. I hadn't acknowledged it to myself, but I was wildly attracted to him. There was something about him that was like Mario. I did try to resist Vincent's 'old black magic,' and tried hard to ignore my tumultuous feelings, but I suppose mine was only a token resistance, a feint.

> *'That old black magic has me in its spell*
> *That old black magic that you weave so well*
> *Those icy fingers up and down my spine*
> *The same old witchcraft when your eyes meet mine ...'* [122]

---

[122] Lyrics from 'That Old Black Magic,' music by Harold Arlen, song lyrics by Johnny Mercer, 1942.

A Quiet Life in Bedlam

It took Vincent forty-five minutes to seduce me. I had been in the kitchen for quite a long time, trying to prepare our drinks, White Russians, but I was so nervous that I kept dropping things and spilling things, until I was about to give it up and go back to the living room where I had left Vincent ... when he came to me on very quiet feet.

I was still standing at the kitchen counter with my back to the door when Vincent came in, in that cat-like way he has, and put his arms around me, taking me by surprise. I was trembling, though I did not notice it. I turned to him.

Subconsciously I must have wanted him to make love to me, was desperately longing for it, but I never thought for a minute that he actually would do it. Why would he? I was undesirable. I was protected by my wedding ring. *He* was, 'an older man.' But if he did, if he made love to me, it would be like all the wonderful things I'd ever heard of happening to other people, happening to me all at once, in one fell-swoop; a jackpot.

Nevertheless, it was too much to contemplate, that I would betray my husband in deed, as well as in thought. I did not have the courage to face myself: my wishes and desires, my true and genuine feelings. My instinct told me that I'd found something more perfect and precious than anyone else had ever found, anywhere, and that I must be very, very careful, or I might lose it.

The way Vincent kissed me had had no equal in my limited experience with men. His kiss was so full of passion and the hope of possession that it was impossible not to capitulate. But I did not capitulate at once. I let him kiss me a little more—it was so delicious—back in the living room on the sofa, and then as if it were someone else speaking, I said, 'I want you to make love to me.'

He didn't have to carry me up the stairs; I ran. So he did make love to me, upstairs in the spare bedroom. I didn't take him into the master bedroom where I had slept with Terry. That would surely be adultery.

After that, it was only a rhapsody of, 'Speak Low':

Chapter Eighteen: *The Planets Collide*

Speak low, when you speak love
Our summer's day withers away
Too soon, too soon
Speak low, darling speak low
Love is a spark lost in the dark
And always too soon ... [123]

Night's egg cracked, and it was morning. There I was with my lover in my arms. He said, 'I missed you while you were sleeping.'

There was no turning back.

After that, I belonged to Vincent entirely, though I don't think I knew consciously that I was in love with him for about a month. 'I am still in love with Terry,' I told myself. I believed my passion for Vincent would cool with time, but it didn't. I had to let my feelings take me over completely before I could let myself love him, plus acknowledge that I did.

By the end of July, maybe before that, I did love Vincent, but I thought I still loved Terry, too. I stopped writing to Terry. I did not have anything more to say to him. My life had changed completely, and in my heart, I had made a commitment to someone else.

I had to stop working in the bar at the Holiday Inn. I could not hide it that I was in love with Vincent. There were too many people who knew him, and would talk about us behind our backs. There was a real danger to my reputation. Norfolk was a small town in those days, with a small-town mentality, and I would be regarded as just another slut, a Navy wife who was cheating on her husband (alas). No one would understand the special nature of our relationship, the depth of my need. And my chance would end too soon.

---

[123] 'Speak Low,' 1944. Famously played by Guy Lombardo. Written for the musical, *One Touch of Venus*. Lyrics by Ogden Nash; music by Kurt Weill.

A Quiet Life in Bedlam

Time is so old and love so brief
Love is pure gold, and time a thief
It's late, darling we're late
The curtain descends and everything ends
Too soon. [124]

It was so hard for me to be working in the bar when Cæsar or Luca came in, and not sit down with them, and say, 'Hey listen; I'm in love with your brother.' Vincent couldn't handle it either, if I continued working in the bar. He became very possessive. He did not want anyone to look at me but him. Those men customers did love to look; one could feel their eyes staring a hole right through one's clothes.

Vincent did not want anyone but himself to touch me. The bar customers could not be prevented from getting in a 'quick one' once in a while; they thought it was their right if they left you a tip! Vincent did not want any other man to talk to me but himself. It hurt his heart if he overheard anyone saying anything rude to me. So I gave a month's notice. What else could I do?

Before I left the employ of the Holiday Inn, two interesting things happened. Number one, I met Delores Delaney. Delores was a stunning blond who worked at the front desk. It was really pleasant to get to know Dolly, because I needed a friend, and I found that she shared my tastes in literature and music.

Many of the men going in and out of the Holiday Inn tried to find a way to have a conversation with Delores, but she wouldn't give them the time of day. The other Inn employees thought this was very funny. None of the men customers could understand why Delores seemed to be so cold—surely (they said) a girl with breasts as large as hers was looking for a boyfriend. Delores was physically magnificent. She looked as if she could try out for the World Cup, or hack her way through jungles, or scale precipices.

---

[124] 'Speak Low'.

Chapter Eighteen: *The Planets Collide*

Delores was really an attraction standing behind that check-in desk. She seemed to take a perverse delight in discovering customers who were trying to use expired credit cards; and these cards, once in they were in Delores' possession, were destroyed with alacrity, right in front of the fraudulent customer's face, causing a veritable fireworks display around the humiliated fraudster. Then the Inn Manager got called out of his office. The Inn Manager was a real easy-going guy—he was always kind to me—and he smoothed over the difficult scenes time after time.

Delores had flashing green eyes that, when one looked at her closely, proved to have brown flecks in them. These eyes were terribly enigmatic; I have seen Delores pick up a man in the grocery store (of all places!), simply by flashing a look, and crooking her little finger. I tried it, but it didn't work for me. She had a magnetism that was really astounding. But usually, Delores presented her 'cold' exterior to the world, and she could freeze you to death with a look that plainly said, 'Touch me not.'

Delores was a package of contained TNT. In a favorite murder mystery, *No More Dying Then,* the British crime writer, Ruth Rendall, has her character, Detective Inspector Burden, speak a line to a woman suspect: 'You use words like dangerous weapons.' That was Delores. She shot to kill. Vincent, who had a penchant for fanciful nicknames, called Delores the 'Amazon.' Me, he called 'Bess,' instead of any derivative of Katharine, as one would expect. I wonder, if he was getting his queens confused? And sometimes, he called me 'Bean,' or 'Princess.' Beats me why.

Delores, after a period of 'retreat' in a convent, eventually made a happy marriage, and was my attendant when I married Vincent, but at that time, in 1972, Delores was just twenty, and was trying to get a divorce. When she was seventeen, she had made an attempt to get away from home by marrying a boy straight out of high school. This boy had already joined the Armed Forces, and was committed to go to Vietnam the minute the honeymoon was over.

A Quiet Life in Bedlam

Delores' young husband had only just returned from his tour of duty in Vietnam, and was found to be a hopeless drug addict. She didn't tell me about this until later, but eventually, Dolly needed someone to confide in. She was by no means as cold as she looked. Delores had the 'street' savvy, and common sense, that I lacked. She proved to be a valuable friend.

One of the last nights I worked at the Holiday Inn was a Friday. Vincent had gone out of town, and I felt desolate. We had seen each other every day since The Seduction. But Vincent had a firm routine of flying out of Norfolk each Friday night, and joining his childhood friends in Queens, New York, for fun and games.

Vincent and his cronies played poker all night, and said things to each other like *'Mo Fak, Cak Sack,'* which is a very rough street slang. (I'll leave you to guess what it means.) Vincent invariably flew home to Virginia on Saturday morning, having gambled his money away. But he never said 'how much.' He was very secretive about money, 'how much and where from.'

Vincent kept up this exit-to-New-York routine until he was so hopelessly in love with me that he could not let me out of his sight; then he took *me*, on a plane or in the car, on Friday evening every week, to some distant city. We had dinner, spent the night in a posh hotel, and drove or flew, back to Virginia.

It was all very glamorous. I was being spoiled rotten. Gone was the stultifying life of a grounded Navy wife. I was excited out of my mind. I used to thrill my friends with tales of what Vincent and I had done 'last night.' Once, I accidentally left behind a new 18 karat gold bracelet in a hotel room in Las Vegas, and never saw it again.

But on this particular Friday night, early in August, Vincent had left me for his New York cronies, and I worked in the bar until 2:00 a.m. closing time. Then I drove home alone. I didn't have far to go. I noticed somebody's headlights following me all the way, but I didn't think anything of it.

I hadn't been inside my house more than a few minutes when there was a knock on the front door. Surprised, and sud-

Chapter Eighteen: *The Planets Collide*

denly excited, I thought it might be Vincent—he had been known to watch my house until I came in, and then ask for admittance. To think that it was Vincent on this particular Friday night, though, was irrational, because I knew he was out of town. That's what a love affair will do to you—make you leap for your lover.

It wasn't Vincent. It was a bearded young man who had been in the bar until closing time. He seemed pleasant and nice enough in the bar, though he had not impressed me as anyone I would be attracted to, or have any interest in whatsoever. Well, while I was standing there nonplussed, he shouldered his way into my house. I was still not afraid; he had not given me any reason to be, though I felt a little uneasy about the way he had followed me home.

The young man said he 'wanted to talk,' so I asked him to sit down. The next thing I knew, he had grabbed me, and was trying to force me down onto the carpeted floor in my living room. He did not have a weapon that I could see.

Somehow, by the grace of God, I managed to struggle away from his grasp, and ran into my dining room, separating myself from the malice in his eyes by the length of my dining room table. I had beautiful colonial-style high ladder-backed chairs, which, with the six-foot dining table, were the only protection available to me. I kept my wits about me, and though he pursued me into the dining room and around the table, I managed always to keep a piece of furniture—usually one of the ladder-back chairs—between him and me.

The man clearly wanted to attack me, you could see his fingers itching, but somehow I had thrown him off balance when I bolted away so precipitously. With the distance of the six-foot table between us, I said to him very quietly, very calmly, 'If you don't get out of here, I'm going to call the police.'

He said, just as quietly, 'I'm not going to let you call the police.'

Then he said, 'Now why don't you submit to me, like a good girl?'

A Quiet Life in Bedlam

I replied, still calm, 'I want nothing to do with you, you scum. Can't you get a girl without having to force her?'

He said, 'You work in a bar; I thought you were available.'

'What? Are bar girls prostitutes, too?'

This exchange of words and hard looks took only a few seconds, but it seemed like long minutes. My scalp was prickling, but I consistently kept the table and chairs between us as he circled, always alert for any new move he might make.

I said, 'You thought wrong. I am not available; I just have to work, like anybody else. Anyway, I'm married, and my husband is due home any minute. You better be out of here—my husband weighs two hundred pounds, and he'll throttle you for sure.'

The man said, 'I don't believe you. I heard you tell someone that your husband is in Vietnam.'

I countered with, 'I don't care what you heard! My husband is due home, and if you don't get out of here immediately, I won't answer for the consequences to your person.'

Well, I was astonished that my bluff worked, but the would-be rapist turned around and left by the front door. Trembling, shaking with fear, I double-bolted the door behind him, and called the police to report what had happened. The potential assailant sat in my driveway in his car until a squad car turned into the street, then he got out of there quick.

He did come back, several times. He must have been crazy. I had to be very careful for several weeks, because this man would come up to my house unexpectedly very often, late at night, and ask me to open the door and let him in. It was very frightening. After the first incidence, I had a 'peep-hole' installed in the front door, then I could see who it was; plus, I could hear his voice plainly through the wooden door. It was the second time I had been 'stalked.' It wasn't the last.

I could not figure out why the man would not stop bothering me. Each time he came to the door, I said, 'My husband is at home; you'd better go away.' Each of those times, I was alone with no defense if he should have decided to try to break in. Thankfully, he never did.

Chapter Eighteen: *The Planets Collide*

The last time the stalker came to my house, Vincent happened to be with me, and showed himself at the door. The presence in the house of a man, seemed to convince this fellow that my husband was indeed at home, and he never came back. Thank God. I still had Terry's Lugar pistol in a drawer upstairs, but I did not know how to use it.

The experience was enough to teach me a lesson. I never worked in a bar again.

CHAPTER NINETEEN:
Since I Fell for You

I loved Vincent, and I told him so, though he would not say that he loved me. Every action, every look of his told me that he did in fact love me, but I wanted to hear it from his lips. He would not say it, no matter how I begged or cajoled; I suppose he had some scruples about admitting love for a married woman.

I told him that when Terry came home, I would have to break off our affair, but he didn't believe it, and neither did I. I had confessed to Vincent about my lack of a conjugal life with Terry; and Vincent, who is deeply intuitive, almost clairvoyant it seems, knew in his heart that I would not be able to leave him—which, in the end, I couldn't—but Vincent was years making any sort of commitment to me. I suppose he had been burned once, and was twice shy.

'I love you,' I said.
'You always say you love me after I've fed you.'
'I do love you, truly.'
'You need a lot of help, Bess, but I can't afford to give it to you.'
'What kind of help, darling?'

Chapter Nineteen: *Since I Fell for You*

'I just want to put a little money aside, so that I can take you out of the booby-hatch after they lock you up. I know they won't take American Express.'

All I could do was laugh. His sense of humor really tickled my funny bone. I can still picture him standing there in his paisley-print silk shirt and Gucci alligator loafers, dark hair slicked back and thinning a little on top. Vincent was a peacock, the sort of man who wore white bucks, a white sport coat and a pink carnation when those clothes were in style, in the late 1950s. And blue suede shoes! Yeah, man, Vincent was a real cool hep-cat.

He seemed always in a good humor. The closest he ever came to flying into a rage was when someone asked him, as they sometimes did, if he was an Arab, or a Greek, a Jew, or an Iranian—yes, an Iranian! For he's a very Mediterranean-looking man. His profile is like one you would see stamped on a Roman coin.

I get a kick out of it when he makes cracks, as he often does, about the size of his own nose. I think it's to cover his insecurities, because he is very sensitive about being a first-generation American. Even with his ethnic background, Sicilian down to the ground, Vincent firmly contends that he is an American, and not an Italian, even if he looks like one. He says his roots are in the U.S.A., even if he was plainly reared in the European fashion.

I heard that his mother and aunt had tried to marry him off to one of his spinster cousins who had a mustache on her top lip and didn't shave her legs; but Vincent refused. At least he has some sense!

But the truth is, the Scandellari family had no plans for Vincent to marry; they just didn't talk about it. As he was the quietest and most passive of the four sons, he was earmarked to stay at home with his parents. It was an old Sicilian custom, and rigidly adhered to where Italian populations were most dense, like New York City.

Usually, it's a girl that is chosen to care for her aging parents, but there were no daughters born to the Scandellaris.

A Quiet Life in Bedlam

Before I left the Holiday Inn job, I went to work as secretary for an interior designer in downtown Norfolk. There I met one of the loveliest and most original girls I have ever set eyes on. Her name was Lynette Mckinnon, and she had brown eyes that actually sparkled when she talked. And she had a wonderful talent for mimicry; I never laughed so much. Lynette was a riot. Her routine based on Lady Bird Johnson was priceless: *'Just plant a tree or a shrub!'* We all fell about, laughing.

Lynette had a sweet smile, and a genuine, sweet nature. Her dark hair was long and wavy. Her make-up was perfect. Her fingernails were like daggers, well-shaped and polished with red lacquer. She was as physically perfect as a fashion model would have to be, but she wasn't as thin as models usually are. She did, however, dress fit to kill, and must have spent all her money on clothes.

I never saw such a wardrobe as Lynette Mckinnon had burgeoning in her closets. She had more pairs of shoes than Imelda Marcos. Each pair was neatly placed in the original shoebox, with a Polaroid photograph of the shoes taped on the end. She had more accessories than a department store.

Just as I felt I was getting to know her really well, Lynette suddenly left her job as bookkeeper, to get married. This took everyone at the firm by surprise. Lynette had not mentioned a pending marriage before. Our boss, the interior designer, who was a very high-strung and hyper man, immediately had some sort of seizure which the paramedics said was a heart attack.

As the ambulance took the man away, he looked Lynette in the eye, and said, 'This is your fault, for leaving me. You caused your father to have that heart attack, and now, you've done it to me, too. I hope you're satisfied!'

'Jesus, Mary and Joseph!' slipped out of my mouth before I could stop it. Lynette looked as though she might faint.

Well, not one of us who witnessed this scene could figure out why the man would say such things. Lynette was only the bookkeeper. True, she hadn't given any notice of leaving, but then, these things happened in business. Was the interior de-

Chapter Nineteen: *Since I Fell for You*

signer fiddling the books in some way? The resignation of a bookkeeper shouldn't cause a heart attack, for Christ's sake.

Lynette felt crushed by the man's remark about her father—not a month previously, Lynette's father had died of a coronary thrombosis. She was not out of mourning yet.

My job ended the same day because my boss was in the hospital, critically ill, and his wife dismissed the staff, not knowing when her husband would recover. Lynette did not change her plans, but went on to Richmond to marry a young attorney whom she had known for a couple of months. I was happy about her marriage, but I hated to lose her before our friendship had had a chance to begin. There was something special about her; I wanted to know her. I felt I could say anything to her, anything at all, and she would understand.

I gave Lynette my address and telephone number, and told her that if she ever came back to Norfolk from Richmond, that she should come and see me.

It was July 31st, a Monday afternoon, and the scene at the interior designer's office had happened on the previous Friday. I was without a job, but I felt I would die before going back to the telephone office. I was down on my hands and knees, pulling weeds out of my flower garden, when I felt a presence near me.

I looked up. It was Lynette, and there were tears streaming down her face. Her dark thick hair hung limp around her shoulders, and though she was dressed perfectly nicely by anyone's standards, for Lynette she looked curiously disheveled. She was dressed in a very formal manner, too. She wore a long-skirted velvet suit in *rose du Barry,* a kind of hot pink. It was simply gorgeous, and very unusual.

My heart stopped. I said, looking up at her. 'Lynette! What a surprise! Why are you here?' Her tragic gaze reminded me of Countess Dracula, though I don't mean to imply that Lynette seemed frightening in any way. She was the kindest of women.

Lynette said nothing.

Then I asked, 'Where's your husband?' She had just gotten married, hadn't she? Her husband must be nearby. But Lynette

A Quiet Life in Bedlam

just cried some more—this time sobbing audibly. It was very strange. Was this a dream?

I said, 'Come into the house,' and I took her arm.

We got into the house, and I seated Lynette in one of my beautiful brocade wing chairs. The chair was blue, and she was in pink, so it was quite a picture. There she sat until I brought her a Scotch and water—Johnny Walker Red—to see of it would help to calm her down.

Lynette told me this bizarre story about her lost weekend. She had gone to Richmond on the Friday night with her mother and three brothers, and was married in a small church ceremony to a fellow by the name of Don King. Stylish as always, Lynette wore a pink velvet two-piece fitted suit with a full-length split skirt. She had a sparkling engagement ring on her finger, and the wedding ring that came after.

Lynette recounted, 'Don and I spent Friday night at Don's apartment as man and wife. Don claimed that he could not afford to take me on a honeymoon, because he had just set up a new law practice and money was short.

'But I was satisfied just to be with my new husband, married at last, and beginning to feel secure.'

Lynette had been like me, not really able to find her place in the world, and needed to be married to establish her identity. Also, like me, she was sensitive and artistic, and not a terribly good money-manager—so she needed a husband, just like I did. We were birds of a feather.

Lynette was twenty-one, but everyone thought she was older, because of the fact that she had been married the first time at only thirteen years old when a twenty-five-year-old creep by the name of Mckinnon had persuaded her to run away with him and get married. The marriage was strictly unlawful, because the legal marrying age in Virginia without parental consent was eighteen. Lynette's mother would never have allowed such a thing, but she was not able to catch her in time.

So this weirdo, Mckinnon, who must have been a pedophile, altered Lynette's birth certificate to show that she was five years older than she actually was, and the two were mar-

Chapter Nineteen: *Since I Fell for You*

ried in North Carolina. The lie about Lynette's age followed her throughout her life, and now she's not particularly happy about it! Hah.

Mckinnon had to be some sort of pervert to marry a thirteen-year-old girl anyway, and that was what he proved to be within a short time. Mckinnon had been married twice before, and had custody of his five small children by his previous marriages. It was to be Lynette's job to care for these children. She was hardly more than a child herself. In addition, she was to be Mckinnon's live-in lover and housekeeper.

Mckinnon showed his true colors when he began to abuse Lynette both emotionally and physically. Lynette had run away from her mother's home because she was unhappy there, and now she seemed to have gone from the 'frying pan, into the fire.' Poor baby.

Lynette continued her incredible saga, 'My mother and father were so disappointed by what I had done, marrying an older man without their consent, that the relations between us were strained for quite some time, and though I was desperate many times to escape from Mckinnon, I felt as if I didn't have any place to run to.'

God, what a mess, I thought to myself. *Is everyone in Virginia as mad as the ones I have met so far?*

'Finally,' Lynette said, 'at the age of eighteen, I had the courage to leave Mckinnon, and have the marriage annulled. I kept Mckinnon's name, however, because the Norfolk Circuit Court judge had the same name! It was like an ace up my sleeve. That name was powerful, and it could get me things. For example, I could speed, and the police who stopped me did not give me tickets. "Judge Mckinnon?" they would ask. His niece, I would say!

'I could get credit from local firms, because of the Mckinnon name. I even turned away a would-be robber once by saying, "My father is Judge Mckinnon." But I had a gun under the front seat, too.'

'How exciting,' I said. 'You carry a gun?' Hers was a different world. My world had been so drab—before the Scandellaris came along.

I told her about Vincent. 'Grab him!' she said.

'No,' I replied mournfully. 'I have to give him up in October when Terry comes home.'

'Why?'

'Because I want to be married and respectable.'

'Won't Vincent marry you?'

'I doubt it. He's Catholic. I'm Protestant. And then I would be divorced from Terry, you see. His family would never approve.'

'Oh, you could bring them around.'

'I don't know.' The Scandellari family was a hard nut to crack.

After Lynette's first annulment, she lived at home with her mother for three years, but she was unhappy. Her mother treated her like a child. A financial settlement made with Mckinnon at the time of their separation allowed Lynette to finish school, and graduate from a business college. Then she met Don King, and married him in Richmond on that fatal Friday night.

Suddenly Lynette exclaimed, 'I'm hungry!' like she a monstrous appetite. I didn't have any food in the house, and not much gasoline in the car. I was broke.

She said, 'Not to worry,' and we drove away in her ruby red Dodge Monaco, that she called the 'Mon-NAH-ka!' always with that exclamation point, as if it were some special car—and I guess it was—it was paid for.

Over a fantastic 'Hawaiian' dinner, and a bottle of Rose Mateus wine at the Chinese restaurant, Lynette continued her extraordinary story. I was still so young and inexperienced, even at twenty-six that I believed every word—and I reckon the most of it was true. Why did I attract crazy people?

'So, back to my sudden marriage and the precipitous ending!' Lynette had definitely perked up. 'By Saturday afternoon Don was acting strange. I had some shopping to do, and I

Chapter Nineteen: *Since I Fell for You*

thought Don just needed to be alone for a while to think. That was what he needed all right, but it was not going to be to my benefit when Don finished his thinking.

'I didn't suspect any problems, and went off happily to shop. My favorite department stores are in Richmond. Norfolk is almost a backwater when it comes to fashion!'

Obviously. I had never seen clothes so swashbuckling and romantic as hers were. I began copying her style right away.

'When I came back to the apartment building about four hours had passed, and I found the door to the apartment bolted against me. I knocked and knocked, and rang the bell. No reply. Finally, just as I was beginning to feel panicky, Don opened the door, and I walked into the place that I thought was to be my home.'

I was listening intently, trying not to chew so I wouldn't miss any of the juicy details.

'Don was moody and withdrawn. He didn't want to talk about what was wrong. He wouldn't kiss me, or even come near me. I was bewildered. The situation stayed like that all through Saturday night—Don shut me out of the one bedroom, and I slept on the sofa in the living room.'

I couldn't wait. 'What did you do?!'

'Wait a minute. The next morning at breakfast, I was nearly beside myself with anxiety. I demanded that Don tell me what on Earth was the matter. He said, "I've made a big mistake. I married you only to make my girlfriend jealous. I didn't know what I was doing".'

'Was he on drugs?' I asked.

'I don't know. I was astounded at his behavior. It was totally unexpected. On Saturday morning a young, attractive woman had visited the apartment, and Don talked to her privately, and at some length. I didn't think anything of it—I just assumed the woman was one of Don's clients. After all, we had just been married the night before.

'While I was still speechless with shock, Don said, "I want a divorce".'

My jaw dropped. 'I think I have to order a drink,' I said.

'I need one, too,' Lynette agreed. When the waiter came, we ordered Johnny Walker Red Scotch and water on ice. Lynette advised me, 'Always drink scotch and water, nothing more fancy; then you won't get sick.'

Words of Wisdom. Lynette lit up a cigarette. She handled it beautifully, like the cigarette was some delicate thing—a Japanese fan, perhaps. Lynette managed to talk a lot with her hands, waving the cigarette around, almost as if she were dancing like a Hindu *natch* girl.

'What about drinking White Russians, with vodka, Kahlua, and half and half?' I asked her.

'You're living dangerously.'

'Oh.' White Russians were my favorite.

Lynette wasn't finished with her tale. By this time, she had begun to show a decided flair for drama. 'Then Don rose from his chair at the head of the table, walked across the room, seated himself at his typewriter, and began typing up the divorce papers. He explained, "No need to pay a lawyer when I can do it myself".'

'Jesus Christ,' I said. Lynette's story was a good example of the old adage, *fact is stranger than fiction.*

I asked myself, 'Is there no limit to what Virginia lawyers will do?' They were different creatures altogether from the ones I knew in Key West.

By the Monday, Lynette had packed all of her belongings into her car, The Mon-ah-kah, and gone to see a lawyer in Richmond about her annulment. She received one, but it took some time, and Lynette found herself to be in something of a legal limbo. Lynette didn't feel as if she could face her mother, so she came to me! She was still wearing the pink wedding outfit.

Why she chose me, I'll never know. She must have had other friends. We barely knew each other. But nevertheless, there she was, and I couldn't turn her away. Lynette had a penchant for romantic misadventures. There were instances during the time I knew her when Lynette was Moll Flanders or even

Chapter Nineteen: *Since I Fell for You*

Fanny Hill. She didn't seem to have a conscience about whom she went to bed with.

However, she proved to be a lot of fun. I was getting another kind of education. Lynette knew all the places to go, the people to see. I began to enjoy pretending to be single. I had been feeling very guilty about my affair with Vincent, so in a futile gesture, I suggested to both Vincent and Lynette that perhaps they should date each other—maybe they would hit it off. In that way I could return to my status as 'respectably married woman'—become constrained by the veil, as it were.

I reasoned, 'If I can't have Vincent, at least he would belong to a friend, and I can keep tabs on him.' It was a way of being righteous and unselfish—and I didn't mean a word of it. Vincent and Lynette *knew* I didn't mean a word of it, and they just laughed at me. Gosh, sometimes I could be so obtuse. I can only say in my defense that intellectuals do not understand practical realities.

Now, sometimes, Vincent would get into a mood where he was playing hard to get, and he would stay away from me for a couple of days—not telephone, not come by—that sort of thing. Though he wanted more than anything else to be in my arms, he thought perhaps it was unhealthy (not to mention unwise) for me to be enamored of him, for us to be seen so often together, though Vincent did everything he could to take me places where we would not be seen by people we knew.

We sat in dark restaurants and drank cocktails, like Brandy Alexanders or Pink Ladies, resembling the illicit and naughty couple in the song, 'Me and Mrs. Jones.'

'Me and Mrs. Jones, we got a thing goin' on ...' [125]

The waiters were still 'carding' me to find out if I was old enough to drink (twenty-one). That was a giggle. After I showed the waiter my I.D. and he went away, I would say, 'Do you know I love you, Vincent?'

And he would say, 'You never told me.'

I would say, 'What would I do without you, Vincent?'

---

[125] Lyrics from 'Me and Mrs. Jones,' 1972, sung by Billy Paul; written by Kenny Gamble, Leon Huff, and Cary Gilbert.

And he would say, 'You'd find some sap.' There would be a guffaw from me. We were like Laurel and Hardy.

Ours was a relationship filled with an easy companionability and a stream of meaningless banter; it was as if we had nothing better to talk about. Vincent only laughed at my literary pretensions and my longing for a real education. He was afraid of growing old, and wouldn't talk about age or aging.

Vincent didn't like black, which he associated with death, so I was not allowed to wear little black dresses. Vincent was afraid of water, would not swim, and regularly went to the barbershop to get his hair washed and cut, so that he wouldn't have to immerse his face in that dangerous liquid, H2O. Neither of us drank much alcohol when we were together. We wanted to save our ardor for the bedroom, and not the booze. But if it was a question of who would drive, I would say, 'I'll drive.'

Vincent would answer, 'No, I don't trust you.'

'Why? I never have any accidents!'

'Yes, but it's unknown how many cars you've run off the road.'

Wasn't he just the limit?

I suffered when Vincent was away from me. I still was hurting because he would not tell me that he loved me, and by the end of August, I was beginning to feel very nervous about the prospect of Terry coming home again.

Whenever Vincent ignored me, Lynette and I went out together to dinner, for drinks, to dance, just as if we had every right to be young and have fun. I never descended to the deceitful depths of putting my wedding ring in my shoe, as others did; but the gold band almost did not exist. One night when I was at a nightclub with Lynette and her brothers, the four of them were feeling devil-may-care, and they got up and began dancing on the bar! I didn't know whether to say, 'Fie!' or 'Excelsior!' It was very daring.

Lynette and I ran into Cæsar a few times. Cæsar followed us with his eyes. I cared very much for Cæsar's good opinion since he was Vincent's brother. It made me happy that he seemed to like me, and was clearly impressed by my gorgeous

Chapter Nineteen: *Since I Fell for You*

friend, Lynette. Cæsar had been watching my house too, or having it watched, and he knew about my affair with Vincent; he also knew that Lynette was living with me.

One summer's day when I was home alone, Cæsar showed up at my door, and asked if he could come in and talk. I said, 'Sure. Glad to see you.'

The long and short of it was that Cæsar was looking for a mistress; he thought I might make a good one. He proposed just that to me. I was surprised and bemused. *Has the world ever changed!* I thought. Was I mistress material? I didn't know what to say.

One doesn't refuse a man as rich and powerful as Cæsar appeared to be, but I was in love with Vincent. *Really,* in love with Vincent. Terry was not even a consideration by this time—though he was a prop I could fall back on, if the need arose. I guess I knew I was being beastly to Terry, but at least he knew nothing of it.

So, I said, 'Cæsar, I'm honored that you would think of me; but didn't you know that I've been seeing your brother, Vincent?'

Cæsar brushed aside the mention of Vincent as if he were a fly on his jacket lapel. 'Vincent can't do anything for you,' he said, 'and I can. I could make you very comfortable. You would never want for anything.'

I was flabbergasted. It was a dilemma. How could I say, 'Thanks, but no thanks,' without hurting his feelings, and without making an enemy? Cæsar was a powerful man. Was he making me an offer I shouldn't refuse?

Finally, I said, 'Look, Cæsar. It's a very tempting offer, and I'm flattered by it. But I really believe it would make my life too complicated. My husband is due home in October.'

Caesar was gracious, as he can be when he wants to; and he left, looking as proud, and arrogant, and cynical, as he did when he came in. I had to sit down. I was hyperventilating.

A few days later Lynette was in the house alone when the doorbell rang, and it was Cæsar. He had, of course, known who was there, and he knew she was alone.

The big man put the same offer to Lynette, who was caught completely off-guard, and didn't really know what he was talking about (or offering). She refused him without a proper hearing.

Cæsar left again, and he's never had anything to do with me, or any of my friends, since. He never even acknowledged it when Vincent and I were married. Cæsar was a proud man and not used to being refused. In fact, he fired Vincent from his job as site superintendent one more time.

Cæsar finally decided on the barmaid at the Holiday Inn, Debbie, to be his mistress, and they have had a hugely successful relationship for many years now. Though Cæsar has not always been discreet, Cæsar's wife has never confronted him with it, though she must know. They're Catholic, have five children, and she wants to stay married. I would say she's a wise woman.

Summer drew to an end, and autumn began to cool the days. Vincent and I were still going at it hot and heavy, but he wouldn't allow me to get too close to him emotionally; he held me at arm's length, as it were. Vincent would come to see me real often; then he would stay away for days and days. I got my feelings hurt. I was like the woman in that famous story by Dorothy Parker,

> 'Please, God, let him telephone me now.
> I won't ask anything else of You, truly I won't.
> It isn't very much to ask. It would be so little to You, God, such a little, little thing. Only let him telephone me now. Please, God. Please, please, please.'

Vincent had his own key, and often he would walk in unannounced and unexpected. His key was not one I gave him—he had a master key to all the houses in that development—but I didn't argue with him about it.

One day he came in by surprise when Lynette and Delores were cooking collard greens, a Virginia delicacy. Lynette and Dolly were real Virginia girls, and liked all those Southern foods, spinach, Virginia ham, even okra.

Chapter Nineteen: *Since I Fell for You*

Lynette always loved to cook, and still does. She said, 'Cooking makes me feel secure.' I began to wonder if I did *really* understand her. Cooking makes me feel like a slave. So when she was living with me, she did all the cooking. It was great. Dolly contributed baked sourdough bread and bottles of wine, Mateus Rose and Blue Nun Libfraumilch.

What fun it was to run with that fast crowd—as I realized later it must have been. But the days of my Rose Mateus were running away too soon, too soon. It was not so long anymore, before Terry would come home.

Oh, dreaded day.

Now, in my opinion, the odor of collard greens cooking is enough to knock down a strong man, it's true. It is really repulsive, and poor Vincent, who had only made it into the house as far as the foyer, was at first overwhelmed, and then nauseated.

He shouted, 'Who, in God's name, is dying from diarrhea?' And he left without a word to me.

I was very upset. A man in love is not normally put off by collard greens. Then I became more and more upset when Vincent stayed away for several more days. I was trying hard not to call him, though I wanted to, badly. It often happens that a woman in love has no pride, and I was one of those, God help me; I would have kissed his feet. But I didn't call him. I had given and given in the relationship with Vincent, and he had given little back, except for some torrid lovemaking. Well, there was that trip to Rome one weekend ...

Then I heard it through the grapevine that Vincent was seeing another woman who lived on the other side of the Lake Edward development. Her name was Mrs. St. Germaine. I was suspicious. One day, I followed him on my bicycle to see if it was true. Sure enough, he stopped at the woman's house, came out with her, and took her off somewhere.

Scream! Think girl, think.

Well! I had been faithful to him, after my fashion, but he was not being faithful to me! It just so happened that I ran into Vincent's brother, Luca, that evening when Dolly and I were out getting pizza. Luca lived in a Lake Edward apartment nearby.

Luca said to me, 'I've just returned from a trip to the Bahamas, and I've brought back some excellent black rum, one hundred proof. Why don't you come up to my apartment later, and we'll have a drink.'

I said I would. I was feeling rebellious and devil-may-care. I was feeling jealous.

Luca was going through his 'man-about-town' stage. He had plenty of money, a mother who adored him, all the women he wanted. He had his own airplane, lots of men friends, a collection of valuable guns, and many other expensive hobbies—such as scuba-diving equipment, and keeping a horse stable.

It was rumored that Luca had a friend who liked snakes and owned a houseful of exotic ones. The snakes were allowed to run loose. There had to be something twisted about a man who liked snakes. But generally, I took people at face value, and did not see any 'guilt by association,' as it were. Theoretically, Luca would be a catch. Surely there were no boa constrictors in Luca's apartment.

Anyway, I had to be flattered that a man like Luca Scandellari had asked me to socialize with him—even though I would never desire him for my own; too many other women wanted him. That was definitely a turn-off for someone of my temperament. I had to feel as if I alone belonged to a man. He had to want just me, and no one else. It would have been hard for Luca to limit himself to only one woman, what with the way all the Virginia Beach girls were flinging themselves at him.

Luca was at that time twenty-nine—probably the most attractive of the brothers. He had a cerebral way of flirting that was very appealing. I'd like to say though, here and now, that I never observed in Luca a tendency to think that he was God's Gift to Women, which trap would have been so easy for him to fall into. He seemed down-to-Earth and sincere. I didn't know it then, but he was looking for a nice Catholic girl to marry. Of course, I wasn't it.

Chapter Nineteen: *Since I Fell for You*

I went up to Luca's apartment. I was dressed in low-slung brown corduroy jeans with flared legs, belted at the hips with knotted rope (the better to hang myself with), and a thin-ribbed nylon short-sleeved sweater, and loafers. It was September, and the evenings were already cool.

Luca was sophisticated, gentlemanly, suave, urbane—all the things those devils, the Scandellaris, are noted for. I used to throw that word, 'suave,' into my conversation sometimes, just to spice things up, and the Scandellaris would scream with mirth and shout, 'SWAVE! SWAVE!' I never got any respect for my astounding vocabulary. But Luca, even more than the others, exhibited a droll humor, and it was fascinating. If I hadn't had my wits about me, Luca could have swept me off my feet.

We sat on Luca's sofa. He plied me with Bacardi rum and cokes. I liked rum. I drank it, and it only took one and one-half glasses-full to finish me to the point where I could not resist his advances. The image of Vincent's sad face (he perpetually wears a melancholy look anyway) flashed itself in front of my poor, whoosey, intoxicated eyes. Luca had my glasses off, and he was—I kid you not—biting my breast, right through the ribbed sweater.

What was I doing? Fear flashed through me, I came to my senses, and pushed Luca away. He thought I was just being coy, and pulled me back to him again.

I pushed him away a second time and said with all earnestness: 'Luca, I'm in love with your brother.' I didn't have to say which brother; I suppose he knew. Immediately he stopped his amorous advances. He picked me up off the sofa, handed me my pocketbook, and showed me the door. He was an honorable man, after his fashion. I left, feeling as if I had been rolled over by a tidal wave.

Luca has never had too much to say to me, either. I have always complained about the Scandellaris ignoring me, which I would not have expected, but I guess I made my own troubles right from the beginning, and the memories of those things that

A Quiet Life in Bedlam

happened with the three brothers in the late summer and early autumn of 1972, have neither been forgiven, nor forgotten.

CHAPTER TWENTY:
Total Eclipse of the Heart

Lynette and I had a row late in September, after she took a brand-new white quilt, which had been hand-stitched by my grandmother, to the beach to lie in the sand with her new boyfriend. The quilt came back all grimy and sandy, dirty, and ratty-looking. It had to be washed, and never looked the same again. The smooth finish provided by the sizing in the fabric was gone forever. I was incensed, and I let Lynette have it right between the eyes. My possessions are only a little less precious than my life.

I told Lynette that we did not have the same values, if she could be so stupid as to take a new hand-made quilt to the beach and ruin it. That quilt was probably worth a hundred dollars. Lynette packed up and left immediately. But we stayed in touch. As she exited my front door, she commented, 'I can't sleep in this house anyway, because of all the clocks going off every fifteen minutes!'

Hrrmphh! I *like* Westminster chimes. Good riddance.

In late October, I got word that the ship was on its way back—would be docking in a few days. At first I was in shock. I guess I had hoped the day would never come. Then, I felt myself to be on the verge of an emotional breakdown. I met my *doppelgänger* in the doorway to my bedroom. That was terrifying. I knew it could be an omen of death. I went into a state of psychosomatic paralysis, unable to move.

I must have been there like that for about two days, when Vincent let himself in with his key, walked upstairs, and found me frozen with fear about the confrontation that was coming. I had never been so guilty. I did not know what I would do or say when I saw Terry. I just wanted to take the coward's way out and leave with Vincent for South America. The only thing that held me back was my innocent dogs and cats.

Vincent carried me to his car, and took me immediately to the Navy hospital where the medics gave me a series of shots to relax my muscles that had been locked. The medication got me walking around again, but did nothing to relax or relieve my mind. I was in a quite a state. It seemed as if for many years, I had been unaware of my deeper feelings and natural instincts. Now that I was facing myself, I had no choice but to take the consequences of a drastic upheaval in my life. Now I knew who I really was, and not who I thought I was.

I still tried to hold it off though, the knowledge of that real person, Katharine Bamber, who was someone quite other to what I believed. Experiencing an 'unbearable lightness of being' feeling that I wasn't really *there*, I prepared myself and my house for a reunion with my husband. Terry already knew something was wrong, because, unable to write to him, I sent a cassette tape where I just cried, and tried to talk to him, through half a disastrous hour.

On the day the ship came in, I was deadly calm, void of all feeling, intent on one purpose, and that was to go to the ship and tell Terry I was divorcing him. I had seen Vincent for the last time the night before, made love for the last time, been happy for the last time, though the happiness was short-lived and bittersweet.

When I saw Terry, I felt confused. There was the pale face that I had loved for so long. There were the innocent blue eyes. There was the person that I had endured six years of Navy hell for. There was the man I had married, and given my young life to. Somehow, I just couldn't tell him and break his heart. It

Chapter Twenty: *Total Eclipse of the Heart*

took me a week to break the news that I was in love with another man.

Terry was shocked beyond anything I had ever known him to be. For a man who characteristically did not show emotion, who always walked around with a pleasant, smiling countenance, such an easy disposition, Terry became extremely emotional, and even a little bit crazy and self-destructive.

'Please don't leave me,' he begged. 'I will do *anything* to save our marriage.'

Over and over, he asked me most humbly to reconsider. He was breaking my heart, and I knew that his was already broken. But it was beating, beating, beating, in my heart, in my brain, that I would never feel alive again if I could not see Vincent everyday. Vincent had become my life. I told Terry this.

Terry said, 'I will do anything! I will get out of the Navy.'

'No, no, it's your life.'

'I will see a psychiatrist.'

'Maybe that's a good idea,' I said. 'But what about the danger to your Navy personnel records?'

He ignored that. 'I'm at sea so much—I will allow you to have a lover, to have Scandellari—if you will just remain with me as my wife. I cannot face life alone. I like being married.'

This was not right, not fair, and I knew it. I agreed to give it a couple of weeks, a reconciliation period, to find out how we felt at the end of that period. Terry tried to make love to me. I recoiled from him. We continued together in an uneasy truce. We still slept in the same bedroom.

About a week later, we went to a ship's party, where the crew was separated from us across the big ballroom, so that the enlisted men and their wives were on one side of the room, and the officers and their wives were on the other side of the room. It was everything that I found disgusting about the Navy. Terry asked me to dance. Other couples were dancing, all married, all happy to be reunited; Terry and I were in agony.

As we danced, I was looking over Terry's shoulder, thinking how odd it was that he had seldom agreed to dance with me at any time during our married lives (the dance at the USO had been practically the only one), but he was willing to dance with me now. I knew even then that people don't really change, though I thought that Terry would try very hard.

I almost resolved to give him another chance, just for the security the married state offered; and to save more trauma and tears to one that, essentially, I loved, but in a brotherly way. Then I happened to notice the faces of the other Navy wives as they danced. Happy, sleepy, as contented as cows, the wives leaned on their husbands, and danced their way into my consciousness as *dead people, who forgot to lie down,* to put it in Vincent's quaint phrasing. And I knew that it was no good.

I craved the excitement of being with Vincent, the passionate lovemaking provided by Vincent, the deep emotions that showed on his face, the glamorous, gad-about lifestyle that I had lived with Vincent over the past few months. I couldn't give that up for another stretch of married life that would only end anyway, just as soon as the ship left for another trip to the Mediterranean, as it was scheduled to do in the spring of the new year 1973.

I think I may have been going through what astrologers call my 'social butterfly stage' that Lunar *Aquarians*—that was me, the Moon in Aquarius—experience at some time or other in their lives. Practical realities don't come into it. Social life and fun are all that matter.

Of course, my commonsense was battling with that dragging, paralyzing loneliness and body hunger, the impulse to break away from a way of life that seemed likely to kill my soul if not my healthy woman's body. Though this sounds contradictory, I wanted permanence and stability, the establishing of roots. I had a need for predictability that the Navy could not give, nor Terry, since he was Navy in blood and bone, and gold stars and bars. Living with my lover would not give me peace of mind, but that is what I ultimately sought.

After the party, I told Terry that it was over between us, and that I wanted him to move back to the ship as soon as he could do so. I could give him some time to arrange things. We verbally divided up our belongings. We gave Pretzel and An-

Chapter Twenty: *Total Eclipse of the Heart*

heuser away to a kindly couple who lived in the country; that way they could run as much as they wanted, enjoy their lives as dogs without seeing me crying and moping around. Pretzel had become quite nervous and high-strung, though Anheuser was as laid-back as ever.

During the next week, Terry and I visited a psychologist daily. There weren't so many marriage counselors then. For each session, Terry and I would hold hands and sob our eyes out as broken-heartedly, we told the doctor about the failure of our marriage. The doctor's professional opinion was that Terry and I should get a divorce.

Terry moved his belongings to the ship; the Christmas holidays came. On Christmas Eve, I was alone, not having the one, or the other to spend the evening with, and I slept on the sofa in my living room, watching the Christmas tree lights blinking off and on. I was in some kind of emotional wilderness. *Lover boy, oh where can you be?*

Vincent had not said that he loved me, or asked me to marry him. I was leaving my flanks unguarded. *And* I was stuck in Virginia. I should have picked a better place than that.

Terry Muszyka came to see me on what would have been our wedding anniversary, December 30th, to beg just one more time to try to patch up a marriage that had been irretrievably broken. Of course I had to refuse, but I did it as kindly as I could. When Terry left, he was crying. We had taken out the separation papers. Everything was winding up.

According to the peculiar laws and social customs of the times in Virginia, I charged Terry with 'desertion.' That was a farce. He was so good to accept it.

Alas, 1973 was a disaster for me personally from the first days until the final tragic end. There were times when I thought perhaps I had made a mistake in leaving Terry so precipitously. Vincent made no move towards forming a lasting partnership with me, and he did not seek a divorce from his estranged wife, Cathy. We could not stay away from each other, and were constantly together, but Vincent did not say he loved me, or make any marriage plans.

A Quiet Life in Bedlam

I did not see the obstacles to a union that he obviously saw, and for the most part, he refused even to talk about it. Verbal communication had never been a strong suit between Vincent and me; we were on common ground only in the bedroom. For me, marriage was the one thing I had in mind when I began my liaison with Vincent, and it was still my goal, pure and simple. I suppose you could say I was very middle-class in my 'marriage or nothing' attitude. 'Living in sin,' was not the life for me.

Vincent had not become any less possessive. He did not move in with me, but he made sure he knew where I was every minute; and when he slept with me at night, he wrapped his whole body around me in a way that made me feel as if I were going to suffocate. If loyalty had been what I wanted, I got that.

Terry showed up once in a while in the early months of the year, and said how lonely he was, and how he couldn't get any girls to go out with him; so I decided to fix him up with Lynette. They were both *Aquarians,* so I thought it might work. Lynette went out with Terry just as a favor to me, but her heart wasn't in it—neither was Terry's. Finally, he left on the cruise to the Mediterranean.

I hadn't thought that I had a right to ask Terry for any financial support, circumstances being what they were, so money was very tight. Terry signed over the car and the house to me. I had a place to live and something to drive, but that was about it. Vincent, though he was kind and fed me often enough, never lent any monetary support, even in emergency situations, of which there were several.

One particular emergency stands out in my mind. Late in 1972, just before Terry arrived back from Vietnam, I had traded in the Volkswagen fastback for a metallic blue Mercury Montego, a much more stylish car. I had Terry's power of attorney, though not his specific permission.

I thought I had to trade cars, because Vincent kept making fun of the VW, calling it, 'a tomato eggbeater,' referring to the color and the noisy Volkswagen motor. It was so embarrassing.

Chapter Twenty: *Total Eclipse of the Heart*

He drove a black and white Pontiac Grand Prix. All the attention I was getting from the 'higher-ups' had quite turned my head, and I made a very unwise investment in buying a big, gas-guzzling car, even though I felt more beautiful in it, more glamorous—like Lynette in the Dodge Monaco.

The 1973–1974, gasoline crisis was looming. For me, it came right out of the blue, that gasoline shortage, and was brought about by an Arab blockade and other economic factors—for example, the end of the Vietnam War in 1973—I never really understood it—but whatever happened caused an acute gasoline shortage around the world. Gasoline prices went up, up, up.

Suddenly, my Mercury Montego became a very expensive car indeed, and very unwanted by anyone. It was not paid for, and I advertised for someone to take over the payments. A married couple from Florida did 'take over the payments,' drove the car off to Florida; then proceeded to run it all over the place with the hardest possible usage, until it was nearly a wreck—and they never made one single payment against the loan. I had to get the police to fetch my car back from the crooks, catch up the payments, and save my credit rating.

The Scandellaris, whenever I happened to meet them, treated me politely, but with a thinly disguised contempt. I had met Paula Scandellari by this time, and she took every opportunity of meeting me, to advise me to go back to my husband; also, to tell me about the clever way in which she had broken up Vincent's first marriage—it was as sordid a story as I ever heard, but Paula Scandallari was proud of her part in it.

'Ma' Scandellari seemed to think that she had done what was best for her son in breaking up his first marriage. 'Ma' had done to Cathy the same thing she was doing to me: she invited the unsuspecting victim to her home in a seeming gesture of friendship and good will. Then, in the case of Cathy, Ma was careful to give Cathy all the liquor she could drink from a supply kept by 'Ma' for that specific purpose. Then Paula laughed at Cathy, and watched while the poor woman made a spectacle of herself, falling all over everything, becoming helplessly drunk, foolish, and sick.

Finally, Paula telephoned Vincent to come get his sot of a wife, knowing that he would be so embarrassed and humiliated that there was a good chance he would 'come to his senses' and admit defeat, long before he actually did.

In my case, Paula Scandellari simply wanted to tell me her stories about the ways she had manipulated her family, so that I could find out first hand the power she had, and what I was up against; also, she wanted to probe me for personal details that she could use against me. She picked at me, picked at me.

'Treena, go back to your husband!' she would say. Ma Scandellari could not say Katharine, and didn't like 'Kate'; so she called me Katharina, or ultimately *Treena,* and I hated the sound of it. It was like fingernails scratching on a windowpane. If I'd had any sense, I would have stayed away from her.

I wanted so much for Mrs. Scandellari to accept me that I probably played right into her hands at times. Fortunately for me, she was basically a stupid woman, all cunning and guile, and little intelligence, and she did not do me much damage (I don't think), except that it seemed to be through her ill-will that the family continued to ignore me; and I was not invited to Luca's wedding when he was married, later that year, to the 'right sort of girl,' even though Vincent and I had had dinner together with the engaged couple at Ma's house every Sunday for six months.

It was really a slap in the face, not to be asked to the wedding; I was sick over it for days. My goal of reaching 'respectability' seemed still at a dismal distance. I attended Luca's wedding as Vincent's 'date,' but first, I went to Thalhimer's Department Store and bought myself a white gold engagement ring with a one-carat simulated diamond in it. Without the ring, I would have felt naked, defenseless. With the diamond, I could say I was 'engaged.' Vincent wouldn't care, anyway.

That wedding was lovely. I still remember it. The new Mrs. Luca Scandellari wore a scrumptious wedding dress, and an even more stylish going-away suit with knee-high velvety pur-

Chapter Twenty: *Total Eclipse of the Heart*

ple leather boots. I was so envious. But I tried to smile, laugh, and charm as though I didn't have a care in the world.

I changed jobs several times in 1973. I was beginning to resemble a 'bolter'; that is what the English call a woman who runs away from her husband. I seemed to be running away from jobs. I was as unstable financially as I ever had been. It began to worry me that my house would be foreclosed by the bank.

Each job I got ended in some sort of strange or unpredictable way. In May, I walked into the supply closet at the office where I worked, only to turn around and find my boss was in the closet with me—the door closed against my escape, and he in the process of putting his arms around me. I could not have been more shocked. I truly had not done or said anything to precipitate that situation. I socked the (otherwise handsome and personable) man in the belly, and got myself out of there.

Now that I am older and wiser and can think about these incidents objectively, I believe I must have been a little sexpot; but I swear, as God is my witness, that I never realized it, never consciously used sex to further my interests. I only wanted to look good so that Vincent would not look at anyone else. In my own mind, sneer if you will, I was as pure as the driven snow, honorable in my intentions, true to myself, with a little chimney soot in rough spots.

I *wanted* to be honorable, but events kept going against me. It was a time of social upheaval and rapidly changing values, and I was confused; I bet I wasn't the only one who was at a loss. Men were befuddled too, and they were using the sexual revolution, and women's equality movement, for all it was worth, to get as much extra 'sex' as was possible, before the whole Glorious Age came to an end. And they got a lot of it, by all accounts.

Naturally no one considered, or had ever even heard of, 'sexual harassment,' in 1973. From the way everyone behaved, you would think that fumbling with the secretaries was part of the perks of the job. At least our salaries should have been commensurate, but they weren't. And how did these men keep their infidelities from their wives?

To offset the employment woes of that ghastly year, I had some lovely times with Vincent. He took me to New York, and introduced me to his 'poker' friends. An odder assortment, you have never seen! One of them fairly bristled with weapons that he carried in every conceivable place on his body. Another one was a bookie (strictly illegal), and another had a habit of turning up in beautiful, expensive new cars on a regular basis, and no one knew where he got them from.

They would say things to each other like, 'He's depraved because he's deprived!' I was getting a rare glimpse of a world I did not know existed. The Underworld? I couldn't imagine.

One of Vincent's friends was called 'Bob Paternoster,' such an odd name—Bob Our Father. These 'Queens' guys, all of whom Vincent had known in childhood, seemed to enjoy playing practical jokes on one another, and I never knew what was going to happen next. Usually, it was that they all left for Las Vegas on a whim, to gamble and, except for Vincent, womanize. It was a laugh a minute. I was certainly out of my depth, but they seemed to enjoy my wide-eyed ingeniousness.

Those Italians, they ran in packs. They wouldn't let anybody in that didn't belong to them. The Sicilian blood was very thick. They were cliquish, ultra-conservative, reactionary, right wing: very contradictory. I was dazed. They only looked like gangsters because of their five o'clock shadows, I told myself. Anyway, Vincent swore to me that there was no such thing as the Mafia. I wanted to believe him. *They are Sicilians*, I thought, time and again. *No, it couldn't be. Stereotypes.*

The pick of the crop, Bob Paternoster, seemed to be particularly adorable, and was entirely more presentable than Vincent's other friends ... as far as I know; they were a secretive bunch. Bob Paternoster did not *seem* to have anything odd about him or his way of life. He didn't carry guns, or drive around with car trunks full of bottles of liquor that he had received as 'gifts.'

Chapter Twenty: *Total Eclipse of the Heart*

Bob Paternoster was Vincent's age, and not married. We introduced him to Lynette. He fell for Lynette like a ton of bricks as soon as he set eyes on her. They were two free spirits, and we had to hold on to their shirt-tales to keep them from dancing away from us into the ethers. *Speak low when you speak love* ... They were a pair.

There was no question of marriage, however, because Lynette was not a virgin. Bob wasn't either, but he was a Catholic.

For days at a time, Lynette and Bob, Vincent and I, traveled together to every resort in the northeastern United States, having barrels of fun, tons of laughs. I still would rather have gotten married, but one takes what life gives. Once, at a honeymoon resort in the mountains of Pennsylvania, Vincent and I slept in a heart-shaped bed! I kid you not; everything in that place was heart-shaped. It was almost tacky.

One night, on our way back from a seedy racetrack in the wilds of West Virginia, the four of us found ourselves without adequate accommodations when we arrived at the northern Virginia hotel where we had planned to stay. The place was over-run with Shriners, who hung about from the chandeliers, or leaned drunkenly against the lobby pillars, intoning *'humma, humma,'* and grinning broadly as Lynette and I sauntered by.

Bob and Vincent thought it was awfully funny, but instead of falling down laughing, as they usually would do, they were too preoccupied with what the four of us were going to do about beds for the night. There was only one room available that had not been taken over by Shriners. The one available room had two double beds. So we all slept in there! What else could we do? It was far, too far, to drive to Virginia Beach so late at night.

We felt deliciously decadent, though we behaved as if we were two devoted old married couples with gray beards—the four of us have laughed about it ever since. Nowadays, no one would even blink an eye at such a harmless situation, but we thought that if anyone who knew us found out, they would think we had been into an episode of wifeswapping, which we

A Quiet Life in Bedlam

definitely had not! Vincent would have killed Bob, friend or no, if he had ever even looked at me cross-eyed.

Still, it was unnerving to undress in that soft darkness for bed, knowing that there are three other people who are not related to you by blood standing near, and you can hear them breathing! But like I said, we behaved ourselves—except for the fact that Vincent wrapped himself around me like he always did, and I was immobilized until morning. Vincent had a mother-complex, and I was his womb.

Lynette and I have never parted ways, though I have disapproved of her lifestyle and choices from time to time. I remember when, in 1973, Lynette filed personal bankruptcy because she had run up some credit card accounts. I was something like 'horrified,' and felt a kind of dread and panic, as any Taurean would do, at the prospect of the law taking away personal possessions. I said to Lynette, 'Aren't you afraid the sheriff will come and take everything you own?'

She said, 'I don't own much. They won't take my clothes. You can't get blood out of a turnip.' I had never heard that expression, but it was interesting. What did it mean, exactly? As I was obviously discombobulated, Lynette said, 'You can't get blood out of a stone.' How true, I had to agree with that. But didn't she want to run and hide?

Lynette Mckinnon and Delores Delaney saw me as something of a 'little mother' to them, since I was five and six years older than they were. 'I insist on a certain standard,' I said, like a sergeant-major, and I expected them to follow suit—anyway, if they were going to live at my house!—as they did off and on.

Lynette and Dolly believed I had good judgment (!) except perhaps when it came to my passion for Vincent. But anyway, we all became bosom friends, almost like family to each other, because they didn't have any sisters.

Delores herself had some troubles that she didn't want to share with anyone else but Lynette and me. Dolly was having problems with her parents, not too different from what I had experienced at my own home in Memphis; but she, being a more conservative person than I was, felt that she couldn't af-

Chapter Twenty: *Total Eclipse of the Heart*

ford to move away from home. Delores had set herself up an 'apartment' in her parents' garage—a garage that was not insulated, not carpeted, heated or cooled. It was all steel and concrete. She must have been very uncomfortable in extreme weather, but Dolly bore it all quite stoically. She had the ability to make a dollar stretch a mile, so she was like my mother in that way.

Once or twice, my two bosom friends said boldly to Vincent, 'Do you love Kate?' and he replied, straight-faced, 'We're pretty tight.'

'But do you love her?'

'It's a secret,' he said.

'Prevaricator!' They had him pegged.

Lynette, who was not by any means Jewish, finally married Dr. Winterstine's Jewish medical practice partner, and now has been a pillar of Jewish society for years. They had a wonderful wedding where everyone had to smash something and shout, *'Mazeltoff!'*

Lynette, with her dark hair and eyes, looked every inch the American Jewish Princess in her ivory wedding gown. The men were dressed in the extravagant male fashions of 1974. They wore soft as velvet, wide-lapelled tuxedos, with lots of ruffles around the neck and sleeves, and floppy bow ties. Their pants legs were flared. Their hair was long, with sideboards (sideburns) and mustaches to match. They looked as romantic as cavaliers. Lynette is now more Jewish than the Jews. She is adaptable, all right. Lynette is a survivor. I am proud of her. God bless Lynette.

Before Lynette married the good doctor, she used to bring her boyfriends to me for vetting, and I actually had to turn away a few; it was my responsibility. Dolly, on the other hand, kept her boyfriends away from me. I don't know why.

If I happened to run into Dolly when she had a new man in tow, she would say, 'This is my new Ha-ha,' meaning, he's just for amusement and a good time 'dating.' Dolly was out for love, but she wanted money along with it. Who can blame her?

A Quiet Life in Bedlam

Those girls, Lynette and Delores, are two of the most captivating people I have ever known, though they are hardly 'girls' any more. We laughed, played, frolicked around like fillies. We even smoked marijuana once. We taught each other many useful things in our long, long childhood. We gambled with life and love, lived by our wits, and made as much as we could out of the unstable and often unhappy times we lived through. I sometimes wonder how typical we were for our generation.

In 1973, I had to deal with the death of my mother. It is something that I am not completely reconciled to, to this day. I will never understand why worthless Daddy was allowed to live, and vital Mother had to die.

In April of that year, I drove home to Tennessee to take Mother my trio of Siamese cats: Kahlua, Rajah, and Anastasia. Mother already had Drambuie, who was the mate of Kahlua and father of Rajah and Anastasia. Vincent didn't like my cats, and though I hated like hell to part with them, I wanted to please Vincent if I could. So I gave them away. I had them back again before the end of the year however, after Mother died.

Vincent is reconciled to my menagerie now. It's a good thing, too! I can't live without him or them. Anyway, I found out that he was only pretending not to like animals. He is as mushy over them, as I am.

When I arrived in Memphis that April, I found Mother and Daddy in the same old quagmire, just as hopeless as before, but now Mother had the additional grief to bear that I was divorcing Terry, who turned out to be her favorite son-in-law. The divorce would not be final until November.

Mother, obviously mystified as to my reasons and greatly saddened at the prospect, said to me, 'Katharine, I just can't understand why you are divorcing Terry. I know he loves you truly and devotedly. To my knowledge, he always supported you; he never drank or ran around with women. He never gambled or beat you.'

'That's true,' I agreed.

Chapter Twenty: *Total Eclipse of the Heart*

'He has treated you with the honor a husband should. What can you be thinking of to divorce him, and break his heart?' With those words, I think she sounded like mothers everywhere. Mother did not ask about the condition of my heart; as usual, she assumed I had been the erring party. I guess she wasn't far from right.

It upset me too much to try to discuss my reasons with her; she was obviously physically ill and sick at heart. For a year she had been having some peculiar burning sensations in her left leg, 'sort of like molten lava being poured,' she told me, 'down along my veins.' It was the first indication of the cancer that killed her within months, a voracious, greedy cancer that was eating her alive.

It would have been really difficult to convince someone who was as selfless as my mother, about the restless spirit within me that was looking for more love than Terry could give. But I did try, without going into too much detail. I tried to tell Mother that Terry left me alone too much, and that he wouldn't make love to me.

My mother could not fathom these reasons at all—she had never been a day without Daddy, and in addition, he had always pressed himself upon her most ardently. They had five children to show for it. Such a life as mine had been was totally alien to Mother's experience. Above all, she was practical and sensible, and feared for my future as a divorced woman. Divorce was still a stigma, a bad one. How would I maintain myself?

'Good question.' I had no answers.

Certainly there was no one in my family who could understand why I divorced Terry. It simply wasn't done! My grandmother was scandalized, and took an oath never to admit me into her presence again. And when family or friends asked for my reasons in their truly concerned way, how could I tell them what the *real* reasons were? It was so personal. How do you say 'My marriage was never consummated?' It was forbidden. How do you say, 'I took a lover?'

A Quiet Life in Bedlam

I don't know about other people, but I wasn't interested in getting stoned to death. The divorce happened well before all the open talk about sex, and people just did not discuss such things. St. Paul, in his many writings had said plainly that you shouldn't.

And there were two real snags, if I did tell any of them:

1) Who would believe it that my marriage had gone unconsummated? Who had ever heard of such a thing?

2) No one would have thought non-consummation to be such a serious problem, when weighing it against the fact that Terry was such a fine fellow otherwise; he was universally well liked.

And I know that not one of my hometown family or friends had ever lived the Navy life, had ever been lonely, or had so utterly been responsible for their day-to-day routines without help or companionship of any kind. They did not understand where I was coming from; they had never walked a mile in my shoes.

Mine was just another of those divorces that happened in the Seventies, which some of us have later had cause to regret. I was the first person in my family to ever be divorced (except for Aunt Lizzie, the family tear-away), but it seemed that my divorce was the icebreaker; after me, most of my cousins, one brother and one sister got divorced, and my Aunt Mildred left my Uncle Landon.

As nearly as I can make out, everyone I knew (save a few staunch souls) got divorced during the 1970s when social pressures were overwhelming to find one's own separate identity, no matter what the cost. Many of us were immature and selfish, and we often found, when it was too late, that the price very high. Those stalwart souls who managed to stay together through it all, like Annabelle and Ralph, deserve a medal for stick-to-itivity.

Mother even tried to divorce Daddy shortly before she died. It was in 1971, or 1972, and she actually had gone so far as to have some legal papers drawn up. Sherry and I, both of us married and living far away from Memphis, received frantic

Chapter Twenty: *Total Eclipse of the Heart*

communications from Daddy, begging us to fly to Memphis, and talk Mother back into her senses. Actually, Mother was in her senses, and we were talking her back into insanity.

I don't know why Sherry and I felt sorry for Daddy; maybe we had forgotten the pain of living with him in that household; I don't know. I do know that we should not have interfered. Mother dropped the proceedings, and ended a defeated woman. It was not more than a year or so later that she was diagnosed with a virulent type of cancer that kills within a few months. Sherry and I will be sorry all our lives that we did not let Mother divorce Daddy.

Before I left Mother behind in Memphis that April of 1973, I knew that she looked sick, but I thought it was just the general depressed state of affairs she had to live with, that was causing her to look so inexpressibly sad. Cancer was not diagnosed until late July. The doctors amputated Mother's leg at the hip in an attempt to keep the cancer, *fibrous sarcoma*, from spreading. But when I left her house in April, neither Mother nor I knew what her fate was to be.

I got back to Virginia, and I sat down to write Mother a letter, thinking that perhaps I could express my innermost feelings in writing, if not in speech; I hoped at last, to make her understand:

May 1, 1973

Dear Mother and Daddy,
I don't know what to tell you about Terry. I know that you love him, and are concerned about him. I am aware that you still regard him as your son. I am concerned about Terry, but no longer love him. I don't mean to run down his character, as you say I do; it's probably true that I have done it, but the words tumble out before I know what I am saying.

I have a very deep resentment towards Terry that I would give anything to be rid of; but unfortunately, it will probably only get worse if Terry and I continue to see each other. We have tried to be friends through this, but divorce seems to bring out the worst in people, and we both have found ourselves saying and doing things that we don't mean. We don't want to end up hating each other. Terry, who has always been so unemotional, has let his emotions completely take him over, and it is not attractive. I have already been through my emotional 'thing' and I only feel empty and sad, and exhausted. I have no more feelings towards Terry except for the resentment. I suppose I must feel that he has failed me, in some way.

The psychologist who talked to Terry and me said that the only way we could keep from hating each other was to get completely apart, and never see each other again except in rare instances. The doctor explained that when an emotion as strong as love is no more, another strong emotion has to take its place. Terry and I are both trying hard to keep anything like 'hate' from setting in. Probably neither one of us is capable of hating, but it's best not to take chances with our lives.

Please be patient with me. Let me find my own way through this. Terry and I are both still hurting. We have to get the pain out of our systems. Yes, hard as you may find this to believe, Terry did hurt me—more than anyone could ever know. The decision to divorce him was the hardest one I ever made.

I do not know if I am doing the right thing, and I may yet regret it, but I had to do it. The trouble between Terry and me, at this juncture, was not nearly so bad as it would have been later on, and I felt that it was best to make an honest break of it while we both had a chance to get out with a minimum of trauma. Terry is suffering, I know, but I can't help it. He is an adult; he will have to pull himself together.

I don't know how important physical lovemaking is to you, because you never discussed it, or even alluded to it with me; but, somehow, you have turned me out to be the way I am, a woman who needs to love, and wants to be loved in return. To turn to a body that did not turn to mine, became intolerable; each time Terry refused me, I felt my heart harden towards him. It was an involuntary reaction, but that's how it was. Eventually, that vital organ, my heart, became dry, and withered, at least towards my husband. I felt less and less like a woman, and began to see myself as some unlovely, undesirable thing. I wondered if I was unlovable. I got so that I needed to see the psychiatrist, thinking it was me that wasn't normal!

Chapter Twenty: *Total Eclipse of the Heart*

The frustrations that began in the bedroom worked their way into other parts of our marriage. Anyway, we didn't have much of a marriage—Terry was always gone. I lived our lives for both of us: established our homes, made our friends, pursued our interests, created a life for us within the community—but no one ever saw my husband, though I said I had one, because he wasn't there!

Yes, like you say, Terry was a good, decent, fair man to me, and to the world. But he was not a good husband. I was the one who had to be married to him—not you, nor Grandmother, or anyone else. The lack of a physical relationship was not the only thing wrong with the marriage; it was just one of the more obvious things.

Please understand. I remain your devoted daughter,
Katharine

Mother passed away on November 18th, the day before her 47th birthday; so I always say she died at the age of 46. Before she died, she suffered dreadfully. The pain, both mental and physical, was very great. She had intended to adjust to the disability, and get an artificial leg; but before she could do that, the cancer entered her lungs. A woman who did not smoke, the cause of her death was lung cancer.

In earlier days, I have been keen to blame my father for my mother's death. Why? Well, I have described the physical and emotional trauma she endured at his hands. Research shows that *fibrous sarcoma* originates in old bruises. Whom do you think gave my mother bruises? Who made her stay up all night so that she never had enough rest? And even worse, before she died, Mother was confined to a wheel chair, was in extreme discomfort, and needed someone to see to her simple needs. These were eating, and resting, taking her morphine periodically, and relieving herself when that need arose.

Daddy, her only attendant, lay on the sofa in front of her, drunk most of the time; and tormented her with vile words and even viler actions. She could not defend herself. Daddy hid the morphine from her, and let her scream with the pain. He could not get himself together enough to feed her or bring her water, so she did without. Daddy did not care enough to see that Mother got to the bathroom to relieve herself, so she had to sit in her own filth. Each day, my brother Duane found her passed out from the pain when he came home from school.

Wherever my mother went, heaven or hell, it cannot have been a worse place than what she left, and was probably quite a bit better. She must have been relieved to die. My father still rots in that house, and cries for her, but he deserves nothing, nothing, not even the release of death. I won't see him now.

I visited Mother shortly before she died. She was connected to a breathing machine in hospital. Mother said to me, 'I don't want to die.' I'm crying now as I write this. Oh God, I am so sorry.

There was a strange incident that happened on Interstate 40, on the way driving from Memphis to Nashville. It was hot, and we needed a little fresh air in the car in spite of the air conditioning. Cats begin to pant in a hot car. I could hear mine panting heavily. So I rolled down my window slightly for a breeze.

As I was driving along, I had this uncanny feeling that one of the cats had jumped out of the window, but I didn't think it could be possible, because the car window was open so very little, just a slim sliver. But after a few hundred meters, I pulled over to the side of the road, looked in the back seat, got out of the car, and ran back along the Interstate towards Memphis, just on the off-chance I could find Anastasia, who was clearly missing.

It didn't seem likely that I would ever see Anastasia again, and she was 'in kitten.' There were no friendly houses around there; the landscape was quite rural and unpopulated.

Well, it's hard to believe, but a man in a truck pulled up right behind my car, and he jumped out with Anastasia in his arms. The young cat was jolted by her long jump from a moving vehicle, but she was totally unharmed. The angel-man-saint said, 'I saw her jump, and I didn't think you would want to go farther without her.' What a miracle!

Chapter Twenty: *Total Eclipse of the Heart*

A further miracle occurred when I was back in Virginia. One day soon afterwards, I came home from work to find that Anastasia had given birth to a purebred Siamese kitten at the foot of my bed. She was lovely, a lilac-point. We called her Olga.

So in November of that year, my mother died. And in November, Terry made the divorce final by paying the legal fees. I really had not expected that he would cut the cord like that. I believe he had met someone, and so far as I know, he married again in about 1975. He and his wife produced a daughter, and I was very glad for Terry's sake. All of this information came to me via Terry's family.

For years, I carried around a burden of guilt for causing such suffering, unintentional though it was, to a man who certainly deserved better. For a while, my grief was intolerable; I finally had to shrug it off and get on with my life. I was very hard on myself, always my own worst critic, and I wore a figurative 'hair shirt' for at least five years after the divorce was final. I sought help from a counselor to deal with the feelings of guilt, and was finally able to forgive myself, as Terry forgave me long ago.

Terry Muszyka died in a December of a not so long ago. I did not hear about it for quite a while, since Terry and I were no longer married. Thankfully, one of his cousins notified me of the death. Terry left a wife, a daughter, and a grandson.

Months before I received notice of Terry's death, I dreamed vividly of him. I have learned to study dreams. Dreams give many messages, if one just pays attention. In the dream, Terry was young and handsome, smiling broadly, wearing a Hawaii shirt like he did in our best days in Key West.

In the dream, Terry had a solid gold *lei* around his neck, and was dancing the Jerk to 'Joy to the World' as sung by Three Dog Night. He was so cute!

I could remember when Terry had asked me if 'Joy to the World' was a Christmas carol! Lah! Innocent, unworldly Terry!

He said, 'I want us both to be glad of the happy times we had together, though they are finished for this lifetime.' Then he said, 'We may meet again in another incarnation, when things will be easier for us.'

Well, thank God for that, I said when I woke up. The dream was so real, and in gorgeous technicolor. I was there with him as I am here with you now. After that dream I could not resist believing in reincarnation anymore, and I subsequently left Christianity.

CHAPTER TWENTY-ONE:
The Edge of the Precipice

The year 1973 was one secretarial job after another, with nothing jelling into a permanent job, but I would *not* go back to the telephone company—not that they would have me. Anyway, I never applied, so I didn't find out if I was still telephone company material. I guess it wasn't likely. I didn't want to be disciplined anymore. But more important than that, I *had* to do something that allowed independent thought.

Vincent and I were devoted to each other, but he still had not filed for a divorce, so there was no wedding pending. My paramour was very romantic and generous that year, and he showered me with gifts and flowers. It was the 'mistress' treatment all over again.

Taking a chance, I bought a gorgeous wedding dress that I saw in a shop window, and hung it in my closet so that I could be ready double-quick if the spirit ever moved Vincent. What inspired me to do this was that Vincent bought me a ring. He said it was not an engagement ring, but to me, it immediately assumed those dimensions, and I wore it around town feeling like the Queen of Sheba.

In January of 1974, I went to work for a nationally known health and beauty aids company as sales merchandiser. The brand name was very well known, and had been around for a hundred years—an American institution. The firm was closely identified with sports. I was the first woman they ever hired to work in a 'territory,' and drive a company car. But women were slowly getting liberated. I blessed that man to high heaven for hiring me—at last I had a chance to show my mettle.

Mel, the District Manager of the health and beauty aids company, said, 'A woman has never done the job, but I don't see why a woman can't do it,' and I agreed with him. I knew I could do it. I was delighted at the prospect.

My territory was from Virginia Beach to Richmond, about a hundred miles; and sometimes, I had to drive to Washington, D.C., Baltimore, Maryland, and even Boston, Massachusetts. I soon discovered that my friendly nature, beautiful smile, and easy laughter made me welcome anywhere. The merchants teased me though; they said, 'What do *you* know about razor blades?'

Blushing, I answered, 'Well, I shave under my arms, don't I?'

It was exciting for a while, but I found that I did not like being away from home so much. Living out of a suitcase, in even the most glamorous of circumstances, quickly got old—I missed Vincent, and I missed my cats. I missed my flower garden that I was planting up with perennials. I longed for a more stable life. 'What a contradictory person you are!' I said to myself. 'When will you know what you want?'

My employer was generous with the expense account, fair with its working conditions, and fast with promotions and pay raises. Once I got to know the ropes, I settled into a regular routine, and Vincent, who did not have to work because he had an income from his mother, traveled with me, or followed me by car wherever I had to go. My district manager, Mel, did not know about Vincent of course, but Vincent paid his own way, and he made a traveling life more tolerable for me.

Vincent traveled light, with only a change of clothes, and what he called his 'douche kit' (shaving kit) while I was loaded down with every conceivable thing. Our lives together in the

Chapter Twenty-One: *The Edge of the Precipice*

hotel rooms was the most 'living together' we had done to date. Occasionally I asked him, 'Vincent, why won't you pick up your clothes and hang them in the closet?'

He answered, 'Because my mother always does it for me.'

I was indulgent. I wasn't so good at hanging up my clothes, either.

Vincent said, 'This motel is really *Far From the Madding Crowd.*'

'Oh, Vincent,' I gurgled, 'I didn't know that you knew about *literature!*'

'Yuk, yuk, you're really sick, Bess.'

I whooped. 'I don't know why I love you,' I retorted.

'It's because I feed you in the best restaurants.'

'You stinker. Why can't you take me seriously?'

'What is there to take seriously?'

That conversation was going nowhere, but it was like that with us.

Sometimes, in the middle of the night, as I lay clutched in an embrace that was tighter than an oyster shell, Vincent would say, 'I miss you, Princess.'

And I answered, 'But I'm here, Vincent.'

'That don't cut no ice. Yuk, yuk.'

'Promise me you'll never leave me, Vincent.'

'I can't afford to gas up and go.'

He made me laugh inordinately.

So, 1974 passed in a flurry of traveling, and it was not such a bad year. There was a sales meeting in Boston at midwinter, and I used my 'company' air-traveling card to pay for the round-trip flight. Boston in winter! Wow! What a sight. It was so white that I expected to see Santa Claus and all his reindeer glide across the extensive grounds of the conference center. And it was cold, colder than I had ever experienced. My eyelashes froze.

Most of my colleagues were young men, and they were sweet to me, and full of good fun. On the nights when our whole 'health and beauty aids' district tribe was in Boston, we went out, danced, drank mixed drinks, and felt hung-over the next morning so that it was hard to concentrate on what the boss, Mel, was saying about the sales pitch. But the 'boys' just took it all in their stride, the carousing, the drinking, the staying up all night. They were used to it. But I wasn't. Still, they had accepted me as one of them, and I tried to do my best.

Sometimes, it was hard to be a 'man.' The others expected me to eat a 'cannibal sandwich' when they were having that for lunch. It was something similar to steak tartar, finely chopped raw beef mixed with raw egg, onions, capers, possibly anchovies, and other seasonings. I didn't care for it.

And then there was the evening in Baltimore when we sat at rough tables and watched while a huge amount of freshly steamed crabs was dumped onto newspapers in front of us, and—that was our dinner! We had to break open the crab shells, somehow, with 'crackers,' and finagle out the crabmeat. My colleagues thought it was tremendous fun, a riot, but I hated it. I got crabmeat under my fingernails and in my hair. I had to take two showers that day, and it didn't help when it turned out that my hotel room was fitted with a waterbed, the first I had ever seen.

The waterbed was cold, cold, cold, like sleeping in the depths of the sea. I couldn't get warm all night. I was miserable. Like a fool, I had left my hot water bottle at home! A person shouldn't need a hot water bottle at the Hilton. I complained bitterly to Mel the next morning, and, trying to suppress a smile (he always tried to take me seriously) he said, 'There is a thermostat connected to the waterbed that heats the water to just the right warmth. Turn that on tonight. Then you'll like it.' But I didn't. I changed rooms.

One night the group of us was at a discothèque under a glittering, whirling crystallized ball, and Mel asked me to dance. The popular dance then was the *Bump*, to Gloria Gaynor's 'Never Can Say Goodbye' [126] or perhaps, Yvonne Elliman's,

---

[126] 'Never Can Say Goodbye', Clifton Davis, 1974, Jobete Music Co. Inc.

Chapter Twenty-One: *The Edge of the Precipice*

'Love Me' [127] I was mortified that I was expected to bump hips or bottoms with my boss, Mel. That was the dance—jiving and bumping. Was it respectful? It certainly wasn't dignified. But I liked to dance, and he was the only one who asked me.

> *Love me, please, just a little bit longer*
> *Together we can make it.*
> *Our love is much too young to break it.*

To give me courage, I drank several different kinds of mixed drinks, one after the other, and Mel said, 'If you don't want to be sick in the morning, keep it to Scotch and water.'

Where had I heard that before?

Because I was traveling so much, I got a roommate named Barbara. She was there specifically to look after the cats and tidy up the house. One time, I arrived home after a week away, to find Barbara naked on the living room floor with whipped cream all over her, and her boyfriend ready to pounce. It was like a scene out of an X-rated movie.

I shouted at her, 'For Christ's sake, Barbara, you can do that in the bedroom! You're ruining my carpets!' Barbara moved out of my house soon after, and married her partner in crime. It was the obvious end to such a scene as I witnessed. With all my faults, I had never actually been a libertine.

After a year and a half with the health and beauty aids company, I began to think about other work I could do that would allow me to stay at home. My sister, Sherry, was having great success in Nashville, selling real estate, so I began to study for my real estate license. That was fun, but it would take some time, and I would not leave my secure job until I was good and ready.

In studying for my real estate license, it was difficult to do the mathematical calculations, but Mel had given me a new-

---

[127] 'Love Me,' Robin Gibb, Barry Gibb, Gibb Brothers Music, 1976, RSO Records Inc.

A Quiet Life in Bedlam

fangled gadget called a 'calculator,' so I aced the examination in April. I was proud.

In May and June of 1975, I worked for two weeks around the Beltway of the Metropolitan Washington, D.C., area. I seemed to go round and around and around, passing the Mormon Cathedral many times. I always loved glimpsing its spires looming through the trees. It was a long two weeks in Washington, and I was more than ready to go home at the end of it, even though Vincent had been with me most of the time.

On the one or two nights Vincent was not with me at the hotel, I dreamed vividly of him. There he was, as clear an image as if it were my Zenith television screen. He said, 'I love you so much.' And I replied, 'I know, but I am surprised that you would tell me.'

On the Friday afternoon that I finished my work, Vincent headed out for Virginia Beach in his own car about 4:00 p.m. 'Bye,' I said, and kissed him. I was to follow in my company car later that evening after doing some shopping and having dinner with friends who lived in the area. So, for the last evening, we were just four girls, my friends and I, and I was to drive the two hundred miles back to Virginia Beach alone, leaving the Washington area at around 9:00 that evening.

My friends wanted to go see a fortuneteller who displayed her sign by the side of the road. I was game; this gypsy lady read palms, and tarot cards. She 'read' the other three girls first; they were thrilled and excited. They believed every word.

Then, it was my turn. The gypsy looked at my palm, then she took out the tarot. Saying not a word to me, she scribbled something on a piece of paper, folded it up, handed it to me, and bade me wait until I got home to read it.

Well, home was Virginia Beach, two hundred miles away, and I got on the road after 9:00 p.m., as I had expected to do. I had a four-hour drive in front of me. I reached Richmond after midnight and was sleepy, very sleepy, and dog-tired. I thought to myself that I had been foolish not to stay in Washington for the night. My hotel room was paid for until Saturday morning; but I wanted to be with Vincent.

Chapter Twenty-One: *The Edge of the Precipice*

I stopped at the Richmond Howard Johnson's to have a cup of coffee. I hoped that, with a little rest stop, I could stay awake for the two hours that it would take me to finish my journey. Having no idea that someone was watching me, I got into my car and drove on.

There was a stretch of Interstate between Richmond and Williamsburg that was lonely and desolate. It was heavily wooded, had only a few exits, and featured deep gullies on either side of the four-lane, divided highway. As I quitted Richmond, I noticed that there was a man in a truck following me. His headlights were on high beam. There appeared to be a woman in the truck with him, but I couldn't tell for sure. It was just a shape in the darkness.

Presently, the man pulled into the other lane beside me, and kept the motion of his truck timed to stay right alongside my vehicle. He was shouting, and banging the side of the truck with his arm. He dropped back behind me again, and flashed his lights. I just ignored him. I had been harassed like that before, in the past. I remembered something like that happening late at night in Jacksonville. But I had driven alone all over the eastern United States, and never had any real problems.

The man was very persistent about trying to get my attention. He obviously was indicating that there was something wrong with my tires or my car. I became apprehensive. I had always had a subconscious fear of experiencing car trouble when I was alone on the road, and this man played upon those fears.

Pulling up beside me again, the man motioned for me to roll down my car window. We were still moving at about fifty miles an hour. The man shouted to me, 'You've got a wheel about to fall off; you better pull over.' I didn't pull over, so he banged on the side of his truck, and blew his horn again.

Even with the strange experiences I had had in my life, I still did not expect evil from people, and I wanted to believe that he was genuinely trying to help me. For my wheel to fly off at those speeds like people drive on the Interstate, would have put me in mortal danger—those weren't just gullies beside the road, they were deep, dark, wooded ravines. I figured that if I lost control of the car, and it flew down into one of the ravines, I wouldn't be found for a few days.

Where could I get help at this hour? It was after one o'clock. There was no place that was lighted for stopping. There were no rest areas. We had recently passed a single, lone exit that led to a Virginia nowhere. The stranger seemed to want to assure my safety. He yelled, 'Lady, you better stop or you'll have an accident.' I decided that I had better trust him. The last thing he shouted before we both stopped was, 'There are sparks flying from around the rim of your tire.'

I was afraid to stop, but not very, and I was very nervous about going on further with a bad wheel. I pulled over to the right shoulder. The man pulled up close behind me. It was a big truck. There still was that dark shape in the seat next to the driver's position—somehow, I thought it was a woman. But it wasn't a woman. The man was alone.

The following series of events happened so fast that it makes my head spin to try and sort them out. Thinking to be cautious, I stayed in my car, and only lowered the window a little way down. The man jumped out of his truck and came to the window.

He said, 'Lady, I don't mean to cause you any trouble, but you've got sparks flying from your right front tire. You better have somebody look at it, or you're going to be in trouble.'

I asked, 'Why? What kind of trouble?'

He said, 'Let me check it for you.'

I nodded okay, but I did not get out of the car. The man went around to the right front tire, pulled off the hubcap, and shook his head. He came back to my window and said, 'Lady, that tire looks really bad. The rim's all burned up. It's going to have to be fixed.'

I said, 'Where can I get it fixed?'

He replied, 'I don't know. There's nothing open this time of night. But you can't drive much further like that.'

'I'll go back to Richmond,' I said.

Chapter Twenty-One: *The Edge of the Precipice*

'You better not try it. There's no place to turn around, and if you do, that tire's going to fall off, and you'll run off the road. Besides, nothin's open in Richmond, anyway.'

'I'll drive on until I find a service station, then.'

The man said, 'Lady, you're takin' a chance. That tire's in pretty bad shape.'

'Okay,' I said. 'Thanks for warning me. Some truckers were blinking their lights at me on Interstate 95 out of Washington. I wondered if something was wrong.'

He repeated, 'Get it fixed as soon as you can.'

I said, 'Okay.' And drove on.

I had driven another two miles when the man started blowing his truck horn again, blinking his headlights, and pointing to the tire. His truck had stayed to the side of me, or to the back of me, never to the front. So, again, feeling apprehensive and suspicious, I pulled over to the shoulder.

The man pulled up close behind me, and jumped out of his truck. He came to my window, and said, 'Lady, there's still a lot of sparks flying from out of your hubcap. You better let me look at it again.'

I said okay. He went around the car again, and took off the hubcap. He looked at the tire again, shook his head as if it looked really bad, then came around to my window and *said* it looked really bad. In all this time, there had been no other traffic on the road but us.

I asked, 'What do I have to do to get it fixed?' still speaking through a small opening in the window. The man insisted that the tire would have to be changed; and that would give me a new rim to replace the other one that was so worn and dangerous.

'So, I will have to drive to a service station to get it fixed.' I had no mechanical talents whatsoever. I knew that.

The man said, 'Lady, you just can't go very far on that tire. You'll run off the road and be killed if that thing comes off there. I'd hate to see you be killed. How far are you going?'

I answered, 'Virginia Beach.'

The man told me, 'You'll never make it to Virginia Beach. The wheel will be gone way before that.'

I asked, 'What am I going to do, then?'

He said, 'I'll tell you what. I'm going to Williamsburg. I'll follow you there to be sure you're all right. But you better drive *real slow*.'

I asked, 'What speed?'

He replied, 'Certainly not more than twenty-five miles an hour.'

Then he said, 'I'll follow you there to be sure you're all right. I'd hate to see you run off the road and be killed. I'll follow you; then, if anything happens, I can help you.'

I said okay, and drove on very slowly. I passed a sign that said, 'Next services, 22 miles.' A disc jockey on the radio said it was '2:01 a.m.' The man stayed right on my bumper. Then all at once, he started flashing his lights again, and blowing his horn. He flashed his right-turn blinker to indicate that I should pull over.

He ran up to my car, obviously in a panic, and said, 'You cannot drive further, or you'll be killed. There's a lot of deep ditches on the side of the road, and you're sure going to end up in one unless that tire is changed. Have you got a spare?'

'Yes, but I can't change it.'

'Well, you can wait for a state trooper to come by, or I can change it for you.' Then, he asked for my car trunk key. His expression was very grave.

I was so tired. Vincent was expecting me home. I decided that I would just have to trust him. I got out of the car, and handed him the keys.

He said, 'Come here; let me show you what's wrong with the tire.' Then, without stopping at the trunk to remove the spare tire, the man led the way around my car towards the offending tire. At that point in my dark journey, I sincerely believed that something was wrong with the tire, and that the man really wanted to help me. All I could think of was getting home with as little delay as possible.

Chapter Twenty-One: *The Edge of the Precipice*

When we got around to the dark far side of the road, there on the grassy shoulder of the lonely road, that was when he grabbed me.

'NO!' It was the worst shock of my entire life. Nothing had ever prepared me for such a thing. I immediately began screaming, and trying to break away. But he had me in an iron grip. I almost got away once, but the man was too fast and too strong for me.

As he pulled me behind the car, and forced me down on the ground, I kept on screaming and struggling. Cars and trucks were passing by about five feet away, but no one stopped—probably, no one could hear me, even though I was screaming at the top of my lungs. I kept screaming and struggling, and fighting him, and I almost broke away another time.

He said to me, 'I've got a knife, and if you don't settle down and stop screaming, I'll use it on you.'

The feel of a cut was only too real already because I had cut my hand on the sharp gravel the first time he pushed me down. But I kept screaming, and he pushed me flat down on the grass and gravel there on the shoulder of the road beside my car. Then he started hitting me hard with his fist. Still, I kept screaming. I swear, it was a primal scream.

Still, cars and trucks were going past, and no one stopped. I kept on screaming. It was my only defense against the abomination. I was a good screamer. My ability had heretofore gone untried. I'm surprised they didn't hear me in Richmond, but we were in a desolate and lonely place, surrounded by trees that blocked the sound.

Then the man said, 'If you don't stop screaming, I'm going to have to hurt you. I've got a knife, but I don't want to hurt you.' I kept screaming, but he hit me a hard blow, and I stopped screaming.

He said, 'Now, are you going to cooperate?'

I answered, 'Yes.' By this time, he had me pinned to the ground with all the weight of his body. He was a big man.

The man said, 'I just want to touch you. I just want to touch you.' But I knew he was going to rape me. He ripped my white linen slacks right off me, panties and all. There I was, lying in the weeds and the gravel, nude from the waist down, except I think I still had on one white shoe, and what was left of my slacks around my ankles.

He kept saying, 'I just want to touch you, you're so pretty.'

He still had me pinned to the ground harder than if he were nails. I was desperate, trying to think of how I could get out of this alive. I said, 'Don't, please don't. Please let me go home. I just want to go home.

As he was doing things to me, touching me, he left my arms free for a moment though my legs were still securely pinned down by his body. I saw headlights coming, and I raised myself from the waist, and waved frantically, screaming. But the cars didn't stop.

This defensive action of mine seemed to inflame him, so he forced me back down, and said, 'I was just going to touch you, but since you've acted this way, I'm going to do the whole thing.'

I said, my voice dripping with the contempt I felt for him, 'You were going to do it anyway.'

He replied, 'No, I wasn't, but I'm going to do it now.'

I started screaming again, and he hit me again. He tried to get me to move further over towards the underbelly of the car, because I could clearly see headlights coming, and I tried to wave. The gravel was cutting my backside, and I told him so.

Hating him with all my might, I said, 'What's the matter with you that you can't get any girls of your own without raping somebody?'

He said, 'Girls don't like me.' Then he began trying to kiss me. I resisted, and kept trying to talk to him. I didn't read psychology for nothing. I hoped I could talk him out of it. I tried to think of everything I'd ever read about rape, and what one should do to try and prevent it.

The man was trying to rape me, but he couldn't get a proper erection. Seizing on an idea, I pleaded, 'I'm pregnant!' He didn't say anything.

Chapter Twenty-One: *The Edge of the Precipice*

I said, 'My husband is waiting for me at home, and if I don't get there soon, he will come looking for me.'

He asked, 'Are you going to tell your husband?'

'I don't think so.'

'Why not?'

'Because he'd be so upset.'

'Would he be really mad?'

'Yes.'

'Would it kill him?'

'No, it wouldn't kill him, but he'd be really upset.'

At about this juncture, the man had pushed up my knit shirt, and ripped off my bra. He finished pushing off what was left of my shredded linen slacks, and kicked off my last shoe. He was fumbling with my breasts, and I think this may have been when the actual rape took place, but I am not sure. He still seemed to be having trouble.

To find out something, I asked, 'Did you come yet?'

The bastard, he said, 'Do you want me to?'

I replied quietly, calmly, 'I don't care. I just want you to be satisfied and get this over with so I can go home.' But I don't think the man was having any luck with the main part of his mission. In my estimation, he was having an impotence problem.

I pulled my shirt down, as my arms were free for a minute. He pushed it back up again. I told him, 'My husband is in the Mafia. He'll get you.' For all I knew, the Scandellaris were connected with the Mafia. People had told me they were. There was certainly something unorthodox about them, and I wouldn't put it past them to take revenge on anyone that crossed them.

The man ignored my remark about the Mafia. Oh well, it was worth a try. He asked me did I want him to do this thing, or that thing to me (I refuse to tell what, exactly), and I replied, 'No, please don't.' He seemed to be trying to be considerate as long as I would cooperate.

After he fumbled some more, he asked, 'Do you like it?'

I said, 'I don't like being raped.' I said again, 'I am pregnant.' No reply.

I said, 'I know my husband will be looking for me.' No reply. The man was still rutting against me.

I said, 'I have syphilis.' No comment from him.

I said, 'I've been exposed to typhoid fever.' Nothing.

I said, 'You're cutting off the circulation in my arms.'

He flipped me over on my stomach and began trying to sodomize me.

Up until that point, I had remained fairly calm, and had been concentrating all my thoughts on how to get away unharmed. It flashed through my mind that tomorrow or the next day, someone would find me in the ravine, stabbed to death, and wonder who I was.

When the man began trying to insert his penis in my rectum, I panicked a little, because I could not imagine how much that would hurt. So I said, 'Please don't do that. It will hurt.' I said, 'I'll do anything, if you'll just let me go home, but please don't do that.'

The man still had me solidly pinned, and was cutting off the circulation in my arms.

He asked, 'Will you give me a blow job?' meaning fellatio.

It wasn't my favorite thing, but I said yes, because it occurred to me in the same instant that it would be the opportunity I needed to escape: I would be in the superior position.

The man asked, 'Will you promise to be good?' meaning, not run away. I said yes.

And with that promise extracted, he just let go of me, rolled over on his back and lay prone, with his penis sticking straight up. By that time, he had quite an erection, though it had taken him a long time to get it. I was thinking I had always heard that rape was over with pretty fast, and this guy sure was taking his time. I wondered when it was going to be over, and whether I would live through it.

So there he was, lying on the ground, expecting me to give him a blowjob, and he had turned me loose completely. The man actually seemed to trust that I would do what I said. He

Chapter Twenty-One: *The Edge of the Precipice*

remarked, 'Make it a good one!' I was twenty-nine. What a mercy I had knowledge of men, that I could string him along this way. A virgin wouldn't have stood a chance.

I was thinking fast, 'This will be my only chance to escape, but I have to time it to run when there are cars approaching.' I took hold of his penis, and put my mouth to him as if I were going to do it. Then, I heard cars approaching, and saw headlights.

I waited until the cars were close enough, which was only a matter of seconds. When I felt that the cars were almost to us, I jumped and ran. He lunged for me, but didn't quite reach me. There were no garments to grab, only bare skin. It was an advantage to be naked from the waist down.

I was barefooted, and wearing only a lightweight, unbuttoned cotton shirt, but I knew I had to run in front of those cars, scream for help, and hope that one would stop. I ran across two lanes of I-64 to the grassy median strip, all the while waving my arms wildly, and screaming, 'Help me, help me.' To my great misfortune, that was the very year, 1975, that many of the college students had been 'streaking,' or running nude in public places as a practical joke, and usually on a dare.

No one stopped. My heart sank. This was it. Death.

My attacker was running between my car and his truck, and I was sure he was coming after me, but somehow he didn't. He jumped into his truck, and screeched away, very much in a hurry.

I stood there, naked, raped, cars going by, and no one stopped to help me. I think that's when I finally lapsed into shock. All I can remember is that I was terrified that the man would come back for me. I had to get away.

I crossed back over the two lanes of highway to my car and groped around on the grass for my keys. During the attack, I had asked him if there was really anything wrong with my car. He replied, 'No.' And I asked him, 'Where are my keys?' He said, 'Beside the wheel.' But I just couldn't find them in the dark.

A Quiet Life in Bedlam

Miraculously, I still had my glasses on, and they weren't broken. The glasses were probably what kept him from hitting me in the face too much, and I was thankful that I had the glasses, and could see.

I tried again to find my keys beside the wheel, but they weren't there. I had an extra set in a magnetic box under the left front fender, so I pulled them out, started the car, and then remembered that I didn't have any clothes on.

I opened my suitcase, which was in the back seat, and pulled out whatever was on top. It happened to be a white wrap-around skirt, so I wrapped it around me, and started off home. At that point, I didn't know that I was hurt. I was on the Interstate, in the middle of nowhere; I didn't have enough presence of mind to dress myself properly, and go look for a highway patrolman.

I barely had enough strength to drive the car, which was thankfully, an automatic. I knew I had to get out of there quick. I was still barefooted, but that couldn't be helped. In a cockeyed sort of way, I remembered I had heard that it was against the law to drive barefooted; and for the first time since the ordeal began, I smiled to myself, and thought, *I do hope someone stops me and gives me a traffic ticket.* Any policeman encountering me would get a shock!

The next road sign said, 'Twenty-five miles to Williamsburg.' Jesus, if I could only get there ...

Then I came to Hampton, and to the Hampton Roads Tunnel. The man on the radio said, '4:00 a.m.' The ticket taker in the tunnel was so sleepy that he didn't notice that anything was wrong with me, that my face was black and blue, and I was only partially dressed. There wasn't too much blood, thankfully, because it was a company car. I grimaced at the bloodstain on the pale yellow upholstery just beside my head. How would I explain it to Mel?

I finally reached home in Virginia Beach about 5:15 a.m. I do not remember anything at all about the trip home, apart from what I have related. I had the sole idea in my head that if

Chapter Twenty-One: *The Edge of the Precipice*

I could just get home and into Vincent's arms, that I would be safe, and all would be well.

So, I was home. But my keys were still laying in the dark at the side of the Interstate near Richmond. I had an extra house key somewhere—where was it? Oh, yes, in my purse, still in the car. I fetched the purse, opened it up to find my house key. I noticed the piece of paper I received from the gypsy fortune teller in Washington. It was folded up, waiting for me to read. It was just light enough for me to make out the penciled words she had written. There was one sentence. It read,

'You have no future.'

For the first time that awful night, I began to shake. I got myself into the house just as the sun was rising. I had met my fate on the road that night, but the hand of God had reached down and plucked me out of it. It put a responsibility on me to do the best I could with whatever days were left to me. As bad as the experience was, I wasn't going to let the memory of it kill me. It would take some time, but I would resolutely put it behind me.

Let that be a lesson to you, my grandmother said inside my head.

Shut up, Grandmother, I whispered.

My grandma and your grandma, were sittin' by the fire
My grandma told your grandma, I'm gonna set your flag on fire
Talkin' 'bout hey now, hey now, Iko! Iko! an dé [128]

I could hear the drumstick beating against the Coke bottle.

Vincent came sleepily down the stairs. 'Bess …' he said. He had waited up all night for me to come home.

---

[128] 'Iko Iko,' traditional folk song of New Orleans, sung by the Dixie Cups in 1965, accompanied only by a drumstick being struck on a Coke bottle.

I looked up. Immediately, shock and concern registered on his face. He took the remaining stairs at a single bound. I walked into the circle of his arms.

Well, the experience didn't finish me, but it nearly killed poor Vincent. As dark complected as he was, he turned chalk-white when he saw me. But he tenderly ministered to my needs, and put me to bed. When day came, I insisted on reporting the incident to the State Police, though Vincent was dead-set against it. The Scandellaris never went to the police for anything. But I had to go, I had to do it, I had no choice.

Vincent did not want me to face a rape trial, but it didn't come to that. I was never able to identify my assailant. I blocked out his face. On the same day that I arrived home much the worse for wear, I presented my battered, black and blue body to the State Police, and they took a full statement, made photographs. I kept my own copy of the statement, and sealed it up in a file cabinet.

After I visited the police, I was admitted to the hospital, thoroughly examined and counseled by a psychologist to within an inch of my life. They were more worried than I was. Then I was released from the hospital within a few hours, relatively unharmed—but completely black and blue all over. That was the one and only time after my maturity that I thought I looked ghastly.

One of my front eyeteeth was chipped, but that was the worst of it, other than the cut on my hand. I was very lucky.

The police did everything they could to help me. I drove with a State Trooper back to the stretch of road outside Richmond, and we drove up and down, up and down, until finally, in the hot summer sun, I spied the glint of metal and a white rag. The metal was my keys; the rag was what remained of my slacks. My white shoes were there too, a little ways down the ravine. I knew I was lucky to be alive. An attacker who would go to such lengths to perform a rape was capable of much else.

It was like being in a bad dream, but over the next few months, the information came to me from the police, who were still investigating—I had been to several line-ups—that the

Chapter Twenty-One: *The Edge of the Precipice*

man who waylaid me, or at least a pathological rapist who was working in the same way on all the state highways thereabouts, had murdered a total of six women within a hundred mile radius. It really happened, and I still shudder to think of it sometimes, but mostly I am detached now. It is finished. I survived.

CHAPTER TWENTY-TWO:
No More Crying Then

Traveling had lost its appeal for me, and I left the employment of the health and beauty aids company in December of 1975 after obtaining my real estate license. Mel was sorry to see me go; I had been his experiment in hiring a woman for a man's job. Certainly, I had not been an unqualified success—'Don't kid the kidder,' he used to tell me—but Mel found another brave girl to take over my territory, and we were both satisfied.

Mel, whose nickname was short for Mr. Mellow and Laid-back, was a brick. A *Sagittarian*—and I thought I didn't like them—he taught me a lot, and I was thankful. I still think of him, even though it is all many years ago now. It seems as if anybody I have loved, I still love them, no matter where they are, or how we parted ways.

When I gave up my company car, I bought a Chrysler Cordoba two-door coupe. It was a burgundy metallic with a leather top, an early kind of 'personal luxury car.' Of course I couldn't afford it, but I didn't think about that. The Cordoba was cool, low-slung and sexy-looking. Vincent loved that car, but he kept on driving a Pontiac, by this time, a blue one.

I enjoyed selling real estate, and had my broker's license within the year. Vincent got his license too, but he really had no interest in it; he just wanted to follow me around.

Chapter Twenty-Two: *No More Crying Then*

I bought a new townhouse in Kempshire Manor off Princess Anne Road, and Vincent lived with me a little more, and then a little more, but he never actually moved in. Our neighbors would laugh when they saw us come out of the front door in the mornings, Vincent with his valise that had nothing in it but the morning newspaper, and me in my little swingy dresses and peek-a-boo clear vinyl platform shoes—both of us bound for work at the real estate office where it was 'nine to five.'

As a couple, we were gorgeous, glamorous, mysterious. When I see photographs of us as we were then, oh! One of the inexplicable things about Vincent was how he stayed so slim on a constant diet of manicotti. That was one of the mysterious things about me, too. Vincent's mother, even though she wouldn't 'accept' me, cooked huge pots of pasta, and meatballs that would melt in your mouth, any day of the week for us that we cared to attend her. But I had a secret: I was still taking diet pills, and birth control pills. It was necessary, believe me.

One of my first real estate customers told me plainly, upfront, that she was a call girl. Well, by that time, I knew that the world had call girls in it, but I hadn't considered it likely that I would meet one. What a novelty! This girl was very pretty, and she wore hot-pink hot pants, plus knee-high, white vinyl go-go boots. Her only flaw was a large dark mole on her right cheek.

Wow. I thought. *Sock it to 'em.* The prostitute clearly had street-savvy and chutzpah—everyone used to use that word 'chutzpah,' like it was something you ought to have—and she earned a lot of money. Because she did not have a bank account, once a week the prostitute came to my house and stuffed a lot of cash money into my hands so I could save it for her, for a 'deposit' on her house.

The girl, her name was Garnet, was going F.H.A. I wondered what she would say to the mortgage company about her 'ways and means.' There has to be a clear source of income to buy a house. That money the call girl handed me, made my hands very itchy! There was so much of it, it added up so fast, and it was so green! Garnet eventually bought a townhouse off Princess Anne Road, not very far from mine.

Vincent was in trouble with me by this time. His divorce from Cathy Scandellari had become final late in 1975, but he still did not marry me. So, I began to date other men. It seemed eminently fair. This hurt Vincent's poor heart so much that he would nearly suffocate with the pain of it. To his mind, I had belonged to him from the day he set eyes on me, and it was 'adultery,' pure and simple, for me to go out with other men.

But what was I to do? I turned thirty in 1976, and I could not wait for Vincent forever. His family was still just as opposed to a marriage as they had ever been, and Vincent himself seemed to think that I would turn into some sort of wild-eyed shrew, the minute he put the ring on my finger. So we were at a standoff.

Vincent became more romantic than he ever had been though, writing me wonderful love letters, and sending me lacy greeting cards by the hundreds, showering me with gifts and flowers. Then when I didn't respond, he backed off, deeply hurt. We broke up and made up, broke up and made up.

I took him to meet my brothers and sisters in Tennessee. We were back and forth to Nashville and Memphis during 1975 and 1976. Vincent pretended disdain for my family, and said he was not comfortable with them. He did not like sitting outside, he said, for example at a picnic or a barbeque or a family reunion, the kind of occasion my country relatives prized the most. Muttering and cursing, he would try to settle on a lawn chair, but the bugs kept him twitching and jumping and straightening his trouser-leg. He would say sincerely, his eyes full of soul, 'I'm afraid they will seal the borders, and I won't be able to get out.'

'What? Of Tennessee?'

'It's a loony bin,' he said. This was a rare public outburst from Vincent. I looked around to see if anyone was listening. They weren't. So I said, 'Well, I know that. That's why I choose not to live here.'

Chapter Twenty-Two: *No More Crying Then*

'Yuk, yuk, you're really sick, Bess. You were born in a thunderstorm.'

I giggled. That was what I used to say about Sherry. Vincent didn't like Sherry! He said, 'She has a squeaky voice.'

'But people find that charming about her.'

'The two of you are a lot alike, but thank God you don't have a squeaky voice!'

Thank God.

Around other people, Vincent pretended he didn't care for me. But everyone knew the truth from merely glancing at his luminous eyes. Those eyes expressed the emotions he tried too hard to keep under control.

In May of 1976, I met another real estate broker who lived on the quaint, otherworldly 'Eastern Shore of Virginia.' The Eastern Shore is a long peninsula of land that reaches out into the Chesapeake Bay, and it is a world apart from the mainland of Virginia; it is like stepping into a fairy tale.

I spent some time on the Eastern Shore with my new boyfriend, and all the time, I was trying to figure out the complicated relationship between my boyfriend Charles, and his best friend, George, who lived in the nearest house. The 'Shore,' as the natives called it, was very rural, scattered with real 'plantations,' and harbored a nest-full of what I like to think of as the First Families of Virginia. They were rich, landed, and from old stock; and they thought of themselves as part of Virginia's elite, as they were.

Charles and George moved with this select set, and it was illuminating to see how such people lived. The old Georgian, Revival, and Antebellum manor houses were huge with high ceilings, and elegantly and expensively furnished. George delighted in explaining the provenance of each and every house and item of furniture. Some of the houses had elevators, and all had servants. There were peacocks on the lawns, and oysters in the creeks just outside the back porches.

Charles and George both had houses on the famous Cherry Stone Creek. George had given Charles the land to build his house on. It was right next-door. Ladies and gentlemen in their set, dressed for dinner; life moved at the pace of the rich and idle. The whole thing was overwhelming for a simple girl like me. I even had to buy special clothes to cope with the social life. But I enjoyed it. It was new and rich experience to add to my already vividly colored tapestry of life.

I had a major setback in my relationship with Charles when one day he was visiting me in Virginia Beach. We were just getting ready to go out, when who should walk through the front door, using his own key, but Vincent. Vincent, so he said later, had come to ask me to marry him. He and Charles were stunned to meet face to face. They knew about each other, of course, but this was too much.

Vincent left my house immediately. Charles left shortly after.

Charles said to me before he left, 'Kate, I don't know why you're fooling around with me, when that man really loves you.' I guess I really didn't understand love at all.

I was feeling very stubborn, and I went on dating Charles for several months. I was seeing Vincent, too, of course; we really could not seem to separate our lives, just in the same way as if we really *were* married.

By the January of 1977, I was beginning to see myself as 'Lady of the Manor,' presiding over my own little estate on the Eastern Shore. Nothing in life is a sideshow for me. I was always looking for the 'main chance.' This seemed to be it—marriage to the right man. Was Charles the right man? I was willing to gamble on it. I wasn't getting any younger.

Though George, Charles's friend, was always gracious to me and cordial when I visited his home, he seemed to get very red in the face and throw a lot of temper tantrums during the few days of my visit.

'Hell's Bells!' George would cry out, 'Are you here again?'

His was a jocular manner, but he was lashing about with willow switches as he said it.

Charles seemed to worry about George at such times, wondering if George were going to have a heart attack. George was

Chapter Twenty-Two: *No More Crying Then*

about twenty years older than Charles, which made him about fifty-five at the time. George used to say to me that he was born on 12/12/12— December 12, 1912. I thought that was a noble date on which to be born. *A Sagittarian* again. Hmm, interesting. I would have to study that Sun Sign. The 'fire signs,' Sagittarius, Leo, Aries, had never mattered too much to me, before.

I had become such a frequent guest, and so familiar with the surroundings and their habits, that sometimes I drove over to the 'Shore' for a surprise visit. John seemed to be at George's house as often as he was at his own, so I usually went straight to George's house, and walked in through the back door. George liked to cook, and sometimes could be found in the kitchen ladling out clam chowder or oyster stew. The doors were never locked; I didn't need a key. For the people who knew each other on the Eastern Shore, it was an open-door community.

It was April, shortly before my thirty-first birthday, and the weather was lovely. April can be like early summer in Virginia. It was pure pleasure to drive across the Chesapeake Bay Bridge's seven miles length, and soak up the blue sky and green sea. The lawns around George's house were always beautifully manicured, and I couldn't help but think how lovely it would be to spend the rest of my life living in such a place. A white peacock screamed and strutted around.

What a perfect paradise! I thought. It was almost as good as Key West.

Letting myself into the house, I found no one at home. That was surprising. I walked through the spacious rooms, admiring again the genteel beauty of it all. There were plasterwork patterns on the ceilings and the walls. There were bronze busts on pedestals. That house was Virginia at its Colonial best. I loved it. The house was about 200 years old.

'Halloo!' I called.

Everything was very quiet, except for the buzzing of flies and the cries of peacocks in the gardens. Then, I thought I heard voices upstairs. Then I heard a man laugh. I walked upstairs. It was a spiral staircase. One could look up to a domed cupola. I admired it, once again.

The upstairs was small compared to the downstairs—the foyer ceiling vaulted to the roof of the second story. I peeked into the spare bedroom; no one there. I walked into George's bedroom. No one there. The door to George's dressing room was standing ajar, and I could plainly hear George's voice, and also Charles's.

My heels clicked on the hardwood floor as I tripped across to the dressing room and pushed the door open. The dressing room opened through an arch into George's old-fashioned bathroom, where there was an enormous old enameled tub that stood up on four legs, and had silver taps. In the tub were George and Charles, the two of them up to their necks in bubbles, their arms around each other. Why didn't I see it coming? I must have been stone-blind.

I rushed out of the house and drove straight back to Virginia Beach. I told Vincent that I wanted to get married immediately. He thought I must be going through one of my emotional, unstable periods, and I guess I was. Everything was at sixes and sevens.

Vincent refused to marry me that day, but said if I were feeling more rational by my birthday, which was a week away, he would marry me then. On my birthday, we drove to Nag's Head (marry in one day with no three-day wait!) in North Carolina. I was more than ready to marry Vincent. I had even purchased a white-gold wedding ring to go with the diamond ring I had bought so long ago—just in case Vincent forgot to get one. I couldn't get married without a ring!

Well, Vincent didn't marry me that day—said I was still too changeable, too unpredictable. 'I want you to be sure first,' he said.

I was sure, but it didn't budge Vincent. Then too, Vincent had no desire to be married a second time by a justice of the peace in North Carolina. He wanted to be married in church. Well, so did I, but that would take so LONG. We were both

Chapter Twenty-Two: *No More Crying Then*

divorced. Divorced people were not allowed to be married again, in church. We would have to get annulments.

In the end, we came to an agreement that we would begin pre-marital counseling at the church where I belonged, St. Savior Episcopal, with the hope that at the conclusion of it, six month's time, the diocese would allow—it had never been done before—two previously married people to pledge new vows at the Anglican altar in the sight of God and some witnesses.

Vincent and I went through a terrible time with the Reverend Mr. Vermillion during the next few months. It was like sitting in front of Jehovah. Vincent and I were interviewed individually and together. I felt very shy about facing Stephen Vermillion alone, because he had been kind enough to talk to me often about many things, emotional problems, problems of faith and belief and doctrine; existential questions that I tried to come to grips with before I left Christianity. I cried a lot, because I wanted my life to be better, and I didn't know how to fix it.

I believe Stephen Vermillion thought of me as a very silly woman, and there I was again, asking for help, when really what I needed was a psychiatrist. At times, I have been a solemn little thing with no sense of humor, and a fear of oddments that has kept me crippled and unable to laugh at life, a valuable lesson that I should have learned ages ago. It was with trepidation that I approached his office door.

It was something that I could not understand, it blew away all my comfortable conceptions of life within the church (and challenges me to think again), that Mr. Vermillion had hanging on the wall of his study, right over his desk for all to see, a wonderful painting of *The Laughing Christ.* I swear, as God is my witness, that I never knew Christ could laugh. What a strange thing. It was as if the Church Fathers knew how to tell jokes.

Mr. Vermillion obviously did not think Vincent and I could stick the course. But we did, and at the end of it, Mr. Vermillion presented our petition to the bishop, and it read like this:

... being perfectly candid, it appeared from the beginnings of our discussions that this was a proposed marriage which I would *not* be willing to perform. As we talked, and I must say, we spent a considerable number of hours together, it was the most complicated and confusing relationship that I had ever encountered. But as we continued to work together, it very slowly dawned on me that there were many strong points about their relationship.

The couple has been in deep relationship for over five years, and I began to realize that there appeared to be an amazing knowledge about one another between them. There is no question in my mind that they are perfectly aware of the limitations, weaknesses, and idiosyncrasies of one another, and yet, they are bound firmly to the relationship.

Although on the surface, the relationship has many unusual characteristics, it is my *very* firm conviction that underneath, there is an extraordinary woven fabric of commitment. The long courtship has allowed their commitment to be tested and buffeted by all manner of concern, and it has withstood.

In addition, their commitment to this process of approval for remarriage within the church, which has been long and arduous, speaks well of their convictions about the sanctity of this relationship. In pondering over this proposal, it is very clear to me that in relation or comparison to other couples who seek a first marriage, they are in many ways more clear about the nature of themselves, and the proposed ...

Well, you said a mouthful, Mr. Vermillion, so let's just leave it at that. It is hard to believe, but after that six-month

Chapter Twenty-Two: *No More Crying Then*

ordeal, a trial by fire as it were, Vincent still wasn't ready to get married: Mr. Vermillion could have solemnized the marriage at any time after the end of the counseling in October of 1977.

Vincent would not agree to get a blood test, which was necessary by law, because the sight of blood causes him to faint, but when the first cold weather set in, in November, he developed bursitis in his left arm, and had to see the doctor anyway.

So, I went with him to the doctor, afraid he might escape. Vincent is afraid of doctors—says they're all quacks—but I saw to it that we both got blood tests during the same visit. I had to hold Vincent's head against my shoulder as they drew his blood. He was deathly pale again; that was only the second time I had ever seen him so faint.

Time passed, and I was really worried that the blood test would expire before we got our marriage license—Vincent was still refusing to make the necessary trip to the Court House to apply. But finally, I caught him in a weak moment, just after he returned from New York where he had attended his Uncle Vincent's funeral. It had really upset Vincent when he saw the gravediggers set the stone on the grave of his uncle, because it read: Vincente Scandellari, died, November 1977. All at once, Vincent began to feel his mortality.

Then it was December, and still no wedding plans, Mr. Vermillion was piqued that he had gone to all that trouble, and still no marriage, and I didn't blame him: I was piqued myself. I received a phone call from Stephen on December 1st, and he said that if he didn't marry us soon, he wouldn't be able to do it until after Christmas.

Well, I couldn't bear to think about putting the marriage off until the New Year. So I asked Stephen (we were on a first name basis by that time), 'When can you do it?'

'December 5th,' he said.

I replied, 'I'll check with Vincent and call you back.'

'Fine.' He hung up. *God bless that good man,* I thought.

Vincent still wasn't ready. December 5th was too soon, he said. I was very upset.

I asked him, 'Vincent, do you love me?'

Vincent's heavy-lidded brown eyes regarded me with weary irony. He said, 'I got it bad, and that ain't good.'

'It is too,' I replied.

I called Stephen Vermillion back, and stated that December 5th was no good. Clearly annoyed, he said it would have to be after the New Year.

I said, 'Wait!' and making a firm resolution, I asked him, 'What other date in December might you have available?'

He looked at his calendar and answered, 'December 15th, which is a Friday evening. I can marry you at seven o'clock.'

I said, 'Fine. We'll be there.' Clearly, I had to take the bull by the horns. The bull (Vincent) was resisting with all his might, but he eventually agreed to go through with it. He complained petulantly that he didn't see why we couldn't go on as we were.

Man, you must be joking! I stood, arms akimbo, feet firmly planted on the floor, and said, 'Absolutely not. I am the marrying kind.' But I still wasn't sure, right up until the Day that Vincent would do it. I was Jane Eyre, and Vincent was Mr. Rochester; and I was afraid that at the very altar rail, some quirk of fate would snatch him from me. He still said, 'You are rushing me.'

Christ!

At 7:00 p.m. we arrived at the church, attended by my friend Lynette and her doctor husband, and my friend Delores and her fiancé. The girls were dressed in similar, apple-green silk evening dresses, which was a surprise to me, for I had only asked that they wear long gowns.

My wedding dress came out of the closet after all those years of just hanging there waiting, and Vincent wore a blue suit.

Lynette brought flowers for everyone, including a bridal bouquet for me. This too, was a surprise, and a really nice touch. Delores was to take the pictures.

Chapter Twenty-Two: *No More Crying Then*

The church was lighted with candles, and Mr. Vermillion was standing at the altar end of the aisle. Vincent had asked me not to invite anyone, so the church was empty, except for we seven.

So, Reader, I married him. A quiet wedding we had. The vows were said, and Vincent and I walked out together into the clear, cold December night, a husband and his wife. He'd made an honest woman out of me. I was married with the white-gold wedding ring I had bought myself.

During the days that followed, love descended over me like a balm—serene, calm, secure. I knew that as long as there was breath in his body, Vincent would look after me and love me. I had found my home, at least for a while.

Vincent said, 'By the laws of nature, we shouldn't be together. We are opposites in every way.'

'That's what makes it so rare and wonderful,' I answered.

He didn't say anything.

'What's the matter, Vincent?'

'Yuk, yuk, yuk.'

I smiled.

'I'm sorry we're poor, Bess,' he said.

'I'm waiting for your ship to come in.'

'My ship hit a reef, and went down with all hands.'

Hah, hah, hah.

'Kiss me,' I said.

'Where?'

One morning I said, 'Last night was perfect to conceive, Vincent.'

'That's just what we need, a baby. Hmmm ... we could sell him on the black market for forty grand.'

'Vincent, you don't mean it!'

'I do.'

'Oh, Vincent!'

'I still think of you as my child bride.'

'Lovely.' I rolled my eyes.

A couple of years after my mother died in Tennessee, my sister Sherry forwarded a letter my mother had left. The letter had been found among her papers. I believe it is appropriate to end my story with this, for it shows that she did indeed love me after all, and that I have been deluding myself. But it wouldn't be the first time.

I think this letter is particularly sad and prophetic, in the light of what happened after.

October 1968

My dear Katharine,

At one time or another we all have to face a cruel fact that all things must end, the good, as well as the bad, and we must accept this as God's will. I have not accomplished all that I wanted to, but time also expires. My heart is heavy with guilt for the things I didn't do, whether it was lack of time, or just negligence. I know that I neglected to tell you often enough how much I loved you, and as time went on, and you grew into a teenager with so many interests, it became increasingly hard to be patient, and take time to express the love that was always there.

One of my biggest regrets is that with the wear and tear of work and home, I gradually dropped out of church, and while I always felt guilty about it, it seemed all I could do to get all of you there. And somehow, we never had the closeness of family Bible reading and prayer that we should have had. But time always seemed to be running away, and it is hard to get into the habit of some things that one hasn't been brought up to do, and in that respect, I have failed you, as I was failed. Not that I blame my mother, for as a farm woman with seven children, she had an even harder time, except that the public didn't expect so much of her.

As the eldest, you were the one and only for a time, with all the attention, but it was over so soon, you can't remember, and then, you were given too much responsibility too soon perhaps. Remember, I too, was the eldest, and so, often, felt I was blamed for everything, but that is something that is hard to avoid in a large family.

Chapter Twenty-Two: *No More Crying Then*

I am so glad that you have had the chance to enjoy a little freedom, before having a family. Do you know that by the time I was your present age, I had given birth to my third child? That is quite a handful for a woman of only twenty-two and a half years.

I hope that you will always love your Daddy, and forgive him for any injustices you feel he has done to you; and I know he has, many times, though he really didn't mean to. It may be hard for you to remember how many wonderful years we had when you children were small. Adam worked so hard, day and night, and he wanted to give all of us so much, and he was always so dissatisfied with himself, that over the years, it broke him down. Your Daddy grew up in more poverty than you will ever know, and he had to drop out of school very young. With determination and hard work, he overcame the obstacles, except for his inferiority complex. Your Daddy never could relax and be satisfied with a day's or a week's work, even when well done. He worked harder the next week to do more. He hardly ever drank—a little beer now and then. He almost never stopped off on the way home; and when he did, I'd be out of my mind for fear something had happened to him.

Of course, that was in the days before insurance selling, when I still knew when to expect him. But, it was no different for years after he went into insurance, except that I didn't know what time he'd be home.

But, if you remember, he still came straight home; however, not soon enough to keep me from walking the floor for fear that one of you would be late getting to one of the places that you had to go so many times a week. And I know that your Daddy must have felt neglected in those years—after a hard day's work, I met him at the door, complaining because he didn't get home sooner; and then, I would rush off to take each of you in different directions; and then staying up way into the night to do odd jobs and sewing your costumes and dresses. And yet, he never complained.

But, the years of driving himself, and the pressure of work that was never done, along with age and failing health, got the

A Quiet Life in Bedlam

better of Adam. Love your Daddy; he needs it, and love and take care of your husband. I hope you have many wonderful years together.
I love you,
Mother

The letter speaks for itself.

Across my dreams, with nets of wonder, I chase the bright elusive butterfly of love. [129]

---

[129] 'Elusive Butterfly,' Bob Lind, 1966.

Lightning Source UK Ltd.
Milton Keynes UK
17 May 2010

154303UK00001B/68/P